I0675630

The Secret History of the Palace Theater

John Urbancik

The Secret History of the Palace Theater

John Urbancik

Copyright © 2024 John Urbancik

All rights reserved.

Cover art © 2024 John Urbancik

Design Copyright © 2024 John Urbancik

This is a work of fiction. Similarities to persons, living or dead, are neither intended nor should be inferred.

ISBN: 978-1-951522-18-6

For more information, please visit www.darkfluidity.com

The Secret History of the Palace Theater

John Urbancik

SECRET HISTORY
PART I

1.

Maybe it was lightning: a stray thunderbolt let loose by the gods. Perhaps an errant wish gone wrong; radiation; cosmic activity or seismic activity or occult activity. Poisonous gases. An uncontrolled radical particle, an ionized electron, a fluctuation in the magnetic field. Maybe the convergence of a rotten anti-inflammatory after a preternatural headache and something more sinister, perhaps Scarlet, on the other side. Maybe it was just because they looked into the same mirror at the same time and noticed the same crack. Maybe it was bad magic.

Whatever the reason, they switched.

They switched, and Nicholas found himself in a place both utterly familiar and completely bizarre. The walls were where his walls had always been. The old apartment was his, but the color was gone. In its place, the walls were blacks and whites, black like charcoal and white like chalk. Everything in the room, the desk and tables, the chairs, the lamps, all sketched in variations of these. The bulb glowing on the lamp gave off a bright, distinct white light, more substantive than should be, thicker, cleaner.

First thing, Nicholas went into the bedroom and changed clothes. Out of the jeans, out of the tee shirt, into something more likely to provide camouflage this side of the mirror. Coal jeans, chalk shirt, coal jacket. The streets were his streets, though the color was different. The cars were the same shapes he'd left behind. The sidewalk was just as cracked, the buildings just as old and crumbly. The Nicholas on this side of the mirror had done no better for himself than he had. The apartment was a hole, the neighborhood bordered on ruin, and the sound of passing subways shook the world.

The people on this side of the mirror were painted with the same dust as the rest of the world. That would take some getting used to. He wasn't sure how long he'd be here. What if it was a permanent switch?

He explored the neighborhood and found the same deli at the corner. Inside, it was the same clerk, or a variation of him. Nicholas had never learned his name. The guy looked up. "Hey, Nicholas," he said, tilting his head in a funny way. "You don't look well. You need something to make you better?"

"Always."

"I got just the thing." The clerk called back to someone in the kitchen. "Hey, Jerry, guess who's dropped in for your pastrami."

A big guy emerged, Jerry, wiping his hands on a towel, but he stopped and froze entirely the moment he saw Nicholas. His eyes narrowed. "*You.*"

Nicholas hesitated. What had his mirror self done?

Jerry threw the rag and ran around the side of the counter. Nicholas didn't wait. He fled. Out the door, down the street, toward an alley. Jerry was big and slow, but Nicholas was no Olympic runner, speed or distance. He turned left, then right, then bumped off the side of a chain link fence.

It was hard to run through all the blacks and whites. The lack of color, the sketchiness of everything that was visible, played with his sense of depth. He crashed into a set of garbage cans. He ran like a drunk man, a madman, a freak.

"I'll kill you!" Jerry kept yelling behind him. It wasn't the welcome he had hoped for. Around another corner, he ran into a wall.

So the geography wasn't exactly identical.

Jerry caught him, got a fist around his throat, foam spraying from his mouth as he snarled. "We thought you'd learned," Jerry said, bringing a fist back to throw a punch. But he hesitated. "What the hell's wrong with your face?"

Nicholas grinned, but the grip around his windpipe did not let up. He tried to say something, cough something, draw any breath at all. He kicked, maybe caught a shin, maybe didn't manage to catch anything. He tried to punch. He'd never been a fighter. Didn't learn until college not to keep his thumb tucked inside his fist. Hitting Jerry was like hitting slabs of meat. He quite suddenly understood *Rocky*.

Jerry forced him backwards, against the wall, cracking Nicholas's head against the bricks. Nicholas was able to breathe again, at least a breath, and that was all he needed. "Disease," he said, gasping, not needing to exaggerate the sound of it. "Terminal."

Jerry flinched, let go, stepped back. "What do you mean, disease?"

"I'm dying," Nicholas said, staring into the pasty white face of the big man. "Days, maybe a week. It's highly contagious." Every word increased the concern in Jerry's expression.

"I don't believe you."

"It's terminal."

"They'd have you locked up," Jerry said. "Quarantined."

"I escaped," Nicholas said. He stepped forward. "To find you."

"You're crazy," Jerry said.

Nicholas grinned. "Yes." He touched the back of his head. There was blood. Red. Brilliant and bright on this scratched side of the mirror. Jerry's eyes went wide. There wasn't much blood, but it was the most vivid color this world had ever seen. Nicholas shoved the fingers forward. "See?" he said. "I'm a walking deathtrap."

"I don't know what you are," Jerry said, "but I'll be glad when you're dead." He walked away, dignity intact, straight and tall and satisfied, a man who'd meant to kill and did so. Nicholas, meanwhile, struggled not to hyperventilate. When the big man was out of sight, he bent over double, coughed, wiped his brow, felt the back of his head again. He looked back at the brick wall behind him. A smear of red.

In a nearby open window, a white cat, staring at him, swished its tail and licked its paw.

1.

Maybe it was lightning: a stray thunderbolt let loose by the gods. Perhaps an errant wish gone wrong; radiation; cosmic activity or seismic activity or occult activity. Poisonous gases. An uncontrolled radical particle, an ionized electron, a fluctuation in the magnetic field. Maybe the convergence of a rotten anti-inflammatory after a preternatural headache and something more sinister, perhaps Scarlet, on the other side. Maybe it was just because they looked into the same mirror at the same time and noticed the same crack. Maybe it was bad magic.

Whatever the reason, they switched.

They switched, and Nicholas found himself in a place both utterly familiar and completely bizarre. The walls were where his walls had always been. The old apartment was his, but the colors were changed. In its place, the walls were sick with color, lurid, nearly overwhelming. The bulb glowing on the lamp gave off a pale, dirty variation of light.

First thing, Nicholas went through the apartment, pocketing anything he thought might be useful or valuable — cash in a funny hue but with the same Presidential portraits, a ring that might be gold, a pocketknife. A jacket. There wasn't much. The Nicholas on this side of the mirror hadn't done any better in life than he had. Outside, the neighborhood was the same, if garish, but he was getting used to that. The sidewalk was just as cracked, the buildings just as old and crumbly. The colors of the people would take some getting used to. What if it was a permanent switch?

He explored the neighborhood. The same deli at the corner. He thought about going in, demanding pastrami on rye, just to test the stock of the people on this side of the mirror, and then went in, nodding to the clerk as if everything was normal.

"Hey, Nicholas," the guy said, tilting his head in a funny way. "You don't look well. You need something to make you better?"

Nicholas grinned. "Always."

"I got just the thing." The clerk called back to the kitchen. "Hey, Jerry, we got any of your momma's soup left?"

A big guy emerged, Jerry, wiping his hands on a towel. His eyes reached Nicholas, eyes full of color, and he said, "Yeah, I think so."

"I bet you do," Nicholas said, thinking how easily a man could slip a bit of cyanide into soup and watch his enemies choke and gasp and die. "Not today, thanks. I've got other plans."

"You don't look right," Jerry said. "Pale. Pasty."

"Yeah, I'm sick," Nicholas said. "Diseased and dying. Probably it's contagious as all hell. You'll probably want to burn this place down after I'm gone."

He left with an apple. A solid, real apple he'd slipped into his jacket pocket. He wondered how something so red must taste. He tossed and caught it once as he walked away from the deli, then took a bite. There was so much juice, it spilled over his lip and down his chin, and it was damn sweet.

"I could definitely like this place," Nicholas said to no one, and took another bite.

He wondered how the Lissa on this side of the mirror would respond to him.

In a window as he passed, a black cat, staring at him, swished its tail and licked its paw.

2.

Before he reached Lissa's apartment, Nicholas stopped outside the Palace Theater. On his side of the mirror, it was a crappy, rundown place closed years ago. Here, it maintained all that crappy rundown appeal, but it hadn't been closed. There were posters in both spots, one for some sort of choir and the other for a magician. The name wasn't written in very big letters, and the face wasn't clear, but he had stared at that face in the mirror's reflection for the entirety of his life.

"I'm a fucking *magician?*" he said aloud. Even with the colored face, and all those gaudy reds and golds, no one could hide his own face from him, not even the backwards face from the other side. He stared for a moment, leaned closer to get a better look. The assistant, pictured even smaller—was that Lissa? Impossible.

He knocked on the window for the ticket seller. Though no one was immediately visible, through that door someone might be working. When no one answered, he tried the front door. Locked.

He let himself in anyhow.

The lobby was as wide as the building but not very deep, and there was a stand for selling assorted candies and sodas. He couldn't read the names because the cacophony of color blinded him. He walked through the doors into the theater itself, at the far end of the rightmost aisle. There was a mirror, one of those standalone types you could move from house to house and spin around until it shattered, on the stage. What would be the point? There was also a box of some sort, and a bag full of stuff, but he didn't get closer to investigate.

According to the poster, the show started at 8. Hours from now. What would happen when their precious little illusionist failed to show up and make with the tricks?

He exited the way he'd come in, not bothering to lock the door as he left, and headed for Lissa's apartment. Now, he absolutely had to see her. She lived on the third story of a walkup just a few blocks away—on both his side of the mirror and here. He saw her name on the mailboxes, pressed the buzzer, waited for her voice over the loudspeaker. It sounded no better here than on his side. "I'm not expecting anyone."

"Nicholas," he said, answering the unanswered question. He wondered, briefly, if his voice sounded the same on both sides, but apparently it was enough. She buzzed him in.

She wasn't waiting in the hall when he reached the third floor. When he turned the knob, it was locked. He knocked. No use in picking it if she expected him. After a moment, she opened the door only as far as the chain would allow.

"Lissa," he said.

She looked gorgeous, even in full color. He smiled and held out his arms with palms up, essentially asking what was up with the chains.

"Show starts in three hours," she told him. "Call is in two. I'm not ready, and I don't want to see you here."

"What gives?" he asked. "You should be thrilled to see me."

"Is there something wrong with you?" She squinted from behind the door. "You look...dry. Flaky."

He frowned. "I merely wanted to see a familiar face," he said. "A lovely face like yours. A face I see when I close my eyes."

"Have you got a fever?"

"We're a team, you and me," Nicholas said. "Why are you keeping me out?"

"Nicholas," she said, distinctly, enunciating every word. "We work together. We do. But you've never been to my place alone before, and I don't think now's the time..."

"Now," Nicholas said, "is definitely the time. Obviously, I've wasted enough of it."

She smiled in spite of herself. He was glad to see it. He was on his way to fixing things. Because despite the apple, there were things wrong with his life on this side of the mirror, things horribly awry, and he intended to fix them.

Averting her eyes, she said, "Give me a moment." Then she shut the door.

While waiting, Nicholas looked up and down the hallway, at the rich, shiny woods, the green and white tiles, the yellowish tint to the walls. He could take the colors in muted tones like that. He might even grow to like them.

When Lissa opened the door again, she pointed an Oliveri 9mm at him. From behind the barrel of the gun, she said, "Trust me, this is for the best."

2.

When fully recovered, Nicholas escaped the alleys and returned to the streets. It was too dark back there, with the streaks of black and spots of white. If he looked at anything in particular for too long, it gave him vertigo.

Nicholas made his way to the streets and did the only thing he really thought he should. He had a show that night. The Palace Theater was only a few blocks away, if he hadn't gotten too disoriented. It took a few minutes to figure out where he was and make his way in the right direction, but when he got there the marquee with his poster in it was empty except for the chalky threads of a spider's web and a good supply of dust. The ticket counter was barren. The doors were not merely locked, but chained shut.

He knocked anyway. The echoes bounced back, but obviously no one was inside. He didn't understand. Was there another stage somewhere else?

Lissa would know.

He'd been to her apartment only a few times, for parties and such, and didn't know if he could find his way back. The city sounded the same. People on the streets ignored him, mostly, though one or two nodded in acknowledgement of another human being. Their faces were either black or white, the same as everything else in this world. It was beginning to be unnerving.

He found Lissa's apartment, climbed the stoop, and pressed the button. After a moment, she buzzed him in, no questions asked. She lived at the top of a three story walkup. He climbed through the darkness and found her door standing open.

He stopped at the threshold and knocked on the open door. "Lissa?" he called. When she didn't answer, he looked around the side of the door and called her name again. The door opened onto the kitchen at one end of the tenement. Next was a living room, where Lissa sat wearing a sleek black dress with a high slit. Her legs were crossed, her lips twisted into a rictus smile. She pointed a 9mm Oliveri at him. From behind the barrel of the gun, she said, "Trust me, this is for the best."

3.

Nicholas held up his empty hands. "Isn't that a bit of an overreaction?" He didn't back away. If she meant to shoot him, she'd have to risk getting splattered by blood. Murder was always a messy business.

"Back away," she said, "and never come back here."

"What'd I do?" Nicholas asked. It was a stupid question. She wasn't going to tell him.

Lissa gestured with the gun. "I want to see you outside and walking away inside sixty seconds," she said. She didn't issue any further threat. She didn't have to.

"I didn't mean anything by it," Nicholas said. "I was just thinking...I mean, I didn't want to lose you."

"I was never yours to lose."

"Which is the same as losing you," Nicholas said. When she didn't immediately respond, he added, "You're beautiful,

Lissa, you always have been, and I've been a fool not to see it before. Look at me now, here, risking my life to tell you this."

"I quit," she told him.

"One more show," he said. "Please."

She eyed him, still from behind the gun. Her aim was steady. Her eyes steady. She said, "I have a headache."

"One more show," he said. He didn't even know what a show would entail. Probably magic. Illusion. Lissa stepping into a box and disappearing. He must've been to a magic show at some point in his life. What should he expect?

"You," she said, "promised me real magic."

"I did?"

"Said you'd make me a star."

"I must've been drinking."

"You," she said, "don't do a damn thing on that stage. I do all the work. I do it."

"I understand, I do."

"I've wanted to quit for a while now," she said. "I've wanted to shoot you for almost as long."

"Well, you've already done one," Nicholas said. "Just one more show, and I'm sure we can work things out."

"You don't know how to work things out. Did you see your audience last night? Did you see it? Thirteen people. *Thirteen*, Nicholas, and three of them didn't even pay for a ticket. You know what my share of that is?"

"Insufficient, I'm sure."

"Ten dollars."

"No one can live on ten dollars a night," Nicholas said.

"And how much did you make?"

Nicholas shook his head. "I honestly don't know."

"No fortune, I can tell you that much," Lissa said. She gestured with the gun again. "Go. Go, or I swear to every god you've ever known, I'll pull this trigger."

Nicholas didn't turn. He didn't want to give her his back. He'd rather see the bullet coming when it did. He backed toward the stairs, took the first step carefully, then said, "After the show tonight, Lissa, I'll make everything right. I swear it."

She said nothing. If anything, her trigger finger tensed. Nicholas hopped down the stairs. Once he started moving, he ran, taking the steps three and four at a time. If something broke inside her, if Lissa came out after him, he'd already be out of range. He spun around at the landing and went down the next flight, down until he was out the front door, on the street again, with all its overwhelming colors. He felt lightheaded. He glanced up at Lissa's silhouette in the window.

Long shadows stretched across the street, swallowing some of the vibrancy of everything. He went in a random direction, not sure where he'd go next. He had no real desire to put on a magic show. The only tricks he knew involved lifting wallets and watches and fancy gold-tipped pens. However, if he was some sort of illusionist on this side of the mirror, maybe it was time to work some real magic.

3.

Nicholas held up his hands, showing empty palms. "Whatever you think I did, I didn't," he said. "Honest." He didn't back away. If she meant to shoot him, he'd never get back out to the hallway in time.

"Closer," she said, gesturing with the gun. "I never expected to see you again."

"I'm not who you think I am," he said.

"I suppose not. An escape artist as well as a thief?" She grinned. It was a carnivorous grin. He didn't like it. This was not the Lissa he knew.

"Something happened," he said. "I'm on the wrong side of..."

Lissa gestured with the gun again. "Sit." She flipped the end of the gun, briefly, toward the couch. "I trusted you."

Obviously, she expected an answer. Nicholas said, "I don't know what to say."

"You can't talk your way out of this, *Nicholas*," she said. He didn't like the way his name sounded off her tongue, like that of a pet who had done something wrong. He sat at the edge of the couch like a coiled spring. She rose. Holding the gun at her side, she stepped toward him, making a show of it. "I've let you slide on a lot of things," she said, "because I've always liked you, Nicholas. I've always found you...I'll say attractive, in a not so obvious way." She towered over him now, all black and white and metal. Her finger never left the trigger. "So I asked you to do one simple little thing to make it up to me, Nicholas, and you couldn't manage it, could you?"

"There's still time," Nicholas told her.

"I'm not so sure," she said. "You look...pasty." She made a face to show her disgust. "Like you're coming apart."

"It's not like that."

"Quiet, now," Lissa said, tapping his knee with the barrel of the gun. "I'm talking."

He didn't respond. Even when she seemed to want a response, he didn't. It had been a mistake, going to someone he had known. Everything was different on this side of the mirror. The people he trusted couldn't be trusted. The people he loved would be filled with loathing and contempt. He had seen *Star Trek*. He should've known what would happen.

"So what," Lissa asked, "are you going to do..." She paused here, leaned close, raised the gun again to point it at his chest. "To make it up to me?"

When he didn't immediately answer, she moved her arm slightly and pulled the trigger. The bullet tore into the couch next to him. She returned her aim to him and narrowed her eyes. He could practically see smoke drifting out of the barrel, though that might've been his imagination. "Only thing I can do," he said, trying to sound like he belonged on this side of the mirror. "I'll make some magic."

She smiled. It was a beautiful smile. The gun took nothing away from that. "Oh?"

"At the theater," Nicholas said. "I can set everything up there." He had no idea what he would set up. He was only trying to buy some time. The longer she waited before shooting him, the more likely he'd survive. When his chance to escape came, he'd take it.

"There's no theater."

"The old Palace Theater."

She seemed to recognize it. "Kinky," she said, winking. Then: "Sure, why not? Lead the way." She swung the gun again like a beckoning finger. He hoped she wouldn't accidentally shoot him.

Outside, long shadows stretched across the street, disguising the starkness of chalk and charcoal, and lights had started to be lit—neon lights, not bright but certainly vibrant. He was in no frame of mind to put on a magic show. However, if he was any sort of an illusionist, it was time to work some real magic.

4.

Nicholas ran through an array of possible tricks he could perform. He only needed a distraction. Then he could run. He could worry about a destination when he was on the move. Of course, Jerry had caught him. There was a good chance Lissa, not his assistant Lissa but some otherworldly variation thereof, would catch him too. Catch him and shoot him.

Card and coin tricks seemed out of the question. Rope work might be appropriate, if he could somehow entangle Lissa in it. The only real solution, of course, was either to trap her—but none of his boxes would actually be in the theater—or take the gun.

Nicholas knew as much about guns as he knew about cameras: point and shoot. Hope for the best.

As they walked, the gun wasn't visible. She had it tucked in her bag, at the end of her hand, which still clutched the weapon and pointed it at him. The bullet would go right through the bag if she shot him. So he did nothing to incur her wrath.

The walk to the theater was only a few blocks, but it had been a long day already. Nicholas felt drained, physically and emotionally. And in some other way, too, that he couldn't describe, something to do with being on the wrong side of the mirror.

The theater looked rotten and neglected. The walls were brick, too thick to break in, but crumbly and dusty. With enough time, a person could dig their way inside. The doors, locked and chained, didn't look like they would easily move under any circumstance. They were heavy, wood and metal, the hinges rusted into place.

Nicholas was beginning to discern differences in the shades of white and black. These were not grays, but variations in thickness and intensity.

And the neon lights confused him. They didn't shine like a sun or a flashlight, but as night fell more neon blazed. Signs with words, outlines around doors and windows, even the electric lines to traffic signals buzzed. He tried not to spend too much time noticing. But he noticed.

He looked up at the top of the theater. The three stories were topped with architectural flourishes worthy of movie palaces from the 1920s, but such outcroppings had always been weak and were clearly eroding.

"I am intrigued," Lissa said.

"There's an entrance in the back," Nicholas said.

"These locks too tough for you?" She was teasing him. What was he on this side of the mirror?

"Less conspicuous," he said.

An alley ran alongside the theater. The building was straight and featureless from the alley, completely lacking in extravagance. Also, the side lacked windows, doors, platforms, anything that might allow entry. Nicholas still had no real plan other than delay.

The back doors were as big as the front but plain, thinner wood, without the glamour that faced the public. The chains were not as thick. And there was a window. With some effort, Nicholas pushed the window open. He would've broken it if necessary, but this seemed better.

"I'm almost impressed," Lissa said. "Too bad you couldn't put your talents to better use for me."

"Everything," Nicholas said, climbing through the window, "is for you." It was a tight squeeze, but he made it inside. Lissa squirmed through even more easily, making quite a show of it in that silky black dress. Together, they crept through the darkness behind the stage.

The green room door stood open, and the room beyond looked empty. The various set pieces, whether being stored or in use, were gone, though a couple of unrecognizable backdrops had apparently been too large to remove. There were sandbags and lighting rigs and a few chairs scattered around. They passed through the curtain onto the stage.

It was so dark, Nicholas could see nothing. The stage, the auditorium, all the seats—if they were still there—were swallowed by darkness. Lissa held him by the shoulder, her grip firm, not out of fear but to keep him from running.

With a heavy thud, a spotlight came on. It caught the two of them on the stage. A voice from faraway, perhaps the balcony, perhaps aiming the light at them, said, "Welcome to *my* Palace Theater."

4.

Nicholas went back to the theater. Not intentionally. That was just the direction his feet took him. He stared at his face in the poster. The face that stared back at him from the mirror. As night fell, the color seeped away, making it almost exactly like him.

And this, he realized, would be his greatest theft. Not merely cash, but a whole life. The Nicholas on this side of the mirror lived differently than he did. He would claim that as his own, even if it meant performing tricks on a stage. He would find a way to make that work, then twist this whole world to his will.

He entered the theater. Though old and in disrepair, it was not the wreck he remembered. There was still no one around. The show didn't start for hours. How did a magician prepare for his act?

He probably started by learning what the act was.

He needed Lissa for that. Or a videotape.

He strode into the auditorium, down the aisle between plush red seats, and climbed onto the stage. He pointedly did not look at the mirror. It seemed somehow wrong. He didn't even know why it was on the stage. Approaching it sideways, he pushed it toward an angle so he wouldn't accidentally catch his reflection.

He didn't want to know what his reflection was doing.

Backstage, still he found no one. He passed various props and set pieces for a variety of productions, some of which he might've recognized if they were named. He walked into the green room, which wasn't green at all, where there were trunks and a suitcase and a rack of clothes—suits for the magician. A second, adjoining room had outfits for the assistant, for this side's Lissa—outfits which were impossibly small.

She'd said she did most of the work. But she also wasn't

likely to show up tonight. Maybe a better plan was to steal this Nicholas's life and run away with it, maybe to Vegas, and put his skills to work. He could clean up in a town like that. All those drunk tourists throwing cash at the roulette wheel and blackjack tables. He could deal. He had the skills.

He went through the contents of both rooms searching for books with instructions. But of course there weren't any. It was all sleight of hand, right? He could manage that. He couldn't settle on a course of action.

Eventually, he realized he was being watched. He looked up. "Lissa."

She stood in the doorway, arms crossed. "I need more money," she said.

"I can do that."

"I need some now. Today. This moment."

Nicholas pulled the cash he'd taken from, ostensibly, his own apartment. In the low lighting, the green almost looked normal. He had never counted it, and didn't now. "Everything I've got," he said.

She took it. She did count it. She did not seem impressed.

"I can do better," he said. "I have a plan."

The lights went out.

He didn't think Lissa had arranged it, but he didn't want to take any chances. He rushed her, grabbed her, covered her mouth, whispered in her ear. "You still have that gun?"

She struggled, but only for a moment. She nodded.

"Where?"

She didn't answer.

With one hand, he took her bag. Though small, it was just large enough to hold a 9mm, and certainly heavy enough. He didn't have a lot of experience with guns. It wasn't part of his line. But he could point. He could shoot. How difficult did it have to be?

Still whispering, he asked, "Are you alone?"

She nodded again. Effectively a lie, since she was with him, but they both knew that wasn't what he meant.

"If I let go," he said, "you have to be quiet."

She nodded.

He let go. She slapped him. Hard. Not quietly at all.

"Fine," he said. "I deserved that. Now quiet." He crept out of the green room. The backstage area was dark and shadowy with only the red light of an exit sign. He went toward the stage, Lissa immediately behind him and holding his shoulder. On stage, he bumped into something, a crate, some part of the act. It was so dark, Nicholas could see nothing. The stage, the auditorium, all the seats were swallowed by darkness.

With a heavy thud, a spotlight came on. It caught the two of them on stage. A voice from faraway, perhaps the balcony, perhaps aiming the light at them, said, "Welcome to *my* Palace Theater."

5.

Trapped by the circle of light, Nicholas—and also Lissa, he assumed—stared defiantly at its source. "You might," Lissa said, "come down here and introduce yourself properly."

To that, the response was laughter. Good, hearty, from the belly laughter.

"I don't like the sound of that," Nicholas said.

"You're a brazen one, I'll give you that," the voice said. It seemed to echo from everywhere at once, as though it owned or was possessed by the theater itself.

Pinpoints of light emerged from the darkness. Eyes. Crouching low and hanging from the rafters and crawling on the walls, all at once a hundred dog-like creatures turned their attention to the stage—and to Nicholas and Lissa upon it.

"Now," the voice said, "would be a good time to *run.*"

Then he laughed again, the maniacal laugh of a madman, and Nicholas found himself entirely in agreement.

Nicholas retreated off stage, Lissa immediately after him. The creatures chittered behind them, and above them, and alongside them; and the creatures smacked their claws against the walls and floors and ceilings; and one of the creatures howled.

Lissa, even in that dress, leapt straight out the window, feet first, landing perfectly on the uneven broken alley floor in heels. Nicholas caught himself, almost didn't make it out at all, and nearly landed flat on his face.

The face that appeared in the window behind them snarled and slavered and showed teeth like spikes, and its eyes burned neon red. Lissa and Nicholas ran. It didn't matter where they went, it only mattered that they got away. They turned random corners, they drove deeper into the labyrinthine alleys into the center of this city.

It was not the city he thought it was.

Eventually, he couldn't run anymore. Lissa dragged him forward. When they stopped, they hadn't escaped anything. They'd been let go. Lissa wasn't even out of breath.

"They're after you, not me," she said.

"How do you figure?"

"The same red eyes."

"My eyes aren't red." He shook his head. With so little color to reference, maybe she mistook brown for red. The neon lights here were not brighter, but they buzzed more loudly, and there were more of them. He didn't know where they were. He recognized none of the buildings, none of the alleys they'd raced through, not even this version of Lissa.

When he'd caught his breath, or at least thought he'd been panting long enough, he managed to stand. Lissa looked at him, into him, examining and appraising him. If she'd been as afraid as he'd been, she hid it exceptionally well.

"Now what?" he asked.

She kissed him. Hard and rough and fast. It was over before he knew it had started. She grinned, all mischief, and said, "I have no idea where we are."

Nicholas looked around. Nothing made sense. The slashes of white and black, the powdery look of everything, the lines of the buildings, the lines of colored light. The disorientation threatened him with dizziness and nausea. He focused instead on Lissa, who had smeared her black lipstick on his lips.

That wasn't focusing.

"It's too dark," Nicholas said. Even in daylight, it was too dark, but the sun had gone and left them somewhere else. He tightened his fists. He said something, he wasn't even sure what, a word or two from an ancient language he'd never known, and created a ball of light out of nothing.

5.

Trapped by the circle of light, Nicholas—and also Lissa, he assumed—stared defiantly at the source of that light. "You might," he said, "want to come down here and introduce yourself properly."

To that, the response was laughter. Good, hearty, from the belly laughter.

"I don't like the sound of that," Lissa said.

"You're a brazen one, I'll give you that," the voice said. It seemed to echo from everywhere at once, as though it owned or was possessed by the theater itself.

Pinpoints of light emerged from the darkness. Eyes. Crouching low and hanging from the rafters and crawling on the walls, all at once a hundred dog-like creatures turned their attention to the stage, and to Nicholas and Lissa upon it.

"Now," the voice said, "would be a good time to *run*." Then he laughed again, the maniacal laugh of a madman, and Nicholas found himself entirely in agreement.

Nicholas retreated off stage, Lissa immediately ahead of him. The creatures chittered behind them, and above them, and alongside them; and the creatures smacked their claws against the walls and floors and ceilings; and one of the creatures howled.

Nicholas tried to dive straight out the window. It wasn't pretty. He caught himself, twisted in midair, and landed hard on his shoulder. Lissa managed the window with an acrobat's grace.

The face that appeared in the window behind them snarled and slavered and showed teeth like spikes, and its red eyes burned. Nicholas and Lissa ran. It didn't matter where they went, it only mattered that they got away. They turned random corners, they drove deeper into the labyrinthine alleys in the center of this city.

It was not the city he thought it was.

When he thought they weren't being followed anymore—not that they'd gotten away, but that they'd been abandoned—Nicholas stopped running to catch his breath. He slumped against a brick wall. Lissa grinned at him. She didn't even seem to be out of breath. "What were those things?" he asked her.

"They're after you, not me," she said.

"How do you figure?"

"They were the same dusty black you are. With the same red eyes."

"My eyes are not..." He didn't finish, because he didn't really know. The colors here confused him. "If they wanted us," he said, "why the warning? Why tell us to run? Those..." He didn't know what they were. "Those *dogs* could've ripped us to shreds right there on stage."

He pushed himself back to his feet, away from the wall, and faced Lissa directly. Was she responsible? Had she unleashed this? She stared back at him with genuine fear.

Anger, frustration, annoyance, all sorts of other things mixed in there, but definitely fear. He pushed aside the idea that she might be responsible.

"Now what?" she asked.

"I don't know where we are," he admitted. It might've been true on his side of the mirror, as well. Forget the hues and saturation; it was dark enough now, those didn't matter. But the shapes were wrong. The architecture seemed crooked. He wasn't sure how some of these buildings managed to continue standing.

Lissa looked around. "Neither do I." Then she grinned. Pure mischief. "It's too dark," she said, and with a twist of her fingers she created a ball of light out of nothing.

6.

The ball of light glowed and sizzled. It gave off no heat. It moved when she moved her hands, responding like a marionette might, in ways Nicholas couldn't quite understand. "Impressive."

"I didn't know I could do that."

The ball lit the entire alley. It was a harsh light, and it threw hard shadows. She shifted it and played with it and, after a moment, made it spin.

"And how, exactly, does this help us?" Nicholas asked.

"We can see, for one," Lissa said. She narrowed her eyes at him. "When I told you, months ago, that I could do actual magic, you didn't believe me, did you?"

"You conjured that ball of light from the spirit realm?"

"Something like that."

"What, then?"

"It's tricky," she told him. "Involves math. You wouldn't understand."

He stared at her, but only for a moment. He looked back, toward the theater and the creatures. They didn't seem to be in pursuit anymore.

Lissa tossed the ball into the sky. Over the buildings, it exploded into one and one thousand white sparkles which drifted down and away. She was staring at it and smiling. Briefly, Nicholas did the same. It felt childlike. Naïve. Even innocent. But it felt good, and he liked it, though he didn't think it was a feeling that would last.

As the sparkles scattered and winked out of existence, darkness returned to the alley. Nicholas tried twisting his fingers and saying whatever word it was Lissa might have said, but nothing happened. Lissa, meanwhile, created another, bigger and brighter, ball of light.

"Okay," Nicholas said, "so you're a magician."

"And you," Lissa said, "are an imposter and a fool. What the hell did you think you were doing, anyway?"

"I don't know what you mean."

"You must've tried something, to have sapped all your color. You look positively ghastly, Nicholas." She grinned. "Although I admit, there's a certain appeal to the starkness of you. Are you dying? Did you sign a contract? Did you read something you weren't supposed to read? Dammit, Nicholas, did you at least get the pronunciation right?"

Nicholas was shaking his head to answer her questions. "I have no idea what you're talking about."

"You lie."

"Often," Nicholas admitted, "but not this time."

She regarded him for a moment, seeming to peer right into him. Surely, she realized he wasn't the Nicholas she knew from this side of the mirror. "Apparently," she said, "my magic works better now. It's easier to manipulate." She rolled the ball around her hand like a juggler with a clear glass sphere. "Which means it's stronger, Nicholas, and therefore more dangerous. Less predictable. Volatile, even." She looked as if she blamed him.

"And more fun, I hope," Nicholas said.

"You are exasperating."

Nicholas flashed a grin. "You'd be shocked, how often I hear that."

After a moment of silence, Lissa said, "You're not supposed to be here, right? I mean, you're some other version of the Nicholas I know?"

"You know me, now," Nicholas told her.

"You have to go back."

"I don't think so."

"You brought this trouble with you," Lissa said. "You have to bring it back."

"Oh, no," Nicholas said. "All this is unique to this side of the mirror." He looked up, at the thick, roiling clouds, gray things that soaked up all the colors and made a sort of soup. "We don't have clouds like that."

"Neither did we."

Nicholas tightened his fists. "Can you magic the weather?" he asked.

"No."

"How do you know?"

"I wouldn't know where to begin," Lissa told him.

"Okay, fine, we'll deal with that later," Nicholas said. "For the moment, we need to break into one of these apartments."

"What?" Lissa blinked. "Why?"

"Those dogs won't be far behind us," Nicholas said. "I for one would feel more comfortable behind the safety of a door."

"Even if it's a door you break open?"

"I've got skills," Nicholas said. "I can do a bit more finesse than *breaking open*."

"Then we can find a mirror," Lissa said, "and see about switching you back."

"I don't think so."

Lissa smiled. "We'll deal with it later."

"You're forgetting who has the gun here."

"You're forgetting who has all the magic."

Nicholas took a breath, acknowledged—at least inwardly—that he had no idea what the extent of her power might be, and nodded. "Okay, then," he said. "Which way?"

Lissa looked around. She said, "None of this is familiar." She looked back the way they had come, turned to a different direction, and said, "This way."

6.

The ball of light glowed and sizzled. It gave off no heat. It moved when he moved his hands, responding like a marionette might, in ways he couldn't quite understand.

Lissa stared. "Impressive."

"I didn't know I could do that."

The ball lit the entire alley. It was a harsh light, and it threw hard shadows. He shifted it and played with it and, after a moment, made it spin.

"Do you have any idea what you're doing?"

He caught the ball. Palmed it. Hid it behind his back, which threw his own shadow over Lissa and swallowed this black and white powdery version of her. "None," he admitted, but he smiled. "I mean, I've practiced all sorts of magic, not just illusion, but never with much effect."

"Much effect?"

"A thing here or there, maybe," Nicholas said. He whipped the ball around him, levitated it over his open hand, then sent it into the sky. When it passed the top of the building, it exploded like fireworks, but soundlessly, with a shower of sparkles in every color across the spectrum. He stared up and smiled. Lissa did the same. For a moment, only a moment, he felt like a child discovering all the things.

As the sparkles scattered and winked out of existence, darkness settled again on the alley. This time, with purpose and intention, Nicholas created another ball of light. This was bigger. Brighter. Again, it burned without burning. It radiated no heat whatsoever.

"Maybe my magic works better here, this side of the mirror," Nicholas said. "Maybe it's more likely to work in this world."

Lissa stepped closer, so there was no real space between them. "That might make it more volatile," she said. "Less predictable and more dangerous." Her grin flashed at full intensity. "And more fun."

"So what I have to do," Nicholas said, "is figure out how to return to my side of the mirror."

Lissa frowned. It was exaggerated, but it was honest. "I like this version of you better than mine."

"I don't know what's going on here," Nicholas said.

"Aren't you missing something obvious?"

"What's that?"

"If you came through the mirror, and my version of you went through the mirror, aren't the two of you facing the same problems simultaneously? If you look into a mirror, won't you be there doing the exact same thing?"

Nicholas slumped. All of him, all at once. The logic was terrible and terrifying. "What do you suggest?"

"Verify it."

"Do you happen to have a mirror on you?"

"No."

"Your apartment?"

She shook her head. "I have no idea where that is anymore."

"What do you mean?"

"Look at the sky," Lissa said. There were clouds above the city, thick and roiling, charcoal black clouds reflecting the colors of neon. "It's changed."

Nicholas tightened his fists as he stared. Lissa added, "That's not an ordinary weather system."

"So where do we find a mirror?" Nicholas asked. "And what do I do if..."

"One thing at a time," Lissa said. "Does it have to be a mirror, or just anything reflective?"

"I was working a spell," Nicholas said. "I didn't think it would work, really. I just wanted to peer into the mirror, that's all. But it was definitely a mirror. It's shattered now. Impassable, I would think."

"Any apartment should have a mirror," Lissa said. "We can just break into any..."

"I'm not a criminal."

"You're a thief, here," she told him. "And a killer, or a would-be killer. You still owe me a body, you know."

"One thing at a time," he told her, not even wanting to address what his reflection had gotten into on this side of the mirror, a little afraid of what he might learn. "We can knock on someone's door, ask for help."

Lissa laughed. "That might work on your side of the mirror," she said, "but not here."

"No, you're right."

"You just have to open a lock." Lissa grinned again. Put a sexy spin on her voice. "We can knock first, if that makes you feel better."

"I can't pick a lock," Nicholas said.

"Of course you can. You could here, why couldn't you, there?"

"You know, that means we're not identical," Nicholas told her. "On my side, my Lissa is my assistant."

"Assistant?"

"In my magic act."

Lissa laughed, though it was short. "I'll pretend that doesn't hurt me."

Nicholas glanced around. They were at the crossroads of alleys, surrounded by fire escapes and alcoves and garbage bins and windows, but no stoops with doors or doorbells, no true entrances of any sort. "Which way?" he asked.

Lissa looked around, said, "This way," and led Nicholas down an alley they hadn't been running through.

7.

Not far down the alley, Lissa stopped under a fire escape. The ladder had been lowered, so it was a short jump to reach the bottom rung. The ladder was black, the bricks were black, the mortar between the bricks white like chalk, and the sky above a mix of variations on the same. Nicholas couldn't help but see the sky when he looked up. He didn't really want to.

"Here's as good as anywhere," Lissa said. "Start climbing."

"I can't just break through a window."

"It's easier than picking a lock."

She had a point, though it wasn't a good one. "Can't we just find a door?"

"Do you see any doors?"

"At the far end of the alley," Nicholas said. "Surely, that's the street, and all the front doors are there."

"The back doors are just conveniently missing?"

Nicholas ignored her. He walked forward. He brought his light with him. Lissa stayed where she was, arms crossed, gun dangling in her hand. "Fine," she said. "I'll wait here."

The alley stretched forever, possibly for miles. Nicholas walked ten minutes without reaching the end of it. The bricks weren't merely the same bricks repeating. Some of the fire escapes were rusted and crumbling. Some of the garbage bins overflowed. White rats scurried in the corners of the shadows, running from his light. Eventually, Nicholas conjured a second, smaller ball of luminescence, reared back like a pitcher, and launched it ahead of him. The ball streaked forward, well faster than he could have thrown it, with a tail like a comet, losing colored flakes of light as it moved.

The ball of light shattered at the end of the alley when it hit a wall. Something ahead groaned, or grumbled — something too far for Nicholas to see.

He sighed. He turned around and started walking, but whatever he'd heard behind him made him run. Nothing chased him. But whatever moved back there, it was large, and briefly there was the sound of wrenching metal.

It didn't take ten minutes to reach Lissa. She stared down at him from the fire escape. "You know you're wearing a dress," Nicholas said.

"And heels," Lissa added. "Get up here."

Nicholas leapt for the ladder. On his first attempt, he missed. He tossed the ball of light up to float level with Lissa, then jumped again. It was a hard climb. He was far from the height of physical perfection. The first few rungs were all upper body strength. Lissa watched, leaning against the railing, and was polite enough not to laugh.

Whatever had made noise behind him sounded closer.

His feet reached the bottom rung, which made the rest of the climb easier.

"There's an open window on the top floor," Lissa said, taking to the stairs.

In total, it was a five story climb, a switchback at every level. The fire escape creaked under their weight but felt steady. At the top story, they could have climbed higher, to the roof, with an easily reached ladder. Lissa slipped into an open window. With a deep breath, Nicholas climbed in after her.

The television screen glowed in a variety of neon colors. If those meant to convey shapes or figures, Nicholas couldn't see them. It was the first thing he noticed in the room. Neon lights lined the corners of the walls and ceiling in an otherwise white room with black flourishes. A man sat on the couch in front of the screen, so mesmerized he at first didn't notice his visitors until Lissa stepped in front of him and pointed the gun at his face. "We'd like to ask, very politely," she said, "to use a mirror."

"Is that a gun?"

Her trigger finger twitched. "It's not a rolling pin."

The guy looked from Lissa to Nicholas, then back to the gun. "I haven't got no cash."

"Mirror," Nicholas said. "Bathroom, perhaps? Bedroom?"

"Hell, I ain't got the money to buy me one of them reflecting glasses."

Nicholas and Lissa exchanged confused glances.

"Listen," the man said, "there's a guy I know, he can get you a mirror, and some Scarlet pills or something while you're at it. He can do you up real good."

Lissa stepped closer, pressed the barrel against the man's forehead. "That guy you know," she said, "works for me."

"Then why the hell do you come to me looking for a fucking mirror?"

She wanted to pull the trigger. Nicholas could see it. He wanted to, too. He left the living room, walked straight into the kitchen, which was useless, and found a bathroom so small he could fit it in his closet. There was a shower stall, toilet, and sink, and behind the sink a black frame around a wash of white. He tapped it. It might've been glass, but it certainly didn't show anything.

He went to the bedroom. It was small enough for one, and a woman slept entangled in the sheets. There was a closet, a dresser, an assortment of clothes—nothing fancy—and makeup in shades of black and white—no gray, no neon—but no mirror.

The woman sat up suddenly. She stared straight at Nicholas. "Your eyes," she said.

"My eyes?"

"They're red."

Nicholas wanted to shoot her, too. Instead, he returned to the living room and told Lissa, "They haven't got a mirror."

Lissa frowned. She had stepped away from the guy on the couch and no longer pointed the gun straight at him. "That doesn't make sense."

"I've been trying to tell you," the man said. "Reflections, they ain't easy to find."

"Last one I saw," Lissa said suddenly, though she frowned as she said it, "was on stage at the Palace Theater."

"We just left there," Nicholas said.

"We did."

He didn't add, *And that's where the dog things are.*

7.

They walked.

They walked and they walked, but the alley stretched infinitely ahead—and possibly infinitely behind. The walls were monochromatic enough, especially in the night; they no longer made Nicholas vertiginous.

Lissa lit the way, and led the way, but there was no place to go. Finally, Nicholas stopped walking. "We're going the wrong way," he said.

"There isn't any other way."

"Up," Nicholas said, looking to the top of the five story building beside them. "Or down." Small windows at foot level indicated basements, maybe basement apartments, and maybe only the top level of multiple basements.

Lissa shook her head. "Not down."

"Fine. Climb."

She hesitated, weighing options. Which was safer, climbing before or after him? She pushed the ball of light into the air. It reached the first level of the fire escape and spun in place. She jumped, caught the bottom of the ladder, and quickly reached the first level. Nicholas shoved the gun into the waistband of his jeans and followed. He kicked as if it would give him momentum. When he reached Lissa, she had split the ball of light into three and was manipulating them around her hand.

"They're surprisingly agile," she said.

"Up," Nicholas said. "To the roof."

They climbed stairs to the top floor, then a ladder to the roof. It was rooftops in all directions, some higher or lower, dotted with vents and shafts and little sheds and air handler units and all manner of unidentifiable machinery, stretching as far into the darkness as Nicholas could see.

"This ain't my city," Nicholas said.

"It's not mine, either," Lissa said. "But I think I can..." She folded the three balls into one again, reared back as if to pitch a baseball, and threw it into the sky. It sizzled and grew and dropped flakes of light as it rose, and lit the city rooftops.

Essentially, she created a sun, or at least a moon, under the clouds, bright enough to extend their vision a long way. But what they saw—Nicholas saw an endless sea of rooftops. People gathered on some. On others, he saw the dogs, the red-eyed dogs of the theater, creatures he never needed to see with any detail. They were jagged slashes cut from the fabric of reality, black and white and neon and smoke and emerald and crimson, fur sharp like knives, and so many teeth. They sat, alone or in small groups, and every single one of these things, without fail, stared straight back at Nicholas.

All at once, to the left and to the right, north and south and every other imaginable direction, the dogs—that name was insufficient—got up and started, without hurry, walking in their direction.

"This," Lissa said, "doesn't look good."

"Down," Nicholas said, headed back to the fire escape. Lissa beat him there, and rushed down the ladder. It was like looking into a well; no matter how far he looked, no matter how well he squinted his eyes, the bottom never emerged from the murk. The light of Lissa's little moon slowly faded, but even at full capacity it never stretched deeply into the city canyons. Something moved underneath those shadows. Something swam through the darkness.

As they descended from the roof, the darkness rose. Rather than give themselves to whatever hid there, they slipped through an open window on the top story of the building.

The television glowed in a variety of rich, sumptuous colors, none of which Nicholas's eyes were able to translate. If they meant to convey shapes or figure, Nicholas couldn't see them. There was plenty of color in this room, from the deep green blanket to the extraordinarily yellow walls, the bright red toaster in the kitchen, even the purple tee shirt on the man sitting in the couch. He was so mesmerized by what he saw on the screen, he didn't acknowledge his visitors until Nicholas stepped in his line of sight and pointed the gun at him. "We need your help."

"Is that a gun?"

Nicholas's trigger finger twitched. "What the hell else would it be?"

The guy looked from Nicholas to Lissa, then back to the gun. "I haven't got no cash."

"Then it's your lucky day," Nicholas said, "because I ain't looking for any."

"Then what do you want?"

Nicholas didn't actually know. He looked to Lissa. She said, unhelpfully, "A mirror." When no one said anything, she added, "Bathroom, maybe? Or the bedroom."

"I can't say I've got one."

"What do you mean, you haven't got one?" Nicholas asked.

The guy shook his head and scratched his cheek. "I can't say I remember ever looking in a mirror. Dirty frightening things, they are. Who knows who you'll see staring back at you."

Lissa made a noise of frustration and marched into the kitchen, toward the bathroom at the corner of the tenement. Half a minute later, she came back, and walked straight through to the next room, the bedroom.

"Man, your girlfriend's gonna be mad," the guy said to Nicholas.

Nicholas wanted to shoot him. Instead, he looked up when Lissa returned. She said, "They haven't got a mirror."

Nicholas frowned. He lowered the gun. He didn't know what he was doing, and he didn't like not knowing. "That doesn't make sense."

"Why should any of it?" Lissa asked.

"Hey," the guy said suddenly, nearly popping up from the couch, restraining himself only at the last minute when Nicholas raised the gun. "I know where I recognize you from. You're that magician guy, down at the Palace." He smiled. "Hey, that was a great show. Your assistant was gorgeous." He glanced at Lissa. "Hey, that was you, wasn't it?"

She smiled to say yes.

"You're gorgeous," he said.

"This isn't helping," Nicholas said.

"Oh, no, but it is," the guy said. "See, it's like this. Reflections, they ain't easy to find. But the last one I saw, the last time I saw a glass like that, it was on your stage, man. It was part of your show."

"We just left there," Lissa said.

"We did," Nicholas said, but he wasn't happy as he said it. The dogs were everywhere now, but that's where they'd come from.

8.

Into the hall from the apartment, they found long halls with walls slashed white, cheap linoleum, art deco frames every fifty feet, but no pictures, no glass, and no mirrors. The doors were labeled, but not with numerals of any sort Nicholas recognized. The symbols were all wrong. Even Lissa frowned at one of those signs before they retreated back to the apartment.

"Yeah," the guy there said. "It looks rather rough out there."

"Can I get you some whiskey or something?" the woman from the bedroom asked.

"No, thanks," Nicholas said.

"Actually," Lissa said, "I could go for a double."

"It doesn't look rough," Nicholas said. "Just different."

"Man, all I've got to do is sit here and watch the TV. Nothing to concern me, right?"

"There are dogs," Nicholas said. "With eyes like mine. And a temper."

"What do you need?"

The woman returned from the kitchen with whiskey and glasses. She poured for everyone, even Nicholas. He stared at the floor, the cheapest kind of carpet he could imagine, white with flecks of black. He glanced at Lissa. She nodded. Encouragement? He decided to take it. "Okay, I've got this," he said. "I need—a glass. Empty."

Lissa downed hers and handed it over.

"Clean," he said, "and dry."

"Coming right up."

"Fill it with—what kind of herbs have you got?"

"Man, my lady can cook."

The woman smiled shyly. "I can make a thing or two."

"I need some herbs. The more different kinds, the better."

"Sure."

"And from me?" the guy asked.

Nicholas smiled. "We're just getting started. We need a map."

"I ain't got no map."

"Not of this place, you wouldn't," Nicholas said. "I'm trying to make one. Have you got, I don't know, a shirt, a button up shirt, one you'll never need again?"

"That," the guy said, "I've got." He went toward the bedroom.

"White," Nicholas called after him, "if you've got it."

Lissa handed him a glass. The woman returned with an assortment of jars on a plastic tray. Oregano, sage, tarragon — they were all whites or blacks.

"I hope you know what you're doing," Lissa said.

Nicholas shook his head as the guy brought out a white shirt with black buttons. "I'm making something," he said. "Step back. And get me a lighter."

"No lighter," the guy said.

"Matches?" the woman suggested.

"That'll work."

She hesitated. She asked, "Will all this fix your eyes?"

Nicholas paused. He didn't know exactly what he was doing. He drew from a variety of the arts he had practiced and played with, but mostly the best he could do — even here so far — was a little bit of light. Okay, here there had been a substantial amount of light, beyond anything he'd ever conjured before. But he needed something big now, something unique, and since he didn't have a spell to make precisely what he needed, he was improvising. What it would accomplish, in the end, he didn't know. He didn't have a plan that stretched so far as fixing his eyes. He suspected they were their normal brown, and there had never been reds other than neon on this side of the mirror.

From outside, from on the roof, one of the dogs howled.

Everyone froze, if only for a moment. The guy went to shut his window. It had already let Nicholas and Lissa in, wasn't that enough? The howl was wolf-like. It was answered, and the answer was none too distant.

"Yes," Nicholas answered, because anything else would require the same explanations he needed. But he paused again. "Hey, what's your name?"

"Us?" the woman asked.

"Don't think anyone's ever asked us before," the guy said.

"You're kidding."

"Honestly," the woman said, "he doesn't remember much. He's Dale. I'm Devi." She gave a white jeans curtsey.

He smiled. "Thank you, Devi. Dale. This means a lot to me."

"Yeah," Dale said. "It's a crazy world out there."

"I'm Nicholas. The woman with the gun, she's Lissa."

"I'm dangerous," Lissa warned them.

Devi shook her head. "You ain't as dangerous as you think. Have you seen the sky?" Everyone glanced toward the window, the one which had been open a few minutes ago. One of the dogs stared in at them, salivating, growling from the back of its throat, black barbed wire fur matted back. It was raining. The rain was neon red, like the dog's eyes.

Devi drew the curtain over the window. "Enough of that," she said. "You've got work to do."

Nicholas filled the glass with the herbs and mixed them with his forefinger. They didn't have to be evenly distributed, just plentiful and pungent. He dumped some of the herbs on the front of the shirt, between two mother of pearl buttons, and the rest on the other half of the shirt, between button holes.

Everyone watched in silence—well, in the pounding silence of the red rain—as Nicholas struck the match and brought the flame down to the herbs on one side. They

41

caught quickly, unnaturally, and burnt in a flash. He lit the other side off the same match. Each side left stains in the shirt, one representing this apartment, the other the abandoned Palace Theater. He drew the two sides together and fastened the two buttons, so that the two locations were adjacent.

"I see what you did," Devi said.

As another dog howled outside, Nicholas said, "Let's just hope it works."

Lissa went to the apartment door and pulled it open, revealing not the stage or auditorium of the Palace Theater, but a small apartment, with the abandoned spring frame of a twin sized bed and a table which might once have supported a lamp: the manager's apartment over the theater, all the different shades of black overlapping.

"Welcome," Nicholas said, echoing the words they'd heard earlier, "to the Palace Theater."

8.

"How," Nicholas asked, "do you think we're going to get back there? You saw what happened on the roofs. You saw there's no place to go."

"Down," Lissa said.

"Underground?"

"There's more to this world than you imagine," the guy said, lounging back on the couch. "What you need, if you want it, is a map."

"Have you got one?"

"Damn straight, I do. Hey, Devi!"

A woman emerged from the bedroom. "You rang, *master?*" The sarcasm was vivid, but her smirk cut it back to something playful.

"No, baby, I didn't mean nothing like that," the guy said. "I just need to know, have you still got those pamphlets?

From the subway?"

She eyed him, then looked at Nicholas with his gun. "You ain't as dangerous as you think," she told him. "Have you seen the sky?"

They all glanced through the open window. It was dark out there, not just nighttime dark but strangely iridescent, burgundy or maroon, a color Nicholas could barely register. He went to the window and looked up, over the alley, into clouds that were bubbling, spinning and whirling, with tendrils of smoke dancing like tentacles in a New England speakeasy. And closer, on top of the roof, looking down at him, were the dogs, a dozen or more, staring, salivating.

The rain started then. A red rain. Nicholas slammed shut the window, drew a curtain, and said, "We should focus."

Devi had found the subway map. They laid it out on the floor, over the impossible color of the carpet. They unfolded it. They spent forever unfolding it. It hadn't been that thick, but there was as much paper as there was space. On one side, in the tiniest letters imaginable, were the timetables for a variety of rail lines. On the other, a map that resembled a circuit board.

"I can't do anything with this," Nicholas said.

"We're here," Devi said, pointing with a razor sharp red fingernail and poking a hole in the map.

"And you want to get here," the guy said, also pointing. His finger was dirty and smudged and dull, and did not put a hole in the paper. Nicholas thought that was significant. He thought a lot of things were significant, including the fact that the guy had no name, and was therefore expendable. When he looked at Devi, she met his eye, and he couldn't catch the details of her through her perfection.

"Hey," Lissa said, snapping her fingers in front of his face. "Focus."

"Right." Nicholas swallowed. "I don't see the theater on this map."

"Trust me," the guy said, "that's the right place."

"Of course it is," Lissa said. "Have you never taken the subway?"

"I like to give my legs the exercise."

"You're infuriating."

"The alleys are all twisted," Nicholas said, "and the rooftops looked like they never break for streets. How do we know we can trust this map?"

"I never said you could," the guy said. "But it's all you've got."

"No," Lissa said. She turned to Devi. "Have you got gloves? I don't mean winter gloves, I mean..."

"I know what you mean." Devi went for the bedroom.

"You," Lissa said, putting out a palm, "I need a bullet. From that gun."

"You need a bullet?"

"Actually, I need the gunpowder." Then she turned to the guy who had been watching TV. "I need thread. Have you got any?"

"If we don't, we can pull some off one of my old shirts. Them things are just unravelling."

"I'll make that work," Lissa said.

"What is it you think you're doing?" Nicholas asked.

"I'm not entirely sure," Lissa said, "but I think I only need one more thing." She looked at Devi again, who had returned with a pair of gloves like you might see on the fancy ladies at a 1929 opera house. "Thimble?"

Devi shook her head. "Not here."

"I...I don't want to get blood on this," Lissa said. "I'm not that good a seamstress."

Devi sat opposite Lissa. "Enough of this," she said. "You've got work to do."

Lissa spread the gunpowder over the pertinent section of the map. It seemed like a long distance. From outside, from on the fire escape, one of the dogs howled. Everyone froze, if only for a moment. The howl was wolf-like. It was answered, and the answer came from the roof above them.

"A lighter?" Lissa asked.

Devi got a book of matches from the kitchen. Lissa struck one, then set the little flame to the gunpowder. It burned in a flash, distorting the map, obscuring the parts that weren't needed and leaving a clear path from this apartment to the Palace Theater.

Lissa produced a needle, apparently plucking it from the air unless she'd had one hidden in her jeans or hair or something. She ran the thread through the eye of the needle, then went to work on the map, stitching with crazy speed. With a tug, she pulled the two locations together on the map. With the last stitch, she drew blood, and a drop smudged the ink on the map.

"Damn." Lissa sucked at her finger. "That hurt."

"I see what you did," Devi said. "That's not a good omen."

As another dog howled outside, Nicholas said, "There are no more good omens."

"Did it work?" Lissa asked.

Nicholas got up, went to the apartment door, and pulled it open onto a room that had clearly not been there before, a room with a neatly made bed and a table with a lamp: the manager's apartment over the theater, in soft pastel colors Nicholas couldn't even register. "Welcome," he said, echoing words they'd heard earlier, "to the Palace Theater."

9.

The step across the threshold made them all dizzy. The four of them swayed and shifted. They grabbed each other for support. Nicholas held onto the wall. It was like an elevator suddenly plunging beneath him. He barely kept his footing. He stumbled into the abandoned apartment, through a whorl of dust and cobwebs. The floor creaked under his step.

Lissa patted down her dress. "*That*," she said, "was impressive."

"We still have to get downstairs," Nicholas said. "Through the dogs."

"And the man with the spotlight," Lissa said. "Maybe we should go after him first."

Nicholas shook his head. "I doubt he's still there, but since I don't know the way—let's see what we see first."

"Man, that certainly was something special," Dale said.

"We're just getting started," Lissa said. She went to pull the door open and had to really work at it. Time had warped the wood of the door, had settled it into place, and it was not happy to move. Devi came alongside her to help. When the door gave way, it gave all the way, and swung open wildly.

On the other side: a dark hallway. Nicolas pushed the ball of light ahead of them. It might draw attention, but it would also prevent surprises. Under his breath, he said a few words he didn't even know, ancient words of protection borrowed from shriveled memories. He must've read a passage in a book at some point.

As yet, they had no idea which way the stage was. The hall might be on a side, directly above, or all the way at the back of the auditorium. Nicholas chose a direction at random. There was no subtly in walking on these floors, as they creaked, cracked, and squealed with every step. The dogs had made no noise. Nicholas considered casting something for stealth, but he didn't know how much he could do before depleting himself. Any little thing might be one thing too many if it came to a confrontation.

At the end of the hall, stairs led down and a door led to the right.

"Could be the lighting," Lissa whispered. She pointed the gun as Devi opened the door.

It was, in fact, the spotlight, still aimed directly at the

stage. The mirror stood there, grungy and facing away, unguarded.

"He had been here," Lissa said.

Nicholas nodded. "Now, he's probably at Dale's place." He looked over his shoulder. "Did we shut the door behind us?"

Nothing moved in the hallway, nothing emerged from the manager's apartment, nothing made a sound that could be heard over the drumbeats of the red rain.

"We've got to assume they're coming," Lissa said.

"All we have to do," Nicholas said, "is reach the mirror on that stage."

"What's so special about the mirror?" Dale asked.

Devi smacked his shoulder. "Isn't it obvious?"

Nicholas took a breath and started down the stairs. These had never been meant for the masses. They were the opposite of grand and opulent, and each step seemed to sag beneath his weight. He didn't want to touch the walls, and his ball of light, bobbing along beside him, revealed nothing comforting. They descended to a storeroom. The skeletons of big old desks leaned against the walls. A few crates had been left behind. Mice, maybe rats, scurried out of the reach of the light.

The storeroom led to an office. On top of the desk, on a sheet of fresh paper, someone had hastily drawn circles and triangles. The cracked remnants of pencil leads littered the desk.

"Someone's been here," Dale said, peering at the desk.

"A ghost?" Devi suggested.

"Something else," Nicholas said, as additional shapes formed on the paper. They were rough, they were incomplete, they were crazed, and they were leaking to this side of the mirror from someplace else, someplace where the Palace Theater still entertained guests. "It's a good sign, I think."

"An omen?" Lissa asked.

Nicholas didn't answer. He didn't know how. But the pencils that were making those circles, and the circles themselves, were not the same charcoal black as everything else in this world.

Through the office, they reached the lobby. Nicholas wanted to run. He wanted to race. He said, "I'll have to face the mirror alone."

"No," Lissa said, grabbing his hand long enough to give a reassuring squeeze.

The lobby seemed to be a geometric impossibility, folding in and around itself, curved in ways Nicholas didn't understand. It wasn't an exact duplicate of the Palace Theater lobby he had known. It was something else entirely, something strange, something unsettling.

"The illusionist," voices said, voices that didn't really reach across from the other side of the mirror. "The artist." "The virtuoso himself." It sounded vaguely hostile. "Do a trick. Give us a preview."

"Am I the only one hearing that?" Nicholas asked.

Dale said, "I don't hear nothing."

"Do us a magic!"

Dale jumped, startled.

"We all heard *that*," Devi said.

"Ghosts?" Dale asked.

Nicholas shook his head. Lissa said, "We must be getting closer."

"This way," someone said, someone solid, someone on this side of the mirror. An usher stood at an open side door. "What do you think you're doing out there? Someone will see you."

Nicholas blinked. "Who?"

The usher waved them into the room. "They'll simply eat you alive if they find you."

"That can't be a good thing," Nicholas admitted.

The usher showed his teeth in what was meant as a grin. "Of course not."

"You realize," Lissa said, as they stepped into the side room, "you're an usher in an abandoned theater."

"The Parliament of Ushers," he said, "never allows a theater to be forsaken."

"Do you know what's going on?" Nicholas asked.

The usher shook his head. "I had hoped you might. I'm here only to protect the theater, and I will do what I can to stop this. At first, I thought *you* were responsible."

"Me?"

"Wielding all that magic," the usher said, shaking his head. "A natural assumption."

"We need to get Nicholas to the stage," Lissa said.

The usher shook his head. "Right now, no place in the Palace Theater is safe, especially not the stage."

"And this room?" Devi asked.

The usher shrugged. "Not exactly a place in the theater."

"The stage," Lissa said again.

"You'll have to go through the Throne of..." The usher checked himself. "You'll have to go through the auditorium. I should warn you, there are stairs on both sides of the stage. While there's no real altar for the orchestra, there's still a pit in front for the organist."

"Right," Nicholas said. "The sides."

"You may have to fight your way through," the usher told him.

"And who are you, exactly?" Dale asked. "I mean, it seems like you're trying to help and all, and man I can dig that, I can, but I ain't never heard of no Parliament of Ushers."

"Call me Algernon," the usher said. "I've got sigils in place to contain the theater's ghosts, but anything from the outside, I cannot control." He looked at each of them in turn, deciding something, and finally nodded. "Good luck, and good hunting." He leaned closer to Nicholas and added in a whisper: "I would have constrained the lot of you if I thought it would resolve things."

9.

Crossing the threshold delivered a wave of dizziness. Nicholas grabbed the wall for support. Lissa held onto him. It was like a roller coaster hitting its first decline at ninety miles an hour. He stumbled into the apartment, into another vast explosion of color. But it wasn't as harsh as it had been, and he managed to keep his feet and not get sick. "That," he said, "was impressive."

"We still have to get downstairs," Lissa said. "Through the dogs."

He smiled for her, and for Devi. The guy from the apartment led the way into the hall. The hall was dark, but there was a light at one end of it, so when they started in that direction Nicholas didn't complain. He wasn't as interested in the mirror as he was the man who had sicced the dogs after them.

They moved silently across the carpeted hall until they reached stairs and a door. Without discussion or delay, Nicholas pulled open the door and went through, onto a small landing where the spotlight was still warm. The rest of the auditorium was dark, but the mirror remained on stage, angled just so that he couldn't see it.

A mirror—not that one—had been the source of all this, hadn't it? Nicholas didn't want to consider it too closely.

Lissa pulled shut the door. "What if the dogs were there?" she asked in a furious whisper. "What if their master was there?"

"I was kinda hoping he would be," Nicholas said.

"If he was following you," Devi said, "then he's probably

in our apartment now."

Lissa looked back. "Did we shut the door behind us?"

The hall remained empty. Quiet. Unmoving. Nicholas tightened his fists in anticipation and lowered his eyes. Half a minute passed. An entire minute. He was beginning to feel foolish.

"If the magic is sympathetic to us," Lissa said, "then perhaps they can't get through."

"Or they're not in our apartment yet," the guy said.

"We've got to assume they're coming," Lissa said. "Behind and ahead. All we have to do is reach that mirror."

"What's so special about the mirror?" the guy asked.

Devi smacked his shoulder. "Isn't it obvious?"

Through this, Nicholas tried to listen, maybe to something inside the theater but maybe something inside himself. He considered options. He considered the weight of the 9mm. It felt lighter, now—by one bullet. With the red rain pounding the roof, all other sounds were hollow. Nicholas said, "Downstairs. To the stage."

Nicholas went first to the stairs. These were not meant for the public; those stairs would be grand and sweep them onto the balcony. These were stairs for the workers, straight and unadorned and direct. They didn't lead to the lobby where people would gather before the event and buy fancy wine, but to a storeroom. Boxes. Desks. Ledgers. Maybe money, too, but Nicholas wasn't alone and didn't appreciate an audience. He only had to look at her to remember this wasn't his Lissa.

The storeroom led to an office, where a man hunched over the desk scribbling furiously on paper. He looked up, just for the moment, and said, "Come to pay your respects, have you?" The voice was enough to tell Nicholas this wasn't the man who had aimed the spotlight earlier. A glance at the papers showed he was making circles and triangles and breaking the lead on a lot of pencils.

Through the office, Nicholas reached the lobby, Lissa and Devi and the guy from the apartment immediately behind him. He wanted to run. He wanted to race. He needed to face the mirror alone.

But the lobby wasn't empty.

Nicholas tried to back up, but there were too many people behind him. And too many in front of him. The lobby was filled with them. Men, women, children, all suddenly making noise, talking, laughing, drinking champagne. Some were in tuxedos and fancy dresses, others torn jeans and tee shirts, and all levels between. The lobby seemed to fold in over itself so it could fit more people.

Then someone pointed and said, "There he is!"

A thousand pairs of eyes turned toward Nicholas. "The illusionist!" someone cried. "The artist!" "The virtuoso himself!" That was followed by, "Do a trick! Give us a preview!"

Nicholas glanced at Lissa. She winked. "You were never the talent," she told him.

"Do us a magic!"

Lissa snapped a finger and the lights flashed off. When they came back on, streamers were falling from the ceiling. The crowd cheered and raised their hands and danced.

"This way," one of the ushers said quickly, guiding them away from the stairs and away from the auditorium to another office. The usher wiped his brow and demanded, "What do you think you're doing? These people haven't bought any tickets!"

Nicholas blinked. "What?"

"No tickets," the usher said, "no show. That's how it works."

"We don't need any tickets," Devi said.

"Of course not, I know that," the usher said. "You're with the performers. I get that. I do. But all those people out there—they'll simply eat you alive if they can."

"That can't be a good thing," Nicholas admitted.

The usher showed his teeth in what was meant as a grin. "Of course not."

"And who are you, exactly?" Nicholas asked.

"Call me Ignatius," the usher said. "I'm here only to protect the theater. I thought *you* might be responsible, but..." He hesitated. "You don't seem to be."

"Do you know what's going on?" Devi asked.

"We need to get to the stage," Lissa said.

"You can't go around through the back," Ignatius said. "You'll have to go through the Throne...the auditorium. There are stairs on either side, but I can't vouch for their safety. And though there's no real altar for the orchestra, there is still a pit in front, and the Wurlitzer."

"An organ," Devi said, "might return some powerful magic of its own, wouldn't it?"

Ignatius narrowed his eyes at her, then turned to Lissa. "You may have to fight your way through."

"I've got a little bit of magic of my own, apparently," Lissa said.

The usher shook his head. "I've constrained the ghosts of the theater, but as yet, I can do nothing about outside influences. There are...a great many of them. The people in that lobby, they are real, as best I can tell, actual people, not ghosts and not from elsewhere, but they are not in their own minds."

"We'll be careful."

"Be more than careful," Ignatius told her. "Be swift."

"Man, can I run when I have to," the guy from the apartment said.

Devi swatted his arm. "Shush."

Nicholas withdrew his gun and said to Ignatius, "We'll be doubly careful."

Ignatius looked at the gun for a long moment, then met Nicholas' eyes. He considered something, decided something, finally even nodded to himself. "I would have restrained the lot of you, if I thought it would resolve things. Don't make me reconsider."

Nicholas grinned. "You don't have to worry about us."

As Ignatius stepped back, he raised his hands as if to say he had no part in this. "Good luck."

10.

The four of them waded back into the lobby. The crowd pressed close, jostling, spilling their drinks, apologizing, recognizing the magician out of uniform. Music piped in through tinny speakers scattered in the ceiling. They called for tricks, they called for magic, they called for tickets so they could see the show. They pushed and pulled and made a roadblock, driving them away from the auditorium doors.

"Do something," Nicholas told Lissa, "or I will."

She nodded. She split away, headed toward the center. Devi and her man flanked Nicholas, but the tide was impenetrable and constantly in motion.

With some distance between them, Lissa lifted her hands and announced, "Butterflies!" Her voice broke through the noise of the crowd and brought an instance of silence, a brief and beautiful lull in the cacophony. Many eyes, maybe most—but not quite all—turned to Lissa. She started flicking her wrists, tossing quick butterflies out of her hands. They were slashes of neon green and pink. They crackled with electricity. They fluttered for just a few seconds before dissipating.

But it was enough. Faces turned at the spectacle. Lissa threw the butterflies up and in every direction. She threw them one at a time, then in pairs, then in triplets, and the ozone smell of them filled the lobby. That wasn't a natural neon smell, but a result of Lissa's magic.

Nicholas used the distraction to push forward. At the

double doors to the auditorium, an usher—not Ignatius—
gave Nicholas a brief nod and pushed the door open only
enough for a person to get through. Devi and her man
followed him into the brightened auditorium.

A sea of burgundy seats greeted them, thick burgundy
drapes, brilliant gold accents and architectural flourishes—
the combination of which momentarily blinded Nicholas.
This wasn't his side of the mirror, and the sudden explosion
of colors, even these rich, dark colors, impacted him. Devi
and her man caught him from either side. Supported him.
The guy said, "We're almost to the stage."

This wasn't Nicholas's idea, but he didn't know what else
to do. He staggered forward, and that's when he heard the
dogs. The growling and snarling. They were in the seats, and
in the aisles, and everywhere Nicholas could see.

He drew the gun and shot the dog directly ahead of him.
Like thunder, the shot cracked the night, and cracked the
sounds of the theater. Behind them, the lobby went silent.
Lissa burst into the auditorium from the other set of doors.
An usher pulled the doors shut against the swelling audience.

"Run!" Lissa yelled, and she tossed a bolt of her own,
lightning, a jagged arc of it that split and struck three of the
dogs. They yelped. Nicholas stepped over the fallen dog
ahead of him, the guy staying beside him. Devi, however,
remained at the back of the aisle. They drove forward,
through the screaming animals, creatures so unlike dogs he
no longer understood the comparison. They snapped at him.
The guy caught one as it leapt through the air, caught it with
his forearms, struggled to keep its jaws from clamping shut.
Nicholas shot another. Lissa conjured another volley of
lightning. It came so close, it scorched Nicholas's nose.

The steps alongside the stage were blocked, so he went
up the middle. He almost leapt over the pit, but it was wider
and deeper than he'd expected. He'd never get up before
those dogs tore him apart. So he leapt onto the organ stand

instead, crashing onto the keys of the organ, sending a tumultuous sound resounding through the pipes on either side of the stage. He clamored over the Wurlitzer, shooting one more dog directly in his path, and leapt onto the stage.

Nicholas lost his balance.

He tipped backwards, but the guy from the apartment was there, right behind him, and stopped Nicholas from falling. Then the dogs got to Devi's man, one on his leg, another on his arm, and a third going for the throat.

The man without a name stumbled backwards, off the organ stand, into the pit where a dozen dogs fell instantly upon him. Another jolt of lightning, a cry from the back of the theater, even three more shots from the gun in Nicholas's hand, were not enough to save his life.

The rest of the dogs, smelling blood, moved more swiftly.

Nicholas reached the mirror on the stage. Turned it so he could look directly into it. Lissa reached him then, so the two of them stared into the mirror at images of themselves staring back, which, honestly, should have been what they expected.

"Do something," Lissa said from inside the mirror.

Her Nicholas, the one on the other side of the mirror, reached forward. Nicholas reached, too. When they both touched the surface of the mirror, Nicholas didn't feel the cool smooth surface but his warm flesh grasping back. The Nicholas in the mirror pulled. Nicholas pulled back. Lissa pulled with them on both sides.

Lissa muttered something magical.

The other Lissa said, "We're ruined here. *Pull us through.*"

And that's what they did.

The mirror shattered as the reflections of Nicholas and Lissa joined Nicholas and Lissa on the stage. The dogs suddenly scattered. The lights dimmed noticeably. Nicholas, having used up as much of himself as he could, slumped, and only Lissa's support kept him from crumbling to the floor.

Lissa and her reflection went to Devi, who seemed ready to drop into the pit after her man. The dogs were gone, but they'd left only a mess.

"I didn't even know his name," Nicholas whispered.

"Dale," his reflection told him. "His name was Dale, and he died protecting us."

Devi, makeup streaked down her face, looked up at the two versions of Nicholas. "He was mine," she said. "Mine, and mine alone. You—your enemy—had no right to take him from *me*." With that final word, the theater rumbled.

"I'm not sure what we accomplished," Lissa said to Nicholas. "Whatever's wrong with the world, it's still wrong. And now..."

"Now," Lissa's reflection said, "there are two of us."

"And what happened on our side of the mirror," Nicholas's reflection said, "was terrible. We lost everything. All of it. The whole world collapsed, and only we escaped it."

Nicholas stared at his reflection. He wasn't full color like the rest of this world, but of a similar palette, if darker and in higher contrast. He said, to everyone, "This may be bigger than we thought."

10.

The four of them returned to the lobby. Nicholas could smell the ozone of the ghosts in the darkness. This theater had once been vibrant. Exciting. Now, memories and inertia were all that held it together.

Nicholas heard the crowds from across the mirror. He didn't know how he knew the source, but he knew. They called for tricks, they called for magic, they called for tickets so they could see the show, but they did so elsewhere. Nicholas's fists crackled with electricity. Little pastel butterflies leaked from his hands, tiny things that fluttered once and ceased to exist.

Devi put a hand on his shoulder when he paused to look at these. "Energy leaks," she said, her voice suggesting this was some sort of reassurance.

At the double doors, Nicholas pushed, and put some muscle into it, to force the door open enough for a single person to slip through. He went first, and sent a ball of light ahead to the center of the auditorium. It rose above the seats, all ragged black, like the shredded remnants of drapes. The architectural flourishes and accents were all in white, the color palette familiar now and expected but no less stark.

They were not alone in the theater. There were the dog things. A hundred dogs or a thousand in the seats, in the aisles, at the top of the stairs leading to the stage, all growling and salivating.

Lissa lifted her gun and shot the first dog.

That set them all into motion.

Nicholas twisted his fingers and launched spectral variations of himself down the other aisle, fooling some of the dogs. He launched arcs of electricity from his miniature sun at the center of the theater. The beasts, which could hardly be called dogs, howled and yelped and avoided the blasts, but still came for them.

"We're almost to the stage," Dale said, pushing forward.

The dogs snapped their toothed jaws and lunged and seemed intent on protecting the stage. This, as much as anything else, propelled Nicholas. It confirmed they were moving in the right direction.

So Nicholas drove forward. Lissa shouted curses as she spent bullets on the endless dogs. Nicholas launched two more balls of light into the theater, from which bolts of lightning helped clear their path, but the effort nearly made him lose his balance. Devi and Dale caught him, from either side, and helped him keep his feet.

Then Dale caught one of the dogs in his hands. Caught it at the jaws. Before it could tear him apart, Lissa shot the dog, but her next pull of the trigger rang hollow.

At the stairs, all of six steps, they kicked at the dogs. Lissa smashed one with the butt of the gun. Nicholas muzzled one with a pastel construct that would linger no longer than the butterflies. Dale, trying to catch another, toppled over, fell to his knees at the very front of the stage, and tumbled into the orchestra section, where more of the dogs, like alligators, waited with open jaws. They fell on him. A blast of electricity from Nicholas's hands—which burned his fingers—and a hellish cry from Devi, were insufficient to save him.

The rest of the dogs, smelling blood, moved more swiftly.

Nicholas reached the mirror. He shifted it so he could look directly in. With Devi at the edge of the stage watching the dogs rend Dale in a frenzy, the mirror reflected only Nicholas and Lissa. The two of them stared at themselves. What else had they expected?

"Do something," Lissa said from inside the mirror.

Her Nicholas, the one on the other side of the mirror, reached forward. Nicholas reached, too. When they touched the surface of the mirror, Nicholas didn't feel the cool smooth surface but the warm flesh of his own hand grasping his. The Nicholas in the mirror pulled. Nicholas pulled back. Lissa pulled with them on both sides.

Nicholas muttered something magical.

The other Nicholas said, "It's ruined here. *Pull us through.*"

And that's what they did.

The mirror shattered as the reflections of Nicholas and Lissa joined Nicholas and Lissa on the stage. The dogs suddenly scattered.

Lissa and her reflection went to Devi, who had reached the stage and seemed ready to drop into the pit after Dale.

The dogs were gone, but they'd left a mess of the man.

"I didn't even know his name," Nicholas's reflection said.

"*Dale*," Nichols told him. "His name was Dale, and he died protecting us."

Devi, makeup streaked down her face, looked up at the two versions of Nicholas. "He was mine," she said. "Mine, and mine alone. You—your enemy—had no right to take him from *me*." With that final word, the theater rumbled.

"I'm not sure what we accomplished," Nicholas admitted, kneeling beside Devi and putting an arm around her. "I'm so, so sorry. I wish I could have done something to prevent this."

"We couldn't prevent any of it," Nicholas's reflection said. "On our side of the mirror, the whole world fragmented into dust. We were barely able to get out, and in the end, we only escaped because of you."

Nicholas and his reflection stared at each other a moment longer. The reflection was not black and white like this world. He was almost darker than Nicholas, but of a similar color palette. Nicholas said, "This may be bigger than we thought."

11.

Devi and the two Lissas looked at Nicholas and his reflection.

"Isn't it obvious?" Nicholas's reflection asked.

"This reflection didn't come from your side of the mirror," Nicholas told Lissa.

"And this reflection didn't come from your side," Nicholas's reflection told Lissa's reflection.

"Here," Nicholas said, "the colors—if you can call them that—are all black and white, but scratchy, dry, brittle looking."

"Looks normal to me," Lissa said.

"Because it is normal for you," Nicholas said.

"But not," Nicholas's reflection added, "for me. Our colors are sharper, richer, more thorough."

"Then this," Lissa said, "was the wrong mirror."

Nicholas shook his head. "How can there be a wrong mirror? Wouldn't all mirrors reflect the same thing?"

"Of course not," Devi said. She wiped tears from her face with the back of a hand. "In the long history of glass, there have been innumerable variations in the strength of mirrors, the chemical composition, the amount of mercury or aluminum, even the thickness of the glass. Even from a machine, even when they are mass produced, every mirror is its own thing. And every mirror has something like what you would call a soul."

Everyone stared at Devi. She rose as she spoke. "In times past, men sought to travel the paths between mirrors, but they were fools, or foolish, and they failed to understand a basic fact about mirrors, the same basic fact you've failed to understand today. Each mirror is unique."

"But," Nicholas said, "the mirror where this all started— it's been shattered."

"On my side, too," Nicholas's reflection said.

"Can we repair it somehow?" Lissa asked.

"With what?" Devi asked. "Glue? Adhesive? That would change the mirror's nature, and therefore its reflection."

"I have a question," Lissa's reflection said. "If there's more than one of each of us, on every side of every mirror, how do we know your mirror is the one that started it all?"

"I would think it was mine," Nicholas's reflection said, glancing at the fragments of mirror on the stage floor. "But there's nothing there."

"That," Lissa's reflection told him, "was my world that was destroyed, not yours."

"It's a good question," Lissa said, "but it's philosophical, and we need to do something practical."

"Go back to my shattered mirror?" Nicholas asked.

"Not your mirror," Lissa told him, "but your reflection's mirror." She glanced at his reflection and added, "Not yours. The reflection he switched with. Yours is on the other side of that."

Nicholas took a breath. He was weak, but not defeated. "What's it like outside?"

"Doesn't matter," Nicholas's reflection said. "We still have the map." The balled-up shirt was in his hand.

Nicholas accepted the shirt. It was very similar to Dale's shirt, the one he had worked on. The map had been made in the same way, with the same ingredients, and it felt warm in his hand. He reflection smiled at him. No, he grinned.

The map included Dale's apartment. The map included the theater. And the map included Nicholas's apartment. His hadn't.

"It needs," Nicholas's reflection said, "a bit of magic."

Nicholas laid it out on the floor, over the dark, dead mirror shards. He spread it out, examined it, and realized what was wrong. "It's backwards," Nicholas said, "and backwards again." He shook his head. "I can barely read it."

"Make it yours," Nicholas's reflection said.

Nicholas considered this. This map might be relevant, but not here. They could go back and get the one he'd made, but it didn't include his apartment. He hadn't thought that far ahead.

He picked up one of the shards and, quickly, pricked his finger. A thick drop of blood rolled free. He squeezed it over the cloth map until it fell. The blood splattered their current location, the Palace Theater, and briefly the whole theater flashed neon red. Something rumbled outside, a low, long, deep threat of thunder.

He rubbed the blood into the shirt with his wound,

saturating it, spreading it as far as it would go, from apartment to apartment, then undid the button. As he did this, Lissa and her reflection cleared the jams in their 9mms—apparently, they each had one last bullet. He pulled the edge of the shirt down, and realigned the holes so that the apartment next to the theater, on the other side of the shirt, would no longer be Dale's but his. His reflection's. He took a deep breath, closed the button, and said, "That should be it."

Algernon watched from the rear of the theater as they left through the stage door.

On the other side: Nicholas's apartment, utterly familiar and completely unknown. The walls were where his walls had always been. The old apartment was like his, but without the color. The walls were black like charcoal and white like chalk. Everything in the room, the desk and tables, the chairs, the lamps, all sketched in variations of these. The bulb glowing on the lamp gave off a bright, distinct white light, more substantive than should be, thicker, cleaner.

"This looks vaguely familiar," Nicholas's reflection said.

There were books, and a deck of cards which Nicholas pocketed as he and his reflection walked through the apartment.

"It's not exactly mine," Nicholas's reflection said, nudging a basket full of credit cards and cash.

"Nor mine," Nicholas said. They came around to the side of the table, to the notebooks and pens, the compass, the burnt out candle, the standing wall mirror and the sea of broken glass beneath it. Nicholas and his reflection knelt simultaneously and stared into the pieces. A dozen other reflections stared back.

"What were you trying to accomplish?" Lissa asked.

"I wanted to walk through the realms of mists," Nicholas's reflection said.

"I was trying to perfect a piece of true magic," Nicholas said.

"What kind of magic?" Lissa asked.

"Transportational," Nicholas said. "Step from one side of the theater to the other without...well, without the traditional use of mirrors."

"That," Lissa's reflection said, "sounds dubious."

"It was," Nicholas said. "Obviously. It led us here. All of us." There were four of them now. Devi had remained in the theater.

Nicholas looked down at his reflections again. Some reached for him. Some were turning away. Some were screaming, pounding against the glass. Some were simply staring. "I did this."

"No," another Nicholas said, emerging from the bedroom with two of those dogs straining at their leashes. "I did this."

11.

Devi and the two Lissa's looked at Nicholas and his reflection.

"It's obvious," Lissa said, looking directly at Nicholas's reflection. "You're not the Nicholas I knew. Neither of you is."

"How many sides of the mirror are there?" Nicholas asked.

"How many sides are there to a snowflake?" Devi asked, looking up at them and wiping tears from her face with the back of her hand. "The quantity and purity of the quicksilver, its intensity, its elasticity and its volatility. Alchemists have tried to tame it, scientists have tried to define it, madmen have ingested it in search of magical curatives or visions. And glassworkers have harnessed its reflective properties to build better mirrors. But the lead also contributes to the makeup of a mirror, and the glass contributes to its traits, and every mirror, even when they are mass produced, is its own thing.

Every mirror has something like what you would call a soul."

Everyone stared at Devi. She rose as she spoke. "You, Nicholas, on this side of the mirror and the other, were a fool to try to tap into something beyond comprehension. You failed to understand the same basic fact every other practitioner and maven and adventurer has failed to understand. Each mirror is unique."

"My mirror was shattered," Nicholas said. "The mirror where all this started."

"Mine is lost," Nicholas's reflection said, looking down at the shards scattered across the stage.

"Well, we can't simply glue it back together," Lissa said. Then she looked at Devi. "Can we?"

Devi shook her head.

Lissa's reflection held up a piece of the broken mirror. "This is inert, now," she said. "Dark, non-reflective. Dead. The world on the other side of that mirror, my world, the place where I was born and lived and studied and strove, is gone." She put a hand on the shoulder of Nicholas's reflection. "Yours, too. That's why we tried to come here. We wanted to...help."

"Help how?" Nicholas asked.

"Uniting," Nicholas's reflection said. "And to do that, we need to get back to your shattered mirror. Or through that mirror, to the other side, where it all began."

Nicholas glanced at Lissa. His Lissa? He didn't completely understand, but Lissa was nodding as if this all made perfect sense.

"We still," Lissa's reflection said, producing the subway pamphlet, "have a map." She laid it out on the floor. The two Lissa's knelt next to it. Nicholas and his reflection leaned over to watch.

"It's a reflection of a reflection," Lissa said, shaking her head.

"Make it yours," her reflection told her.

"I can barely read it."

"It needs," her reflection said, "a bit of magic."

Nicholas pointed. "That's my apartment, or my reflection's apartment. My other reflection."

Lissa's reflection handed her a needle.

Lissa nodded, then pricked her finger. A drop of blood swelled there. She squeezed it over the paper map until the drop fell. The blood splattered on their current location, the Palace Theater, and briefly the whole theater flashed red. Something rumbled outside, a low, long, deep threat of thunder.

Then she unraveled the previous thread and re-used it, connecting the theater with Nicholas's apartment.

As he watched, he and his reflection glanced at each other. They shared a grin. They shared a wink. They were of one mind.

Ignatius watched from the back of the theater as they left through the stage door.

On the other side: Nicholas's apartment, utterly familiar and completely unknown. The walls were where his walls had always been. The old apartment was his, but the colors were changed. In its place, the walls were sick with color, lurid, nearly overwhelming. The bulb glowing on the lamp gave off a pale, dirty variation of light.

"This looks vaguely familiar," Nicholas's reflection said.

There were books, cards, coins, rope, boxes, and wands. Inwardly, Nicholas sneered at the collection. Had he, on this side of the mirror, no spirit of adventure, no taste for romance? "It's not exactly mine," he said.

"Nor mine," his reflection said. They came around to the side of the table, to the notebooks and pens, the compass, the burnt out candle, the standing wall mirror and the sea of broken glass beneath it. Nicholas and his reflection knelt simultaneously and stared into the pieces. A dozen other reflections stared back.

"What were you trying to accomplish?" Lissa asked.

"I needed a way of entering places unseen," Nicholas said.

"I was attempting to look in on my rival," Nicholas's reflection said.

"Who's your rival?" Lissa asked.

Nicholas and Nicholas's reflection exchanged a look. Then his reflection turned to Lissa, and to Lissa's reflection— Devi had remained in the theater—and said, "You."

The Lissas did something, some sort of magic thing, a conjuration of words and fingers in unison, before Nicholas or his reflection could raise their guns. They each fired one bullet, one they had reserved for such an event, one they had slipped into a pocket when giving Lissa gunpowder for her magical maps. They fired across each other, Nicholas at Lissa's reflection, Nicholas's reflection at Lissa. Their magic echoed through the room, through the whole world, possibly into all the sides of all the mirrors, but it couldn't stop lead traveling at high velocity.

They died immediately, the effects of their magic unraveling already, but it was too late. The remains of the mirror crackled and sparkled. Some of the shards went dead and dark. Some strained at the edges. Some of those multiple reflections were pulled somewhere else. Nicholas and his reflection tried to resist, but they had no magic at their command, no means of escape, and they were sucked into the vortex

12.

"I did this."

"I did this."

"I did this."

Reflection after reflection emerged from the mirror. Some were bloodied and beaten. Some were armed, some with the same 9mm Oliveri Lissa and her reflection carried. Some were full color, or more than full color, while others closely matched this side of the mirror. Some were red-faced, others sickly green, others bathed in shadows. They came alone, they came in pairs, they came in groups, and they dissolved into each other almost as quickly as they arrived. There were a dozen one moment, then a hundred, then a dozen, then fifty, then half that. They arrived in a flurry, and as each arrived, or each set, the fragment of mirror they came through burst, creating more, smaller fragments. Most wore variations of what Nicholas wore. At least one wore Dale's shirt with its map on it and the buttons all done wrong. All of them, or most of them, said some variation of, "I did this," and some used other languages or voices that weren't similar to Nicholas's voice at all. It overwhelmed him, and reverberated more deeply than his bones.

Nicholas's reflection—the one who been drawn from the mirror in the theater—and also Lissa and her reflection— stood beside Nicholas, holding onto him, preventing him from being sucked into the tide. As Nicholas wavered, one other reflection resisted that gravitational pull. He laughed, and the dogs bristled, and his eyes glowed bright, bright red. He was the intruder.

"I did this," he said again, as the other reflections rose— from the mirrors—and fell—into each other and, ultimately, into the intruder. "I will no longer be your puppet, I will no longer flounder in your wake. I am no mere echo, Nicholas, but I am the truest reflection of you."

Nicholas resisted the gravity of the other reflections, the pull and the push of them all, the thunder from outside and the crackling electricity inside. He held his ground, with help.

"So many variations of you," the intruder said. "These echoes all captured a part of you, Nicholas, and the sum total of your reflections is as great as the original. I have been working a long time, in plain sight, to achieve this."

"What, exactly, do you think you're achieving?" Lissa asked, because Nicholas could not.

"I," the intruder said, "shall replace you, and shall cease to be merely your echo."

The individual reflections, and sometimes the reflections of them, the copies of copies, some insubstantial as wind, some as powerful, continued to pour forth. The Nicholas who murdered. The Nicholas who trained boxers. The Nicholas who painted. The dancer. The sculptor. The assassin.

The thief—Nicholas's original reflection—grinned, and winked at the Lissa who belonged here, on this side of the mirror. His coloring matched. Nicholas reached out, grabbed him by the wrist, said, "*You* wouldn't betray me."

The thief laughed. "I already have." Then he stepped into the intruder, another variation folded into the whole, so that he became more and more substantial.

"My *pets*," the intruder said, "were made with your hair, which I collected from the shower while you slept." He released the leash. The two dogs leapt forward, snarling, gnashing teeth. Outside, thunder boomed and lightning flashed unceasingly.

Nicholas did not back down. He caught the dogs by the throat as they leapt, one in each hand, assisted perhaps by the magic he'd been able to tap on this side of the mirror.

"You cannot resist me anymore," the intruder said. "I'm taking over."

Lissa and her reflection stepped forward, guns raised, and shot the dog-like things in the heads. The intruder laughed and stepped forward.

"There was too much of me in you," the intruder said, "to ever survive."

They were face to face now, Nicholas and the intruder. Only one other reflection remained, whom he had pulled from the mirror in the Palace Theater. The intruder reached toward the reflection.

"No," Nicholas's reflection said. "All of the reflections combined may be enough to overpower the original, but you do not have all of them." He stepped into Nicholas, directly into him. The shiver started in Nicholas's skin and resounded in his marrow.

"You're still weakened," the intruder said, grinning.

"And you," Nicholas said, "are just a pale imitation." Nicholas stepped into the intruder—not to join, not to unify, not even to overtake. He stepped in to overwhelm. He focused the magic he had mustered, the storm around them, the residual energies of the Palace Theater. He called upon the memories of loves and losses, of power surrendered and acquired and wasted. He drew from the magicians of the past, the jugglers and escape artists, the prognosticators, the clairvoyants and telekinetics, the cardsharps and hustlers and pickpockets and conmen, the illusionists and wizards and sleight of hand artists. He used his dreams and his hopes and his fears, and he subjugated this mere echo of him until the intruder stopped laughing, until the intruder cracked and splintered and fractured, until the intruder erupted into one and a thousand pieces. They scattered around the room, this chalk and charcoal variation on his apartment, and fluttered to the ground like leaflets from the sky.

One by one, the shards of the intruder dimmed. Briefly, they retained an image of a fragment of Nicholas. They died like the pieces of mirror on the stage, gray and lifeless. The pieces dissolved into dust. The dust scattered into nothingness.

The only piece that remained looked in on Nicholas's apartment, his actual apartment. Exhausted, Nicholas fell to his knees next to it, even as Lissa and her reflection went to the window.

"There's no world out there," Lissa said. "It's collapsing."

"Like mine," Lissa's reflection said.

Nicholas nodded. "One world," he said, "remains."

The three of them passed through the fragment in the moment before everything imploded and the world, on that side of the mirror, ceased to exist.

13.

When Nicholas finally woke, days later, he ached all over. No mirrors remained in his apartment, so he couldn't look at himself to see what had happened. The toll, however, had been tremendous.

His apartment had not suffered on his own side of the mirror as it had on the other side. There wasn't much to clean up, or it had already been cleaned. He didn't know. He found fresh milk in the fridge and swallowed two full glasses of it before venturing near the window. Outside, he saw the street he had always seen, and not a cloud in the twilit sky.

He showered. He let the hot water wash away everything, almost everything, everything he imagined he should lose. He didn't know if it was effective, but he felt more awake, more alert, and more alive after he dressed and left his apartment. Down the stairs, several blocks, straight to Lissa's apartment.

She had been here. Lissa and her reflection. In fairness, they were both reflections. They had come and taken everything worth taking, clothes and jewelry and money, and had left a note on the kitchen table. It said, simply, *Goodbye.*

Nicholas went to the Palace Theater. Over his marquee, over the image of himself as magician, someone had plastered a sign: *Cancelled.* It was no great loss, but Nicholas stared at it a while anyway. He went to the door, tried it, but found it locked. Before he turned away, however, it opened from the inside. Two men stood there. Ushers. One was Algernon.

"It's over," he told them.

"It is," Algernon said gravely. "Your things have been packed and already delivered. You *were* responsible."

Nicholas nodded. The ushers pulled the door shut and locked it, audibly, from inside.

Nicholas turned to walk away. Not toward his apartment. He wasn't sure what he would do there anymore. In his jacket, he still had a deck of cards from the other side of the mirror, a deck colored in streaks of charcoal and chalk. He manipulated the cards as he walked away from everything.

Eventually, he realized he wasn't alone.

"What now?" Devi asked him.

"I don't know."

Eventually, Devi said, "I forgive you. Dale—you weren't responsible for him. You weren't responsible for any of it, no matter what the ushers think."

"And Lissa."

Devi smiled. "She doesn't blame you, either, I'm sure. She had her own thing going on. Maybe you didn't notice."

"I don't know if I did," Nicholas said. "Will I see her—them—again?"

"Maybe," Devi said. "Good luck."

"What about you?" Nicholas asked. "What happens now?"

"To me?" Devi smiled. It was a gorgeous, devious smile. "I go back to being who I am. This wasn't my story, it was yours."

Nicholas stopped walking. "And who are you?"

Devi kissed his cheek, then left him, saying only, "More than I seem."

SECRET HISTORY
PART II

the
GREAT and
TRAGIC
ROMANCE
of DALE
and the
GODDESS

1
CREATION

Before the beginning, there was nothing, and from the midst of nothing flowed a river. The river wound through a vast ocean toward something. On the back of that river sailed the first of the gods: Sereca, the keeper of secrets, who would later create locks and keep the keys; The Master of Winds, who invented music and musical instruments, and invented math; and one other, whose name was never revealed.

In the face of something, they worked to create something spectacular, something extraordinary, something wonderful. Their lesser sisters and brothers followed from nothing, and their cousins, and all the great beasts. Maps were shaped, oceans forged, canyons carved into the earth. And from the mud, the human race was created, shaped by ethereal hands, honed by the gods and their children, tempered in the hearts of young volcanos, and set upon the earth to do as they would.

The human race did things both terrible and tremendous, with and without the aid or consent of the gods, and in time learned to kill those who came before them. During the first great war between the elysian and the temporal, one and one thousand gods were slaughtered, and the first of the infernals came to be. All of existence was cleansed by the great waters of the ocean between something and nothing, and the nothingness was lost. Only the earth remained.

2
DIVISION

After the beginning, universes fractured and fragmented. Reality was split asunder by the proximity of the vast nothingness from which the river flowed. The strong river moved in only one direction. Even the greatest of the first could not swim far upstream. The strongest humans failed to sail upriver. Gods, and the children of gods, trekked the ocean through which the river moved and were lost.

The world in those days was a kaleidoscope made corporeal. Seas, skies, mountains, forests, and the heavens existed united. They were stronger, together, and even amid chaos there would be order but for the nothingness that poured forth.

The cunning of humanity and the strength of gods combined to build a dam that blocked the flow of nothingness, and the first age began. Heroes were born and quests granted, and this age of prosperity and achievement lasted numerous millennia. They diligently kept the dam operating, diverting the flow of nothingness back into the ocean, but the mounting pressure could not be kept away forever.

The dam broke.

The first age ended with a flood of nothingness. Men were split from women. The skies were split from the earth. Mountains rose above the seas. If the first age was one of artisans and heroes, the second was an age of fear. Cities were built, armies assembled, and quests dissolved into struggles against unknown enemies.

The nothingness flowing down the river infected all of reality, and all of unreality, and all the parallel and perpendicular variations. The universe fragmented, and barriers formed organically to keep it divided. A band of heroes came together to sail upriver and stop the flow of nothingness, each renowned for their bravery and their honor. Each had achieved great things before the end of the first age. None returned.

The nothingness had claimed them, but they proved to be the heroes needed to protect this second age. Their bodies never returned, their swords and shields were lost to legend, but the river ceased to flow.

The river of nothingness remains, even today, but is stagnant and, at the behest of the gods, buried deep beneath the surface, under soil and rock and metal.

The beginning of the third age was marked by disease, but not all of humanity was lost.

3
THE TWINS

In the second age, many gods and heroes were born. Not all survive into this modern age. Not all of their stories have persisted. Their heroics, their accomplishments, their essences have dissipated into mist, sunk into the earth, and fell into one of the rivers.

There is the dead river of nothingness, which eats everything. There is the river of forgetting, the Lethe, also hidden beneath the earth. The river Styx, a tributary of nothingness from the first age, divides the living from the dead. There are long rivers and short rivers, underground and above. The waters are often hungry.

In the second age, the gods frolicked and played and gave birth to a great many things: monsters and terrors, shadows, demons, and other gods. Some were borne of fire, some of mud and clay, some of ash. Some of those children were meant to seal alliances. Some were accidental, and some were terrible mistakes.

On a day lost to history, twin gods were born, Devi and Dion, a girl and a boy. From their birth, they were strong, they were restless, and they were inquisitive. Dion roamed the forests. Devi crawled through the skies. They were inseparable. When a tutor suggested there were lessons for boys and lessons for girls, the twin gods, still children, split the tutor into two halves and hid the pieces so they might never be rejoined.

It was an age of gods, of iron and of war, but Dion and Devi had no interested in battle axes and explosive powders. They instead tested the poisons of the earth. They honed the sharpest, thinnest of daggers.

Still children, they were discovered by a farmer stealing fruit from his vines. "I have an idea," the farmer said. "You've stolen the fruits of my labors. Let me steal something from each of you."

"What would you steal?" Dion asked.

"We have nothing you would want," Devi told him.

"You have your potions," the farmer said. "Don't act so surprised, you are known throughout the land. You have your potions, and you have your skills. I will give you, freely, one tenth my crop, if you can devise a way to double what I grow."

"Devise, how?" Devi asked.

"We should have one half your crop, if we double it," Dion said.

"One half the first yield, yes," the farmer agreed, "and one tenth every yield thereafter until my death."

The fruits of his vines were juicy and sweet, so they went to their laboratories and played with their ingredients and made concoctions, the smell of which would strip a mortal man of his bones. They returned to the farmer with a potion and a plan.

"We'll make more every year," Devi promised.

"And you'll grow more every year," Dion told him.

The farmer's crop did indeed multiply. It doubled, and doubled again, and the little gods were pleased. But they were young, and had seen nothing of the first age, and had by this time missed much of the second age. They cared nothing for politics or conquest. When a wandering king's army trampled the farm and set their flags over the land, the gods were upset. When they found the farmer's dead body left unburied amid the charred vines of his fields, they were horrified.

The wandering king found the godlings crying in the field. "What is this?" the king asked. "Children on my battlefield?"

"This wasn't a battlefield," Devi said.

"It was a farm," Dion told him.

"It was, perhaps, once upon a time," the king admitted, "but it's now a graveyard." He instructed his men to bring their dead, and to bury them here, in this very field, under granite markers and statues glorifying the king's long list of victories.

The gods watched as the king's men built their graveyard and buried their fallen soldiers.

"And what of the farmer?" the gods asked.

So many weeks had passed, the king had forgotten they were still there, but he turned his attention on them, ever so briefly, to say, "Let him rot."

This, they answered with fury. The skies thundered. The ground shook. Fires rose from the earth. In the end, the granite and marble of the graveyard was melted and twisted, incorporating some of the wandering king's dead men, and the king himself had been entombed alive in solid granite. The earth opened and swallowed his tomb, and the wandering king's name was lost to history.

They buried the farmer properly, and said all the rites, but history devoured the farmer's name, as well.

4

THE TWINS DIVIDED

A storm came that tore the world apart. It was a violent, vicious, relentless thing, the accumulated anger of a dozen thunder throwers and earth shakers. Never in history had the winds blown so strongly or the rain fallen so heavily.

The world didn't end. The age didn't end. But ships were lost at sea, harbor cities were reduced to rubble, and families were broken. The inseparable twin gods, Devi and Dion, were separated.

The storm drove one into the earth. Dion dug through dirt and rock with his own hands. He dug deep, to protect himself from the winds. And he dug broadly, to escape the rising waters. He created the labyrinth, the very first, on which all others are based. He wandered alone for a thousand years, subsisting on inexplicable pools of water and cave spiders. He drew nutrients from roots that dangled from the ceilings. But no one could tell him the storm had passed, so he continued to dig and he continued to wander.

A mortal hunting party found an entrance to his caves. They huddled in the dark with a fire burning. They watched the approaching god, still young by the standard of gods but no longer a child; but unlike the farmer, they knew nothing of him. They didn't know if they should be afraid.

"You bring fire," Dion said, "but did you bring meat?"

"We're hunters," the leader of the party said, "and we have plenty to share, if you would join us."

Dion smiled for the first time in a hundred years. "Will you tell me stories?"

The hunters obliged. Their leader told of their current hunt, the race through the woods against the great bear, the coming of winter, the storm that drove them to seek shelter in the caves. The bear had eluded them, so tonight they feasted on rabbit.

One of the younger hunters told a story of gods hunting a celestial beast through the skies, a devourer of some type that sought to consume the stars themselves. The gods chased this beast for a dozen years before it finally tired of running and turned to fight. The nighttime sky burned as brightly as day as they struggled. The beast's hide was as hard as the core of the earth. The weapons of the gods were from the first age or the second, not the kind of weapons human hunters could carry. They ensnared the devourer in their golden nets. They stabbed it with their sharpest spears. The devourer, in turn, gorged the gods when they came too close, and made them pay for the wounds they inflicted.

"How did it end?" Dion asked.

"It ended," the hunter said, "with the end of the struggle. The devourer finally died, and a new cloud of stars returned to the night."

"What of the gods?" Dion asked. "Who did they count among their dead?" He hoped his sister had not been lost to this devourer. He missed her more than anything else.

The hunter named five gods, none known to Dion, but added, "There may be more, and the stories may be wrong. I don't really know which gods, if any, died. It's none too easy to slay a god, even for a beast that can devour the stars."

"And you," the leader of the hunters said. "Would you tell us a story?"

"I have no stories left to tell," Dion admitted. "I've been sheltering from the storm for a hundred years, and have seen no one else until today."

"Neither human nor god?" the hunter asked.

"Only the cave dwellers," Dion said, "who tell no stories."

"Then perhaps," the hunter suggested, "we should feed you more."

They told tales throughout the night, even as the fire waned, and Dion told of his sister and of the farmer and of a dozen other things. In the morning, the hunters packed their gear, and the leader said, "You look like you'd be good with a spear. Why don't you join us in our hunt?"

"I will wait for the storm to pass," Dion told him.

"I'm sure it's passed by now."

At the mouth of the cave, the morning sun blazed bright in the sky, cutting through the leaves and sending brilliant beams of light all the way to the earth. Dion reached into one of these, afraid he'd been gone so long it might burn his skin. He had grown pale, and his vision in the dark had been strong, but it felt good to breathe the forest air again. And the sun felt good, if hot, on his skin.

"What shall we hunt?" Dion asked.

The leader of the hunters said, "The bear."

Meanwhile, Devi had sought shelter above the skies. From among the stars, she watched the storm. She ignited nebulae and cracked open planets and gave the earth its moon. And she rode with the hunters when they chased the devourers of stars.

5
THE ORDER OF STORIES

The Order of Stories is under the auspices of the Storyteller, an otherwise anonymous or unnamable god and cousin to Devi. The Order of Stories is not always chronological. Some tales are passed from generation to generation and therefore cannot be trusted.

6
THE GLASSMAKER

A glassmaker born in a small town was apprenticed to a master craftsman of great skill. He was named Dale. One of several apprentices, he labored long hours over the ovens. Dale dreamed of running away and taking his skills with him, but he was still many years from mastering his technique when he was visited by the goddess, Devi.

"I require a bottle," Devi said to him, "more ornate than any you've made, to contain my perfumes." Perhaps such a thing had not yet been done. But she was the goddess of love, and potions of love were to be expected. She allowed the mortal man a generous breath of the aroma she wore on her neck. He was enthralled.

Dale worked for his master during the days. Nights, he returned to the workshop, to the tools and fires, and utilized methods Devi had described to him. He neither slept nor ate as he practiced. After a month of designing intricate jars, which were the envy of his fellow apprentices—and which caused his master a great deal of concern, as these skills were well beyond his ability—the goddess came again to Dale's little room and said, "I would like to see your progress."

Dale showed her the jars and bottles he had forged, in order and starting with the first, to demonstrate his improving workmanship. Devi looked at each and nodded at each and dropped each on the floor after saying, "This is not what I want." She said this of every piece he had made, but he begged her not to shatter the last.

"Allow me to keep that for my mother," Dale said, "and the next piece, the very next, the one I work tomorrow, will be as beautiful as anything that has ever existed—anything other than you, that is. Your vision has haunted me, your eyes have burned into my heart, and if I could have but one more breath of your scent, which you wish to hold within my bottle, I will never be more inspired."

Devi smiled for him and said, "You have already drunk deeply of my fragrance, and I fear your ardor is artificial."

"But I am not declaring love," Dale said to the goddess of love. "I request this favor merely as encouragement and motivation."

Devi did not like being told anyone wasn't in love with her, and her temper was known to be swift. But she did not strike down the glassmaker's apprentice. He had not declared a lack of love. She embraced him, and gave him the full power of her perfume, which intoxicated mortals and the infernal alike.

Dale slept well that night, and late into the morning. He apologized to his master glassmaker, who admitted, "I know you are being influenced by gods, and I can guess by your color which one. Do what needs to be done, Dale, as I would not interfere with the will of gods. But then you should go, leave my house and establish your own. The skills of the gods run through your fingers. Your talent is unprecedented and I can teach you nothing more."

"But I have seven more years of apprenticeship."

"No," his master told him. "You have already exceeded us all."

Dale went to work on the perfume bottle. He labored late into the night, with all the other apprentices watching. They took notes, even when they didn't understand, and by morning he had set the bottle to cooling.

The goddess Devi visited again while he slept in the workshop and asked, "Is my bottle done?"

"Return at dusk," Dale said, "and not earlier. Let the glass cool." The goddess could, of course, handle the heat; but the glass would lose its shape.

Precisely at dusk, Devi returned to the workshop. The goddess wore a moon-colored dress that danced in the winds. The other apprentices had gathered in hiding places up and down the street to catch a glimpse of the goddess, so we see this image even today, of her dress flowing about her, in some of the most ancient glassworks.

The bottle wasn't there.

Devi was furious. She raged, and the skies trembled, and the apprentices fled, but Dale endured all of it. No matter how much she shouted, no matter how much the skies rained down on him, no matter how loud the thunder crashed, and no matter how near the lightning struck, Dale remained unwavering—because he was in love with the goddess of love and in shock that his vessel, on which he had worked many long hours, for which he had trained a month with inhuman techniques, had disappeared.

When Devi ceased ranting and demanded an explanation, Dale said simply, "A thief."

The glassmaker, Dale's master, had stolen the bottle, and had run away with it into the coming night. Devi commanded three white horses and took Dale with her to run down the glassmaker. He cowered at the sight of her and returned the bottle. It was misshapen, but only slightly, by his theft. Devi showed it to Dale and asked, "Is this what you intended to make for me?"

"Almost," Dale admitted.

"Is this a testament to the love inspired by my fragrance?"

"Your fragrance had no effect on me," Dale told her. "I was in love the moment I saw you."

Then Devi showed the bottle to the master glassmaker turned thief. "Is this what you meant to steal?"

"I am awed by its intricacy," the glassmaker admitted.

"Is this a testament to your love of glass?"

But the glassmaker shook his head. "To envy."

Then Devi said, "You will be, thief, the most intricate of all glass to yet walk this realm, but I fear you will not remain so forever." With a touch, she transformed the thief into a statue of glass so detailed, a casual observer could read the fear in its eyes.

"And you," Devi said to the apprentice, "tell me again how you love me."

7
THE GLASS STATUE

In a desert, for a hundred years, stood a statue of glass depicting the flawed glassmaker, the thief of legend, who had tried to flee by foot from the fury of the gods. For some seasons, the sands obscured him entirely, but then the sands dispersed and he was once more revealed. His glass tears were visible in his face, and it was believed that he still lived and therefore suffered.

War came, eventually, through that portion of the desert. The statue of the thief was shattered and the pieces scattered across numerous dimensions and worlds.

8.
THE CAT AND THE GODDESS

A jungle cat travelled far from the jungle, across oceans and deserts, to seek an audience with the moon goddess, Devi, in her temple by the sea. It was an arduous journey. The jungle cat fought a variety of beasts, befriended a seven year old girl, and hitched a ride with a swarm of butterflies who brought him as far as the shore.

Men had built the temple with mountains of gold and rubies and sapphires. Priests had blessed the temple. Oracles lived in it, passing their days in long baths and gentle contemplation of poetics and futures. One of the priestesses, Arachne, read the leaves of her tea and saw the jungle cat's approach.

So all of the temple turned out for the jungle cat's

arrival. They assembled like soldiers for war. The jungle cat strode between legions of oracles to enter the temple itself and stepped straight to the altar.

The oracles and priestesses and their servants and acolytes were warned to wait outside. The temple served a celestial purpose, in addition to being their home, and whatever the jungle cat sought from the goddess, it was not meant for mortal eyes. But Arachne snuck into the temple and climbed to one of the many balconies where she could watch without being seen.

The jungle cat extended his claws and scratched geometric shapes into the floor of the altar. He purred, which from a jungle cat sounded no different than a growl, but Arachne spied upon the cat from a safe distance.

When the jungle cat snarled, it was a sound Arachne couldn't identify. She had heard lions roar and housecats hiss, but this was a kind of cat she had never seen. The jungle cat had come from far away, and instead of the language of cats, it spoke the language of gods.

Devi appeared before the jungle cat. She scratched the jungle cat's chin, then wrestled a while with the animal, until both were tired and laughing. Then she asked, "What's the purpose of this long journey, my friend?"

The jungle cat told her. And even Arachne understood the words. Her brother, lost many centuries ago to an unnatural storm, her brother Dion who had allied himself with darkness and crevices, her brother Dion who was older by three minutes or three millennia—not all words were easy to understand—had returned from the shadows.

Devi was visibly excited. "I feared he was lost forever."

"This brother you'll find," the jungle cat said, "is not the same as the brother you lost."

Devi hugged the jungle cat and whispered something in his ear, then turned her attention to Arachne in the balconies. "Tell your sisters I'm leaving the temple, and I don't know when I'll return."

Devi and the jungle cat left through doors Arachne couldn't comprehend. She had never truly believed the goddess was present in the temple. She fled. And though the oracles and priestesses and visionaries returned to the temple, Arachne followed after her goddess.

9
DALE'S FIRST RESURRECTION

The master glassmaker who had learned from gods lived a long life. He lived far beyond his mortal years. The goddess visited him often, and he made her the finest menagerie of glass fauna and flora that ever existed, before or since. He gave her new figurines and intricately designed eggs, not limited to glass, every time she came to him.

He could not, of course, go to her. She was a goddess, and travelled by means inaccessible to mortals.

This did not stop him from trying.

One time, Dale fashioned a mirror of a size he could enter. There had never before been so large a mirror. The difficult, delicate work required different skills than those needed to create a glass zoo. He tried to crawl through the mirror. He enlisted the help of witches to enchant the glass. He applied nectars and potions, and even traces of the goddess's essence. But the perfume, which had no effect on the glassmaker, had equal effect on the glass.

One time, Dale tried to climb to the moon itself. He acquired the longest of ladders and climbed the tallest of buildings on the highest of mountains, but he could not reach.

He purchased a magic carpet from a travelling merchant. Dale rode the winds that night, and waved to many a god. He attracted the attention of celestials, infernals, and mortals. Most recognized him or understood his quest.

One bowman, however, tried to shoot him out of the sky. The bowman missed, and was punished for missing.

One night, Dale sought the temple of the king of gods. He fought a variety of beasts, and befriended a seven year old girl, and hitched a ride with a swarm of butterflies who brought him as far as the shore. The god's footmen greeted him. Pages guided him into the temple. Knights took a knee as Dale approached the altar. The king of gods, one of many such kings, sat upon his throne and laughed as Dale approached.

"What is it you want?" the king of the gods asked.

"I want to be able to follow where Devi leads."

The king of the gods considered this. He consulted old scrolls, texts from a previous age, and a consortium of wise men. He returned to Dale, in the center of his throne room, and said, "You are merely a mortal."

"I am a mortal," Dale said, "loved by a goddess."

"In love with a goddess," the king of the gods said. "There is a difference."

This, perhaps, elicited the glassmaker's first tear. It slipped from his eye, rolled down his cheek, and dropped to the crimson temple floor.

This caused much commotion. Later, knights would joust for the right to collect that tear. It would be placed in a bottle made by the glassmaker himself and eventually brought somewhere else. But for the moment, Dale still stood there proudly, prepared to prove himself to the king of gods.

"Fine," the king of gods finally said. "But first you must die."

The king of gods smote Dale, who loved the goddess of love, with a lightning bolt as swift as thought. Dale was dead before the ozone smell reached the knights. His burnt corpse was brought to the courtyard and burned in a giant funerary fire on the coldest night of the year.

Devi did not seek vengeance. Not immediately. She

instead sought to retrieve the mortal she loved.

Devi journeyed deep under the earth, with her brother as guide, her brother who despised the idea but loved his sister. They reached the shores of the river Lethe. To traverse it safely, they stored their memories inside glass vases shaped by the dead glassmaker. As they crossed the languid waters on the raft provided, pulling themselves by a rope that had always been there, they marveled at the mists and the clouds and the cavern walls so many miles away in every direction, but they had no idea what they were doing or why. When they reached the distant shore, they reclaimed their memories from the vases.

When they reached the shore of the river Styx, the ferryman demanded payment. But they were gods, or godlings, and pennies alone would be insufficient for this journey. The ferryman made his terms clear: he wanted a jar of the goddess's perfume. When they reached the distant shore, the godlings walked unhurriedly past the guardians, for they were coming to request a favor of their uncle who ruled this underworld.

"To what do I owe this pleasure?" their uncle asked.

"I want the man I love returned to me," Devi said.

"How long ago did he die?"

It had been a long journey. "Seven years."

Their uncle nodded. "I will need someone to stay in his place."

"I'll stay," Dion said. When Devi protested, he told his sister, "I'll only have to stay seven years, and as you know, I can never die."

The agreement made, their uncle gave Devi this warning: "Do not look upon him, do not ask anything of him, do not even seek to hold his hand, while still on this side of the river, or he will return to the mists. And know this, too: when a mortal leaves the underworld, they return with something gained and something lost. He may not be the man you loved."

"He'll be the man I love," Devi said, "and he'll love me as no other has ever loved me."

"This," her uncle said, "is true."

She left the underworld, the wraith of Dale behind her, silent and weightless. He might have been only an idea, a memory, an echo, but she trusted her uncle, though gods often lied. She passed the guardians, who watched and salivated and growled but did not attack. She reached the river Styx. The ferryman returned them to the other side, with Devi always looking forward, never once to the back of the ferry where her lover remained half in the mists.

On the shore, they embraced and kissed and made love like the world was ending. They reached the river Lethe, where they re-used the glass jars Devi and her brother had used, though faint traces of previous memories lingered.

On the shore, when their memories returned, they embraced and kissed and made love like the world was wholly new.

They reached the surface, and Dale, the glassmaker, discovered he no longer had the skills to make glass.

10
THE DUST GODDESS

Devi and the jungle cat, and Arachne behind them, travelled long and far. After leaving the Temple of the Moon, they sailed south and east until they reached a foreign shore where magicians and pickpockets performed in the streets. The merchants and their customers gave a wide berth to the goddess walking with a beast.

As they walked, a woman with a wailing child begged for favors, and Devi healed the child.

As they walked, a ruffian attempted to wet a knife with their blood. The jungle cat consumed him.

As they walked, a circus overtook Arachne. Gymnasts and acrobats and tamers of beasts circled around her. Clowns paraded before her. Jugglers and stilt walkers and, finally, the ringmaster himself, a tall, narrow man, perhaps a god, tipped his hat and said, "Good day to you, madam."

He was the first person to speak Arachne's language in months.

"You travel," he said. "We travel. Perhaps we might travel together."

"I don't think so."

The ringmaster, however, knew things he shouldn't have known. "You're an oracle of the moon goddess, and you follow her now on a quest you cannot complete. I offer…an alternative."

Arachne was losing sight of the goddess and the jungle cat. And she was losing her patience. "Get out of my way before I run you through with my blade."

No blade was visible, but the ringmaster was not a fool. Any devotee to the goddess of love would travel with an assortment of poisons and powders. He said, "They seek her brother, but they go the long way around. There are swifter paths."

For the first time, Arachne looked into the eyes of the ringmaster, and it's anyone's guess as to what wonders she saw within.

The goddess and the jungle cat, meanwhile, continued into the desert. They walked for days. Nomads on camels offered water, for which the goddess gave them fire opals, and pilgrims sheltered them during the nights. But eventually, they reached the great expanse, which no man dared to cross. The pilgrims gave warnings, told them of the great snakes, and spoke of the sand demons. Djinns and tricksters of every sort wandered these mad, dry lands, and every oasis they saw for forty days would be a mirage.

The goddess and the jungle cat thanked the pilgrims and

blessed their relics, then braved the great expanse. During the day, the winds swept sands before them. During the night, they rested, and took water from the moon. At day, skeletal hallucinations taunted them from the horizons. At night, unnatural howlings and growlings surrounded them. Days, they came upon oases that were merely mirages. Nights, they made camp and burned unnatural fires to stay warm.

On the fortieth day, they emerged on the other side of the great expanse. The goddess and the jungle cat had dined on vipers and scorpions. A king and his travelling party greeted them on the other side. "Let us feast tonight," said the king. "It's not every day a goddess appears out of the dust."

Stories of the goddess spread, and in this way Devi became known as the dust goddess, and the sand goddess, and even goddess of the hunt. With skin as light as the moon and eyes as bright as the sky, they said she'd vanquished the seven-headed desert serpent, and that the moon had birthed her during a rare storm, and that she'd arrived riding on the backs of elephants. They spoke, too, of the jungle cat, but in hushed tones, fearful the hunter's beast might hear their whispers and devour them in their sleep.

And they spoke of her intention, to find her brother, returned from the molten core of the earth.

11
AT THE RIVER OF NOTHING

The goddess Devi often walked through marketplaces in disguise. As a moon goddess, she was known to favor opals and pearls. She picked through the stalls, talked with the merchants, listened to unspoken dreams slipping through the winds.

When she found something she wanted, she often asked for it. Many merchants were happy to oblige the whims of the goddess.

One merchant said, "I cannot."

"What do you mean, cannot?" Devi asked him. "I am the goddess of love, a moon goddess, the dust goddess, the dragon of the white city."

"It's that not I don't want to," the merchant said, "but with the recent thefts, I am deep in debt. I cannot afford to give away any of my wares. My wife would leave me, my children would starve, and my creditors would feed me to the lions."

"The lions," Devi said, "would not have much to eat."

And she left him.

In truth, Devi often rewarded those who gave her gifts. But at this time, as at all times, she was a young goddess, and easily offended. She retreated to her palace on the moon and watched the marketplace from her highest window.

She watched for forty nights and days.

One thief returned to the merchant's stall every week, always at the same time, and always snatched a single object when the merchant's attention was diverted. A second thief snuck in every night to lift a single piece. A third thief showed his face only once and took the very glass and golden egg coveted by the moon goddess.

The merchant's creditors, bankers and landlords and lenders alike, loomed.

The merchant's wife, with one child on her hip and another still in her belly, cooked and cleaned their meager home like a slave.

"I can fix this," Devi said.

The moon goddess went to the first thief and admired his collection of stolen trinkets. She requested a private showing, plied him with wine, and left him dead in his hovel. She went to the second thief and took just one finger every night until there were none left to take. He wandered the city as a beggar until his death, many years later.

She visited the third thief. She sent a boy to announce her as a collector of exotic eggs. This thief was a man of wealth who could have purchased everything at the merchant's stall and not noticed the cost. She arrived wearing a cascade of white silk and fire opals. "The truth is," she told him, "I have more than I need, but that's never been enough."

The thief said, "I know exactly what you mean."

"You know what I want," the goddess said. "Give it to me now, and maybe I shan't destroy you."

The wealthy thief laughed. "I am not so easily destroyed."

"We shall see." The goddess left the thief and went to the creditors. With the items taken from the thieves, she paid the merchant's debts. They were happy to take any payment at all, as they feared the merchant would gamble away everything he'd ever borrowed, drink away all he had ever owned, and die pennilessly in the gutter.

The moon goddess asked the merchant, "Would you give me what I ask?"

"Of course, of course," he said, "but the thieves..."

"The thieves are gone."

"And my creditors..."

"Your accounts are all settled."

"And my wife..." But the merchant's heart wasn't in the denials. He hung his head and said, simply, "It was taken."

"Then acquire another," the goddess said. "If not identical, it's equal. Make me happy." She said she'd return in forty days.

The goddess went to the wealthy thief's home, entering through a window in the darkest hour before dawn. She breathed promises into his ears as he slept. She enchanted his dreams and gave him instructions. He woke with a start and didn't even see the goddess in his bedroom. He dressed and took his horse and rode out of town.

How he reached the mouth of the cave, it cannot be said. Within that labyrinth, the wealthy thief reached the bank of an underground river. The smell of it returned his senses. "Why am I here?" he asked. Then: "Where am I?"

"This is the river of nothingness," the moon goddess told him, "from a time before the first age. If you could follow the river back to its source, you might learn how the gods created and saved this world, but the river cannot be followed."

"You!" The wealthy thief pointed in accusation and his whole body shook with rage.

"Have you brought me my egg?"

He did indeed have the glass and golden egg, though he didn't remember taking it with him. "It's a bauble. It's worthless."

The goddess took the egg from the wealthy thief's hands. "I accept this gift with thanks," she said. "And now, your reward. Drink." She dipped a cup into the river and gave the water to the wealthy merchant. He didn't want to. "It is unwise to refuse a gift from the gods," she reminded him, revealing for the first time her full glory.

He drank, and the nothingness consumed him. She led what remained of the wealthy thief to a faraway city. He remembered nothing of his old life. He was given the name *Nil*, and he lived as a beggar—a beggar and a thief—the rest of his days.

When the moon goddess returned to the merchant on the fortieth day, he had obtained a brilliant, ornate egg, comprised of sapphires in every color.

The moon goddess added both to her collection on the moon. The glassmaker had fashioning her first egg out of glass and quicksilver and moonstone. But the glassmaker had died and, though resurrected, no longer worked in glass.

12
THE WHITE CITY

The White City couldn't last forever. Mountains didn't, so how could a city?

The gods of the first age constructed the city with the bones of magnificent monsters unimagined today. Every house was a palace. The courtyards, of which there were a great many, overflowed with mead and wine at every celebration. And even in the closing days of the first age, there were plentiful causes for celebration.

But the White City was envied.

The White City was nothing less than paradise. Only heroes, politicians, poets, and artists were invited to fete with the gods. Outside the White City, in the dark forests, where dwelled indescribable beasts older than time, a legion of warriors, men, and monsters gathered. Denied the pleasures of the city, they intended to destroy it.

The twin godlings, Dion and Devi, partying with the men outside the city, learned of the growing danger.

Dion said to them, "We have no need for those other gods and their city." He coaxed vineyards from the earth and convinced the bees to make honey, and he personally rode with the hunters to slay great boars for the feast.

Devi said to them, "We have no need for those other gods and their city." She cut a sliver from the moon that would only shine outside the city, she personally bartered for the favors of flutists and violinists, and she herself sang.

Within a generation, the carnival outside the White City was envied from within. But the gods were refused, all save the twins, and they were forced to thrown bigger, more lavish festivities that would last months at a time.

It was a type of war, and it continued beyond the fall of the first age.

In the second age, inside the White City, theater was born. Actors took to the stages and gave their tragedies and comedies. Outside the White City, the circus was born. Acrobats took to the sky and magicians stole hearts. Dancers moved freely in and out of the confines of the city. Jesters and harlequins performed both outside and in. The walls that contained the city expanded. The lines separating the gods of the city and the men of the suburbs blurred. There was a long period of intermingling, and the war, if it could be called such, was forgotten.

But the second age reached its end, and the White City was not destined to stand eternal.

With her brother lost, Devi was alone outside the city when the army came. Malcontents, ruffians, mercenaries, and fiends intended to destroy the White City, to end the carnivals, to stop the plays.

"What can I do?" Devi asked herself. "I am but a girl."

She was, in fact, a goddess, magnificent and powerful. Under the light of the moon, she transformed, drawing upon powers she might have had if she'd been born in the first age but that she might never have again. She grew in size, and she sprouted wings. She paled, and she roared, and the sound of her shook the whole of the earth.

She became a dragon.

There had been other dragons, and many might lay under the earth today, sleeping, maybe restless, maybe biding their time. But at the dawn of the third age, there were no dragons such as Devi. Fierce, large as a mountain, breathing plumes of freezing breath, she met the advancing army. She was as pale as the city, with fire in her eyes, and in a single night she consumed half of the army.

The rest scattered. Over time, the dragon of the white city hunted each of the survivors, the cowards, and froze their hearts or shattered their bones.

For only that one night, celebrations at and around the White City ceased, but it was enough. Eventually, the White City would crumble to dust. Its gradual disintegration began that night.

The White City still stands. But it won't always.

13
THE TWINS REUNITED

The king at the far end of the great expanse gave Devi and the jungle cat food, drink, and information: her brother had taken residence in a mountain temple. In the foreign forest en route, they met one of the local cats, who was nothing like the jungle cat.

"I would taste the flesh of a goddess," the forest cat said.

"Only if you kill me first," the jungle cat said.

The cousins fought through the night and all the next day. Their claws were sharp. Their teeth were vicious. Feline blood was spilt, and the other creatures of the forest fled. But the two cats, as different as they were, of different sizes and colors, with different skillsets and areas of expertise, of temperaments that couldn't be less alike, were evenly matched. Finally, Devi stepped between them and said, "This is silly. You cannot win."

"But I cannot lose," both cats insisted.

"You want to taste me?" Devi asked the forest cat. "I should warn you, I am venomous and poisonous and am made more of bone than meat. I would not be a satisfying meal."

"But," the forest cat said, "you would be a meal."

"Are you hungry?" the goddess asked.

"I am a lord of the forest," the forest cat said. "I never go hungry. But I have never gorged myself on celestial flesh."

"I can defeat him," said the jungle cat. "I know his weaknesses."

"I know his," said the forest cat.

To the jungle cat, Devi said, "I *can* defend myself."

To the forest cat, Devi said, "I can *defend* myself."

Through the night, the forest cat tried to eat the goddess, and the goddess tried not to hurt the forest cat. At dawn, the goddess said, "This has been fun. I've even worked up a sweat. But it's time I continue to find my lost twin brother, who has been gone these past thousand years."

The forest cat said, "I feel like I have lost."

"You have," the goddess told him. "Maybe there's a lesson there." She dried her sweat with a cloth and wrung the cloth to collect her sweat in a saucer. She gave the saucer to the forest cat and said, "This will not sate you, but you may find it sweet."

The forest cat accepted her gift without further challenge, and the goddess, with the jungle cat beside her, continued toward the mountain temple.

As the land rose higher, the air grew colder, and winter fell upon them. They crossed a river frozen solid. They slept in caves some nights. When they had to sleep under the stars, the goddess plucked one from the sky so they could have a fire. The land grew white, the ground soft with snow, and the air thin; but soon enough, they caught sight of the temple.

The goddess and the jungle cat climbed over rocks and ice. When they reached the temple, they camped outside its doors, Devi plucking stars to keep them warm. They did not knock on the temple doors, or in any way formally introduce themselves. Devi said to the jungle cat, "If truly my brother is here, he will know I am at his door."

Despite the obvious flaw in such logic, the jungle cat did not dispute it.

They camped outside the temple for seven nights. The jungle cat hunted, and brought back food every night. The goddess melted snow for water in the star fire. After the seventh night, the door pushed open and a servant stood there. "You have come to see my master?" the servant asked.

"Perhaps so, yes," the moon goddess told him.

"My master requests the spoils of a hunt as payment for entry."

"Tell your master," the jungle cat said, "that I will enter as I please, even if the temple preserves the brother of the moon goddess."

The servant looked at the jungle cat and said, "If you do not present the proper gifts, my master will roast me for your dinner tonight."

"Tell your master that would suit me fine."

"No," the goddess said, touching the jungle cat's haunches to soothe him. "Tell your master we will present a rarified feast fit for gods and lords, but we must have access to your kitchens to prepare it."

The servant nodded once and closed the door. The day stretched, though it was the shortest day of the year, and the servant finally returned. "My master accepts your offer." Then he bowed his head so as not to look the goddess or the jungle cat in the eye. "He says there will be one hundred for dinner in four hours."

The servant led the goddess and the jungle cat to the kitchens, which were sparsely furnished but large. There were ovens, pots and pans, and a variety of spices at hand, but no fresh meat, no vegetables of any sort, and nothing canned. Still, the moon goddess prepared a feast fit for a hundred guests. She prepared courses of fish and courses of fowl and courses of red meat. She readied a dozen different vegetables, some steamed and some broiled and some roasted, and countless loaves of bread. She even made dessert.

She and the jungle cat were led to the dining halls, where one hundred visitors were surprised to be dining in the presence of gods. Indeed, some had expected meager meals in huts a thousand leagues away, and others had been wandering lost in the woods. Kings dined at that table, and former kings, and beggars who had never heard of kings. At one head of the table, the moon goddess, Devi, was seated, and the servants kept her wine glass full. At the other head of the table, the moon goddess's brother, Dion, was seated, and the servants supplied him with endless wine and honey mead and nectar.

They ate as though they were at the White City, with jugglers and acrobats and jesters providing entertainment. The feast went on for seven days, during which time the gods amused themselves with the other visitors and the jungle cat amused himself with games of chase. When it was time for desert, the servants brought out a half dozen flavors of ice cream, which until that day had never existed, and a variety of sweets from thirteen corners of the earth.

But eventually, the meal reached its conclusion. The visitors were sent back to their palaces and hovels, or returned to the woods and deserts they'd been roaming. Celestial and infernal guests made their own ways home, and even the jungle cat returned to his jungle and his queen. The servants cleared the tables as the gods sat, appraising each other, from the furthest seats.

Dion spoke first. "You have outdone yourself."

"Where have you been hiding all these years?" Devi asked.

"I sought shelter."

"The storm was never meant to be eternal."

"I have not sheltered for all of eternity."

"I missed you, brother."

"And I missed you."

Devi finished her last glass of wine. The servants were gone. The temple was dark and otherwise empty. Ice covered it. Only the two gods remained. She said, "What will you do?"

"I will," Dion said, "sate my appetites. I am still hungry, and still thirsty, and I will be long after you go."

"And then?"

"And then," Dion said, "I will have my vengeance. One thousand years are too many to lose."

Devi nodded. She accepted her brother's decision. She rose from the table and left the temple. As she descended the mountain, a traveling circus made their way up to give a command performance to the god of mazes and mysteries.

14
DALE'S SECOND RESURRECTION

After his resurrection, Dale, the mortal lover of the moon goddess, retained no skill with glass, though he marveled at the jars and bottles and eggs he had crafted with his own hands. The goddess kept her gifts in a treasure room on the moon, a collection never rivaled before or after, and few were ever permitted to view it. Dale had made half its contents. For many years, he wandered the streets of the earth, from city to city, in search of a new art. He tried writing poetry, but his words lacked vibrancy. He tried sculpting in clay, but could not give his visions life. He attempted juggling, and brought a kingdom to the brink of war.

When he picked up a violin, though, it was like being struck by lightning. He played with fury and fervor and tenderness never before known. He elicited notes from the instrument no one had heard before, and melodies that soothed even the most volatile of beasts. He wandered streets playing, and attracted behind him parades of children and snakes and rats and fainting women.

He hardly noticed any of them.

He played for the moon, night after night, no matter the phase and no matter how bright. He played for love, and for dust, and for dragons. And he played for his lover who came frequently with gifts.

Together, they strolled through parks and gardens. Dale teased the strings and Devi sang. All goddesses, since before the first age, were wonderful vocalists, but the moon goddess was perhaps the most wondrous of all. She sang, and he played, and they cared nothing for audiences or stages or opera houses.

When they were together, he slid his bow across the strings until delirium set in. When he could no longer stand or see straight or breathe, he rested in the palace of the moon goddess.

When she was away, he plucked those strings until delirium set in. When he could no longer stand or see straight or breathe, he rested wherever he happened to be.

One night, he slept in the shadow of a temple. The resident goddess had him brought inside and demanded that he play for her. He did so, because he would play for anyone. When she demanded he play with her, and she presented herself to him in all her glory, Dale did something no mortal man, and perhaps no god, had ever done before. He demurred.

Angeline was the goddess of music and math, the goddess of sunrises and sunsets, and also a goddess of love. There were so many gods, especially in the first age, who shared attributes. Looking into Dale's soul and seeing he would never surrender to her charms, Angeline slayed him on the spot. She cut his throat with a poisoned blade.

When Devi came looking for her mortal lover, the goddess Angeline was kind and gracious and promised to help in any way she could. Maybe she didn't at first know who, precisely, the moon goddess sought. When Devi found Dale's body buried in the temple gardens, she brought down the walls and turned up the earth. She cried, and the clouds poured rain for a month. She screamed, and storms pummeled the countryside and leveled the city. She dragged the goddess Angeline, near death, down to the underworld.

They crossed the infinite rope bridge through the mists, Devi carrying Dale's corpse in one hand and Angeline in the other.

"To what do I owe this pleasure?" Devi's uncle asked.

"I want the man I love returned to me."

"He has returned once already."

"Yes, but he was stolen from me."

Her uncle nodded. "I will need someone to stay in his place. Last time, your brother, Dion, remained, but he did not remain long. This time, I will need someone to stay with me until the end of an age."

Angeline, because she was prompted, volunteered. "I'll stay."

"You may stay," Devi's uncle said, "but you are too beautiful to toil in the fields of death. You will marry me, instead, and be my queen."

Angeline bowed her head. "I will."

"And you will not return from the underneath," Devi's uncle said, "until an age has ended, at which point our marriage will be annulled and you may return to discover whatever the fourth age brings."

Angeline nodded and smiled, though it was a wicked smile. "I agree."

A procession of gods and immortals, monsters, celestials and infernals, and ghosts attended the wedding of Devi's uncle and the goddess of love, Angeline, at the end of which she and he both declared, "I do."

Devi returned to the world with her mortal lover, Dale, but he was hungry and tired when they returned. He would remain hungry most the rest of this life—until he died again.

When he picked up a violin and tried to play, the sound was so disharmonious, so incredibly jagged and broken, ears bled, windows shattered, and the strings flayed themselves in agony.

15
THE PARLIAMENT OF USHERS

After the attacks on the White City, an assortment of gods and goddesses gathered mortals who were not musicians, who did not act or juggle or dance, but who instead had other skills, and entrusted them with guardianship over theaters, playhouses, stages, auditoriums, cinemas, and movie palaces.

16
ARACHNE, ORACLE AND ACROBAT
AND PARAMOUR

A procession of acrobats and jugglers played for the god of mazes and mysteries. Fire dancers and knife throwers dazzled a god who had never before seen a circus of any sort. In his time underground, he had hunted, and he had communed with monsters of dirt, rock, and metal. But he had never tasted spun sugar, nor seen a man whose flesh had been so thoroughly and vibrantly inked.

Sword swallowers and contortionists delighted Dion. He tried swallowing swords himself, but found it quite challenging. A woman tied in ropes and bound in chains was locked in a chest, and then swords were pushed through it. None drew blood. Gymnasts walking on their hands led a procession of freaks. Then a trapeze was raised in the great dining hall.

The flyer, a woman unlike any he'd ever seen, caught his eye. She was special. She flipped and twirling through the air, always to be caught by the strongman on the other end. They worked without a net.

After the performance ended, Dion, the lost god re-arisen, requested an audience with three members of the troupe.

First, he spoke with the ringmaster, and congratulated him on assembling such a fine performance. "The blood of the White City flows through your veins," the god said.

"It does. Many among our troupe trace their ancestry there."

Next, he spoke with the magician, a man of mysteries, but the god had seen through them all. "However," Dion said, "your execution was flawless, your delivery perfection, and your assistants superb. I have a gift for you."

The god gave the magician a trick, something for the act, something no one had seen before, though which trick—the magician had arrived with a thousand and now added one more to his arsenal—no one can say.

Last, the god spoke with the flyer, the girl Arachne, who was barely of age and had travelled many miles before joining the troupe.

"Your line does not descend from the White City," the god said.

"No, sir, it does not."

"Do not call me sir."

"Of course, my lord."

"You were an oracle. You have a talent for futures."

It was not a question, but Arachne curtseyed as she answered. "Once upon a time, my lord."

"Do not call me your lord."

"Of course, your exaltedness."

"Call me Dion."

This, she found curious. "Your twin is the goddess I served."

"What ended your service to my sister?"

"She left her temple to seek her brother, the god of mazes and mysteries. I left to follow, and offer my support, and learn what other futures there might be."

"What have you learned?"

Arachne shook her head, but she could not lie to a god.

"I have learned it is difficult to follow the paths walked by the gods."

"I think I love you," Dion told her. "It may be a short-lived love, as I have been hidden away a long time and maybe do not know. Love is my sister's purview, not mine. But I love you, and if you would stay with me here, I will teach you the ways of gods."

Arachne trembled before the god, perhaps with fear but also with fervor. "I would learn the ways of gods, my...beloved."

And thus, when the circus left the eastern temple of Dion, their freshest recruit remained.

17
THE DANCER AND THE GODDESS OF LOVE, OR DALE'S THIRD RESURRECTION

In a distant past, the goddess of love was presented with a jeweled egg. It appeared plain on the outside, merely unadorned gold, smooth and lifeless. But there were cracks in the egg, three lines descending from a single point at its top. The lines were not precisely straight. Nor were they symmetrical. Two of those lines hid hinges; between them, the egg could be opened.

Inside, the egg was lined like the inside of an oyster, mother of pearl, iridescent in color, and waves of emerald shot through with fire. One entire piece made up the back of the egg, and one piece made each of the doors. They were the finest examples of mother of pearl that could be found, and had been collected by Ama divers off the coast of a young island nation at the edge of the eastern world.

Within the egg, there appeared a ballerina made of painted ivory. Her dress was red and her eyes blue. She stood no more than the height of the goddess's thumb. Since the egg was also a music box, she twirled.

The egg had been made by the goddess's lover, a mortal glassmaker, but he had twice died and twice been resurrected without those talents.

However, Dale could dance.

He'd never received any formal training, and never had a partner of any sort, but upon returning a second time from the mists, he found himself moving every time he heard a note—a proper note, not the kind he would wrench now from a violin. He attended concerts and danced in the aisles. Passing street musicians, he danced beside them, and they would collect double or triple their usual donations. When the head of an imperial dance troupe saw him, she begged him to join her team.

And then she made him work.

While the moves came easily and naturally, it was difficult to put them into the right order, and to dance so closely with women who were not his lover, the goddess of love. But under the tutelage of the imperial dance troupe, he honed his skills and perfected his techniques, and he danced with the wild, reckless abandon of unnatural beasts.

Devi, the goddess of love, attended the first public performance, wherein his name was listed as one of the performers but not as the prima donna. That role, of course, belonged to Anastasia.

Anastasia, born in the imperial court of royal parentage, from the time she took her first steps, trained in full pointe. The most famous and fabulous ballerina of the age, she deserved every accolade. The life of a dancer was hard and lonely, but Anastasia embraced it like no one before her.

The audience, one thousand strong, included celestials and infernals, monsters in disguise, foreigners and aliens, and Anastasia's royal family. The question on everyone's lips—on almost everyone's lips—was where did *he* come from, this man who could dance, who could steal the spotlight from the delightful Anastasia.

In truth, Dale wanted none of the fame and none of the glory. He enjoyed the dance, and thrilled that his performance, as part of the Imperial Troupe, brought tears to the eyes of so magnificent an audience.

When it was over, Anastasia came to his dressing room and wept. She wasn't sure if these were tears of joy or horror. She trembled, she admitted all her fears, and she begged Dale both to leave and to stay. "This is my world," she said. "Yours is somewhere else. But without you beside me, it would be so pale a world."

She wept, and he wept, and they comforted each other, and perhaps they both allowed themselves to be seduced. They danced through the night, in private, sharing and exploring, until the light of dawn broke through the window and Anastasia's father sent his guard to find her.

The king's guard found them intertwined.

The goddess of love found them intertwined.

The sky darkened. Thunder shook the land. The goddess of love cried out and fell at her lover's feet. The king's guard ran him through with their swords. The goddess screamed, and the dancer screamed. But before Anastasia could launch herself from the window, the goddess of love caught her.

Together, they descended to the world of death and decay, where there was no dance and no music. They traveled dark, narrow chasms cut through the hearts of mountains. "Your dancing was divine," the goddess of love said after her fury dissipated. "There was no choice but for the two of you to fall in love."

"It wasn't love," Anastasia said. "We lost ourselves to the moment, each of us, and did what we must, but it wasn't love."

The goddess of love took her hand and said, "I know all the faces of love." She kissed Anastasia, so that she could taste what was left of Dale upon her lips, but the truth was the goddess, also, had fallen in love, however briefly, with the dancer.

They reached the halls of her uncle and his bride, Angeline. He said to the goddess of love, "I can guess why you return."

"Then grant me this favor, once more," the goddess said.

"I should warn you," her uncle said. "Every time you return for your lover's soul, more is lost. You can return to the surface with him this time, yes, and perhaps once more, but after that he must live one last life, however brief, and be lost to you forever." This made Angeline, beside him, uncomfortable; and it made Anastasia, beside the goddess, uneasy.

"I will be careful with him," the goddess said.

"And you, dancer," the goddess's uncle said. "You would volunteer to stay in this gray world, to allow your lover to spend the rest of your life with my niece?"

"You put it so eloquently," Anastasia said, with a smile and perhaps a degree of sarcasm. "It is my fault he is dead."

"It was not your sword which pierced his heart."

"It is my fault there were swords to pierce him at all," Anastasia said. "I will stay, but I must request one favor." She addressed this to both the goddess and the god. "If it pleases you, I would like to dance with Dale once more before he leaves."

So the god of the underworld cleared space in his hall. He plucked the most talented musicians from those who had died, and a performance was staged in the great necropolis. Legions of the dead, demons, infernals, and other forsaken made up the audience, and Dale's spirit was permitted to dance with the prima ballerina. She brought life and vibrancy to the gray lands. She continued to dance on her own, but Dale, resurrected a third time, and the goddess, Devi, did not stay to watch.

Upon reaching the light of the sun, Dion never danced

another step. Devi went to the king's guards, who had been overzealous in their duties, and transformed each of the five of them into mayflies, so that their lives would be brief and pointless. Then she went to the king, and asked if there was any reason she should not destroy him.

After hearing the goddess's story, the king presented her with his sword and answered: "None. I give you my life."

The goddess of love spared the king.

The goddess of love returned to her lover.

18
SHARDS OF THE MASTER GLASSMAKER

Long ago, a master glassmaker had tried to steal the work of his apprentice, who had been favored by a moon goddess. Transmuted to glass, for a long time he cried slow glass tears before eventually being shattered.

Parts of him traveled great distances. In the Antarctic, a piece of the glass master glassmaker was used to create caves of ice sheltering a sunless sea. In the distant west, a piece of the glass master glassmaker was harnessed to erect a city, but only a madman could tell such a story. In the north, a piece of the glass master glassmaker pricked the thumb of a princess. She slept for a hundred years, during which time ice enveloped her kingdom. In the east, a piece of the glass master glassmaker was ensconced in an heirloom passed down to each of the Four Great Beauties.

His essence did, eventually, depart for the land of mists, where he was allowed to rest for a day before being put to work in the eternal mines extracting diamonds that burned when he touched them. He would not toil in the mines forever, but for long enough.

19
THE WEDDING OF ARACHNE
AND THE GOD OF MAZES

After a glorious courtship, in which Dion gifted his beloved with a grand hanging garden populated by marble statues and mechanical automatons, the former oracle of the moon goddess accepted Dion's request for her hand.

Marriages between the elysian and mortals were rare; but the twins had not been born before the first age when the gods arrived from nothing, and Arachne was no ordinary mortal. Under tutelage at the temple of Devi, she had grown extraordinarily beautiful and learned some minor glamours. As an oracle of the goddess of love, she'd witnessed visions of the future and glimpsed the fundamental nature of celestials and infernals. Anyone who saw the couple would testify to their happiness. They were utterly and completely and thoroughly in love.

Invitations were widely dispersed.

When the wedding day arrived, guests included Sereca, the keeper of secrets, and gods whose names are known even today. The Master of Winds presented a gift of music. The Rose Fairy brightened the garden. A delegation of Amazons attended, as well as a legion of infernal soldiers. Nomads from the southern kingdoms traversed the desert. Artisans came from the ends of the White Nile, the Blue Nile, and the Yellow River. The Thunderbird flew across an ocean. Ice giants ventured into the sun.

It was a rare celebration.

Wine, mead, and chocolate flowed from fountains. Puzzle boxes were distributed as keepsakes, designed by the god of mysteries and mazes himself. Even his twin sister Devi attended, escorted by her thrice-deceased and thrice-arisen lover, the former glassmaker, renowned violinist, and dancer extraordinaire, Dale. He was a painter now, and they presented the god and his bride with one of Dale's landscapes as a gift.

The landscape was a type of maze, though not even the god of mazes immediately knew this.

A circus performed, with a new flyer, a Nubian princess—whose father, the king, was one of a hundred kings in attendance. Musicians played newly invented instruments, and the prima ballerina of the mists, Anastasia, returned briefly from the land of the dead to perform.

During the dance, the mortal, Dale, leaned close to the goddess of love and whispered, "She's familiar."

The ceremony itself was brief, officiated by a king of gods. They exchanged vows, they exchanged rings, and they exchanged kisses. The reception went on for seven nights.

Briefly, on the third day, Dion and his sister had a moment to talk privately within the garden. "I deserve happiness."

"I never said otherwise."

"You won't destroy my bride?"

"My oracle," Devi reminded him.

"She left your temple."

Devi only smiled.

Arachne was never alone with the goddess to whom she had pledged devotion. When the newlyweds greeted their guests and accepted their congratulations, the goddess Devi took Arachne's hand—it was the first contact ever between them—and said, "I wish you nothing but joy."

Arachne thanked the moon goddess. But as a seer of futures, she knew things no one, not even the gods, knew.

Later, in private chambers, Dale said to the goddess, "Your brother seems nice."

"Did you speak with him?"

"Not at all."

Devi smile and caressed her lover's cheek. "Don't."

"Perhaps one day we should marry," Dale said.

"I might like that." But Devi did not smile as she said this. "I'm a goddess of love. I'm not sure I'm free to marry."

"Perhaps one day," Dale said again.

After the seventh night, the newlyweds boarded a sailing ship and departed for their honeymoon, bringing with them many of the gifts they'd received—goblets and jewels and tapestries, and one painting of the shore for which they sailed.

They intended to honeymoon on the island three months. The locals, thrilled to have the god and his bride, provided everything the newlyweds might need. But Dion hung the painting, which he had at first been partial to ignoring, and examined it for hours at a time.

"Come to bed," Arachne said more than once. Every time she said it, he was there, at the painting, seeing things her mortal eyes could not see—things Dale's mortal hands should have been incapable of painting. On each subsequent occasion, it took more time for the god of mazes to tear himself from the painting.

It was a seascape, this very island, but there were colors not yet imagined, and there were subtle figures in the sand and in the sea—celestial figures, fiends and freaks in the shadows, monsters that existed only in the depths of the earth.

"Come to bed," Arachne said, but her new husband stared, transfixed, at the painting. She tried to slash it, but no blade would pierce the canvas. She tried to remove it, but even with help from the islanders it remained immoveable. She tried burning it. Painting over it. Nothing worked. Nothing changed it. She tried to bodily drag the god of mazes away, but the struggle was inside him. No amount of pushing or pulling, no expenditure of effort, no quantity of sweat would shift the god of mazes until he worked through the painting himself.

Arachne, being mortal, and knowing how long a god could be trapped in a place, wept.

20
KING OF THE JUNGLE

In his jungle home, the jungle cat was king.

The other cats and the lesser animals, the colorful birds and the swiftest fish, even the gorilla, deferred to the king of the jungle cats. He had walked with the moon goddess and spoken with men, so he deserved reverence and respect.

It rained a lot in the jungle, but on sunny days spider monkeys danced and scarlet macaws soared. On such a day, the jungle cat perched lazily on the strong limbs of a tall tree. He had recently dined and was feeling rather leisurely. Once upon a time, he had strolled through the great expanse of the desert. Forever since, sunny days left him feeling languid. He longed for the sudden, violent rains. Instead, he was visited by an anaconda. She was a large snake, almost as big as the jungle cat himself, and perhaps she had designs on ruling the jungle herself.

"Your perch looks pleasant," the anaconda said.

"It is," the jungle cat said, "and I shan't easily be persuaded to leave it."

"You teeth are sharp," the anaconda said. "Mine are so very small."

"That has never caused you trouble in the past."

"And it will never in the future," the anaconda admitted. "And your claws—you know, I do not have claws."

"You have no need for them."

"You, my liege, are a magnificent creature," the anaconda said. "It is a shame, that you must one day die."

The jungle cat eyed the snake closely. "One day, but not one day soon."

"Perhaps not," said the snake. "I must slither on my belly for the sins of another. But you, the greatest and mightiest beast of this jungle, you stride."

"And I stalk."

"I'm glad we had this talk," said the snake.

"We have, in fact, discussed nothing."

"No?" The anaconda seemed surprised. "And I thought we'd just realized we have so very much in common."

The jungle cat remained vigilant through the day, watching for the return of the snake or her children, but it was a golden dart frog that came in the golden twilight. Unlike the snake, she was small, not even a mouthful for a jungle cat who would never knowingly consume so poisonous an animal.

The frog perched well above the jungle cat without being seen. He dipped in a pool collected in the fronds above the jungle cat. When he adjusted the leaves just right, a trickle of water fell upon the jungle cat's head.

Maybe the jungle cat thought it was rain. Maybe he was merely thirsty. But he turned his head up to catch the droplets in his mouth. Tainted by the frog's poisons, the rainwater was bad. The jungle cat never saw the frog, who was of course the agent of a malicious god.

The frog's poisons worked quickly. The jungle cat died in his perch in the tree. The tree also died, perhaps in sympathy. The frog, glorying in her kill, climbed the jungle cat's fur and declared herself king of the jungle. No one took her seriously. When she sat in the jungle cat's mouth and professed her regality again, the jungle cat, perhaps involuntarily, perhaps in defiance to the end, swallowed the frog whole.

The jungle cat's kin retained the throne. Life in the jungle was little changed. But in this way the moon goddess, Devi, was denied one of her strongest allies.

21
DALE'S FOURTH RESURRECTION

Upon returning again from the land of mists, Dale, once a glassmaker, once a violinist, and once a dancer, retained no knowledge in any of these arts. His skills were lost, his talent withered. In his fourth life, the paramour of the goddess of love became a painter.

He didn't make ordinary paintings. He didn't use ordinary paints. He made his own, collecting ingredients from everywhere, and in this way travelled with some of the greatest heroes of the age. He took students, too, and taught his processes and methods and techniques. He favored paintings of Devi, goddess of love, the moon goddess, the dragon of the white city. He depicted her in all her glory, but those paintings had to be kept from mortal eyes lest they melt in their sockets. He painted her nude and clothed, in sunlight and in shadow. Sometimes she posed, but Dale needed no model. He understood light, he had perfect mastery over his pigments, and his perception of motion was unparalleled.

He painted the goddess of love as though she were glass, to represent the fragility of beauty, and this painting fetched a king's ransom when displayed at a gallery.

He made other paintings, too. Landscapes and seascapes, mountains, forests, children and thieves, saints and scholars. His students grew older and travelled and formed schools of their own. There were rivals, but upon experiencing Dale's work up close in person, each realized their inadequacies and strove to do better. Only one plotted to kill the painter, to remove him from competition, to release that throne so that any might claim it.

Dale never sat upon a throne except in Devi's palaces on the moon, and even then, no other painter witnessed it.

But others did attempt to mimic his style and subject matter. The image of Devi spread. Dreams of Devi spread.

Some mortals were afflicted by the sight of the goddess of love, even the image of her, and some never recovered. The madness caused many to believe they were visited by the goddess in the night, that she crawled into their bedchambers through open windows, that she slid in on beams of moonlight. They would rave and rant and curse her name for stealing their hearts. They pilgrimaged, her temple in the sea their destination, and supplicated themselves. The priestesses and oracles and servants did what they could for the pilgrims, feeding them wines and powders to ease their suffering, but such excursions were often difficult.

Devi hardly noticed. As a goddess of love, this wasn't new to her. She'd had her share of devotees, monks, acolytes, and deviants. But it made Dale uncomfortable.

He lived in a painter's grotto near one of the great rivers. When not painting, he sometimes walked to the shores of that river. He sat in contemplation and sometimes watched the naiads swim. They never seemed to mind him, though they fled whenever others were near.

One day, as he sat upon a rock, dangling his toes in the cold running water, the frolicking naiads suddenly scattered. There had been a dozen of them, splashing and giggling, and quite suddenly they were gone. Woodland creatures had fallen quiet. Even the insects seemed absent.

The rival, who had perhaps been driven mad by tainted pigments, who had seen the moon goddess laughing at him in the middle of the night, crept upon Dale with a black-handled athamé. He thrust the blade into Dale's back, between his ribs. It had been coated with poisons and alchemical powders.

The moon goddess didn't know this until after sunset, when the moon's light reached the edge of the river. The naiads had already arrived to bury him, anointing the body with funerary perfumes proper not for mortals but for gods. Devi descended. She took Dale's body and journeyed, once more, to the land of mists. With her burden draped over her shoulders, she scaled the forsaken cliffs. The beasts that guarded the realm snarled but did not attack.

Once again, her uncle and his queen greeted Devi warmly. "I know what it is you want."

"He was stolen from me," Devi said.

"He has lived a longer life than any mortal has ever dreamt," her uncle told Devi.

"I want him back."

"You know I must have someone or something in exchange."

"I'll send his murderer," Devi said.

Her uncle considered this. "I'll accept it. But I must give you a warning: This cannot be done again. He will retain no memories, next time, no reminder of who he is or who he was. He will be forever dead to you, should he die again. So guard him carefully."

"I understand."

"And if his murderer doesn't take his place," her uncle said, "I will come myself to reclaim him."

"I love him," Devi said simply.

She returned, descending the forsaken cliffs, not looking up because on this side of the mists she was forbidden from catching even a glimpse of her lover.

Devi returned to the river. The naiads told her everything. They told her the name of Dale's rival. They even retrieved his athamé, which he had discarded in their waters. The poisons and powders and blood had been wiped clean by the current. Devi journeyed by moonbeam into the bedroom of Dale's rival and showed him the blade.

"That was mine," he admitted.

"Come with me."

"No."

The goddess raised an eyebrow. It was a word she rarely heard. "What did you say?"

"I said no," Dale's murderer said. "If I follow you, you will no doubt avenge your lover's death. And though your vengeance will be justified, I swear to you I was not in my own mind. I was overcome by unnatural jealousy, not just of his skills, but of his relationship with you."

"Which of these powders and poisons did you use to steal my lover's life?" Devi asked.

He told her. It was quite a mixture. She added all of them to her lipstick and applied them to her lips. Though they burned, and made her ill, they were not virulent enough to snuff the life of a goddess. "I appreciate your honesty," she said. "I'll reward you with a final kiss."

When Devi embraced her lover's rival and kissed him with his own murderous concoction, he surrendered quickly and completely.

When the story of the rival's death circulated, a great many pilgrims, already afflicted by moon madness, agreed there was no better way to die.

22

PUZZLE BOXES

Guests at the wedding of Arachne and Dion, god of mysteries, received a gift: a puzzle box. Each was unique. Most were woods, dark and rich. Many were metals, gold, silver, tin, platinum, and the like. Some appeared more fragile than others. None, however, would break open. Only solving the puzzle would open the box.

They were all of similar sizes, if not exactly the same, less than the length of a forearm at the longest end, as tall as the closed fist of a boxer. They were rectangular, primarily, though a few had rounded edges.

They were not easily solved. After all, the god of mazes had fashioned each with his own hands.

They were, however, very valuable. Five hundred were

made and distributed at the wedding. Only Sereca, the keeper of keys and secrets, had left hers in the reception hall. Perhaps she'd done so intentionally. That extra box was claimed by one of the guests, a minor sprite from the Brittanic isles. She went home with two. And though she marveled at them, she was unable to work out the puzzle. She traded one for an island and locked herself away in a mountain stronghold on the North Sea. She worked at the second box for a long while. She'd kept the golden box that had belonged to the keeper of secrets. It was inlaid with numerous jewels and intricate writing, letters the sprite could not fathom.

She had books brought to her, and consulted local druids and priests, but the calligraphic letters belonged to no known language. The sprite almost invoked the keeper of secrets herself, but decided against it. What if the puzzle box had not been left intentionally?

She tried to pry it open, but the gold proved invulnerable to tools and heat. Touching it made it ring like a bell. Shaking it did not make it jingle. The sprite slept with the puzzle box, and ate with the puzzle box, and braved the tumultuous North Sea with the puzzle box. One random day, for no particular reason at all, she realized the lettering wasn't a language but a set of directions. Turn the box this way, flip it that way, slide it here and there.

The sprite copied the instructions and followed them precisely, and the puzzle box clicked as it unlocked. Alone in the tallest tower of her keep during a stormy gray twilight, she opened the box.

Inside, she found a golden egg, ornate and intricate, with diamonds and rubies and a dial at its crown. Even to the sprite, this inner puzzle seemed simple. She turned the dial and opened the egg.

Not even a magical sprite could survive that explosion. The keep collapsed into the North Sea. The island fractured.

This excited the Mirrie Dancers; the aurora borealis reached further, with a shine of golden fire.

Other puzzle boxes, deemed unsolvable, joined the prized collections of mortal kings in every corner of the earth. The king of an eastern nomadic tribe opened the puzzle box inherited from his father, who had in fact witnessed the nuptials, revealing a pearl egg the size of his thumb. He wove this into his headgear and carried it everywhere.

An Arabian thief acquired a puzzle box, don't ask him how, and kept it in a cave with a great deal of treasure. His four year old daughter solved the box while he was away, revealing a diamond egg almost as big as her thumb. It was the brightest treasure of the cave, and even at such a young age she knew to keep it hidden from her father, as he would no doubt trade it for another lamp.

One of the winds, opening her box, found a mercurial egg. She had no idea how it maintained its shape. It glimmered differently in every variation of light. If it contained something inside—she had no doubt that it would, being a gift from the god of mysteries and puzzles—she never discovered it.

A hundred puzzle boxes were lost to time. Discarded, stolen, destroyed, dropped into chasms or abysses, swallowed by volcanos. Half the puzzle boxes were never opened and never revealed their treasure. Over the course of days, months, then finally centuries, the eggs were found and displayed in great halls, temples, castles, citadels, mansions, and palaces. Each was magnificent, a triumph of beauty and engineering.

In the palaces of the moon, on a beautiful morning while the moon goddess was away, her lover, Dale, who as a glassmaker had made the first and most dazzling jewel egg, easily opened the puzzle box he had received.

23
THE GOD OF MAZES VERSUS THE MAZE

The god of mazes had been trapped within a maze. He had created the first and greatest labyrinth. He had traced cosmic eddies into the mundane. He had burrowed through the roots of the earth. Formerly a forest god, one with the wood, he transmuted into a god of metal and rock. His fingernails were diamond, his teeth granite, his eyes rubies in a sea of moonstone.

He was strong like iron and stone. But he was trapped in a maze unlike any he had ever imagined.

Dion, god of mysteries and puzzles, god of mazes, and forest god, stood on the edge of an island shore staring into the depths of a painting of him staring into the depths of a painting just like this one, in which he was staring into the depths of a painting on this shore. But the painting within the painting shifted and changed, and was never this image. It had been, once, maybe. He had reached into the painting, and into that painting, stepping into each level through the sand and sunshine and gentle island breezes. His mortal bride was lost behind him. If he reached back, he might be able to disentangle himself and touch her.

But Arachne, in all her splendor, with her hidden traits and skills, with her tenuous connection to the goddess of love, remained mortal, and mortal flesh remained weak. If he pulled, she would be drawn into the painting and lost forever.

The painting drew him deeper. He reached back for something, anything, that might anchor him.

Somewhere distant, the first of his puzzle boxes opened, revealing an eye—an egg in appearance, but an eye of the god of mysteries, and a connection. Through the eye, he saw the palace of a god as if through a prism. It was a god of light, a sun god, a voice of the sun, a young and stupid godling birthed in this third age. Gold dominated his palace, but the columns supporting the roof were built with sunbeams. Apollo, on his throne, playing with his toy even as his acolytes fawned for his attention, stared into the amber egg and didn't know the god of mazes stared back.

Elsewhere, under the sea, in the dancing hall of a sunken city, another puzzle box opened its eye. An extraordinarily beautiful mermaid. Maybe she didn't understand how osmium worked or where it came from. It was a marvel to her, unlike any sunken treasure she'd ever discovered, unlike any undersea wonder. She didn't know the seas weren't deep enough to reach the richest deposits of osmium.

A mouse, an emperor over his dominion, whose foot soldiers had stolen a puzzle box from a god of fire, released an egg of ice. The ice came from before the first age and would never melt. It existed under the river of nothingness and nowhere else. When the god of mazes peered through the eye, the flash of light blinded the emperor mouse and all his brethren.

In a palace on the moon, the painter—the former painter, who no longer retained such gifts—opened his puzzle box and discovered an egg, the shell of which was eggshell, meticulously crafted by the god of mazes on the night before his wedding. The pieces came from robin eggs and crocodile eggs, and the eggs of dragons and cockatrices. The mosaic those pieces made invoked every color of the sky, the earth, the sea, and the mists. It was delicate, extraordinarily fragile, and as heavy as phoenix breath.

Each puzzle box had been made with a particular recipient in mind. There were no mistakes.

The painting was a maze, but it was not a maze with an exit. It was a trap, like barbed teeth which do their damage when you try to escape them, but the god of mazes could not easily be contained. He was, after all, a god of metal, and a god of the second age, strong as iron and entirely unstoppable.

He stepped out of the painting, back to that island shore, to his bride weeping on the bed they had shared. When she looked at him, she smiled, but it was a deviously hungry smile, reflecting his own.

"The eyes are opening," the god of mazes said. "Our honeymoon is over, Arachne. You have to go."

"Come to bed," she said, wiping away the last of her tears. "We'll discuss it in the morning."

24
THE REALM OF MISTS

A king of gods descended to the land of mists to ask his brother about thunder. The land of mists was a confusing place, even for celestials, and the king of gods found himself face to face with one of the infernals. It was a hideous thing, physically, but quiet and curious. The infernal begged for release.

"Release from what?" asked the king of gods.

"From the mists."

"I have no dominion over the mists," the king of gods said, "but I'll take you to my brother, the lord of this place."

The king of gods and the cowering infernal delved deep into the land of mists, through eternal graveyards, beyond the guardians. The infernal said little, and shied away whenever the king of gods cast his eyes in the infernal's direction. "I shan't strike you down," said the king of gods.

"So many would," the infernal said. It was smaller than most its brethren, and pathetic. The king of gods rarely felt sympathy, but he felt it now.

"Walk beside me," the king of gods commanded. The infernal had been lurking in the king's shadow instead.

So the two strode, side by side, into the hall of the lord of mists and his queen, Angeline, formerly the goddess of music and math. It was a performance day, so the prima ballerina, Anastasia, was showing off her newest moves, which would have been quite impossible beyond the mists.

The infernals lived and loved and died just as mortal men or gods or monsters, so a legion of deceased infernals lingered in the corners and crevices of the underworld. But none had ever before ventured this deep whilst still drawing breath.

Anastasia finished her performance. An audience of thousands, ghosts and spirits and phantasms among the gods and monsters, and the dead infernals hidden in their cracks and fissures, applauded and threw flowers to show their appreciation.

The king of gods said to his brother, "I've come to inquire about my thunderbolts."

"I know nothing of thunder," the lord of mists said.

"That's odd," said the king of gods, "because my thunder has died."

"Thunder doesn't die."

This wasn't entirely true. Thunderers had died before, and several had even been in Anastasia's audience. Three stepped forward—two of them huge men, one a lithe woman, Tempest—all of whom had wielded the most powerful of weapons.

"And you?" the lord of mists asked the infernal. "What brings you to my hall?"

The infernal grinned. Its face had never contorted into so ugly a shape before. "Vengeance."

The ghosts of infernals fell upon the lord of mists. His queen beside him, Angeline, didn't just turn against her king. She wielded the thunderbolts of the king of gods. She ran her husband through with the edge of the weapon like a sword. It crackled and howled. The thunderers, below, were shocked. Few, even among the gods, could master such a weapon.

She'd had a teacher, of course.

The infernal and Tempest, the thunderer, descended on the king of gods. He fought valiantly. He slayed the infernal, releasing a torrent of murky energy. If it was an explosion, it was felt all throughout the world, well beyond the realms of mist. When the dust cleared, Tempest alone stood in the field; and Angeline, alone, stood at the throne.

Anastasia, the prima ballerina, had witnessed the battle, but had no words to describe it. It was swift, and it was decisive, and in the end two gods walked out of the realm of mists. She went after them, and they did nothing to stop her. She wasn't mortal anymore; nor was she lifeless.

The king of gods and the infernal, however, were not a sufficient trade. The realm of mists trembled. Steam rose from the earth. Dust rained down from the ceilings. Granite gravestones split and splintered. The balance disrupted, a great many demons and beasts attempted escape. Some, no doubt, succeeded. Some were brought down by the gravity of death. Guardians protected all the exits.

The lord of the mists returned to his throne, even in death. But there was only one way to restore balance. Otherwise, the realm of mists might fracture, and such cracks in the firmament of this universe would bring an end to everything.

25.
THE FIRST DEATH OF
TEMPEST THE THUNDERER

During the second age, a thunderer was born. She seemed small, especially for a thunderer, and frail, but as she grew she competed with the strongest and swiftest and always won. The gods named her Tempest, and as a teenager she harnessed the thunderbolt.

During a storm, she scaled the side of a mountain to

watch a thunderer at work. He was a big man, a mountain himself, full of hair and muscle and zeal. He gleefully tossed lightning, striking trees that had dared reach into his sky and villages that harbored his enemies. He relished the action. He kept the thunderbolts in a basket, and was so busy taking and throwing them he never noticed the girl.

If he had seen the child of gods reach into his basket, he would have warned her off with a thunderous roar. It was rare that even a god could handle so volatile a weapon. By the time he noticed, Tempest, already holding one, was asking, "Can I try?"

The thunderer laughed. He really had a jovial nature. "Please."

Tempest tossed the thunderbolt. Her aim was questionable, but she struck the mast of a ship at sea. The mast cracked, the sails tore, and in the midst of a storm, the fire spread quickly. She frowned, of course, as she'd missed her intended target.

"My first throw," the thunderer told her, "hit a goat on a mountain. He was quite surprised, if briefly." Then he knelt next to her—because he towered over her and wanted to show how serious he was. "Would you like to try again?"

Over time, Tempest became not just a thunderer, but one of the most powerful. She threw and caught thunderbolts with her brothers and cousins, and she fought in the thunder wars that threatened to end the second age. A hundred gods were lost during those battles, including the young twin, Dion, who was not even involved.

It was one of Tempest's volleys that sent the young godling underground. So she went after him, deep beneath the surface, through ore and stone, outside of her own element.

When she found him, he said, "I'll hide until your war is over."

"I'll return," Tempest promised, "when it's done."

The war continued for forty nights and ranged across the world and beyond. What started it, no one could say. What ended it? The death of two mighty thunderers, including Tempest's teacher. It takes a lot to kill a god, and even more to kill a thunderer. Mortal cities had sunk beneath the ocean. Rivers changed their courses. Kingdoms were decimated. It had been a horrible and horrifying war, and Tempest was glad it was over.

She retreated into her chambers high in her aerie temple and tended to her wounds.

She forgot about the young godling and her promise. Tempest took mortal lovers, wandered the great expanse, destroyed the palace of an unjust king. She survived the passing of an age. She outlived many thunderers who had fought in the wars; strong though they were, thunder throwers tended to die young.

Tempest did not intend to die young. She tempered her temper. She taught herself constraint and control. She conversed with the wise atop their mountains. She studied with snakes and jungle cats to learn the ways of the hunt. To learn patience.

A travelling circus came to her temple and performed. During their visit, the young godling she had forgotten, Dion, now master of mysteries and mazes, arrived. "I need your assistance," he told her. "And I need your loyalty, even after death."

"I do not intend to die."

"Neither do I," the god of mazes told her. "But I need an ally in the land of mists. And you owe me."

By dawn, the goddess Tempest was dead. Poisoned.

26
THE ULTIMATE DAWN OF THE THIRD AGE

Returned from the realm of mists, the love goddess Angeline, goddess of music and math, and goddess of sunrises and sunsets, greeted the eastern sun as it rose over the horizon. There had never been so glorious a sunrise. Brilliant reds stretched across the sky, golden yellows and bright oranges, and even the sun god in his chariot wondered at the preponderance of color.

Angeline called forth the Mirrie Dancers to revel in the dawn, even so far south as the Mediterranean isles. They came, compelled by the power of her appeal. Though Angeline had never died, she carried the power of death with her. The colors she gave to the sunrise, she stole from the flowers and gardens around her. Gray stretched over the islands, such was her strength. The colors of that dawn didn't merely cross the sky. They lingered.

The sun god descended from his chariot—the horses knew the way—to confront the returned dawn goddess. She laughed at him and struck him down.

The death of the sun god was considered first blood.

War came to the third age, to gods, monsters, and men.

Angeline reinvigorated her former temples, populating them first with the oracles and priests of the sun gods. Apollo was not the only such god, and not the only such god to fall.

Angeline brought her blood red dawn to gods across the world, across the realms, across dimensions. She brought her dawn to El Dorado and Atlantis and Shambhala and Babylon. Her fingernails were razors and her fury unbound.

Half a day, a long day and a long dawn, passed before she remembered the true object of her hatred: the moon goddess Devi, the love goddess who had descended into the realm of mists and traded Angeline's life for that of a mortal man.

Angeline siphoned the colors of sunrise into herself. She didn't return life to the flowers or the gardens or the islands. Indeed, already the volcanos were exploding, swallowing cities and islands and entire nations. Already, the oceans rose to meet molten rock. Ash coated all of reality. She blasted the sun out of the sky, destroying its horses, shattering the chariots, scattered the powers that opposed her. She shoved the day and daylight away, scattered what light remained, and delivered a premature night.

A billion stars emerged. So, too, did the moon, deep on the horizon at the end of day. Angeline set her sights upon the palaces of the moon goddess and said, "Face me, Devi, and I'll show you what it means to be love's bitch."

Before descending to the mists, Angeline, too, had been a goddess of love.

27

THE STORM BRINGER

The ghost of the thunderer Tempest returned to the earth with centuries of fury at her disposal. Her supply of thunderbolts was endless, and time had magnified their power. Her first bolt took out the northern thunderer, who had fought with the opposition during the thunder wars. Her second bolt destroyed the southern thunderer and all his temples and all his followers. A flood of souls descended to the realm of mists. She had never been capable of witnessing that exodus before.

Tempest's thunder destroyed mountains and cities. She brought fire to deserts and scorched the forests. As promised to Dion, a promise she would this time keep, she cleansed the world with electric fire.

She brought storms to the oceans and decimated undersea kingdoms and the dwellings of river nymphs and the fleets of Viking kings.

She reveled in the dawn, but when night fell, when the stars shone bright and the moon gazed upon the earth, Tempest faltered. She dropped to her knees and wept. The weight of those tears dragged her back down to the mists, where the spirit lord of mists grabbed her by the throat. He held back the full extent of his rage. "Balance," he said, "must be maintained."

She thrashed against him. "I won't return!" she cried. "I am not for death!"

"No," he agreed. "Not *for* death." He crushed the wind from her throat and revitalized the flow of death in her veins. He cast Tempest into the deepest pits of the realms, into a cage of iron and osmium, and sealed it with fire and acid and magic and curses. He infused the cage with his own blood, still fresh from the corpse of the lord of the dead, and he buried the cage at the core of the earth. She raged against the walls, throwing and throwing thunderbolts as though she had an infinite supply. As she scorched the walls, she reinforced them. Those walls would hold her for at least the length of another age. Either she would exhaust herself over the millennia, or she would be someone else's problem.

28
DALE'S FINAL DEATH

After his fourth resurrection, Dale, the lover of the goddess of love, was no longer a glassmaker, nor a musician. He had no grace for either the dance or the paintbrush. Indeed, it might be said that he had no obvious talents, no superior skills, nothing but his love for the moon goddess. He wrote poetry in her honor, but they were not the best of poems. He opened the puzzle box he'd received at the wedding of Arachne and the god of mazes, but it was the least challenging of puzzles.

His talents lay in mapmaking, but the only map he'd

made was of the moon palaces. He barely saw the earth, except in the sky. He'd long ago lost track of his blood relations. He wasn't merely human. Nor was he immortal. He was what the goddess of love had made him, and he was unique in all the known universes.

As war raged, the final war of the third age, he watched safely from the palaces of the moon. He saw the colors of war scraped across the skies. Clouds dispersed and disappeared. All the old resentments and rivalries reignited. And there was nothing Dale could do but watch and wonder and cry.

The treasuries of the palaces held paintings he had made in another lifetime, a dozen violins he had once upon a time played, and a hundred eggs he had fashioned of glass and metal. It held, too, the gifts of other gods, another hundred eggs by celestial and mortal craftsmen, piles of jewels, ornate mirrors trimmed in platinum, tapestries, and incomprehensible delights.

One egg, made of eggshell, which had hidden within the puzzle box, served as an eye and also a portal. Arachne stepped through. She was wicked, and wickedly armed, and determined. She hid in the dark, in the treasure; and through nefarious, un-mortal means, she called to Dale. "Come," she whispered. "I have wonders to show you."

The idea interrupted Dale on a palace balcony. He hesitated, but the call persisted. He retreated inside, into the palace where he should have been safe, into the palace where he had lived most of five lifetimes. Down spiraling stairs, he descended to the treasure rooms. It was dark, lit only by the luminescence of the treasure itself. There were lights, though, that should have been burning.

It was the mirror that drew him, a figure in the mirror he remembered but only vaguely. As he approached, Arachne emerged from shadows, poisoned blade in hand, and slid the sharp end between Dale's ribs. At his ear, she whispered, "I will call this vengeance."

The poison worked fast. The blade had cut important arteries. He had three, four breaths at most, so he smiled and told his assassin, "I have enjoyed each and all of my days."

Arachne pushed him forward, into the platinum-framed mirror, shattering the glass with the tip of the knife protruding from Dale's gut. That was not what she'd wanted to hear.

From the mirror, a figure emerged, the prima ballerina Anastasia who had escaped the confines of the mists. She grabbed Arachne's head and whispered, "I hope you have enjoyed yours." Then she kissed the assassin, conveying the kiss of death straight from the land of mists, a quicker acting poison than any coating her blade. Arachne tried to break free, but it was too late for her. Anastasia delivered Arachne, bride of the god of mazes, into the realm of mist.

Dale's strength seeped quickly from him. "Not so fast," Anastasia said, catching him in her arms. "Dance with me once more before you die."

Two breaths remained before Dale's life would slip away, but he clung to Anastasia and danced until he died.

29
THE TWINS, REPRISE

While the last war of the third age raged, Devi descended to the earth's surface to confront her twin brother. "Is all this because of me?"

"Yes," he said. Then: "No. This was inevitable. You were a convenient excuse."

"Your time beneath the earth changed you."

"It changed you, too."

"I found love."

"I found anger."

The two circled each other, twins inseparable from birth, godlings who had survived the explosive conclusion of the second age. The god of mysteries, the goddess of love—they were the same, almost, yet different enough to stand on opposite sides of the battlefield.

Around them, gods died, mortal armies marched, and reality struggled to maintain itself. The third age was ending. Perhaps there had been a prophecy, who could say? Sereca, the keeper of secrets and keys, who had emerged from nothingness as the first of all the gods, as something more resilient than a god, probably knew, but she was not involved.

"I love you," Dion said. "I always have. You're my sister. My blood."

"And I," Devi told him, "am angry."

Their lovers were dead. Each knew. The palace on the moon had shattered, and Dion had been watching through the eggshell eye he had gifted to them.

"Will we fight?" Dion asked.

"We have always fought."

So they fought. They wrestled, and they kicked, and they swiped at each other with blades dripping poison and venom and acid and tears. They struggled in the unnatural night, neither quite capable of overcoming the other. They seemed evenly matched. Their foundations were the same. They shared a bloodline and a perspective.

But Dion threw everything he had into the melee, and Devi restrained herself. He wanted blood. She'd seen enough. A thousand years beneath the earth taught Dion many lessons, but that millennia had also taught Devi.

So they fought through the night, under the stars, while thunder shattered the sky and the earth. They acquired an audience. Gods, godlings, celestials, infernals, mortals, spirits, oracles, priests, soldiers, and children watched the twins. Smoke wafted over the battlefield. The dead paused in their descent to the mists. The moon shuddered. No one interfered—no one, at least, until the love goddess—goddess of music and math, goddess of sunrises and sunsets, recently widowed from the lord of mists—until Angeline crashed down on the edge of the field.

She said to the moon goddess, "It is time for your reign to end. I will take your acolytes and oracles, I will take your precious temples and your palaces on the moon, I will take all the love there is and ever will be, and I will own this world and the next."

Devi said, "You talk too much."

Here, the jungle cat might have stood at Devi's side. Her lover, the near-mortal Dale, would have backed her. There were thunderers and sovereigns and rajahs and generals who might have fought beside her. Even her uncle, the lord of the mists, might have supported Devi in this moment. But all of them were dead, dead from this war or other nefarious means, picked off one by one while she had favored her lover and gave no thoughts to conquest or even balance.

In this universe, she had been meant to stand in balance against her brother. Her failure had led to this battlefield, with opponents on both sides and witnesses who couldn't know if either side was just.

Angeline unleashed everything all at once—the color of sunrise, the fury of sunset—with precision and with style. She unleashed a symphony of chaos and destruction aimed at this other love goddess, the lesser love goddess, the insignificant and insufficient love goddess.

Devi withstood it.

Devi withstood it because her brother stood beside her. Dion, the god of mysteries and mazes, who had forged allegiances and fostered enmities and sparked this conclusion to the third age, lent his strength to his sister. Together, they fell to their knees, but Angeline advanced and intensified her attack.

"When you die," Dion told Devi, "it will be by my hand."

Devi, harshly lit beneath the onslaught of Angeline's

attack, said, "I won't die."

When Angeline was close enough, Devi rose and grabbed her throat. "I am a great many things," she said to Angeline. "I am grateful to you, for giving me my lover. But he has gone again to the realm of mists, and I am not at all pleased." Her other fist, the one not wrapped around Angeline's windpipe, the one hanging loosely at her side, tightened around a thunderbolt as powerful as any ever wielded, even by the fiercest thunderer, Tempest, in her final moments. One of Devi's greatest secrets, which she had never revealed or relied upon, was her truest nature.

She drove the thunderbolt into Angeline's chest.

"But I've never been angry with you," Devi told Angeline's spirit as it fell, in pieces, to the mists. Then she turned on her brother, thunderbolt still blazing in her hand.

"I have no regrets," Dion said. "It was my destiny, to bring an end to this third age."

"You have another destiny."

30
DALE'S FINAL RESURRECTION

At the end of the third age, after the death of numerous gods, smoke covered the world and the colors of the next age hadn't yet coalesced. It took time for a new age to arise from the ashes of the old. Devi the thunderer and her defeated brother, Dion, descended into the realm of mists. The ghost of their uncle reigned, though diminished from what he had once been. He glared at the nephew who had orchestrated everything. "You have no place here."

"That doesn't matter. You know why I've come," Devi said.

"I wouldn't accept him," her uncle said. "I'd take too much satisfaction in the punishments I'll force him to endure."

"He was what the world made him," Devi said.

Dion never said a word. He stared into the mists, through the spirits and the dead, in search of the woman he loved. Like Devi, he had been capable of great love. His acrobat and bride resided here in the mists.

"And as you know, your lover cannot be restored," the lord of the mists said. "He is dead and gone, gone beyond your reach."

The underworld rumbled when Devi spoke. "Nothing is beyond my reach."

Her uncle did not deny her. Anastasia stepped out of the mists, leading both Arachne and Dale by the hand. She said, "I don't know if they're who you seek anymore, but they're here."

Dion and Arachne ran to each other and embraced and kissed. Dale looked at his lover, the goddess of love, and averted his eyes. "Am I worthy?"

Devi's uncle said, "Fine. You've always gotten your way and probably always will. There's too much damage to repair, and the world, all of the worlds, all the universes known and unknown, are out of balance. One day, you'll have to face that."

"One day," Devi agreed. "Not today."

And thus, the god of mysteries and love reunited with his bride, and they were locked in a prison of osmium alloys on an island in the midst of the river of nothingness, so that no one could bother them and they could never again bother anyone else. And the goddess of love, Devi, was reunited with her lover. The glassmaker had become a violinist, and the violinist had become a dancer. The dancer became a painter, and the painter a mapmaker, though he'd only ever made the one map of the palaces of the moon. The former mapmaker returned to the world with the goddess of love. They settled in a city, in an apartment, far from the worries and whims of fate.

SECRET HISTORY
PART III

The Magician's Assistant

1.

There were seven forms of magic—or there must have been seven, because certain numbers carried more significance than others—and if it wasn't seven, it must've been thirteen.

Alyssa had theories. She didn't *know* the seven forms, wasn't fluent in any of them, had tried her hand at three and only ever witnessed one other being put into action.

She intended to master the seven arts of magic. She knew illusion, but that was an easy one and maybe not true magic. She'd played with divination, which had led her here in the first place, and changed the nature of her dreaming forever since.

She cleaned the Maestro's workroom after a night of serious dabbling. He'd fallen asleep in his chair—a little mixture of herbs helped him along—so now she could pick up his books and peruse them at will and maybe learn a thing or two about the art of transformation.

Just keep an eye on the Maestro, she told herself, because if he wakes up…

The night stretched impossibly long. It always did, this far from civilization, this close to the edge of the world. Cold crept in through the stones; no fire, not even one fed by magic, could keep it at bay forever.

She didn't need forever.

She found something interesting in one of the books, an old book written delicately in an old language. Not the original. Someone had copied the words from elsewhere, and she saw where the copyist had gone back and made changes. Not a translation, per se, but whoever had written these words had no knowledge of their meaning. She recognized errors, places where the copyist had obviously done something wrong, but wasn't yet skilled enough to correct them herself.

She cursed under her breath, then quickly glanced at the Maestro to make sure he hadn't heard her. His eyes flicked and flitted beneath his lids. She wondered what pasts the Maestro dreamt about. He was old, very old, and doubtlessly had a number of pasts from which to choose.

Dreams were another form of magic, not the Maestro's area of expertise, and not the reason she had come into his service.

Alyssa made a few notes in her shadow book. There wasn't much to note. She would need the original. If the Maestro's library didn't contain it, the thing might be lost forever.

Might be.

Maybe the Maestro's library held it somewhere. It was possible. If he had needed something specific from this — *translation* was the wrong word — the original might hide on a shelf.

She gathered an armful of books and, with a great deal of stealth, crept out of the Maestro's study.

The house was a strange one. It kept secrets. It confounded visitors. It swallowed burglars and shredded assassins. Halls did not lead to the same place every time. But the Maestro had accepted Alyssa, and she'd made friends with the house — as best as she could — so it didn't always send her the wrong way. This night, it allowed her to enter the library, though the armful of books had been her key for that.

She had never seen so massive a library. The room was wider than most ballrooms and three times as long, divided cleanly into aisles that looked straight, and stretched to a distant vanishing point. But those aisles were deceptive. They twisted and turned when you weren't looking. They would lead you astray. They would suck you into the shelves and never let you go. Twice, she'd come across skeletal remains, one bound in irons and hanging from a stone wall. She knew the risks.

Searching the library was never straight-forward. She talked to herself as she worked, which was almost the same as talking to the walls. "*The Book of Lost Fates,*" she said aloud, returning one rendition to the shelf. Two others were already there. She knew, from past experience, the three books were entirely different yet otherwise identical. "*Sparrow's Book of Shadows.* That's a tough one." She said this, though it wasn't true, to lull the library into helping her. Though familiar with the story of Sparrow, Alyssa had always assumed she was a mythical figure, a legend rather than a person who had lived. The existence of the book didn't settle the matter. "*Aurora Consurgens,*" the next book, was slim, and something else entirely. It was closer to what she sought, and brought her in the direction she needed to go—she had selected the books in a very particular order.

A breeze brushed her shoulders and played with her hair. The nearest windows were, of course, closed and locked, and none of the stained glass panels were missing. She didn't need to look to confirm this. She had studied a great many of those windows—not for the ironwork, or the glasswork, or any of the exquisite craftsmanship that had been brought to them, but for the stories they told, the scenes portrayed, the tableaus invoked. One of these windows— possibly more than one—was a portal, she was sure of it. It depicted a theater, a grand old place where vaudeville and burlesques had eventually replaced the operas. A theater would normally have two masks, one for comedy and one for tragedy, but this theater had a third. The details, however, were lost to her—because of the distance—but one day she might learn the truth of it.

Not tonight.

She returned *Aurora Consurgens* to its shelf, sighed heavily to indicate to the library this was difficult work and surely she neared exhaustion and perhaps the Maestro might let her sleep a full night rather than interrupt her in the hours before dawn with an urgent need of raven feathers and tears of innocence.

"*Transformation and Transmutation,*" she read off the next spine—not the last spine, but this was the important one. She shook her head. "*Wrong edition,* he said. *I need the older one,* he said." She added a curse from a foreign tongue to show she meant it.

Sometimes shelves eluded her, and this was one of those times. It should've been close. This section contained glamour and makeup and alchemy, all types of transformation.

Finally, on a bottom shelf, below a scratched bust of Pallas, she found the earlier edition of *Transformation and Transmutation.* She took it, and slipped the other in its place, and opened it long enough to check a single passage.

This was the original. It contained the markups of the author, the strikethroughs and corrections, signs of fading ink, and random illustrations that, on first glance, appeared disconnected from the text.

She put the other back, then found the home for the final two texts.

The library let her out without a fuss.

She checked on the Maestro, still asleep in his chair, snoring softly, before returning to her own chambers.

The house was enormous, bigger than it seemed to be because some rooms were physically in other places. She had a suite to herself, though the Maestro could summon her any time, day or night, without warning or explanation. Sometimes, she was expected to simply know what he wanted before he knew. She wasn't as adept in divination as the Maestro might have preferred in a *famulus,* but anyone with those skills would likely find a more lucrative means of earning income.

Her suite contained a number of rooms, some of which she couldn't always access, but she settled in an oversized reading chair with her shadow book, a fresh pot of ink for her pen –a ballpoint was ill-suited for this type of work—and *Transformation and Transmutation, a Practical Guide with Warnings and Anecdotes and Firsthand Observations of the Author*—as well as a bottle of wine and a glass.

Alyssa worked well into the night, into the morning, until the first light of dawn slipped through her windows. She attempted a minor transformation herself—wine into cocoa—but ended up with syrupy wine that smelled earthy, like mushrooms from a graveyard which she wouldn't risk actually ingesting.

She made her cocoa from scratch, aware that even this act was a transformation—of beans and cream and sugar into a magnificent restorative elixir. She had nearly finished a second cup when she heard the Maestro yelling her name.

She stuffed the book under the cushion of her chair, checked her face in the mirror, replaced her blouse with something fresh, and ran to the study.

The Maestro was not in the study. He called for her again. Was he angry?

Was he in the library?

She ran there next. The halls shifted to keep her from her goal. "Coming!" she cried, rounding another corner that led back the way she came.

He called her name a third time, shouting this time. Alyssa stopped in the hall and looked at the walls, the tapestries, the sconces, and asked, "Where are you?"

The Maestro said, "Here" as she rounded one more corner. And there he was, in the hall outside a door. He fixed her with a look, his eyes straining to see from beneath his brows. His face had been scarred a lifetime ago. The red slash remained and, as it was doing now, sometimes pulsated. This typically indicated anger, frustration, or excitement. It was impossible to know which.

With a decisive, authoritative motion, he swept into the room.

She followed.

She had never seen this room before. There were a hundred rooms or more she had never seen or never even found. Doors were locked. Doors were hidden. Doors were simply not there until needed or wanted or requested by specialized rituals or proper offerings.

It was a laboratory of sorts. Vials and beakers of various liquids sat on counters. There were sinks. There were Bunsen burners. There were powders and tinctures and all manner of transformative ingredients.

"I mean to attempt something," the Maestro said to her. He never looked at her when he lectured like this. It wasn't a conversation, and there was no need to respond. "I intend to create a doorway."

"A doorway?"

He scowled at her. "I need quicksilver, a good supply of it. I need raw obsidian, and I need whiskey."

All those things could be found in the house. The whiskey, of course, was for drinking. No time of day was too early for that. She'd procure the good stuff; he always wanted the best unless he specifically requested something lesser. Quicksilver and obsidian were often required for divination, but there had been no mention of either in her readings overnight. Why did he need to transform something into a doorway? Why not simply scratch one out of the wall, or change the destination of a doorway that already existed?

2.

An entire wing of the house stored all sorts of things — flour and cream and eggs, rosemary and sage, assorted gems, cash in a number of currencies, and rare ingredients for all manner of spell casting. This included herbs, roots, the dried feet of a dozen birds, spiders and crickets, butterflies in amber, salamanders, and a variety of elements. Quicksilver was easy to find, not so easy to carry, so she took the whole flask. She found a chunk of obsidian the size of her fist. And she grabbed one of a dozen bottles of scotch.

Alyssa balanced all this in her arms, though there was much glass involved and everything—even the obsidian—was fragile, and went through the halls again. She had made a mistake, not learning the official name of the room—names were important in all things—so she told the house as she walked, "I need to bring these to the Maestro." She had been gone a long while, wandering halls and stockrooms, but that type of work was expected to take time.

Around another corner, she stood before her own chambers. The door was open. A wind escaped her rooms. She had closed that door before, and no one—not even the Maestro—was supposed to enter without her permission. She set down the things she had gathered and approached cautiously. Something was wrong. Unsettled. The floors seemed to tilt. Alyssa held the wall for support and felt the pulse of the house, the echoes of its heartbeat, and it sounded fast. Whatever was happening defied easy explanation.

She reached her door and looked inside. It was her anteroom, just as it was supposed to be. The house inhaled— she felt it in the walls, in the air—and exhaled—she felt it in her bones. She stepped inside, walked through the rooms, checked the gardens outside her bedroom window, and rifled through her clothes and books and pens. Pens were a variation on wands, and hers were not without hidden attributes. Everything seemed to be in order—everything until she checked under the cushion of her chair. Instead of *Transformation and Transmutation*, she found a rip, a crack in the universe, a hole that had swallowed the book.

The tear winked at her, then closed, then ceased to exist. The unnatural wind disappeared. The equilibrium of the house returned to its usual balance. Outside, the sun had moved a long way over the sky. Days were short here, but she had lost more time than she'd realized. Dropped time was never a good thing.

She wouldn't tell the Maestro about it.

She locked her chambers as she left, gathered all the ingredients and wandered the house until she found the laboratory.

He looked up from his work as she entered. "I thought you'd gotten lost," he said, "or swallowed by a vortex."

"Vortex?" She always felt dumb when she asked one-word questions like that, but she knew he said such things to make himself feel smarter.

"A little thing, really," the Maestro said. "A dozen of them formed, half a day ago, when I misread a measurement. I think we lost a bedroom in the south wing."

"Was there anyone in the bedroom?"

The Maestro shrugged. "No one who's not resourceful enough to find their way back home. Now give me those things. Yes." He plucked the jar of quicksilver from her arms. "This might not be enough, *Famulus*." He used the word as a title when he was feeling most magical.

"That was all of it."

"I'll need more tomorrow. I'll send a note." He often sent notes. She never saw him actually do so, and she never delivered anything to a mailbox, but the contents of these notes always seemed to reach the right person.

He took the obsidian, tossed it once and caught it, then said, "You know, you shouldn't eat this stuff."

"I know."

He grunted. He looked at her sideways, tilting his head, peering quite strongly with his left eye—the important one. "When's the last time you've eaten anything?"

"I had cocoa for breakfast."

"That's not food. That's not sustenance. How do you expect to maintain the articulation of those bones? When did you sleep?"

"Last night."

"I slept last night," he said, "in my study, again, which is becoming quite the habit since you've arrived." He frowned. "I'd wager you slept not a wink last night."

"I was reading." She liked to tell the truth when she could.

"*Reading?*" He arched an eyebrow. A lot of hair waggled when he did so. He put the chunk of obsidian on top of a book on the counter. The book was not *Transformation and Transmutation*, though that wouldn't have surprised Alyssa. It was *Measurements of Light.* "Do you have any idea what I'm doing?"

"Transformation, Maestro." She threw in the honorific—she never called him by his name, *Gris*, as that would be unseemly—whenever she felt it was necessary. He was lecturing now, not because he was mad but because he suspected he should be. Long before she ever came into the Maestro's service, she had learned to withhold what she could.

"*Transformation.*" He said it dismissively. "Define the term."

"Is this a lesson, Maestro?"

"I didn't hire you on to learn from me, Famulus. But tell me, what have you been learning?"

"Transformation," Alyssa said, "is the magical art of changing the intrinsic value of a thing so that it becomes something else."

The Maestro took a deep breath and let it out slowly, trying to decide if she had purposefully simplified her definition to illustrate a false lack of knowledge.

Alyssa added, "The stovetop can be a tool of transformation. The chrysalis. The paintbrush."

As the Maestro looked at her, a smile—more properly, a grin—stretched his lips all out of proportion. "Go read, then, or do something else. I don't need you here now. Fetch me for supper."

She left him to his work. She wandered the halls a while, testing behind tapestries, pausing to talk with the cook, and even stepping into the courtyard to consult with the statues.

The statues of Aphrodite and Queen Isabella never revealed anything Alyssa didn't already know, but she sometimes enjoyed the feel of sunshine on her flesh. She sat on a marble bench but didn't read. The book she'd wanted to read was gone, possibly forever, but possibly merely returned to the library. Whatever she went to retrieve now, the Maestro would know, and while it was okay for him to know she increased her overall knowledge of the world and even the magical world, it would never be safe to let on how much she truly knew.

The Maestro was a powerful magician. Her knowledge, thus far, seemed primarily academic, and this was the wrong time to test it.

The sun crawled toward its western horizon. It didn't really have far to go. In this place, the sun was a poor method of determining time. It moved at its own leisure, sometimes consuming hours in the space of breaths, sometimes refusing to slip forward for days. The Maestro's house sat at an edge of the world, one of the corners, and no windows faced north. You could listen to the soundless singing ocean repeatedly strike an unseen shore. You could listen to the sea birds, and taste cold salt on the air, but a person would go mad trying to apply reason or logic to the location. The house sat amid the clouds, high up the side of some mountain bordering a thick, shadowy forest. How could there be ocean sounds?

Alyssa closed her eyes briefly and, without meaning to, slept on the marble bench under the protection of Queen Isabella and Aphrodite. She dreamed of flowers, and she dreamt of mirrors, and she dreamt of a man she hadn't yet met but would. That was the risk of playing with divination. It seeped through unintentionally.

"Alyssa!"

The Maestro was screaming. This wasn't his usual sound or his usual voice. The sky above had grown dark and close. Clouds swirled. Stars flickered. Isabelle's eyes reflected concern. The courtyard, surrounded on all sides, quivered. It was subtle. Someone less adept than Alyssa might mistake it for their own trembling.

She ran into the house.

The corridors were crooked. Servants ran in every direction. Some ran in multiple directions. The laboratory door was not merely open; its hinges had been twisted, the wood of the door splintered, its iron skeleton exposed. Inside, the Maestro faced a whirling maelstrom — a gaping hole in the universe, akin to what had swallowed *Transformation and Transmutation* but of a much larger scale. It emerged from the face of a mirror like a tornado. It whipped and struck, but the Maestro held it back like a lion tamer, baton instead of chair, eyebrows instead of whip.

"Alyssa!" he screamed again. The maelstrom lunged at her. He deflected it with a fluid motion of the baton. Once upon a time, presumably, he had conducted orchestras with that piece of ivory.

"What can I do?" She shouted to be heard over the cacophony of raging winds.

He glanced at her. He looked straight at her, not cocking his eyebrows or tilting his head or any of the other things he often did to show amusement or dismay or anger or anything else. His face was blank. All of his energy was on the vortex he had somehow created. He said, as simply as he could, "Run."

The maelstrom lashed out at the Maestro. A tendril of wind grabbed hold of the baton and refused to release it.

When the Maestro moved his hand, the tentacle moved with him. The room expanded, the vortex swallowed glass vials and bottles, notes, books, and the ivory wand. Briefly, it paused. Someone else might have assumed the worst of it was over.

Alyssa did not make that assumption.

She ran.

The maelstrom grew behind her, and raged, and struck blindly at the walls and the ceiling and the Maestro. The house shuddered. The walls cracked. Alyssa ran to her rooms to grab her pens and her shadow book and whatever else she could carry. But there was, really, no place to run. The forest and tundra and ocean outside stretched forever. Sky and ceiling alike roiled. Wherever the Maestro had built his house, the entirety of it was collapsing.

"Get me out of here," she said to the house. The walls warped. Lights crackled. Electricity spilled from frayed wires Alyssa had never seen. The rugs unthreaded themselves. Lions roared within the tapestries. Servants disappeared through secret passages only available to them. Alysa reached the library.

The floor buckled under her feet. Books tumbled off the shelves. One by one, the panes of the nearest stained glass window shattered—red first, then blue, green, gold. The ironwork glowed white with heat.

Alyssa ran down the outside aisle, alongside stained glass, toward the theater. She knew she could go through and find a real theater, a real palace of cinema and theater, a real place beyond the reaches of the Maestro's maelstrom.

As she reached it, all its glass exploded. Every pane fragmented. Every piece shattered. The whole thing— theater, window, portal—vanished.

Other windows also splintered. The tiled floor crackled. The books disappeared, one after another, as though they had their own means of escape.

One stained glass window remained. It pictured a cathedral in the mountains. It might have been this house. It shimmered. It trembled. Alyssa ran for it. She had no words, no incantations, no preparatory salves. She ran, and she leaped, and she crashed into the stained glass.

The iron tore at her. The glass cut her. The house itself screamed. It was a sound Alyssa desperately hoped she'd one day forget. The last thing she heard was the Maestro screaming her name one last time. She could see him, in her mind's eyes so it was questionable as to whether it was a true vision or an imagination, leaping into the portal he'd created, the unstable vortex, and ending up someplace not unlike the place Alyssa ended up.

Through the portal, it felt like her nerves were ripped from her skin, burned with molten metals, then threaded back into her. The blood in her veins froze. She held her breath. She had read somewhere you should hold your breath. The author had been insistent. She didn't remember, not in the moment, whether she should have taken a deep breath or expelled everything from her lungs.

She crashed into the thick trunk of a tree.

3.

When Alyssa regained herself, full consciousness and equilibrium, she examined her wounds. Scorch marks that weren't burns, as though she'd been wandering through a forest of ash. Cuts and scratches that were mostly superficial but at risk of infection. Her clothes were torn, but not immodestly so. Her shadow book was intact. She'd lost all her pens but one.

Around her, the forest stretched thickly in all directions. The trees were taller than reality, dense and vibrant green at the tops, pregnant with sap, smelling of cinnamon and cloves and even a hint of vanilla on top of the expected cedar and pine. There was no obvious path. Only forest sounds surrounded her.

She took a deep breath. She sat, consulted her shadow book, and listened to the world. Breezes frolicking. Leaves rustling. A gentle fall of water—not a falls, but a cascade trickling into a creek. Squirrels tramping through the trees, birds of a dozen species, something big—not wolves, which she had feared, but a bear. Alyssa was at the edge of winter. The bear should be seeking hibernation. She was safe, relatively safe, if uncertain of what to do next.

The sun arced across the sky at a relatively normal angle and speed. Near nightfall, a handful of fireflies blinked on and off. She smiled. She whispered to the fireflies, "I know you've no reason to trust me, but I don't want to be here, in your woodlands. Would you lead me away, to safety, to people like myself?"

That was a very big ask. Away was easy. Safety was fleeting. People like herself? There weren't any, not really, but she meant *people*, humans, bipedal beasts with the power of speech. The request was loaded because the answers were often contradictory.

The fireflies gave no answers.

She closed her eyes and sat with her palms up. She'd never spoken to animals before, much less insects. She had no reason to expect they would listen, understand, or care. The house was a different kind of beast. The house was its own thing. There was nothing like it in all of Alyssa's experience.

In the dying light of dusk, she wrote questions in her shadow book, questions about butterflies but also other creatures. Stories suggested communication was possible and sometimes welcomed. Maybe wolves would have been more helpful.

She climbed some distance up the tree, careful in the swift dark, and wedged herself into the crook of a branch. She slept all through the night, despite the nocturnal creatures prowling beneath her, despite the owl that settled a foot from her face. She was only dimly aware of these things, but none threatened her. She didn't sleep deeply. She woke hungry.

With the morning light, she climbed. She was strong, fit, and agile. The tree was a challenge. Its bark wanted to puncture her skin. Critters she never saw scampered up, down, and around in anticipation of her ascent. As she neared the leafy canopy, the light grew brighter and the birds more vibrant. She broke through the top, barely, holding herself to the tree and wishing she had access to some sort of magic that might make this easier. She surveyed the forest, looking over the tops of trees sloping up and down the mountainside. So it wasn't just a forest, but a mountain forest. The earth here was jagged and hilly and rocky, but the trees ascended quite a ways before reaching the snowline.

Before the snowline, there was a break in the trees.

A highway.

It was distant, too far to hear, but now that she was aware of it, she would hike to the highway, then pick a direction. She descended the tree and, without breakfast, set off. She didn't trust the berries here, or the mushrooms, and her hunting skills were subpar. She had no weapons, anyhow, so she'd have to catch and kill by hand, which would take too much time without the promise of success.

She drank at the stream when she crossed it. The water was fresh and clear, full of fish, and she watched other animals drink at its shore before concluding it was safe. Alyssa had no spells. She could not detect poisons in the water or the berries. She could conjure no guide to lead her out of the woods. Her skills were in illusion, the lowest form of magic. Deception, misdirection, sleight of hand. All her years of study in the libraries of great magicians like the Maestro, and she'd never managed to even pluck a flower from the air.

After nightfall, Alyssa slept again in the trees, this time

waking when a pack of coyotes yipped beneath her. She watched for them, unable to see the animals through the dark, and eventually went a little higher before sleeping. She dreamt restless dreams. In the morning, hungry again, she climbed to the treetops to confirm her position. She'd managed to stay mostly true to her intention, and made only a slight course correction when she reached the forest floor again.

By the third nightfall, highway sounds guided her. Massive trucks and souped-up sports cars and the occasional motorbike. Her senses were not so fine-tuned she could differentiate between a Fiat, a Volkswagen, and a Chrysler. She still knew only that she was in a forest. She didn't know the country or the continent or the hemisphere.

She didn't take a third sleep. She was more excited than exhausted. She stopped several times to drink at streams or creeks, but never risked food. In her mind, she was confusing the issue. In realms of fairies, it was dangerous to eat, lest you be forced to remain forever. She didn't know where she was. She knew of no fairy realms. It was the first sign of delirium setting in. She was surprised it had taken so long.

At the break of day, she clamored up the final embankment to stand alongside the highway. It was not a busy road, but it was well-traveled enough. The lines in the road were old and faded. The two-lane highway wound through the mountains like the serpentine river at the dawn of time. She picked a direction — one was as good as the other — and started walking.

A few cars passed, nondescript vehicles made dazzling by the low angle of sunlight filtering through the mountains. They might have been mechanized beasts that had swallowed their drivers to live in a near-symbiotic relationship until the flesh grew weak and needed to be expelled for something fresh.

She put out her thumb. She'd never hitchhiked. She didn't even know if that was a thing anymore. She checked herself. She didn't know *when* she was, either. Just because she didn't know time travel was a definite thing didn't mean it wasn't possible. The Maestro's vortex had been angry, and maybe it had somehow disrupted the normal path of stained glass mirrors through space and time. Maybe she should have landed in this spot a hundred years earlier or later and discovered a safe house stocked with supplies and food and hunting rifles.

The first driver who passed her thumb did so with their hands firmly on the horn. The sound reinforced the reality around her. Alyssa opened her eyes—they'd been physically open but inactive—and took in her environment. Highway. Two lanes. Random automobiles. Hunger and exhaustion creeping in on the edges of her sense of self.

As she watched the road, an old Jaguar—old being relative to Alyssa's expectations—stopped just ahead of her. The driver pushed the passenger door open. There were only the two seats. Alyssa opened the door all the way to peer inside. The pen she carried might not be the best weapon, but it was effective. She was strong and fast and agile like a mountain goat. She could get down the side of this embankment and back into the forest at the first sign of danger.

The driver was a smartly dressed lady of the grandest type. She might've bought this car brand new fifty years ago with money earned lighting up the silver screen. She had lost the false beauty of youth, but had attained every other kind. Her hair made her look like Veronica Lake. She smiled at Alyssa and said, "You look a mess, sweetheart. Get in."

Alyssa got in.

The car was comfortable. The hum and vibration of the engine might put her to sleep. The leather was well-cared for. The windows were down. "My name's Rony," the woman said, "I used to be Veronica, but that was a long time ago."

"I'm a little delirious," Alyssa admitted.

Rony said, "My husband, my third husband I think, maybe my fourth, he used to say we're all a little delirious on the highway of life, but it's all okay if you can ride it with *style*. Do you need food, honey? You look pale. There's water in the back seat."

It wasn't really a back seat, not much more than a ledge, but there was, indeed, a bottle of water. Alyssa swallowed it greedily. Was it really safer to drink from plastic? She doubted it. She drank more, half the bottle, before saying, "Where are we?"

"You wouldn't believe me if I told you," Rony say. "But I've got a room, a hundred miles up the road. We can get you cleaned up, and while you're in the shower I'll order us some room service. Would you like that, sugar? Pancakes, perhaps, or pasta. Do you eat meat? You look positively ashen. I think you need real sustenance. How does steak sound?"

Alyssa finished the water and held onto the bottle "Why are you being so nice to me?"

Rony shifted gears and put on some more speed. "Don't you worry none, darling. Everything is under control."

In some crack deep within Alyssa's mind, that sounded reasonable. She clung to that pretense of hope, knowing it was false. She had no money, no prospects, and still no idea where she was. If they passed any road signs, they were either noncommittal or in another language—though Rony's accent was tinged with the American south. Something about Rony seemed completely honest and sincere and real—something, not everything. Mostly, she was a distraction. An illusion. The kind of magic Alyssa knew best.

"Did you go off the road, love?" Rony asked. "I never saw your car, or any skid marks in the road. Did you have a fight? Did a *man* drop you off in the middle of nowhere hoping you'd just die?"

Alyssa didn't have to answer any of these questions. Rony never slowed down.

"My first husband, he was a mistake," Rony said. "Not like the others. He kicked me out of the car outside of, I think it was Baltimore, back in '67 or thereabouts. He was, if you'll pardon my language, a real sweetheart of a man, by which I mean only the worst possible things. I killed him later. Shot him point blank in the face with a .38 Special. He earned that lead, he did. And the jury? They agreed with me."

"Did you kill all your husbands?" Alyssa asked.

"No. No, of course not. Only the one. And what about a sweet young thing like you, have you had to fight off many suitors? Have you counted their ribs so you know where to slide the knife? Have you mixed poisons to put in anyone's tea?"

Alyssa laughed. She couldn't help it. She'd done almost exactly that—mixing herbs for tea—but not all herbs were poisonous and not all poisons were meant to kill.

"Say no more, *mi cielito*," Rony said. "I understand, I understand completely, I really do. This is our exit."

The exit came out of nowhere. Alyssa hadn't been paying attention to the road. She tried to maintain her focus on Rony, formerly Veronica, who borrowed her look from a famous Veronica and whose voice was addictive like sugar and candy.

Off the highway, through a small mountain town, Rony guided the Jaguar into the parking lot of the biggest, most spectacular hotel for a hundred miles in any direction, tossed the keys to a valet she knew by name, and led Alyssa into the lobby. She flashed a smile for the concierge, waved to the gentlemen at the counter, and whispered something in the elevator jockey's ear as she surreptitiously slipped him cash after he lifted them to the penthouse.

Alyssa didn't know if hotels still had elevator jockeys.

Through her delirium—she hadn't been sleeping or

eating properly for days before the Maestro had conjured that angry vortex—Alyssa consciously realized something she'd already known: Rony was a magician, and a damn good one.

4.

Alyssa showered under the hottest water she could stand. Some of the scratches itched and some of them hurt, and some were starting to blacken around the edges. The soot washed away grayly, swirling down the drain as if into a vortex. Alyssa watched it, and blinked, and maybe briefly lost consciousness. She wasn't well and wasn't getting better. She toweled dry and found clothes Rony had hung for her on the back of the bathroom door. They fit as if bespoken.

When she emerged from the bathroom, returning to an enormous living area complete with a gleaming grand piano, Alyssa found a feast on the table: plates of meats and vegetables, three gravies, bowls of fruits and nuts, an assortment of cheeses.

"You must eat," Rony said, "and I haven't a clue what you might prefer." She poured wine—or something like wine. It looked and smelled like brandy, but Rony poured it from a kind of wine bottle and into wine glasses. "This, of course, I must insist."

"I'm not sure…"

"Oh, posh," Rony said. "You're ill, girl, anyone can see it. You're worse now than when I found you. You don't even know what day it is. I'm not sure you know your own name."

Alyssa opened her mouth to say it, but hesitated.

"*This,*" Rony said, continuing regardless, "is special. It's a restorative. An elixir, you might say. Oh, don't look at me like that. Bottom's up, ducky."

The liquid spread though Alyssa like lava.

"And eat," Rony said. "I hired the chef personally."

"This is your *house,*" Alyssa realized.

"Well, no dear, it's not a house, but it is my *home*." Despite the denial, Alyssa was right. This entire hotel belonged to Rony in the same way the Maestro's house had belonged to him. The halls might lead to multiple places, even other hotels. There was probably a library, and maybe a vault containing other treasures. Of course, the books interested Alyssa the most. She might've said something about them, something aloud, but she wasn't quite herself yet. The warmth of the drink stayed with her, searing at the points of infection, as though burning it out of her from the inside.

Rony was flipping through Alyssa's shadow book, not smiling, nodding once or twice, throwing glances in Alyssa's direction. Alyssa didn't have the strength to protest. It was the first time since she'd climbed into the Jaguar that the woman had remained silent for more than a breath. Without looking up, Rony said, "Eat, eat. The elixir can't do its magic without food."

So Alyssa ate. Her stomach demanded it.

She ate with gusto, and she ate her fill, and when she was finally done Rony snapped the shadow book shut and stood. "Would you like to see something truly spectacular?"

"Yes."

"Come onto the balcony."

Rony led Alyssa to a balcony overlooking the entire town, the trees, and the mountains, They were quite high. The elevator hadn't seemed to rise that far. "I had the balcony installed for my first husband," she said, "in case he ever felt the burning desire to fly again, but alas, he never made the attempt."

There was a bar, at the moment untended, a number of tables, several places to lounge, and a pool, which Rony walked around to get to the marble balustrade that separated them from a long fall.

"Do you like fireworks?" Rony asked.

At the edge of the balcony, Alyssa was careful not to lean out too far. She didn't trust her sense of balance. She didn't entirely trust any of her senses at the moment.

"C'mon, *ma chérie*, it's not a party if you don't answer me."

"I love fireworks."

"Great. Look" Rony waved her hand to take in the entire scene, town and mountain and clouds and all. Lightning sparkled silver and gold in the clouds. Streamers shot from the mountaintop and exploded to form giant butterflies and dragonflies. It was a small, quick display, without music. At the end, Rony pointed there, there, there, three times, each time igniting a small explosion of light and sound.

Rony leaned so close to Alyssa, she almost thought the woman would kiss her. "I read your book, sweetie. I know what you want, and I'm unwilling to give it to you. *However.*" With this, she clapped a bracelet onto Alyssa's wrist. It clicked into place. It was obsidian, or something similar, sheer black and reflective. "I have an idea, and I think it will benefit the both of us."

"I don't know what you mean."

"Sleep, child," Rony said. "Let the restorative restore you, why don't you, and leave the worrying to me, okay?" She touched Alyssa's cheek.

A weight of sleepiness collapsed upon her. Alyssa stumbled, but Rony was there to catch her. "Yes, yes, I know, you're positively *exhausted.* Let's get you into bed, warm and safe under the covers, and don't worry about a thing."

Alyssa wasn't entirely conscious all the way into the bedroom. She remembered swimming through the bed, it was so massive and so soft. It enveloped her and moved with her and would have dragged her into dreamland even without Rony's magic. She dreamt, but her dreams weren't entirely her own, and each dissipated when it was replaced. The infection sites burned underneath all of this, but they healed, and the scars they left were practically invisible. She slept for most of two days, over forty hours. When she woke, Rony was there in a sparkling gown with two tall pitchers of fresh ice water. "Good morning, cinnamon. I bet we're famished, aren't we?"

The servants were just finishing loading the table with a new feast. They wore featureless black pants and shirts and shoes and belts. They all averted their eyes from Rony, and only a few risked a glance in Alyssa's direction. When they were gone, Rony said, "Good help is hard to find. They don't know what to make of you, you know that? Neither did I, not at first. How are you feeling this evening?"

"Fine."

"You should be. Not a trace of the infections linger in your blood. Your bones are solid, which is good to know." She grabbed Alyssa by the chin to lift it, and to examine each side of her face. "You're quite fetching. You've got the makings of something, I'll give you that, but I'm not sure if you've got the gift."

"I have it."

"Oh?" Her eyebrow, finely manicured and completely unlike the Maestro's, arched. "Such confidence. It won't make a difference. You want to learn something that cannot be taught. No amount of studying will give you the skills you seek. Darling, you have to take them."

"From you?"

"Not from me, dear," Rony said. "You'll die."

"I don't know what you're saying," Alyssa admitted.

"What I'm saying, child, is that you need a teacher who will give you—let's call it *motivation*. I know a man in need of an assistant, someone to clean up the crumbs after he eats, someone to put away his books, someone to know the minor things so he can focus on what he thinks is important."

"The minor things are important."

"You're well-read. When the time is right, that may serve you. In the meantime, I've arranged a sale."

"What are you selling?"

"You, little dove."

Someone knocked on the door. Rony raised her voice to say, "Please, come in." The doors swung open and a wiry bespectacled man entered.

"Greetings," the man said.

"Are you the assistant?" Rony asked.

"I am, if it pleases you, the emissary."

Rony laughed. "Go away, little man, before I do something rash."

"What shall I tell…"

"Tell him anything you wish, I don't care." Rony smiled. "Wait. Here. Have a fig." She plucked the fruit from a bowl on the table and tossed it to the man. He managed to catch it, though not without some effort. "Mustn't ignore the needs of my guests," Rony said to Alyssa. "And us, too, we should eat."

The man left and the door closed.

"What did you do to him?" Alyssa asked.

"Why, whatever do you mean?" Rony plucked another fig and popped it into her mouth. "They're perfectly safe."

Alyssa didn't believe her, but didn't push it. She imagined the man would die slowly, maybe painfully, victim of some sort of poisonous agent. Or he might be transformed — a vortex somewhere had swallowed *Transformation and Transmutation*, and she wondered if it might be somewhere nearby — he might be transformed into a dog or frog or newt or something silly.

"By midnight, his master will return," Rony said. "He'll be wanting to take a look at you. Never give yourself up to him. You don't want a lover, you want a teacher. But don't let him know."

"I know all this."

"I'm *reinforcing*, sweetie," Rony said. "Be silent tonight, say nothing except when asked directly, and then only answer *yes* or *no*. Protocol must be maintained."

"You're selling me?" Alyssa asked.

"Your life is mine," Rony told her. "You would have died alongside the highway if I hadn't noticed you. Don't pretend any other outcome was possible." She smiled. "I'm only selling what is mine to sell."

"What will you get in exchange?"

"A thing of equal value," Rony said, "or I shan't make the sale."

Magic required balance. That was one of the first things Alyssa had learned. She did, in fact, owe her life to this woman, though she was unclear as to whether such debts were transferable. She couldn't recall any such instances from credible sources, though there were always stories. But there were also stories claiming the moon was made of cheese and the desert hid cities of glass.

"My seventh husband," Rony said, drinking wine and picking at the sweetmeats, "once tried to teach me the ways of economics. Supply, demand, unions, wages. Dreadfully dull, I'm afraid."

"How many husbands have you had?" Alyssa asked.

Rony shrugged and smiled. "I'm old enough to have had as many as I wanted."

5.

Midnight came quickly. Time devoured time. Outside, clouds obscured the moon. Rony, with a wink, twice pointed out past the balcony toward the mountain and made little explosions.

Alyssa hadn't realized it originally, but the fireworks and lightning show were illusions, tricks of light and shadow. Beyond the capacity of self-proclaimed magicians of stage and street. With a little effort, with keen observation and mimicry and practice, Alyssa should be able to set off her own fireworks.

That would have to wait. The clock struck midnight just as it had in Poe's *Masque of the Red Death.* It struck, and the chimes sounded from one end of the penthouse suite to the other, through the bedrooms and the loft, from kitchen to baths. The sounds resonated in the strings of the piano. At precisely the twelfth strike, as though awaiting the signal, the buyer knocked on the door.

He came into Rony's rooms with the confidence of arrogance. He wore robes like a magician of old, but also a flashy expensive watch, a Patek Philippe, polished shoes, and eye shadow. He looked at Alyssa first, a casual glance, before turning all his attention to Rony. His robes flowed with him. His face was clean shaven, like a baby's, and he was extraordinarily young, younger even than Alyssa. She immediately didn't like him. "You've got something you think I'll want?"

"My dear, I've *always* got something you want. The only question is a matter of price."

"We've danced together before."

"And you've lost," Rony said. "Every time."

He smiled like a '70s game show host or a used car salesman. Involuntarily, Alyssa stepped back and drew herself into herself, taking up as little space as possible.

He reached Rony and presented her with an exaggerated bow. Then, finally, but without mercy, he cast his eyes on Alyssa. He looked her up and down and over. His sharp little eyes had been stolen from James Bond and mixed with shark's blood. "And I suppose *this* is what you think I need?"

Rony said nothing. He approached Alyssa, circled her, lifted her arm and let it drop. Alyssa watched him, and merely drew her arm back to her chest. "Do you understand what is happening?" he asked her.

Alyssa glanced at Rony. The older woman smiled and

nodded once. Alyssa said, "Yes."

"Yes?" He grabbed her chin—that had been done before—and turned her head to one side and the other. She slapped his hand away. He looked to Rony. "Has she not been trained?"

"Do *you* understand?" Rony asked.

He didn't respond to that. Physical contact, even for a person magically exchanged, required consent. Alyssa had given none.

He looked directly into the eyes and said, "Show me your throat."

Alyssa opened her mouth. He peered inside. What he sought, she didn't know. She didn't know which of the magical arts he practiced. He was handsome, in a typical and boring way, but he was brusque and unmannered. Even the Maestro at his worst had some level of respect for the people and things around him. She'd stayed with him almost two years. She was convinced she hadn't learned all he could teach. But she hadn't been brought in as an apprentice. She was an assistant. That was something else entirely.

"I have questions," he said.

Alyssa nodded.

"Can you make coffee?"

Alyssa glanced at Rony, who merely leaned against her table and watched. Alyssa said, "I prefer chocolate."

"How many parts bleach to water for a proper mopping solution?"

"I haven't got a clue."

He turned to Rony. "What good is she?"

"She's no fetch girl," Rony said. "Ask her something real."

They looked at each other. For all his swagger, and despite a resemblance, he didn't have the power or authority or regality of the older woman. He was a madman, a hermit, a narcissist. He turned away first, back toward Alyssa, who had no power at all in the present situation. "Fine," he said, "If I require three drops of ox blood, can you obtain it?"

"Do you keep ox blood in your stores?"

"Tell me the root formula for Thyssen's Theorem."

Alyssa had read a lot, and had tried to practice when she had the chance, and she'd recorded all her notes in her shadow book. She hadn't memorized everything, especially not something so esoteric as Thyssen. "He was discredited," she said, "and all his work dismissed."

"That's not what I asked."

"He worked theoretical mathematics with an intention of bridging two disparate points. He sent two assistants and a half dozen peasants through unstable wormholes into oblivion."

"*Oblivion?*"

Alyssa blinked. She wasn't sure if that qualified as a legitimate question. "A state of being and nonbeing existing simultaneously," she said. "An acute, inescapable consciousness of a vast nothingness."

"You've studied transportation?"

"No."

He looked at Rony again. If he had the brows for it, he would have arched one. "How many forms of magic do you know?"

Alyssa hesitated. This was a trick question. "I know of seven," she said.

Briefly, almost imperceptibly, he shook his head. So she was wrong. There were more than seven. She had feared there might be. How was she to master all of them over the course of a single lifetime when she hadn't yet managed to master any?

"How many do you *know?*"

A different question. Alyssa held her breath. She wasn't sure how best to answer this. Lying had consequences. She had to choose her words carefully. She reached behind her ear and withdrew a coin. Nothing spectacular. She gave no story, no soliloquy, no explanation. She simply produced a silver dollar, displayed it, closed her fist around it, and disappeared it. She said, "I have practiced some minor illusions."

Once again, he gave all his attention to Rony. "What do you want?"

"She's been valuable to me, my dear. But I fear I have other obligations now and cannot be bothered with the feeding and caring of a Famulus."

"Other obligations?"

"My affairs," Rony said sharply. "I'll give her to you—her life is indebted to me—in exchange for a certain key I know you possess."

"*A certain key?*"

"You know which."

He considered. He reached into a pocket and withdrew the key—an amazing, ornate thing of obsidian that caught every stray light and fractured it. Rainbows spilled everywhere. As he held it up, Alyssa leaned closer for a better look.

"Done."

Rony smiled. "Excellent." She plucked the key from his hand. "You may retrieve her at first light."

"I want her now."

"You can't have her now. She must be given time to prepare."

"You might have had her prepared before I arrived."

She shrugged. "But I didn't. Now please be a dear, and leave your new assistant to prepare for the rest of her life."

He hesitated, then gave another of those false bows and said, "Till first light, then." When he exited, Rony went to the door and engaged the locks by hand.

"I don't have anything to pack," Alyssa admitted.

"You have your shadow book, your pen—I know it's

special, but it's damaged, and it won't do for you what you expect, not anymore—and you must listen. I have things to tell you. Because your debt is to me, not to Frederick, so you must do as I say."

"I never agreed…"

"Shush, child. You had your chance to object, and you didn't. Frederick has a library, and I want you to infiltrate the place, I want you to become intimately involved with its protections, if you need to. I want you to gain the freedom of his library, and I want you to acquire a book for me."

"Why didn't you just ask for the book in trade?"

"Some books must be stolen," Rony said. "You were wrong, about Thyssen. His theories were rejected in his day, but they turned out to be accurate and useful."

Alyssa smiled. "I know."

"Good. Don't let him know how much you know. Do this for me, find and remove this book, and your debt to me will be paid."

They spent the rest of the night in preparations. Rony gave Alyssa a small chest loaded with a variety of clothes she insisted would fit Alyssa better than anyone else. She showed Alyssa how to access a secret compartment inside, where they put her pen and shadow book, and the silver dollar she'd plucked from the air.

"You'll do well, poppet," Rony said, squeezing her cheek like an overzealous aunt at the holidays. Hotel staff—servants, really—delivered a breakfast feast of eggs and sausages and a variety of breads, fruits, nuts, and juices.

First light broke over the eastern mountains. It didn't shine directly into the penthouse, not from this direction, but even if they hadn't felt it they would've known by the knock at the door.

Alyssa undid the locks, opened the door, and stepped aside to allow Frederick entry.

He swept in like a king entering his throne room. He

looked exactly as he had the night before, as if he had waited right outside the door these past six hours. He announced, "It's time."

Rony said, "She's ready."

And Alyssa was. It hadn't taken much. She didn't need to be adept in divination to know her immediate future would not include any feasts. Breakfast had been something like a last meal for the condemned. Hotel staff came to retrieve her chest and load it into Frederick's vehicle.

"She'll have to prove her worth," Frederick said.

"So I suspected."

"I never understand why you lie." With that, Frederick turned and marched out of the penthouse. Alyssa, after a brief hesitation, followed.

He took her down the stairs. All of them. It was a long way down, and he never once looked at her, never once said a word. The Maestro hadn't been much different when she'd first come into his service. Silent. Consumed by his own thoughts. Always preoccupied, ever observant.

A driver waited with a massive gleaming pick-up truck. The chauffer bowed and opened the passenger door for Frederick, then cast a sidelong glance at Alyssa. "Should I put the girl in the back?"

He must've given some sort of response, though Alyssa never heard it, because the chauffer nodded once, closed the passenger door, then told Alyssa, "Into the bed, *girl.*"

"I'd prefer you not call me that."

"I don't care what you prefer."

She climbed—it was quite a climb—into the back of the truck. It was not meant for passengers and had never been used to haul anything. Her chest sat uncomfortably at the head of it, held in place by a pair of crisscrossing cords. The bed was sparkling and smooth. Alyssa clutched its side as they drove.

The chauffer drove the truck like a man unconcerned by

obstacles. They carved a particular route to escape the confines of the town, which may have been entirely Rony's town—if the Maestro could have such a house, and Rony had such a hotel, why couldn't she also have the entire mountain village?—before barging onto the highway. It was a smooth ride for a while, until they veered off the highway onto an unkempt dirt road. Alyssa felt every rock, and there were a lot of those. She felt every rut, every fragment of dry bone they crunched beneath their wheels. The road became more violent as they drove.

She tried not to think of who had died to create the road. It was a kind of transportational magic, a path from one place to another that skipped physical conventions—not unlike the stained glass window of the Maestro's library.

When they reached Frederick's house, she only got a brief glimpse before they rolled underground into a garage that held a number of other cars and motorcycles, almost all of them black, all of them gleaming. Some sort of glamour kept them pristine like that. Alyssa wondered if that was a misuse of magic or if it served some other purpose she couldn't yet discern.

The trip had been long.

She hopped out of the back of the truck as the chauffer opened Frederick's door. The magician looked at her, then turned away and headed inside. The chauffer grinned and said, "You'll take care of your own things."

She muscled the chest out of the truck and into her room. It wasn't like her chambers at the Maestro's house. This was small enough to hold a twin mattress and a chair. Adding her chest made it crowded. It was a basement room, underground, without windows and without a closet. There was a toilet and shower down the hall in desperate need of cleaning.

She was used to better.

6.

Frederick did nothing to ease her transition to his household. The staff—the chauffer, the cook, the maid—ignored her. They didn't cook or clean for her, they didn't say a word to her, and they spoke about her in hushed whispers when they knew she could hear. She hadn't been brought in with the prestige of a mistress. They had probably never had an assistant in the house before.

As to the house, it was big and sprawling like the Maestro's, but everything was modern, plastic, gleaming hard lines, and airy—except the basement, which had been unchanged despite Frederick's claim of the property. The staff lived in rooms on the first floor. There were kitchens and dining halls and unoccupied studies on the first floor that contained no books, maybe a few pretty knickknacks if there were shelves, often a desk but rarely a chair of any comfort.

Not that Alyssa had time for comfort. He asked for a particular kind of herb one day. When she finally found the stores—she had been given no tour, and no one would direct her—they contained no herbs of any sort. The pantry contained an assortment of spices and herbs, generally in glass jars, but the cook chased her out with a butcher's knife. Alyssa didn't think he'd actually use it, and wasn't sure if he *could*. Did the covenants prescribed for a magician and assistant apply to other members of the household?

So Alyssa went outside in search of the herb. It was cold and getting colder, and a bluish white tint colored the skeletons of birches and ash. She found stragglers of the herb that had persisted into the season and brought them to Frederick in his second story workroom.

"These are nearly dead," he said, scowling at her.

"They're *fresh*," Alyssa said, "and the only I could find."

He asked for crystals, which she was able to find in the storeroom, and he asked for pigments. *Pigments*. She'd never used pigments, and never seen them used, and didn't understand what he might accomplish with them, but she finally found what he wanted in a separate supply closet.

He required her to keep her room clean, and by extension the entire basement, which was really beyond the duties of a Famulus. This kept her busy. Twice, she asked the maid for help—nothing major, just for chemicals and cleaning rags—but after that, she learned the maid would rather suffer the removal of her carefully manicured fingernails than reveal any household secrets.

One day, Alyssa met the butler. "Have you been here the whole time?"

He looked at her like a father might look at a child, then like a father might look at an evil child, and said, "I stay with the house." It was, realistically, the most any of the staff had said to her. However, it was all he said.

"Do you need any books?" Alyssa asked Frederick one afternoon. The sun was low, the light in the workroom saturated orange, and over the past few days he'd only asked for pigments, oils, and roots from the cellar.

The cellar was not the basement, though they were on the same level. She hadn't ever been there before. It contained the herbs she had once picked near the lake, and a hundred others, as well as roots, wines, and cigars behind glass.

Frederick didn't look pleased when she brought him the roots. "Why does it take you so long to do the simplest things? I'm beginning to believe the old witch took advantage of my kindness. You're no better than a wisp of dust smoke."

The cook made meals for the household staff and for the magician, but Alyssa had to make her own. She couldn't use the big kitchen or the good pots, just the facilities in the basement. There was a stovetop but no oven, a set of knives she spent a week sharpening, and access to only basic ingredients. For her first meal, she made a cheese sandwich with day old bread. Later, she was making soups, but upstairs they sometimes ate pheasant or lamb or grand pasta dishes the cook strung by hand.

Nights, she read through her shadow book. She kept her pen close, and sometimes traced the letters as though rewriting them. She memorized every word she'd written, every question she'd asked, and every theory. It wasn't much. Her shadow book, extensive though it may be for a journal, was no library. Alyssa began to wonder if the house even had a library. The second floor was a series of large bedrooms and sitting rooms and closets. The upper floor, where Frederick spent most his time, contained his workroom and a laboratory and a gallery.

"Do you need any books?" She asked several times. He never answered her directly. He kept a small selection in his workroom. She wondered if that was, in fact, his library. He was unconventional in so many ways.

"No," he finally said, "I never need books. I keep my knowledge here." He hit the side of his head. She knew he wanted to hit her. She saw it in his eyes. "Why do you ask so many stupid questions?"

"You brought me here to be your assistant," Alyssa told him, "but never told me where to find the supplies you would ask for, never had the cook make me a meal, never shown me the slightest bit of courtesy."

"You haven't earned any."

"You make demands, and expect me to just *know* where things are, and complain no matter how long it takes to find them."

"You're ungrateful," he told her. "You're obnoxious. You're always underfoot. You want too much, you need too much. I never should have taken you on."

"You have obligations."

"Shelter. Sustenance. You want for nothing."

"I want for *everything.*"

"Go, he said. "To your room, to the library, I don't care. I don't want to see you again until I need you."

He never needed her.

But now, at least, she knew there was a library.

She asked the maid, who told her, "I don't do for books."

She asked the chauffer. He merely sneered.

She asked the cook. "Okay, *fine*," he said. "I'll leave you a plate for dinner tonight." It wasn't the answer she wanted, but the plate contained pasta and cheese and a bottle of wine.

She asked the butler. "Comes with the house," he told her.

"I don't even know what that means."

That night, drunk on red wine, Alyssa took her pen from the secret compartment of the chest. She examined it, the length of it, the nib, the flow of its ink. She took a breath, opened her shadow book, and started writing about pigments. Rony's obsidian bracelet got in the way, and she pushed it up her arm several times. She hadn't learned much, and nothing out of a book of any sort, but her observational skills were not insignificant. She wrote about the powders, the grains and rocks from which they were ground, the pastes that could be made by mixing the right ingredients.

She didn't really know anything, but it was a foundation of some sort.

Alyssa fell asleep sitting in her bed with the pen in hand. She dreamt of feathers and horsehair and other forms of brushes. There was a magic here, something she didn't understand, something beyond the seven arts she had expected to find.

When she woke, her back ached, ink stained her fingers, and she had written an entire page in her shadow book. She read it now, thoroughly and completely, all these truths about color and light she had never imagined. Bending light. Cracking color. Rendering a hue by collectively denying all others. She'd drawn a pyramid and rainbow. She'd

incorporated the seven colors—there were seven, right?—
though she hadn't had the ink to do it.

"*Girl*," he said when she stepped into his workroom. He
didn't look up from what he was doing, "I need a book."

7.

He wanted *Colors of the African Peninsula*. She wasn't
sure where such a place existed. Africa was a continent. But
he didn't tell her anything else, not about its content, not the
author's name, not where it might be shelved.

And still, no library revealed itself to her.

She wandered the bedrooms of the second floor, even
Frederick's, which she would normally not enter. Inside,
other doors led to other places, even a sitting room where a
person might read quite comfortably. She entered every room
on the first floor. When she went into the maid's room, the
maid said, "I have rights."

"I have an obligation," Alyssa told her.

"I ain't never seen no library," the maid said, "and I ain't
never dusted one. That many books all in one place, they
make me nervous."

"I only need one book."

"I told you. It ain't here."

The chauffer was out. There was only one book in his
room, a picture book of classic Corvettes, and keys to every
car in the garage.

Finally, the butler found her and said, "We need to
talk."

He led her to an alcove overlooking the garden and
gestured for her to sit. "You cannot barge into other people's
rooms, girl. They give you your privacy, you should afford
them the same courtesy."

"I have an obligation," Alyssa told him.

"As do I," the butler said. "Next time I hear you're

invading the personal space of any member of this household, I shall see to it that you are expelled." He looked outside. Alyssa followed his gaze. Winter had settled thickly, covering the garden with enough snow and ice to kill a person. "You think what you want is in the library. I'll take you there. To the *library*. To what's left of it."

"What do you mean, what's left of it?"

He wouldn't answer. Instead, he took her there. It was on the first floor, through a door in the ballroom. It was a two-story affair, hexagonal, with shelves all the way to the ceiling, a wheeled ladder, and a platform on the second level.

Like the basement, the library had not been cared for and had not been modernized. The woods were cracked. The shelves were empty of all but cobwebs and dust and ash, the only exceptions being a few leftover objects of presumably no value: a blackened crystal skull, a travel inkwell, an empty picture frame. The scent of wood smoke permeating the air was thick.

"What happened?" Alyssa asked.

"Fear," the butler told her. "Hatred, anger, and frustration. But mostly fear."

"Somebody burned it?"

"Somebody tried."

"What happened to them?"

"*Expelled.*"

"How am I supposed to find the book he wants?"

"I don't think he wanted a book, child. I think he wanted you to stop asking about this place. But search the shelves, if you will. I'll leave you to it."

When he closed the door, Alyssa was alone in an empty library. She stroked the shelves nearest her, removing a thin layer of soot. The shelves, the room, the whole of the house persisted because of magical properties it had absorbed through a lifetime—a house's lifetime—of proximity.

The ladder, though on wheels, wouldn't move. The

mechanics had been ruined long ago. But its wood remained strong and certain. She climbed, looked over and around the room, imagined what it must have been like in its prime. "Beautiful," she said aloud.

A chandelier hung in the center of the room, all crystals and electric filaments showing scorch marks.

Alyssa sat on the top step of the ladder and looked at the empty places, at the shelves that had once contained mystical texts, at the spaces and voids. Now, they held only one backpack, which had clearly not been here during the fire. A tear dropped from her eye. She let it fall. She took a deep breath of the smoky air and exhaled slowly.

Then she made a decision. She would restore the library.

Before she could do that, she would have to find *Colors of the African Peninsula*, if it even existed. Had he sent her on this errand simply to reveal the library's fate? No. He wouldn't. It was out of character. That would involve some sense of mystery, or playfulness, and it would mean he'd wasted even a solitary thought on another person. He wanted the book, and she still had to find it.

Somewhere in this house, there was a shelf—at least— that acted as a library and housed that book. And the book Rony desired.

"I'll come back," she promised the library. When she left, she took the empty backpack. She knew she'd have no trouble finding it again. It was now a part of her rooms.

She hid the backpack in her chest before continuing her search.

If she had the skills, she would have conducted some sort of finding spell, or summoned the book to her directly. She hadn't actually seen such things done, but magic held limitless possibilities. She went to the kitchens, where the cook had at least shown her the kindness of a single meal and bottle of wine. Here, she was surrounded by stainless steel and cutlery and spices. Alone, she closed her eyes and pictured every shelf she'd ever seen in the house, every book, every hole in which one could be hidden.

The cook, when he came, worked around her. She listened, and she teared when he chopped onions. The rhythm of the knife hitting the wood cutting board wove around the rhythm of her pulse.

"Cookbooks," Alyssa said aloud.

The cook stopped chopping. He said, "I don't know what you think you're doing."

She looked at him. She smiled. Though it wasn't meant for him, he wouldn't know the difference. "I'm looking for a book."

"You can't have any of my cookbooks," he told her.

She shook her head. "None of those would do. Can I see them? The books you've got?"

"Why?"

"Maybe the one I'm seeking is hiding among *Mysteries of French Cuisine* and *Spices of the Orient.*"

"I don't believe either of those is a real book."

She shook her head. "*Please.*"

Alyssa looked at the chef. He was older than she, older than Frederick, but younger than the butler by half. He had chiseled cheeks and a dimple and bright brown eyes. When she gave him one hundred percent of her consideration, the grin he typically wore faltered and he lowered his eyes. She might have to reevaluate what she considered forms of magic. "Fine, sure, whatever," he said.

His books were in the pantry. There was only one shelf. He watched with crossed arms as she examined every title, every author's name. Some of these books were ancient. Others were so fresh, they still smelled of oregano and olive oil.

From the middle of the shelf, where it sat upside down, she pulled *Colors of the African Peninsula.*

"I've never seen that book before in my life."

"Considering the dust here," Alyssa said, "I doubt you've seen any of these books since they reached the shelf."

"They don't reach this shelf until I'm done with them."

"I didn't know you could ever be done with recipes."

Whatever magic she had cast over him briefly before was gone. "You are no cook. Now out. Out of my kitchens."

She returned to the workroom, to Frederick hunched over his bench. He didn't look up. "Gods die faster," he said, snatching *Colors of the African Peninsula* out of her hands.

"It was hiding with the cook's books in the pantry."

"Books don't hide."

"No, I suppose they don't," Alyssa said, "but books can be hidden."

He looked up from his work and glared at her. "Are you accusing me of something?"

Alyssa shook her head.

"Are you accusing a member of my household staff? Or my family?"

She had seen no signs of family here. He didn't treat any of the staff as family. He barely looked at any of them, rarely talked to anyone, was content to lock himself up with his experiments. All this time, Alyssa had no real idea of what he was attempting to do. The Maestro had often been forthcoming, if not always talkative. Frederick was downright hostile. As he glared at her now, she thought he might blast her out of existence. Unconsciously, she rubbed the obsidian bracelet that bound her.

"You're a nuisance," he finally said, returning to his work. "And a *spy*."

"What?"

"Leave me," he told her. "To the library. To your room. To the gardens, I don't care. If I want to see you again, I'll summon you."

She left.

She wasn't so easily summoned as a spirit or specter.

She'd have to listen, and listen well, in case this was some sort of test. The Maestro had tested her constantly, but he'd never made her feel that failure would mean dismissal and expulsion.

Rony had promised Alyssa would learn something here, but there was nothing to be learned from Frederick.

She returned to the library. She climbed the ladder and sat on the top rung. She would've brought her shadow book if she'd thought it would do her any good. She weighed her options. Her choices. Her mistakes.

She'd gained the freedom of the library. There were no books to borrow.

8.

She slept late the next morning. She slept past breakfast time and found a tray of fruits, nuts, and bread at her door, and a note from the cook: *I'm sorry.*

"Thank you," she said aloud in the hall. She pulled the tray in, but ate none of it. There were too many possible poisons. Tinctures. Venoms. Potions. He—the chef or the magician—had done something to it. She consulted her shadow book, considered the possibilities, and even wondered why he'd written the note to warn her.

She took bread from her own pantry. It was older, not yet stale, not quite tasteless, but safe. In another place, she might set a trap to capture a rat and see what this breakfast might do to it.

Transformation, she decided. If it was meant to turn her into a rat, a test rat would be unchanged and she would learn nothing.

She opened her chest and withdrew her shadow book and her pen. The rest of it, all the clothes inside, were not really hers. These two things contained a piece of her soul, a portion of her knowledge and memory, a drop of her blood.

Holding the pen gave her a sense of strength. Like the Maestro's baton, it was a kind of wand, and it could be used to channel her magic.

She had no magic. Not really.

She had only illusion. A few tentative attempts at divination. She knew riddles, though she didn't know if they were magical. And she now knew color, color and light and pigmentation, could be harnessed. So she had learned something here.

Alyssa paused to listen. Frederick, in his workroom on the third floor, made no sound she could hear. If he said her name, its echo should reach her, even here. Upstairs, the cook danced in the kitchen with spices and vegetables. The maid slept in an alcove. The chauffer was out driving. Alyssa could go to the garage to determine which vehicle he'd taken, but she didn't care. She knew where the keys were kept. The butler—he moved about the house as a silent presence, like a ghost or a shadow, something somehow not entirely human. He was a mystery she would never unravel.

She searched her room, top to bottom, side to side—eye to the bare floors, hands on the walls—listening to the variations in the house's breath. Something was amiss. She searched her own chest, with all the clothes Rony had provided, a case containing a hairbrush and makeup—she didn't remember the last time she'd used makeup. Glamour was a type of magic, and lipsticks and eyeshadows a kind of glamour. She closed up the kit and shoved it back in its corner. The compartment that hid her pen and shadow book had a twin.

A twin compartment.

The symmetry of the chest could not have been broken by something so trivial as a pen and notebook. She should have looked for such a thing her first night here. It opened easily, as though waiting for her just to try, and revealed a key. But not merely any key. The obsidian key broke the light that hit it and dripped with rainbows. Alyssa stared at it a while before touching it. This was the key she'd been traded for. Rony must've hidden it sometime during that night. Why?

Alyssa took the key. It felt smooth and cold like glass. It pulsed in her fingers, and the bracelet on her wrist pulsed in sympathy. She slipped the key into a pocket, closed up her chest and pushed it back against the wall, and climbed out of the basement.

There were a lot of possibilities.

In the library, Alyssa shut and locked the door. The iron mechanism might be old, and might have survived a fire, but it seemed perfectly serviceable for the task. She needed privacy. She didn't know what would happen.

In the center of the room, she looked at the empty shelves, at the things left behind and spared by the flames. She looked to the corners, to the silk of spiders, to the natural flow of air. She examined the dust on the floor, and even the indications of her own footsteps. Briefly, she touched the ladder, savored the wood, wondered how it might have survived the fire unscathed. Finally, she said to the room, "You have secrets, don't you?"

Alyssa withdrew the key. It nearly glowed, catching light from all directions and spreading colors on every wall. Not merely the red, yellow, orange of the rainbow, but all imaginable colors and quite a few unimaginable. They swirled through the room, through the air, through the knots of the woods. Tendrils of color glowed in each glass piece of the chandelier.

The light revealed echoes of the past by leaving untouched the space where once a statue of the Virgin had stood, where once there'd been a marble Tsarina Alexandra.

The absence of light also revealed the books on the shelves. This library had been stuffed with them. Some of the titles, once embossed on spines, were rendered clearly visible.

She recognized some as legendary, as books that ought not to have ever existed. Alyssa's breath caught in her throat as she read those titles and whirled in amazement. This library hadn't just been stuffed, it had been bigger, taller, stretching not just to the second floor but the third.

In the lightshow, fire swept through the books, through the patrons whose screams echoed silently against Alyssa's bones. A dozen people had been trapped within this hexagon. The fire hadn't been meant to clean just the books, but also the magicians who consulted them. Someone walked through the ash and bone, through the wood, the cracked marble. Someone knelt and swept the floor with their fingers and looked up at Alyssa and smiled.

Startled, she jumped back. The lightshow shimmered and died. She thrust the key back into her pocket, lest it reveal anything more to her—or worse, reveal her to someone or something else.

If it had been the room's memory, and the person smiling was not looking at *Alyssa*, who had they been looking at?

She didn't believe the room would give her more answers.

She got control of her breathing and her heartbeat again. When she touched the ladder, it no longer felt smooth. It hurt. She snatched her hand away, maybe even made a sound. "Fine," she said. "You don't want me. I understand."

She unlocked the door and exited the library.

"Oh." The maid was right there, staring at her, and she seemed shocked. "You're bleeding."

Was that concern? Alyssa looked down at her finger. There was blood, yes, but not much, around a splinter from the ladder. "It's nothing."

"Let me help." The maid grabbed her by the wrist and dragged her around the corner, around another corner, to a bathroom. The water ran icily from the faucet.

"Stop." Frederick filled the doorway. He looked enormous, like a magician of old bringing down the full extent of his power upon a scrawny little mountain village. He thrust a vial at the maid. "Please."

The maid looked at the vial as if she had no idea what it was, then finally took it. Alyssa tried to resist, but the maid was strong and strengthened by the magician's gaze. She put the uncapped vial under Alyssa's finger and squeezed until a drop, two, three fell into the glass.

Frederick took the vial and stoppered it. Without another word, he left.

Alyssa felt weak.

The maid said, "You'll be fine."

But she wouldn't be fine. The maid used tweezers to remove the splinter. She washed Alyssa's fingers, all of them, her hand and wrist, as if prepping her for surgery. "You mustn't worry," the maid said.

But Alyssa worried. Blood was a powerful tool in magic, more powerful than names, more damaging. The absence of it—just the three drops—chilled her veins. "So pale," the maid said. "I'll have the cook bring you wine."

"No."

"Then pick your own wine, I don't care," the maid said, "but you *will* rest." She bandaged the tiny prick in Alyssa's finger, which seemed overkill, but Alyssa was not up to protesting. The maid half-carried her back to the basement stairs, down to her room, and sat her on the edge of her bed. "You should sleep."

"I sleep enough."

"You should see your face," the maid told her.

There was a mirror. It reflected Alyssa's ashen and pale face. "I'll be fine."

"I'll bring wine."

The maid left the door partially ajar. Alyssa listened to her footsteps until she was climbing the stairs, then rushed to the door, shut it, and went to the chest. The key had to go back in its compartment.

She pulled the key out of her clothes. Touching it with her bandaged finger triggered a moment of heat. She put the key away, closed up the chest, and returned to the edge of her bed before she realized a bit of color was oozing from under her bandage like blood. She wiped it on the inside of her shirt before the maid burst into the room with a bottle of red wine and two glasses.

"We girls should celebrate," the maid told her.

"What are we celebrating?" Alyssa didn't trust the maid, didn't know why she was there, but would play along.

"Your survival."

"I don't understand."

"The last assistant in this house lasted eight days before she vanished," the maid said, using a wine opener to get at the cork. She was not having an easy time of it, but Alyssa didn't offer to help. "Took her things and left in the middle of the night. They found her—well, they found her things—in the woods."

"Is that so?"

"That's what they tell me."

"What happened in the woods?"

"She cut herself," the maid said, finally freeing the cork and tossing it aside. She poured two generous glasses. "And you know, there are things, things like sharks, that can track you, track you by *scent*, from a single drop of blood."

Frederick had been quick to appear for those blood drops. But that wasn't even really a wound. It was—it was nothing. Almost nothing. Practically nothing. She took the glass the maid offered. They clinked glasses, and the maid said, "To *survival*."

They drank.

They finished the bottle, but the maid said nothing else interesting. She gave her name, Chloe, which Alyssa filed away; and she said she'd been here since she was a baby. It made Alyssa wonder how they defined family in a place like this.

When the maid left, Alyssa removed the bandage. Her finger looked fine. There was no blood where the ladder had stuck her, but there was the faintest whiff of rainbow.

In winter, night came early, and Frederick often worked late. But this wasn't one of those nights. He was leaving. The chauffer was ready, with his leather gloves and driving goggles. The big truck made a lot of noise. Anyone with working ears could hear it for a mile in any direction.

The maid had apparently found another alcove to sleep off the wine. The cook worked in the kitchen. The butler— he could be anywhere, but she'd have to risk it.

Alyssa retrieved the key again. The wound, barely visible, glowed with striating rainbow hues when exposed to the key. The color drifted away, dissipating in the air, making a kind of path that led up to the third floor. It rounded corners and climbed stairs, following the exact path Frederick must've taken from the bathroom downstairs. It went right past the storeroom and right by the workroom, which surprised her. She'd expected blood to lead to blood, and where else might the magician have hidden that vial?

Instead, the blood trail led directly into the gallery.

Thirty paintings, give or take, occupied the walls of the L-shaped gallery, masterworks by famous hands, vibrant reds and sacred blues. There was a Geographer and an Astronomer set, there were portraits of queens and magicians, there were surrealistic landscapes. Statues stood in some of the corners. A mirror instead of a painting in one place, it had the most elaborate frame she'd ever seen, thick gold overrun with delicately carved curlicues and arabesques. There was even a section of brick wall—cut away from a building in some city—colored with chalk and charcoal but smudged, possibly by rain—an alley scene reminiscent of

Van Gogh's Parisian café. It was probably the least impressive piece in the entire gallery.

The color of her blood drifted around the gallery, around it in circles, as though there was no place else to go.

With a start, Alyssa realized she was directly over the library. This was its third floor. She let the light hit the key, but it wasn't natural light, and the current fixtures weren't the room's original light. She'd have to work harder than that.

"Library," she said, a whisper under her breath. "Reveal yourself."

But she was no spell caster. The library, or the ghost of the library, didn't respond.

She may not be a spell caster, but she had worked hard, and had learned much, and had studied often. She knew illusion. She knew light's trickery. Color was a function of light, she had learned that here. She conjured an illusion, an extension of the library for her eyes only, straight through a floor which hadn't always been here. Alyssa circled that floor, walking where once there had been a platform surrounding the books. She couldn't read titles up here, not under these circumstances, but she could see where the books had been, where they had been moved, where they had fallen as they burned.

They had not all fallen.

Some remained on the shelves.

Some of those books had resisted the call of the flames.

Alyssa paused to catch her breath. She closed her eyes and let the key do its work. She followed its pull, its draw, its magnetism.

She found herself facing a portrait of Anne of Bohemia.

The woman stared back at her. She had posed, possibly for days or weeks, for that painting. It felt lifelike. It was rich and thickly textured. Anne of Bohemia had been beautiful, or at least portrayed that way. She, like every other queen before or since, had kept her secrets.

She had one now.

Alyssa removed the painting from the wall. It was heavier than she'd expected, but came away easily enough. She leaned it against the other wall. There was a spot of color there, a place where a book had watched the flames and— and *what*, protected itself? She wasn't sure.

She touched the key to the wall, which was the same as any other wall but couldn't possibly be. The plaster hid something valuable, something otherwise unobtainable. There might not be another copy in existence. She touched the walls with both hands, felt for the outlines of a hidden panel, whether it was hidden magically or mechanically. Nothing revealed itself. It was a wall.

Using the obsidian key like a spear, Alyssa stabbed the wall.

Plaster came away. She dug at it, into it, through the plaster and into the space between rooms, a place that didn't really exist, except that here, there was a remnant of a shelf that had survived.

She was careful not to hit the book with the key. She didn't know if it would be fragile, its spine easily cracked, its pages like ash. She cleared enough space to reveal the book. *The Making of a Shadow.*

She shoved all the broken bits of wall into the wall. Where else might she hide it? She re-hung the portrait. Anne of Bohemia glowered at her as Alyssa struggled to maintain her balance and not crack the frame or damage the canvas. It was not easy.

She cleared away the plaster dust from under the portrait.

It would take a very talented eye, and at the very least the removal of the painting, to realize anything had happened. As far as Alyssa knew, Frederick never even entered the gallery.

She glanced at herself in the mirror as she left. Her reflection had witnessed her crime. And it was most certainly that: a *crime*. As Rony had said, some books needed to be stolen.

On her way down, Alyssa stopped in the alcove where the maid slept. The girl had been kind to her, but that was not her usual way. Had the wine been a kindness? Had it lowered Alyssa's inhibitions enough to do what she'd done?

It wouldn't be long before she was discovered.

Alyssa whispered, "Thank you," then left the maid.

In her basement room, Alyssa cleaned herself and showered, made a cheese sandwich, packed chocolate in a small bag with her pen and shadow book, then sat on the edge of the bed with *The Making of a Shadow* in her hands. She didn't know how much time she had. Frederick had kept this book hidden, or someone before him had. Rony wanted it, and had sent Alyssa here for no other reason than to steal it.

Where did Alyssa's obligations lie?

She took a deep breath, listened to the house, to the faint echoes of something simmering in the kitchen, to snowflakes landing softly on the rooftop, to a fire crackling in a hearth where maybe the butler warmed his hands.

Alyssa opened the book and started reading.

She paused only thrice, once to lock her door, once for water, and once for the sounds of the truck returning to the house. The chauffer talked, presumably to Frederick, the magician of the house, but his words didn't reach her. She didn't need them. They entered the house, each going to their own rooms. The magician did not bother with his workroom, and certainly not the gallery. Whatever traces of mischief Alyssa had left in her wake, they hadn't been immediately obvious. That was good. She might survive the night.

And she wouldn't have to survive another night in this house.

She read until midnight, until past midnight, when all

sounds of the house were distorted by the hour. The fire crackled in its hearth and threatened to consume the whole house. The maid woke in her alcove and cursed in Spanish, French, and Filipino. The girl had collected such expressions from across the world. No sound reached Alyssa from upstairs. Either Frederick slept soundly, or he sat motionless.

Under any circumstance, it was a risk.

Alyssa put the book in her pack, strapped the pack to her back, and snuck into the basement. Keys to the cars were all kept in the chauffer's room, but not the motorcycles. She snagged a helmet, and keys to the red and black Triumph Bonneville, and rolled it out of the house as quietly as she could manage. Once she reached the street, though her wrist burned under the obsidian bracelet, she kick started the bike.

9.

The winter was cold. The winter was colder on the back of that Bonneville. The single headlight lit up a path of white through the nighttime white. Snow still drifted down, but had been drifting for a long while, eddying in places, so there were snow drifts and, potentially, black ice underneath her.

She rode, she leaned low, she pushed the speed. Somewhere behind her, Frederick would eventually realize she'd abandoned him, and he had paid—if not good money, in good faith—for her. But she had never been bound to him, and life debts, such as Rony had described, were nontransferable. No amount of magic could change that.

She rode, and she trusted the highway to lead her somewhere away. It cut through the mountainous forest, and might've been the same mountainous forest surrounding Rony's hotel and village. It wouldn't surprise Alyssa at all if the road led her straight there.

It didn't.

She didn't know how long she would have before anyone even noticed she was gone. How long before someone found the damage she'd done in the gallery—the secret lost extension of the library?

She might have minutes, hours, or weeks.

Alyssa rode into the snowy darkness, intending to disappear, but she was still close enough to the house to hear her name when it was whispered. The sound of Frederick's voice carried on the wind, bounced off the clouds, and stayed low to the ground. The first time he said *Alyssa*, it was a question, a realization, a concern. The second time, it was a command. It carried so much unsaid, most importantly and unavoidably: *Come here.*

Alyssa, under the helmet she'd taken, gave her response in a whisper: "No."

Anger. Frustration. Fury. Oh, that was not acceptable. Not permissible. Not nice, even. Her name, the third time Frederick uttered it, carried malevolence, and the sound of thunder—not actual thunder, it wasn't a storm of that kind or any other, merely flurries overhead—still, thunder rumbled through the night.

She shouldn't have responded. She pressed forward, increasing her speed, leaning into the curves of the mountain highway. Twenty, thirty minutes after leaving the house, she still didn't know where she was, city or country or continent. If his house was in a pocket of space somewhere, inaccessible without his magic, she would not survive the night. She had considered that, but the risk was low. Most likely, if any sort of portal magic was in use, it worked over the entire road at some point near the house and she'd already passed it.

A truck sounded its air horn as it passed in the other direction. The pitch waned as she went by. It served as an alert, a notification; one of Frederick's spies spotting her.

She hadn't assumed he maintained spies anywhere.

She pressed for more speed. She got off the highway when she could, edging through a road that twisted more tightly, rose and dropped more frequently, and kept its snow.

She had to slow down, and she had to give all her concentration to the bike. If she spilled, he might compel her to crawl back and heal herself the long, painful way. There would be no second chances.

She passed a sign that said *Leaving*. She didn't know where she left, but the nature of the road seemed to change. It widened, and repelled more of the snow. Indeed, there was less snow now, and the air wasn't so thin. She was descending from somewhere.

When she reached a stoplight, a red light, she stopped and looked back over her shoulder. In the distance, rising in the darkness, she saw the silhouette of a dragon through the clouds. Maybe it wasn't real. Maybe her imagination made shapes where there were none. Maybe it was Frederick himself, an alternative form.

No. It was just an illusion. Alyssa had some experience with illusion. She could see how the clouds had been folded over and stretched thin. The dragon was no more substantial than water vapor.

She stopped waiting for the light. She sped forward. The bike responded like a dream, and hugged the road like a demon possessed.

In the snow ahead, spotlighted by the Bonneville's headlight, a woman appeared. White robes danced around her. Hair fell over half her face. Alyssa lurched to avoid her and dropped the bike. She and the Triumph slid across the highway, through the snow and into the darkness, until the road curved and snowbanks swallowed her.

She didn't lose consciousness. She knew the woman in white. Fireworks popped in the sky, in the distance, shattering the illusory form of the dragon.

Alyssa, buried under the snow, waited for Rony, formerly Veronica, to retrieve her. She sat up, ignoring the road burns, the scratches, the blood. Nothing was broken. The helmet had spared her face. She took it off. The brisk air assaulted her. But Rony didn't appear, so eventually Alyssa wiped herself down and stood up through the snow.

The road was empty.

It wasn't hard to find the bike. It wasn't far away from her, and appeared undamaged. All her muscles ached when she climbed onto it. The bike's vibrations hurt her bones. She would endure it. But she would go slower. The apparition had been a reminder, nothing more. When Alyssa left Frederick's house, it seemed all the world had been informed.

Briefly, she wondered what had happened to the Maestro.

She drove the bike down the road, through the dark, ignoring road signs because they wouldn't tell her anything worth knowing. She drove until she reached a familiar town, though she had never seen it under a blanket of snow. She pulled up to the main hotel doors but didn't toss the keys to the young valet who watched her over the top of the newspaper he pretended to read.

She nodded to the concierge as she went by. When the elevator doors opened, the jockey looked at her and smiled sadly and waited silently for her to enter. He took her straight to the penthouse. She was, of course, expected.

Alyssa walked to Rony's door but didn't stop to knock. She opened the door and strode straight in. The older woman sat at the piano, dancing her fingers slowly across the high keys, drawing from its strings a dreamy melody. "Darling," she said, not bothering to look up, "I was beginning to think you'd never make it."

"You never had any right to sell me," Alyssa told her.

She stopped tickling the keys. "You're right, of course. My dear, I never sold you. I made a trade, an illicit trade, and I took advantage of Frederick's naiveté."

"And mine."

"You were under my protection the entire time."

"You know the library in that house was destroyed by a fire, right?"

"Of course I know."

"You expected me to find a book in a library that doesn't exist?"

"You're more capable than that, darling. You have the book with you now. You even still have the key. I'm amazed, actually."

"I want to clean up."

"Of course."

"I forbid you from going through my things."

"You cannot forbid me anything."

Alyssa narrowed her eyes.

"Fine, little bunny, fine. I'm not so wicked as all that. Go, clean up, there's clothes in your room and I'll have room service brought up."

"He's going to come for me, you know."

"Of course he will," Rony said. "Unfinished business and all."

10.

The cuts and abrasions from dropping the bike were wholly superficial. The hot water in the shower, the hottest water she could pull from the shower, was luxurious after hours in the snowy night. She toweled dry. She couldn't remember the last time she'd worn her own clothes. Rony had not gone through her bag as she cleaned up, which was good. She put her pen and shadow book away. They would have no role in what was to come. The first light of dawn broke over the eastern mountains. Someone knocked on the doors to the suite. Alyssa emerged as Rony allowed Frederick to enter.

"I want her," he told Rony. His eyes fixed on Alyssa. "*Thief.*"

"You have no authority here," Rony told him. "But you know how it works. Some books cannot be sold, borrowed, or given."

"She also took the key."

"She always had that key," Rony said. "I gave it to her. Before you took her."

Alyssa said nothing. She held the key in one hand and *The Making of a Shadow* in the other. She glanced at the feast laid out on the table and knew she'd never have a mouthful of the food. All that meat, at least four varieties of cheese that she could see, exotic fruits from across the globe. It looked so good, so inviting, but she had eaten enough from the tables of magicians.

Rony and Frederick looked at each other. It was easy to tell who was the stronger, who was the smarter, who was angry and who was amused. The nature of their games didn't interest Alyssa. Neither did the nature of their relationship. But they weren't going to get anywhere without her, without their *famulus*, the assistant who had never actually belonged to either of them.

"You," she said to Rony, "never had any hold over me. I was never obligated to you in the way you said. And you," she said to Frederick, "should know better than to barter for a life."

Rony allowed a smile to creep into her face. The game was going to end exactly as she'd planned or intended. Alyssa did not appreciate that, but maybe there was nothing she could do. She took a bowl from the table, dumping its strawberries and bananas into a plate of boiled eggs. It was a good bowl, marble, solid and sturdy and strong. "You want the key. It's not yours anymore. You gave it away, and it was given to me." She dropped it into the bowl. Frederick reached for it, as though he might catch it, but made no move forward. "The key caused the fire, didn't it?"

"I don't know what you're talking about," Frederick said.

If he lied, she didn't care. "Your butler knows." She looked down and punched the key in the bowl. The obsidian shattered. It bled colors. The pieces that remained were sharp shards amid some dust, not irreparable, not yet. She punched again, and the obsidian bracelet that bound her cracked into three pieces. They fell into the bowl. After a brief pause—and stunned silence—Alyssa took a thick metal spoon from the table and pulverized all the pieces, crushed them into the colors it had bled, mixing them into a good, solid paste. The obsidian absorbed all the colors, so all that remained was black. She took a spoonful and swallowed it.

The crushed key tasted sharp, and it tasted colorful, and it tasted like magic. It was a dangerous thing to do, but necessary. Frederick dropped his arm as she ate the rest of the obsidian key in two more spoonfuls.

"You want the book. I can't give it to you. You know better. You didn't take it, I did. But for as long as I have it, I'll be in danger, and in fear of you, and I can't have that." She dropped *The Making of a Shadow* into the bowl as well. It was time to perform a little magic.

She didn't say any words or twist her fingers or conjure anything from another world. She simply ignited the flame. Once before, the book had survived a fire. This time, fire consumed every page until all that remained was ash.

For good measure, Alyssa consumed the ash of the book, as well.

Rony and Frederick watched in silence. The ashes were not delicious. They tasted like burnt toast, like over-baked muffins, like blackened garlic bread. Still, she swallowed every dry bite, then washed it down with a glass of orange juice from the feast table. It was pulpy, which was not her preference, but it helped drown out the taste of obsidian and ash.

Finished, she set down the glass. She looked at Frederick, then at Rony, then said, "I think I should go."

"That," Rony said, "would be best."

Frederick almost said nothing. He didn't seem to know what to say. He was angry, he was confused, he was surprised, and he wore it all on a face unused to expressing emotion. Alyssa slung her bag, which contained her pen and shadow book, over her shoulder. Before she reached the door, however, Frederick said, "Wait."

She paused, looked back, and waited.

"You owe me," he said.

She shook her head. "How do you reckon?"

"That key was valuable to me. To *us*. You destroyed it."

"I consumed it."

"That won't give you the magic you seek," Rony told her.

Alyssa smiled. She smiled as if saying she knew something they didn't. Even in all their glory and all their age, there was the distinct possibility they had missed something. There were seven forms of magic, or at least seven, and it was a rare person who had mastered any combination of them, much less all. So she smiled, and she said nothing, but she had never expected to absorb the abilities of the key. Magic was not transferable in that way. She had read a lot about transformation and transmutation, translation, even the quantum characteristics of magic. But she had only ever uncovered real talents in a single form of magic.

Leaving the two magicians with that smile, Alyssa left the penthouse. The elevator jockey took her soundlessly to the ground level, the concierge averted his eyes, the valet had never tried to move the Bonneville.

She didn't have to run anymore.

She rode carefully and slowly out of the town. As she proceeded down the highway and down the mountainside, the snow stopped falling. It didn't take long to reach a place where the snow hadn't fallen at all. There, she increased her speed. She made random turns. She ignored the road signs, trusting in something else to guide her. Fate. Destiny. Purpose. Fortune. Perhaps something no more profound than mere Chance. She was aware of the tinge of obsidian rainbow in her shadow.

By noon, she had traveled a thousand miles or more. She reached a city she had never seen. Its buildings were old and tall, concrete and steel. The bike shuddered beneath her. She'd never refilled the gas tank, and the Triumph had reached the end of its life. Here, she'd abandon it. It wasn't hers and never should have been. Frederick would have been well within his rights to insist she leave it.

So she left it on the side of the road outside a crappy, rundown theater that looked closed. It reminded her of the place she'd seen in the Maestro's stained glass window. Alyssa was too smart to believe in coincidence.

A woman rushed out of the theater. She wore something sparkly, something appropriate for a stage magician's assistant. She slammed the door shut behind her and, in her rush to escape, slammed right into Alyssa.

The woman glared at Alyssa. Her eye makeup was colorful but chaotic. She opened her mouth to say something, thought better of it, then diverted her path and left.

A man, a stage magician, whose face was pictured in the fresh posters outside the theater, burst next through the doors. "Becky, wait!"

But Becky did not wait.

And the man did not chase her.

"Trouble with the help?" Alyssa asked.

The man gave an exaggerated sigh. Even offstage, he was all about the performance. "She's supposed to be my *assistant*."

Alyssa considered her situation. She didn't know where she was or why, but she had much still to learn. The illusions she'd performed at the penthouse had been a good start, but there was so much more to magic than that. She needed a place to live, a place to study, a place to practice. "Is it a paid position?"

The stage magician looked at her. "Is it *paid*, did you say?"

She nodded.

"Of course it's paid. But the show starts *tonight*, we go live *tonight*, and where am I supposed to find someone with the necessary skills?"

"Illusion. Perhaps some contortion work. Disappearances and quick changes?"

"Show me," the man said.

She glanced at the poster and read his name off it. "Nicholas, is it? Sure, I can show you something." She snapped a finger, opened her palm, and revealed a silver dollar—the same she'd produced for Rony a lifetime ago.

He smiled. It was a tentative smile. "That's not *nothing*," he admitted.

She nodded, understanding the challenge. "You know, in a way, I've always been a magician's assistant." *Famulus,* by some translations, meant merely that, though of course it was so much more. She clapped her hands together and produced a book. She didn't merely pluck this from the air. It should have been—it was meant to be—too fast for the stage magician to comprehend. She merely showed him the book, there in the palm of her hands.

He read the title aloud. "*The Making of a Shadow?*"

"So, what say you?" Alyssa asked. "I need cash, you need an assistant...I guess I need an apartment, at that."

"What's your name?"

Names were important. She didn't want to give hers away anymore. So she gave him a variation. "Call me Lissa."

Their first show was almost seven hours later, and though the audience couldn't exactly be called a full house, they were enthralled. Alyssa slept that night in one of the apartments at the top of the Palace Theater. Standing at her window, even if it was only hers for the night, she looked out over a strange and wondrous new city. She counted the stars, those she could see from here, and she counted the people. And she read from her book, her stolen book, which she had vanished right before the eyes of two great and powerful users of magic, by the colorful glow of a fully saturated obsidian key.

SECRET HISTORY
PART IIII

PARLIAMENT
OF
USHERS

1.

"You'll find the contract quite unbreakable."

The paper had been yellowed by time. It was difficult to see in the dim light of the auditorium. Felipe Gris examined it anyway, squinting as though he could read it. There was length and breadth to the document, history to it. It didn't feel like the kind of paper he'd find in stores today.

It wasn't the contract that concerned him.

He'd needed bolt cutters to break through the chains outside. The doors had been closed a very long time. He'd bought the place sight unseen fully aware of how much work would probably be required to restore it. He hadn't even gotten inside the theater yet to answer important questions. Was the Worlitzer still there? Did the chairs need re-upholstering, or to be replaced entirely? He had seen pictures of the theater in its heyday and hoped to find the chandelier. It wouldn't have been easy to move, and where would you move it to?

The state of the theater wasn't a concern, either. He'd gotten it at a steal. The paperwork had included a paragraph that all current contracts were to be upheld—in case there was a play or a ballet or something already scheduled in a theater that had been locked and shuttered over two decades ago.

Ignatius, the man with the contract, had been waiting inside the auditorium, midway between the front doors and the entry to the auditorium, where a concession stand lay under a coating of dust and the gold trim—faux gold leaf, all of it—had lost its shimmer. The man in his clean, crisp uniform, with his tanned skin and strong hands, spoke with an accent from far away and long ago.

"Ushers?" Felipe asked. The contract specified a plural, but lacked names. A court of law might find this omission cause for dismissal. The fine print was too fine, even with a thick flashlight pointed at it.

"Everything, as you can see, is in place," Ignatius said. He had introduced himself, had stepped out of the shadows, had stopped Felipe in his tracks.

"I can't really see much of anything here," Felipe said.

"The lights are old," Ignatius said. "I wouldn't trust the wiring."

"And what have you been doing all this time?" Felipe asked.

"Maintenance."

"The place is a mess."

"We've maintained what's important," Ignatius said. "We are not janitors."

Felipe looked at the man again. At the angles of his face, the sweep of his brows, the dryness of his lips. And the uniform. The thing that bothered Felipe most about the man who presumably had been inside this locked theater all these years was that he had seen him before.

2.

It was the summer the lights went out. Thirteen year old Felipe didn't have much else to do, so when one of the other kids suggested sneaking into the old movie house, there were few good reasons to object.

It was another city, and the summer had done a good job peeling back all pretenses. It was hot, it was sticky, and it was relentless, day and night. No one remembered the last time there'd been rain. Maybe never. It was easy to believe the world had always been this way, and the sun would persist until every brick of every building crumbled to dust. In the not too distant future, the city—which stood in for the whole world—would be reduced to a desert, and shade might only be found underground.

Since the lights were out, they couldn't even go to the

modern movie theater and sit in the air conditioning with Cokes and Slushees.

The old movie house, as everyone knew, had been here before the city, born at the very beginning of time. Neanderthals had watched *Casablanca* here. Cavemen had left their handprints on the basement walls. There was a ghost, of course, because every old building had a ghost. The last projectionist, a dusty relic called Louie, could be found drinking at *The Speakeasy* most nights. Rumors claimed the place had once actually been a speakeasy, and the ghosts of flappers danced there after the final movie let out. Louie would tell stories, sometimes, if you found him outside during the day, about the drugs and the girls and the other things that went on inside the old movie house. "Wasn't always a movie house," he'd tell the kids. "Was an honest theater, back a ways, before Hollywood got their hands on it, before they erected that damn silver screen." He said he drank to its memories. He said if they gave him five bucks, he could buy a drink for Janet.

The old movie house had shown movies until something called *Touch of Evil*. Most of those letters were still on the marquee. All the posters had disappeared before Felipe ever saw the place. The doors had been boarded up and there had never been many windows, but in the alley on the side of the building there was a door with boards loose enough to pry open. They squeezed into the dark theater and had the place to themselves.

Inside, the air was cool, as though immune to the cruelties of summer. The air was stale and unmoving, untouched by light, and you could almost see the trails of the other kids as they spread out in the darkness.

They'd come in through an exit direct from the theater. Louie's silver screen had been shredded, so it resembled teeth hanging limply from the ceiling. The curtains, thick and red, had been drawn open. They seemed to undulate, to almost pulse with a secret heartbeat. Probably rats. Roaches. Felipe only briefly thought it might be the old movie house breathing.

The kids split up. Some went behind the screen. Some explored the edges of the lobby, where you might've gotten popcorn, in search of stairs to the projectionist's room. A few lingered near their escape door. As far as they knew, there were no other exits from the theater.

Felipe wandered alone until he found stairs going down.

His eyes had barely adjusted to the gloom inside the theater, and it only got darker as he descended. Darker and cooler. Very nearly cold. The stairs led to a hall, and the hall contained a series of doors leading to rooms directly under the stage and seats.

That first time in the theater, Felipe hadn't taken a flashlight. No one had, so no one found much of anything. It was dark enough in some places you couldn't see the person next to you, or the wall, or your own hand in front of your face. There might have been monsters in the dark, ghosts, just about anything. In the end, they mostly ended up in the theater, legs propped on the seats in front of them, watching the stage in front of the screen as some of the kids acted out scenes from *Empire Strikes Back*.

Felipe's love of theaters was probably born that summer.

He'd opened one of the doors in the basement. He was alone, but he couldn't tell anyone what he'd seen because there was nothing to see, nothing but darkness, nothing but emptiness, unless you counted the woman applying makeup at a mirror he couldn't really see.

In the reflection, she noticed him. She smiled. When Felipe blinked, she wasn't there.

3.

Felipe returned that night with a flashlight, this time thoroughly alone. He snuck in the same way. Though almost zero light had reached into the theater by day, the dark was thicker in the night. He ran the beam of his light across the shredded screen. It still resembled teeth, but in the night had gotten sharper. The aisle between seats was littered with old and fresh candy wrappers, discarded condoms, who knew what else. Felipe didn't spend a lot of time examining them. He made his way through the theater to the lobby, to the hall where he'd found the stairs, and down into the basement.

With a flashlight shining the way, he didn't know which door he'd opened earlier. It hadn't been the first, so he left that alone. It might've been the second, but it was locked. The third was jammed shut, swollen in place, and would take more than his muscles to move. The fourth door—there were at least two others—opened onto an utterly empty room.

Felipe shined the light where the woman would have stood at the mirror, if this was the right room. He said, "Hello." No one answered. He swept the beam across the room, but it was just dingy walls.

It was the only basement door he could open.

This would require more research, he realized, and there was only one real source of information on the old movie house: Louie. And there was only one place to find the man: *The Speakeasy.*

Getting into the *Speakeasy* wasn't hard as long as he didn't try to order anything. He found Louie alone in a corner booth. Louie smiled, showing his crooked teeth, and said, "Here to buy this old man a drink?"

"I've only got five bucks."

"Is enough," Louie said, holding out his hand.

Felipe handed it over. "I want to know about Janet."

Louie grinned. He looked toward the wall, in the

direction of the old movie house, but Felipe wasn't sure what he saw. "*Janet.* Who even told you there was a girl called Janet?"

"You did."

"Did I?" He shook his head. "Can't say I remember that. Okay, what do you want to know?"

"Everything."

Something in the way Felipe said it made Louie open his eyes. Maybe he'd been dreamy or drunk or lost in memories—his normal states—but for just a moment, he was completely sober and utterly riveted to the present moment. He narrowed his eyes and bit back the side of his lower lip. "What did you do?"

"I didn't do nothing," Felipe said.

"You shouldn't go inside," Louie said.

"I didn't..."

"Don't lie to me, kid." He was raising his voice. Not a lot, but enough to attract attention. Louie crumpled the five dollar bill and threw it back at Felipe. It bounced off his cheek and landed on the table. "Goddamn thief, tryin' to steal my memories. *Mine.*"

The bartender called over. "Hey, enough over there, kid. Get out."

Felipe left the five dollars and the bar. He hadn't meant to attract attention. He didn't know what had made Louie so angry. He went home that night having learned nothing, but there were other ways of doing research.

In the morning, he went to the library.

4.

The library was vast and endless. A thirteen year old might get lost within those shelves, but Felipe didn't venture far inside. He went straight to the reference desk, to the librarian, a pretty woman with jet black hair and eyes like truth serum. When she aimed those eyes at Felipe, his stomach dropped. He hadn't even done anything wrong.

"I want to find out more about the old movie house."

"Excellent," she said. "What have you got so far?"

"That the last film was *Touch of Evil.*"

"That's a little before my time," she said, "but I bet we can find something."

She checked files and catalogs—but the lights were still out, so she couldn't check microfiche or the computer—and found news clippings talking about the fire at *Pitt Theater*, named for Montgomery Pitt, who had built the theater before the second World War. After the fire, the theater had opened again, but a lot of the original fixtures had been lost, and several people had died, including an actress the article didn't name. They found pictures from the grand opening, all black and whites of men in tuxedos and women in fancy dresses like Felipe's grandmother wore when she was young.

What they didn't find was interesting: why the theater had closed.

"That, at least, is probably part of our living history," the librarian said. Felipe must've looked at her funny, because she added, "I bet someone knows."

"Louie," Felipe said, nodding.

"Maybe someone at the nursing home," the librarian suggested. "Maybe someone in the Pitt family. There's still Pitts in town."

He didn't want to see the Pitts. He went back to the theater, *The Pitt*, and snuck in again. It was quieter inside than anywhere else in the city. It was cooler, too, and he liked that, but he eventually realized he wasn't alone. There was already someone in the theater, sitting in the back row, one leg propped on the seat in front of her. She watched him enter, she watched him look around, and when he turned on his flashlight she said, "Turn that off."

He swung the beam in her direction. She squinted,

turned her head, held up a hand to block the light. "Turn that *off*," she said again. "Do you want them to catch us in here?"

Felipe didn't get a good look at her before turning the light off. She was about his age, maybe a little older. He didn't recognize her from school. He said, "No."

"What you looking for?" she asked.

"How do you know I'm looking for something?"

"I'm asking the questions." She dropped her leg and leaned forward. They were separated by a dozen rows of seats, but it seemed to lessen the gap between them.

"There's a ghost," Felipe said.

"There's always a ghost," she told him. "What else? Gonna get high? Meet a *girl*?"

"No."

"You were here yesterday," she said. "With all those other kids."

"Yeah, so?" He didn't mean it to sound so defensive.

He could almost see her grinning in the dark. "I was here the whole time."

"Watching us?"

"Me?" She popped to her feet. "You're the one following me around day and night. You came back last night. So I'm gonna ask again, and this is the last time, what are you looking for?"

"Told you. I saw a ghost."

"No, you didn't tell me."

"I want to see her again."

"So it is a girl." She giggled. "I knew it."

Felipe aimed the flashlight at her but didn't flick it on. "Who are you?"

"Maria. And you?"

"Felipe."

Names out of the way, the conversation seemed to smother under the silence of the theater. She'd spoken too quickly, didn't give him time to think, and his thinking had been pretty messed up since seeing Janet last night. And of course it was Janet. Who else could it possibly be?

"Are you always here?" he asked.

"I like to think."

"You can think here?"

"Can you think anywhere at all?"

He didn't answer that. He looked to the screen instead. "What do you think about?"

"Movies. What else?"

"There's all sorts of other things."

"Nothing so magnificent," Maria said. "Except maybe plays. But they're the same thing. They're *from* the same thing. You going ghost hunting, are you? Are you armed?"

"Why would I need to be armed?"

"Ghosts can be dangerous."

"How so?"

"They eat your heart," Maria said. "They steal your soul."

"None of that's true."

"How would you know? Have you been thinking about it like I have?"

"You've been thinking about ghosts?"

"I live in an abandoned movie house," Maria said. "What else am I supposed to think about?"

"You *live* here?"

She didn't answer right away.

"You live in the theater? Why?" He knew immediately he shouldn't have asked that.

"You'd never understand."

"Then show me around," Felipe said. "Show me the basement."

"Is that supposed to be you asking me out on some sort of date?"

He blushed. He hadn't meant it that way. He didn't

answer right away.

"Relax," she said. "I won't bite. But I'll show you the basement, yeah, sure, why not?"

5.

She insisted he keep the flashlight off. "Scares away the mists," she said, whispering, passing along a secret about nothing Felipe understood. He followed, one step behind her, and she opened the first door. He hadn't even tried that one the night before.

She shushed him, the sound louder than any he'd made. He carried the flashlight like a weapon. He felt more than saw her move to one side, where she flicked a light switch.

He half expected a conflagration of incandescent luminance. A light did come on, a single bulb in a lamp without a shade on a table next to a couch. A folded blanket sat at one edge of the couch, on top of a small pillow, held down by a paperback called *Ghost Story*.

"This is the apartment," Maria said, whispering. "This is where he lives."

"He?"

"The *usher*."

"I don't understand."

"Keep your voice down."

"He's not here." No one was. The walls were bare, the room otherwise empty but for a half-sized refrigerator supporting a few more books. "Who's the usher?"

"What," Maria said. "You should ask *what*. It's the more important question."

"How am I supposed to know that?" Felipe asked.

She gave him a look. It was hard to read her expression in the gloom of that single bulb, but Felipe didn't feel entirely comfortable. After a moment, she asked, "The people stopped coming. That's why the theater died. Someone opened up a new theater on the other side of town, and this one no longer mattered."

"Why hasn't the owner turned it into something else?"

Maria grinned. "It's protected."

"By a ghost?"

She almost laughed. He could see she wanted to. "Where did you see her? *Janet?*"

"I don't know if it was Janet, but it has to be," Felipe said. "Louie mentioned her."

"*Louie?*"

"He used to be the projectionist."

Maria shook her head. "That makes him what we call an unreliable narrator."

"Why's that?"

"They're all flicker and illusion," Maria said. "Can't trust a projectionist."

"He knows things."

"Because he's old? Or because he's drunk by midday?"

That wasn't an argument he could win. He knew nothing about the people who worked in theaters like this, and he really knew nothing about Louie. "You live here? Are you the usher?"

She laughed. It was both light and mocking at the same time. But she didn't answer him. There was a sound upstairs. Footsteps. Maybe a voice. Felipe was about to say something, but Maria held up a finger and shushed him again. After another sound, someone tripping over something and letting loose with a colorful linguistic display, Maria leaned close and whispered. The breath of her words brushed his ear. "Janet," she said, "is probably Janet Leigh, from the movie, and I doubt your ghost is real. But *he* is, whoever he is upstairs, and that is *not* the usher."

"What do we do?"

She fished a key from her pocket. "Only two options. We run, or we hide."

Running would mean getting past whoever was upstairs. They didn't want to get caught, especially if it was the police, so they hid. With all the stealth, Maria pulled shut the door and led Felipe to one of the others that had been locked. Her key opened it, and it swung open nearly silently, but a sudden quiet followed from upstairs.

Before Felipe could say anything—he wasn't planning to, not really, though he may have opened his mouth just a little—Maria put a finger on his lips and held it there. She was saying be quiet, but his stomach did a bit of a twist with the contact. They didn't move. The man upstairs—Felipe assumed a man because of how heavy his steps had been— didn't move. Felipe did his best not to even breathe, though it was hard with Maria's fingers smooshed against his mouth. She was crushing his lips against his teeth. He wasn't about to stop her.

Finally, she dragged him into the room. She shut the door and engaged the lock.

It must've been a closet. It was small, though not tight. There was absolutely no light, just dark shapes in the dark. Felipe imagined brooms and mops and boxes of stale popcorn. Maria held his wrist now, no longer his lips, and kept him close. He reached up with his free hand and, tentatively, grabbed her other arm.

"Don't move," Maria said.

The man descended the stairs. He came slowly. A trail of light blazed briefly under the closet door as it swept back and forth in the hall. At the bottom of the stairs, the man said, "Who's there?" Felipe recognized the voice. Then the man said, "*Janet?*"

With hardly any voice at all, Felipe said, "It's Louie."

The man grabbed the doorknob, twisted it, twisted angrily a second time when it wouldn't open. "Kid, if it's you, if you're playing a joke, I swear I'll rip out your tongue and feed it to the rats."

Another voice, a woman's voice, cut through the darkness. She was further down the basement hall. Felipe knew exactly which room. She said, "It's me."

The man practically ran to her.

Silence followed. The light never returned. Time stretched as though it could reach across all of eternity. Felipe held Maria's arm and she held his. He felt her quickened breathing against his forehead—he hadn't realized she was that much taller than him—but nothing happened outside the closet door. Louie, the projectionist, said nothing else, and maybe did nothing else. The silence was just as it had been, but heavier now with the certainty it wasn't empty.

Felipe and Maria waited in the dark until someone inserted a key into the closet door and turned the knob.

Felipe held his breath. Maria's grip on his arm tightened. The man who opened the door, however, was not Louie. He wore a crisp, clean uniform, not sloppily thrown together rags. His skin was tanned, his hands strong, and his eyes glimmered like a cat's even in the dark of the basement. When he spoke, his accent was from far away and long ago. "Maria."

She released Felipe's arm and bowed her head.

The man turned his attention to Felipe. He carried a flashlight, something far more subtle than Felipe's, and shined it straight into his face. Felipe squinted and turned away, but the man continued his examination, up and down the full length of him, until he finally said, "Name."

It wasn't merely a question, but a demand, and Felipe was incapable of resisting. "Felipe Gris."

"This theater," the man said, pausing in the middle to narrow his eyes, "is closed."

"I know, sir."

"Off limits," the man told him.

"You should go," Maria added.

He wanted to. But the man filled the doorway, and that

beam of light had revealed it was, indeed, just a closet. There was no place to run.

"The Pitt," the man said, "was a beautiful theater, but I'm afraid it's been...truly abandoned." Something about that, the way he said it, the emphasis on *truly* and the delay afterwards, saddened Felipe.

The man stepped aside to allow Felipe out of the closet. His hands, however, were held in fists, and his lips pressed tightly together. Felipe moved very slowly out of the closet, squeezing against the door jamb. Two, three steps through the basement, he glanced back. The man watched him.

Felipe ran up the stairs. He raced through the auditorium, into the theater itself, past the aisles and to the side door through which he'd snuck in. Outside, the sun was harsh. It burned his eyes and his skin. He'd been sweating, a cold sweat all across his forehead and back and hands, but it evaporated instantly, leaving a crust of salt on his skin. He ran all the way home, slammed shut his bedroom door, and didn't come out for anything.

After dinner, after sunset, Felipe was staring out his bedroom window in the direction of the theater. His heart still raced. He'd washed off the salt, he'd eaten chocolate, he'd drunk a gallon of lemonade. He wondered if Maria and the man—the usher—had been the ghosts.

6.

Felipe didn't sleep well. When he did, he dreamt of the ghost of Janet Leigh. She'd been in *Psycho,* which he was sure he'd seen, but the only other film of hers he knew was *Touch of Evil.* Louie had been playing a trick on him, talking about her ghost. It was very nearly wicked. Felipe spent most of the morning working up the courage to return to the theater.

When he finally did, he snuck in reluctantly.

He didn't want to learn Maria had been a ghost. She'd felt real. She'd touched his lips and held his arm. Her skin had been warm, her breath like apple juice, her eyes nearly invisible in the dark. Had they glowed? He didn't trust his senses or his memory, so he had no choice but to go back. To enter carefully. To make sure he didn't attract the usher's attention. How could he find Maria but not—*her father?*

He didn't know.

He had no plan, no real plan, no contingencies in case something went wrong. He went in unarmed, because he'd been unarmed yesterday and the ghosts—if they were ghosts—hadn't hurt him.

No one had done anything to bolster the barricades. He gained entry into the theater as easily as ever. He carried a flashlight again, but wasn't sure he should use it. He stood next to the door for five or ten minutes, waiting for his eyes to adjust, and waiting for the chill of the theater to reach him. It felt different, less inviting but still not foreboding. Finally, he gave up on his eyes and flicked on the flashlight. He scanned the back of the theater, looking for Maria, but found no one. He walked up the aisle, passed the old concession stand, and hesitated only briefly before descending the stairs.

The first door resisted when he tried to open it, but finally gave. Inside, there was no couch, no fridge, no lamp, and no books. He could believe no one had lived here in decades.

The closet remained locked. Eventually, he knocked, and called in a whisper, "Maria?" Nobody answered.

After assuring himself the basement was empty, that all the doors he could open revealed nothing and no one, that most the doors were locked and kept their secrets, Felipe returned to the stairs. He would've welcomed even the shadow of the usher at this point, but as far as he could tell, he was alone in the theater.

Partway down the aisle, the beam of his flashlight passed

across the shredded remnants of the silver screen. It wasn't real silver, he'd always known that. And now, there was someone there.

No, not quite someone. That implied life.

A body hung, suspended by the neck, amid the ribbons of screen. Felipe didn't scream, but he did drop the flashlight. It thudded loudly and echoed throughout the theater, throughout the entire city. After regaining enough control over his legs to know he wouldn't collapse, Felipe knelt to retrieve his flashlight and shined it again on the body.

He had to get closer, but not too close, to be sure of who it was.

"Louie?"

The projectionist didn't answer. He was well and truly dead. His eyes were lifeless and chalky, his face a pale gray, and a shiny puddle of his blood glimmered beneath him. Felipe didn't have to get any closer. He left the theater with more calm than was appropriate, and felt cold under the summer sun in the alley as he considered his options.

Ultimately, he didn't really have any. He went to the police station and told them about Louie hanging in the theater.

7.

Felipe regarded Ignatius, who had introduced himself and provided a copy of this ancient contract and stood there as though he, in fact, owned the place. "What have you been maintaining, then?" Felipe asked.

Ignatius smiled. "The bones," he said. "The heart. The soul."

"How is that done?"

"Carefully," Ignatius said, "and with tenderness."

Felipe looked at the other man's hands, hands he had seen once before, had dreamt might be closed into fists and used on him. "Have we met before?"

"I doubt it."

But they had. Felipe was no longer the thirteen year old boy he'd been in another city—practically another world—but some things were never forgotten. "You live inside the theater?"

"The agreements provide for an apartment, yes."

"May I see it?"

When Ignatius did not immediately answer, Felipe added, "The plans I've seen labeled no special room for *ushers*."

Ignatius nodded. "It's upstairs."

"Not in the basement?"

Ignatius had already turned to lead the way to the stairs, so if his expression revealed any response to the question, it remained hidden. The stairs were in need of carpeting. The banisters needed to be sanded and polished. There was no graffiti inside the theater, which was impressive, and thus far none of the wood showed any obvious signs of rot. The walls were dirty, but not damp. As they climbed the curved staircase, Felipe touched the wall, a brief and non-conclusive test of its strength.

Upstairs, there was a hall for entry into the loge and space for another concession stand, but also lockable doors leading to the private areas of the theater. The hall was narrow and long, with unevenly spaced doors on either side. Ignatius used a second key for one of those doors, pushed it open, and stepped aside.

Felipe entered. He shined a flashlight around the room. A lamp on a table. A couch. A small refrigerator. It all looked familiar, if not in its details. That wasn't the same couch or the same lamp. That wasn't *Ghost Story* sitting on the table, but *A Head Full of Ghosts*.

Ignatius offered, "No two theaters are ever the same, Mr.

Gris. Each has its own history, its own structure, and its own needs."

"What does this theater need, then?"

"Encouragement."

"Can I see the theater itself, now?" Felipe asked, turning away from the utilitarian apartment.

Ignatius opened another door on the other side of the hall. This needed no key. It led to a box overlooking the theater. It wasn't one of the fancy balconies. Its windows were presumably designed to look like ornamentation on the walls. This wasn't a room for the audience. There were no chairs, no lushness, no comforts at all.

Through that window, Felipe first saw the chandelier, a magnificent extravagance hanging over the belly of the theater. Its crystals glittered and gleamed in the light of the flashlight. Below, rows of chairs were intact, though aged, and the stage itself, shrouded by shadows, looked solid.

Simultaneously, Felipe saw three things: the theater as it was now, as it had been in its glory, and as it would be. He had restored others to great effect. This would be a joy.

Ignatius had left him alone. Felipe savored the moment. He still had many questions. But primarily, he had visions.

8.

A few offices had been scattered about the ground level. Felipe took one of these. It was clean enough, and the desk solid. He thumbtacked the original theater plans and elevations to the walls. They fired up electricity for the entire structure. He didn't think about the lamp in the usher's apartment.

There were, in fact, apartments labeled on the original plans, but they were old and mostly faded. He made calls from that office, to bring in an architectural firm, and to begin the search for the Wurlitzer that had originally been here. Only the pipes remained—the lungs of the organ, if he wanted to be colorful about it.

Even with full electric, the lights were dim and scattered. There had never been enough, especially not backstage or underneath. Upstairs contained apartments, offices, storage, and rehearsal spaces. The numerous basements hid rooms that seemed to have no purpose whatsoever. There were small and big rehearsal rooms, wardrobe rooms that had never been emptied, a green room, a music room where someone had left a cracked violin. The strings were gone. Felipe took the remnants of the instrument to his office.

That first week was busy, and Felipe never saw Ignatius—or any other ushers—the whole time. He talked with electricians, an old carpenter who claimed his grandfather had built this theater with his own hands, and other contractors. As Friday bled into the evening and the weekend officially began, Felipe sat again in his office. To anyone looking, he appeared to be absorbed by the plans on the walls—the original plans, as new plans had not yet been finalized. He intended to modernize the theater while keeping most of its original shape, feeling, and details.

He didn't see the sun setting outside, and he didn't really hear the revelers hitting the bars and clubs that crowded this part of the city, but he knew they were out there. And he did hear *something*—something emanating from within the theater.

He didn't think anyone was left. There hadn't been much but demolition done thus far, and even that was minimal. No need for anyone to still be here.

Outside the office, he heard the voices more distinctly— voices and what might be drumming, albeit faint and maybe merely knocking. But no one knocked at the box office door, or the front doors, or any of the doors leading into the lobby. No, the sound came from deeper.

He walked into the theater itself, where the seats had been stripped of their ruined upholstery. The sound echoed from beneath the stage, up from the orchestra section. Not just voices. Chanting?

At the edge of the orchestra pit, looking in, he saw nothing. He climbed down and followed the voices through one of the open doors into a basement hallway. The wood here was two hundred years old. The walls were slate or rock, and more than capable of retaining their ghosts. No lights worked in the hall, but it wasn't completely dark. Some light came from the orchestra pit, and more spilled in from an open door at the far end of the hall.

He had toured through palaces smaller than this theater. It seemed a journey. When he reached the door and looked in, at the moment he should have seen the source of the voices and the steady thumping, the voices and all associated sounds vanished. He found a dozen folding chairs arranged in a circle around a smoldering brazier. The still-red embers released tendrils of sepia smoke.

Someone had left an old, cloth-bound book on one of the chairs. It was tied with a cloth ribbon. It felt as old as the bricks themselves, as the wood, as the air in the lower basements. Felipe held the book, looking about the room, searching for a speaker system—though the noises had sounded natural—or another exit. There were shelves, but no doorways, no windows—and if he trusted the plans, no hidden rooms anywhere within the theater. A single bare bulb, turned on and off by a pull string, provided all the light. The string swayed slightly, as though someone had just walked by it.

He didn't open the book until he got home. In his apartment, under sufficient light, with a beautiful view of the city from his balcony, he flipped through it. Pages were devoted to sketches of theaters—his and others. It included symbology he didn't understand, languages he couldn't read.

There was nothing in it he could read, actually, but he vaguely recognized Spanish, French, Latin, and maybe some Chinese.

He left the book on his dining room table when he went to bed. As he slept, he dreamed.

He believed he dreamed.

He believed he dreamt of Maria.

When he woke, the covers were a haphazard mess and the book gone.

9.

The workers found a variety of treasures—loosely defined—while cleaning out the theater. Trash in the form of fast food wrappers, dead lighters, ragged strips of cloth. Abandoned candles, half burned. Chicken bones, presumably the remnants of chicken wings thoroughly gnawed. Random gloves: children's mittens, fancy silk opera gloves, workman's gloves. A surprising number of paperback books, generally well-worn, spines cracked, pages dog-eared and torn. Felipe started a library - for now, just a box in the office—with a vague intention of establishing it outside where anyone could use it.

They also informed Felipe the plans he'd acquired were incomplete.

"There's at least another basement level," one of the contractors told him. "No electric down there, so we haven't done anything yet, and it's a goddamn labyrinth."

After the chairs were ripped out of the theater, the place felt cavernous. Felipe stood in the center of the theater, looked up at the domed ceiling, and imagined himself at the center, or at the edge, of a universe. The mythological figures painted in the ceiling contributed to this image. He'd already consulted with an art restoration company, but now he consulted the Internet and searched for astronomical charts, especially those highlighting the constellations. Though some of the figures corresponded to the constellations, not all of them did, and none of them were arranged in that way.

He hadn't noticed originally, but the cardinal directions were labeled in the theater. The stage faced east. A tile with a very Romanesque E had been fitted directly over the arched doors leading into the auditorium. North and South had been more difficult to locate, having been incorporated into the engraved woodwork that covered most of the walls. West, however, remained elusive. There was no W over the stage, nor in the curtains, nor in the unadorned wood walls backstage.

From the stage, Felipe found no indication of West. Eventually, he wondered if he was too close, so he went up to the loge to get a view of the entire stage, the curtains, everything.

Ignatius found him there. "Do you like what you see?"

"It's amazing, how much of the work that needs doing is superficial," Felipe said. "You said you'd maintained the bones. I think I see that now."

"Not merely the bones," Ignatius said. "It's been only thirteen years since they closed this theater. The shadows have been thick and thickening, so it's good that you've come to return its breath. Noble, even."

Felipe turned to look at Ignatius. The old usher had been nearly unseen since the crews arrived, a virtual shadow himself. Once upon a time, the man might have smiled, and now his expression betrayed the slightest ghost of one. "You were concerned I might tear the whole thing down and start over."

"It's common enough," Ignatius admitted.

"You've lived inside all these years? How did you get food?"

"Don't be absurd," Ignatius said. "The *front* doors were

locked. You know well enough there are other points of ingress."

"The last show," Felipe said. "Was it *Touch of Evil?*"

Ignatius's lips cracked into something resembling a smile. "This is the sixth theater you've acquired and restored. We've been watching you."

"We?"

"The Parliament of Ushers."

And now, Felipe's attention was riveted. The usher didn't elaborate, but obviously knew Felipe had heard the name before. "That's a myth," he said. "A theater myth. It's not real. Like the Rule of Three Candles, or the Phantom." Felipe didn't believe his own words. "You've been watching me?"

"There's something you should see," Ignatius said. He turned and walked to the back of the loge. Beckoned, Felipe followed.

The public face of the theater was simple enough, but the backstage areas were convoluted and serpentine. Ignatius led Felipe to an iron spiral staircase he'd never seen. It was a long, narrow descent. Though hidden, there were eyeholes through which a person might see most of the theater. Almost no light reached them.

At the bottom, they emerged in the corner of a large room, possibly a rehearsal space. Felipe couldn't read its dimensions in the darkness. He hadn't brought a flashlight with him, but Ignatius struck a match and lit three candles on a candelabra. In the flickering light, he looked like he belonged in a silent movie.

A set of doors led to a hallway which twisted and dipped and branched off in multiple directions before they reached another room where two sides were lined by tiered seats so that maybe twenty people could sit around the round marble altar at its center.

More candles topped the altar, but Ignatius did not light

them. There was a ribbon of silk, an ancient pair of wire-rimmed spectacles, a wide-mouthed champagne glass, and a leather-bound book.

His name, Felipe Gris, was embossed on the cover.

As Felipe reached for it, Ignatius asked, "What do you know about the Parliament?"

"Rumors, legends." Felipe opened the book, but the pages were blank. "Caretakers of old opera houses, ghost hunters or ghosts, scaring off children and the homeless."

Ignatius said, simply, "No."

"A religious sect," Felipe added, looking around the room for icons, idols, and crucifixes.

"We maintain the bones, the heart, and the soul," Ignatius said.

"Why is there a blank book with my name on it?"

"I'd like to show you one more thing," Ignatius said. "If you'll come with me."

Felipe left the book and followed. The room seemed to swell, and even pulse, in the flickering candlelight. The hall, too, seemed to breathe, and the walls were warm to the touch. They made several tight turns, ascended a flight of stone steps, and eventually stepped into a vestibule with a small round window. Ignatius gestured to it, so Felipe looked out. A field of shrubbery and statues stood between them and an enormous gleaming edifice glowing against the nighttime sky. "Is that a palace?"

"*Palazio Real*," Ignatius said. "Madrid."

"I don't understand."

"You're trying to apply logic, geometry, and geography to a situation that defies all three."

Felipe looked out onto the palace again. "Did you drug me?"

"Not yet, no. Come, there's more to see."

They returned almost the way they came, making different turns, climbing different stairs, until emerging in another theater. Here, there was a mirror on the stage—never a good thing in a theater—and a small audience watching a magician and his assistant.

Whispering, Felipe said, "This isn't the opera house."

"No."

"Where are we?"

"Perhaps you've seen enough," Ignatius said.

"Show me another," Felipe said. "Show me *The Pitt.*"

Ignatius shook his head. "You know I can't."

"You can't do what you've already done," Felipe said. "What's one more impossible thing?"

"*The Pitt* has fallen."

After that, they watched the performance in silence from the corner of the theater. The magician was competent, but not spectacular; his assistant carried the show, and the audience clapped when appropriate.

After the grand finale, when the lights came up and the audience filed out through two sets of doors, Felipe said, "This theater is falling, isn't it?"

"It is."

"Why are you showing me this?"

"Come," Ignatius said, slipping back into the secret passageways that connected theaters and opera houses and stages throughout the world. They returned, eventually, to the altar room and the book with Felipe's name embossed on the leather.

There, Ignatius left him alone in the dark.

10.

Back home, away from the theater and its shadows and its ushers, Felipe went to his books. He found little about the Parliament of Ushers because there was little to be found. He searched the Internet, but didn't even turn up rumors or innuendo—nothing that didn't seem to directly involve

British government, which was wrong.

He went to bed without learning anything. Sometime around 3am, he woke. A shaft of moonlight and a slight breeze came in through the window. He expected someone to be sitting in the chair at the far side of the bedroom, someone from his past. Maria or another ghost—Janet or Louie, he couldn't be sure. He expected a figure to step out of the shadows and reveal the arcane secrets he'd been looking for, to issue warnings or advice, to seduce him in his bed. But the light of the moon was enough to leave no corner of the room complete hidden, and he was thoroughly alone.

Still, it was hard, in the middle of the night, to shake the certainty someone had been watching him sleep.

He went through his apartment, turning on lights, checking closets and pantries, and finally verified the home alarm had never been turned off. His apartment was, if such a thing could ever be entirely true, safe and secure.

He didn't get back to sleep that night.

In the theater the next morning, before any of the workers arrived, Felipe wandered the halls. The public face of the theater offered little by way of labyrinth, but backstage was a maze runner's dream. He took a flashlight, and over the next several days never entered the theater without one. He found the room with the folding chairs, but not the book. He was sure it held secrets. He found a locked room that hadn't yet been opened, but when he went searching for Ignatius and any potential keys, the man never answered any knock on his door.

Felipe was tempted to break into the usher's apartment, but the glance he'd already gotten convinced him there was nothing to be learned there. Instead, he broke into the locked room. He borrowed one of the workers, and his tools, to take apart the lock. Inside, they found crates of old costumes that had fallen prey to time, moths, who knew what else. A few props, phantom masks and canes and fake revolvers, remained intact. The rest was a pile of memories reduced to dust.

He found alcoves under arches, solid stone statuary in the lowest levels, and plenty of shadows. He got turned around once or twice, but never so thoroughly lost as he had been that day followed Ignatius.

Saturday afternoon, without workers, with only silence echoing through the corridors, he ventured into the tunnels with the flashlight turned off.

It was nearly impossible to see. He guided himself by hand, touching the walls as he walked, and made slow progress. It surprised him, how much there was beneath the theater. Dressing rooms and rehearsal spaces, he'd expected. Offices and storage closets. But he found a room large enough for a stage of its own, and he wondered what other performances might have happened underground. In a coat check, his flashlight revealed empty hangers and cubbyholes and tokens to indicate which was yours. He found an old program for a play called *The King in Blue*, and a ledger with names of patrons who had left their minks and topcoats.

He was familiar with stories of *The King in Yellow*, but this meant nothing to him. Most of the program's cover had faded, and time had pasted the pages together into a single thick plate he couldn't open. The playwright's name was unreadable.

He found a utilitarian kitchen filled with big pots, ladles, and spatulas.

Eventually, he found himself lost, off the map if there had ever been one. He wondered which turn had led him to this new place, wherever it might be—could it be Carnegie Hall or The Globe or Teatro Colon?

Or was he still in his own theater?

He heard footsteps on the stone floor. He found no source with his light. "Hello?" he said. Then: "*Hola? Bonjour? Ni hao?*"

Felipe walked in that direction. He heard voices, a number of them, not raised but speaking in a murmur. These were the types of voices that would share secrets or issue threats. He reached the door, ajar only an inch or two to show the dimmest possible light. He leaned close and listened. Most of the voices were unintelligible, too quiet, masked by languages Felipe didn't understand. One voice rose above the others. "Tuesday next, then." This was met with general assent.

Felipe took a breath and pushed the door open another inch, then another, until he could see the hooded figures seated around a great mahogany table. There were goblets and candles, and a man seated off to the side scribbling in a ledger.

"It's a sacrifice we must make," one of the people said. Hers was a dark voice, old and older, ancient. She turned in Felipe's direction and lifted the hood off her head. Her face was wrinkled, leathery, dry and cracked. Her red lips and green eyes shined in the weak light of the room. She smiled, a slow process of curling her desiccated lips, and said, "We have a visitor."

A dozen hooded faces turned toward Felipe.

The man with the pen and ledger hopped off his chair and swung open the door even as the woman said, without urgency, "Seize him."

Felipe turned to run, but the man, younger, stronger, and faster, caught Felipe by the arm before he managed a single step and dragged him inside. Felipe tried to resist. He might have had better luck escaping the pull of a black hole.

The woman came around the table to see him. Her wire-thin hair was white and utterly lifeless, but she smelled of Shalimar—like Oriental flowers, like youth and beauty. The scribe held him from behind by both arms. Felipe was, essentially, presented for the old woman's scrutiny.

She grabbed his chin, turned his head, sniffed at his

neck, and peered into his eyes. He didn't know what she saw, but he recognized the echo of Aphrodite in her eyes, a hint of who she might have been a century ago. Now, her eyes were icy green, like a rainforest flash frozen in the prime of its verdancy. Her voice sounded like powder. "And tell me, who are you?"

He told her.

"I don't think you belong here," she said.

"I bought the theater," he told her. "I'm restoring it."

"To what?"

"To glory."

It seemed to be the right answer, because she smiled again. He heard the snap of her skin as she did so. But she said, "There is glory, even, in desolation."

Felipe was out of his depth. "While she still maintains her soul," he said, "I would facilitate the effort."

The woman said, "What exactly do you think it is we do, Felipe Gris?"

He shook his head. "I don't know."

"Guess."

"You preserve the theaters."

She laughed. It was not a pleasant noise. It was not a sound of mirth or joy or anything good. "Have you got a background in magic, Felipe Gris?"

"No."

"None whatsoever?"

"No."

The scribe dragged him bodily toward a coffin on the side of the room. It wasn't really a coffin. It was a chest, big enough for a man but the wrong shape. It smelled of fresh pine as Felipe was forced inside. It had seemed big enough, but it was cramped. The lid smacked his head as they closed it. The other men and women whispered as they crowded closer. Felipe protested, but no one seemed to care.

"You might want to learn something," the woman said.

A padlock clicked into place, and all other sounds vanished. Felipe heard his heartbeat, and heard his breathing. It was a terrible time to learn he wasn't good with enclosed spaces. He could barely move his arms and couldn't extend his legs. He tried kicking the side of the chest, but couldn't get any momentum or strength. He had been forced in facedown. There wasn't space enough to flip onto his back. He pushed upwards with all his strength. The solid lid gave maybe half an inch, but it was something. He pushed again. The lock was strong, the wood was solid. The chest wasn't going to break open.

Felipe took a breath. Tried to calm himself. She'd said something about magic. Houdini had escaped from worse than this. There must be a way. A lever, maybe. He probed the edges of the chest with his fingers, and found a small key.

Even pushing the lid as far open as it would go, he couldn't reach the padlock. He couldn't search the inside of the chest with his flashlight, either. There just wasn't enough room to get it and use it. No longer panicking, sure he had a means of escape in hand, he sought a keyhole.

It was inside the lid next to the padlock. He wasn't a contortionist, so it proved difficult to insert the key without losing it. Twisting, he released the upper plate where the padlock was fastened. He pushed the lid open, rose like a monster gulping its first breath, and faced an empty room.

A few candles had been left burning on the table, but there was nothing else.

The magic trick hadn't been his escape; it had been their disappearance.

11.

Felipe's flashlight was dead. He took one of the candles so he could maneuver through the theater's underground. He didn't know where he was, not precisely—not even remotely—and he couldn't possibly retrace steps he'd made in utter darkness. But he set out with an intention: to return to his own Palace Theater.

Cold wafted through the tunnels. He felt thirsty and hungry and weak, but he pushed forward. He hadn't been underground for more than two hours.

At one point, he heard the drip drip drip of water. He heard mechanical movements like exaggerated gears inside a clock. Around certain corners, he detected a trace of honey in the air, or vanilla, and in one place was nearly knocked down by a thick jasmine aroma that disappeared as quickly as it had appeared.

He climbed steps, sometimes two or three at a time, sometimes an entire floor. He opened doors and travelled halls unseen in an age. The color of the bricks shifted in places. The flooring changed, brick here, dirt there, tile, gravel, even glass. He brushed through dry webs hanging limply from the ceilings. He put all his strength and weight into forcing open a door. He was thoroughly lost. That seemed to be the way to get home again.

Through one door, he saw a troupe of actors running lines, all wearing capes, all wearing masks. He didn't recognize the language. The masks were white, porcelain, featureless except around the eyes where geometric eyeshadow matched the color of their capes. A woman in orange broke character when she saw him. The others seemed not to notice as she backed out of the circle and approached Felipe at the door.

She removed her mask.

Her face was a patchwork of scars, her skin almost rust in

color, her eyes flecked in amber, and her smile a cubism nightmare. She said something. He didn't understand the words. She touched his cheek. She wore orange satin gloves, and even through the fabric her fingers were like icicles.

Felipe backed away and her smile faltered. She asked something, and asked again with anger. When she lifted her hand again, she thrust a long, thin dagger at him.

Felipe fled.

She did not follow.

Through another room, he found a library. It was old, all the books were old, and every shelf was draped in dust-flecked cobwebs. The room was two stories high, every shelf from floor to ceiling crammed with books. Three tables occupied the room, with three chairs around each. On one of those tables, Felipe found the cloth-bound book. This time, he was able to decipher the title embossed on the cover: *Parliament of Ushers.*

Briefly, he went through the book. The symbols inside, the amalgamation of languages, confirmed it was unquestionably the book he'd found before.

Six corridors fed into the library, one from each of its six walls. Three had closed doors. One had an open door. The other two, including the one he'd entered through, had only doorways. Reasonably sure he was alone, Felipe went down the other doorless corridor. It seemed, through that attribute, to be somehow connected.

He didn't know where he was going.

Finally, he reached a door that entered a theater, but it wasn't his. The rows of seats were upholstered in black with gold trim. The curtains were the same. Everything else, however, was decrepit, rotting or missing, scarred and scratched. Graffiti covered the walls. Half the chandelier was missing. There was nothing on stage, but after a moment the faces of the audience turned their heads, one by one, to look at him at the side of the orchestra section. Their eyes all glittered redly. When someone near him smiled, it only barely resembled humanity. The teeth gave them away. Those were predators' teeth. Wolfish. Tinged with blood.

Felipe went back the way he came, twisting through corridors until he was dizzy, until he was exhausted. Finally, on a stone bench in one of the hallways, Felipe set down the candle and then sat himself. His legs ached. His eyes burned. Every muscle welcomed the respite, however brief it might be.

In the middle of this hall, he listened to the sound of the single candle flame flickering. The blood pumping through his ears. The whisper of a distant wind. The rattle of chimes, the beat of a lonely drum, a soprano's voice so distant it was merely a dream. Footsteps. A woman sighing. A woman sitting next to him on the bench and saying, "Hello, Felipe Gris."

He barely had to look at her. How many years, how many decades had passed since he'd left The Pitt Theater? "Hello, Maria."

Maria snuffed the candle. She took his hand. She led him through the darkness, through a door, into a plush greenroom meant for a featured performer. Dim golden lights dripped from the ceiling. She sat Felipe on a plush emerald couch before a table filled with bowls of fruits and nuts and a bottle of champagne on ice. She said, "I was expecting you." She popped the cork, poured two wide-mouthed champagne glasses, and handed one to Felipe.

He said something, or meant to say something, but she touched his lips with a finger and shushed him and said, "They'll be another time for words." Then she sipped her champagne, and kissed him with champagne lips, and laid him back on the couch to strip him.

They made slow, gentle, and exhausting love on that couch. They dozed intertwined, and when they woke explored each other again. She was no longer the teenaged girl in the theater. He was no longer the thirteen year old boy. She fed him strawberries and grapes and macadamias, they dozed some more, and as they made love a third time, someone rapped three times on the door. "Five minutes to show time!"

For a moment, they looked at each other. Felipe saw all the essentials for life in Maria's eyes: magic, mystery, romance, passion. He wondered what she saw in his. She said, "This is not a performance we want to witness." She dressed quickly. He dressed slowly.

When she picked up the book, he grabbed it, too, and said, "This is mine."

She looked down at the book, then into his eyes. She smiled and kissed his lips and said, "If that's what you believe." She released the book. "Now, hurry. We don't want to be here when they knock on that door again."

A minute later, they were fifty meters down the hall when someone knocked on that door again and said, "Showtime."

She led him through the darkness as though she could see. She made definitive and deliberate turns at intersections, opened doors without any hint of hesitation. Every time he tried to ask a question, she said, "Don't spoil it."

"Where...?"

"Don't spoil it."

"Why...?"

"Don't spoil it."

"How...?"

She pressed her finger to his mouth and smooshed his lips in. "Stop."

Another turn revealed a distant light. Here, she let go of his hand. "Go," she said. "You'll find me again later, I'm sure. Next time, we'll have wine and words." She sealed the promise with a kiss and disappeared into the darkness.

Felipe stumbled forward on his own, toward the lights of

his theater's basement. He knew these halls and these doors, and he knew those stairs led to the backstage. But when he got there, he didn't see what he expected.

Work had been done.

The backstage was lit in a way it had never been before, and there were people in costumes, some twirling and some running and some mouthing words they read from script pages.

Felipe made his way to the stage and saw the chandelier shining pristine and polished, the rows of seats fully upholstered, the walls gleaming with carven images of Greek heroes and Shakespearean tragedies. In the audience sat a handful of assistants orbiting a director.

Someone tapped Felipe's shoulder. When he turned, it was one of the contractors. "Good to see you again, sir," he said. "But I think we should get off the stage before they do their final rehearsal."

Felipe and the contractor left the stage. "When did you finish all the work?"

"Only yesterday," the contractor said. "But I'll be staying on as a kind of consultant."

"Will you?"

The contractor gave him a look. "Ignatius said you insisted."

"Of course I did," Felipe said. "I'm just—it's early, isn't it?"

"Not really."

"How long has it been? Since I was last here?"

The contractor frowned. "Three or four weeks, I think. Are you okay, Mr. Gris?"

12.

Twenty-four days.

Looking at his calendar in his office, checking his e-mail and messages, Felipe discovered he'd lost twenty-four days.

During that time, work had progressed exactly as planned, with Ignatius taking point when necessary. Everything had been completed on a quickened schedule, a troupe of actors had been hired, and a play was set to debut tomorrow night: *The King in Red.*

He knocked on the door to Ignatius's apartment, but the usher didn't answer.

The contractor, Greg, merely shrugged his shoulders. "Nothing to do with that."

Felipe wandered the backstage, stepping around the actors and the stagehands, but stopped to speak with the director. "Have you seen Ignatius?"

"A bit busy here," the director said.

"I own this place."

"Ah, well, in that case," the director said, "I am. A bit. *Busy.* Curtain rises tomorrow, and we cannot disappoint."

It was midday on a Monday. Felipe tried to get a copy of the script, but found only parts stapled together for the individual actors. Each included pages with that actor's lines, and none included the third act. Felipe took the pages he'd gathered and retreated to his office, where he could be out of the way. He pieced together what he could, but was missing more than half the script. Something about a new arrival, a stranger to the court, and plenty of gossip about the king and his mistresses. Doorways and portals and madness and an apothecary with wicked intentions.

Felipe could make no sense of it. He gave up on the script and returned to the book he'd retrieved in the theatrical underworld. He leafed through the pages, sure it contained some sort of revelation.

And finally, he found a page he could comprehend.

He couldn't read the words except for the title, *The King in Yellow*, but the *yellow* had been crossed out in another pen and three other words had been scribbled there. *Modrý. Azul*, which he recognized as *blue*. And finally *rouge*.

Red.

A compass rose had been sketched in the bottom corner of the page, with West the only cardinal point labeled—and facing straight up, where you normally found North. There was also a series of little stars, perhaps in the shape of some mysterious constellation, and a theatrical mask—like comedy and tragedy, but different, neither a frown nor a smile but a straight line, and eyes that seemed almost emotionless. There was a word beneath it written in letters Felipe had never seen.

There was a whole paragraph, in an old, tight cursive, so small the meaning had faded. Was it Latin?

Someone knocked on his office door. She didn't wait for an answer but pushed it open. "Are you Mr. Gris?"

"Felipe," he said. "And you are?"

"Reina," she said, shutting the door behind her. "I play the king."

"Not the queen?"

She shrugged and said, "Genders." Then she said, "I saw you before, trying to, y'know, figure out the play." She nodded toward the pages on his desk. "We've all been wondering the same thing."

"What thing?"

"The third act."

"What about it?"

"Have you read it?"

Felipe gestured toward the pages. "I don't have the third act."

"That's just it," Reina said. "There is no third act."

"Maybe there's not supposed to be."

"Then why would there be a second intermission?"

Good question. Felipe knew nothing about a second intermission.

"I'm supposed to be the *star*," Reina said, "but I think Todd's got something else planned."

"Todd?"

She dropped back into one of the empty chairs. The chair sighed for her. She said, "The *director*," as if it was a burden.

"I don't know anything about your play," Felipe admitted. "I...didn't know we were putting it on until earlier today."

"I would think, being the money man, you might pay a bit more attention to what goes on around here," Reina said. "I hoped you'd know something, like if there was another troupe of actors for the third act. But I supposed you don't know jack, do you?"

"That's about it."

"That's too bad," she said. Then: "You're cute, but I prefer men with something more in the skull cave, y'know what I mean?"

She was half his age. "I'll...try to get over it."

"No worries, Mr. Gris," she said. "*Felipe.*" She hopped to her feet. "Anyways, I hope you enjoy the play tomorrow. I make a killer king, I really do, and maybe I'll see you at the after party."

"Maybe."

She was already gone.

Felipe closed the book. He sighed. He finally got up and left his office, but the theater was empty. The cast and crew had left. As he approached the stage, someone clicked off the house lights. The chandelier continued to sparkle above him, reflecting every other light—the Exit lights, the backstage lights that spilled onstage, the lights from the orchestra pit. It was like a three dimensional model of the heavens, all those stars breaking through the darkness, casting their prismatic lights—in the form of little rainbows—throughout the theater.

There wasn't anything left to do, really, except return the next day for the premiere performance of *The King in Red*.

13.

All seats were sold, orchestra, loge, and balconies, though a balcony had been reserved for Felipe and his guest. Another had been reserved for Ignatius. Chaos reigned backstage. Stagehands ran this way and that, assistants wrangled the actors, musicians polished their brass. The director sat on a couch with his fingers tented before him. It was hours before the show.

Ignatius sat alone in his balcony for two. The rest of the seats were empty.

Ignatius sat virtually motionless. Felipe watched him from below. There were other ushers, in entirely different uniforms, marching up and down the aisles, preparing for their part in the performance. It seemed ludicrous to assume any of them were members of the Parliament of Ushers. Ignatius, and the hooded ushers underground, carried a sense of stoicism, a rigidity built upon a foundation of secret traditions and ceremonies. Many of these were teenagers, maybe college kids, ill-fitted in black pants and black shirts that barely constituted a uniform. But every once in a while, one or more of them would sneak a glance at Ignatius in his balcony, a quick glance before hurrying away to do whatever else it was they needed to do.

People manned the concession booth and the box office. A crowd already gathered outside. At one point, there had been roughly a thousand seats inside, though that may have changed during renovations. How had so much happened without Felipe here to oversee it?

He let himself into his office. He hadn't usually kept it

locked, but with the public milling about, someone—possibly Ignatius—had deemed it appropriate. He still had the book. Someone had removed his script pages from the room but left a dozen copies of the program. Felipe sat as he leafed through one.

Advertisements for local businesses. A cast list, Reina as the King at the very top. The director was listed, and Felipe was given special thanks as the proprietor. There was no listing for Ignatius.

The description of the play was brief: *Thought lost to time, original pages of The King in Red were rediscovered under an old Detroit theater. This wasn't anything like The Gris Theater, but a simple collection of chairs around a stage with a single spotlight, an unscrupulous manager, and a man called Raz dealing scarlet out of a backroom. The opening performance was interrupted when a drug deal went wrong. Raz and the manager were both shot and killed. Also, tragically, the King in Red himself, Phillip Bass, was caught in the crossfire. He bled out onstage at what was meant to be the start of the third act. The King in Red script had been found in its basements, and would have been left to molder, disintegrate, and probably disappear during the subsequent demotion if an usher calling himself Algernon hadn't saved the pages and passed them on to an art history student at Wayne State University. After that, the story gets twisted and mysterious, but it ends tonight, at the newly refurbished Gris Theater, with a true premier performance of The King in Red.*

A lot of that, most if not all of that, was meaningless to Felipe, but in the back of his mind he wondered if he had met Algernon. Perhaps he had been underground and under hood, but Felipe had to wonder how the play had gotten all the way from Detroit to his theater—which he had never intended to call *The Gris*. It already had a name. If Algernon had been, as the program said, just a name he allowed people to call him, it didn't require much of a stretch to make the same assumption about a name like Ignatius.

When Felipe left his office, the audience had already been allowed in. A crowd of people were buying wine at the bar and chocolates at the concession stand and otherwise milling about waiting for the theater doors to open. Ushers stood like guards at each of these doors.

Felipe went upstairs to the balcony level. He found Ignatius's box and entered. Ignatius looked down on the stage, as though watching a spectral performance only he could see. Felipe sat in the other chair. "I've never heard of *The King in Red.*"

"In some circles," Ignatius said, "it's as legendary as *The King in Blue.*"

"I don't know that one, either."

"It's rumored to have had a single performance in New York," Ignatius said. "Not at a theater, but on the City Hall subway platform."

"That's...strange."

"Indeed."

Felipe waited for more. When nothing more came, he said, "Why *The King in Red?*"

"You'd have to ask the director."

"But I'm asking you."

Ignatius turned toward him. "It's an old play, written in the eighteenth century by a madman, performed one time and then hidden away after the main actor died midway through his performance."

"That happened twice?"

Ignatius shook his head. "The play went on, anyhow. The madman rewrote entire parts as the play went on. He interrupted the actors. He ingested hemlock on stage, presumably as part of the show, and died at the start of the third act."

"What happened after that?"

"All copies of the play were burned, the theater was burned, the audience dispersed, and no one ever admitted to having been there."

"And it happened again in Detroit?" Felipe asked.

"I doubt it," Ignatius said. "If you understand the nature of stories and legends, you'll realize *The King in Red* has built a reputation largely on whispers and shadows."

"There is no reputation," Felipe said.

"Because you're familiar with every play every penned by the hands of men or gods?"

"I didn't say..."

"The story behind the story *is* part of the story," Ignatius said. "If they ever truly put it on in Detroit, I'm sure they had a story about its spectacular failure in Cincinnati. And they, before them, told of a ruinous night in 1871 Chicago that ended with fire."

"Where was I for twenty-four days?"

Ignatius smiled at that, if the slight crease of his lips could be said to resemble a smile. "A great many people wonder at that. But the work got done."

"And the theater was re-named?"

"Only colloquially. The marquee still proclaims it *The Palace*."

Felipe had other questions, but they crumbled away. The usher wasn't really revealing much of anything. He started to get up, but paused and asked one more question. "Why did you show me those other theaters?"

"We thought you might understand," Ignatius said. "But you lost your way."

"I lost three weeks."

"The labyrinthine connections between the theaters unifies the physical constructs into a single body that spans the globe," Ignatius said. "But there are other connections, other mazes that must be traversed, and it's enough to simply walk from *The Palace* to *The Globe*. Think of the mazes as the veins of the earth, feeding the body of collective humanity. When one vessel is corrupted, another must be made to provide vitality to that part of the body or it will wither or die."

Felipe was shaking his head. "Your metaphor is getting a little out of control."

"Remember *The Pitt*," Ignatius said. "It persisted even after its decay, but it wasn't really tainted, it wasn't truly lost, until murder."

"I thought it was a suicide," Felipe said.

Ignatius shrugged.

"You've been watching me since then?"

"No," Ignatius said. "I don't watch *people*. I watch auditoriums and concert halls, arenas and opera houses, barns and drive-ins and assembly halls. I care for *theaters*, Felipe Gris, not *people*. Now, you should take your seat and enjoy the performance. *The King in Red* should be a rare treat, and you should not leave your guest alone for it."

"My guest?" Felipe couldn't clearly see his balcony, but now that he looked beyond the usher, he realized the theater had started to fill up. Its audience had arrived. Ignatius adjusted, turning away from Felipe, almost turning his back on him, so that he could better survey the audience instead.

Felipe thought about asking something else, but couldn't compose anything useful, so he left. A short walk down the hall took him to his private balcony, another two-seater, where Maria waited.

14.

When he sat, Maria took his hand. "I was beginning to think you wouldn't show."

"What are you doing here?"

"That's the question you ask?"

"I lost time under the theaters."

"Time is a slippery thing. You're lucky."

"Lucky?"

"You might have lived a lifetime within the basements and emerged the same afternoon, old and decrepit, dazzled and destroyed."

"Am I destroyed anyway?"

"Is that what you think?"

"What's going on?"

She held up a copy of the program and pointed to the title. "*The King in Red*, apparently. You're much braver than I expected."

"Why's that?"

"There have been twelve attempts to perform this play," Maria said. "All of them ended in blood."

"What happened back at *The Pitt?*"

She smiled and squeezed his hand. "You've had over twenty years to figure that out. You tell me what happened."

"We broke into a theater."

"*My* theater, don't forget."

"Why are you here now?"

She shook her head and smiled sadly. "The Parliament of Ushers is watching you."

"You're not one of them?"

"Me? Of course not."

She was more beautiful than he remembered, but no more forthcoming than Ignatius. He asked, "Then why are you telling me?"

"Why do you assume it will end in blood?"

"*The King in Red.*"

She smiled again. "Sometimes, you do manage to surprise me. But it's too late now, the show is about to start." She turned to the stage as the lights dimmed.

Reina, the King, strode out to center stage. She looked onto the audience, left and right, up and down, then declared, "You will make for a mighty country."

It didn't get better after that.

Actors stumbled onto the stage, delivered their lines, received the expected laughter and the occasional gasp of shock. As King, Reina dominated the stage. She wasn't good, but she was by far the best of the lot. She owned every step, she delivered her lines as though they were spontaneous.

Halfway through the first act, as the King looked out at her subjects, the audience, a new character rushed out from backstage. He wasn't costumed in the same faux finery, but wore a disheveled three-piece suit and a hat. "Wait!" he yelled. "Stop! There's been a change!"

Everyone stopped. Everyone waited. He handed Reina a page from the script—presumably a new page. She looked down at it and frowned, then spoke directly to the audience. "There's been a murder!"

"Whose murder?" one of the other actors asked.

She looked expectantly at the man in the suit—the writer, presumably, albeit another actor in the play. He handed her another page. "You'll have to forgive the manner of my appearance," he said to the audience, "but I've only just now learned how this play is meant to end."

"With murder?" Reina asked, reading up and down that new page. "*Mine?*"

A swordsman drove his blade through her back. It emerged bloody and red, like her cape, like her gloves.

Felipe started, but Maria squeezed his hand and whispered, "I don't think there's anything you can do for her now."

It wasn't fake blood, and the blade hadn't been a trick prop. The tip glinted in the spotlight. The writer watched the swordsman, disarmed now, run off stage, then said to Reina, "Stand, stand, stay on your feet, Your Highness. Stand and rule."

Felipe had not seen this in the pages he'd read yesterday. The audience, for its part, had gotten very quiet. He still heard the swordsman running further and deeper into the basements. He glanced toward Ignatius, but couldn't see the usher. Felipe said, "I can't just sit here," and pulled his hand out of Maria's grip.

She followed him out of the balcony. The hall was quiet, dark, but not unoccupied. They might have been ushers earlier, but now they were additional assassins, all armed with blades not as long as the onstage sword but just as sharp and just as real. From either side of the balcony entrance, they turned toward him and, though their faces were obscured by smears of black and red makeup, met Felipe's eyes with all kinds of threats.

Only three actors played assassins, according to the program.

Maria whispered, "Probably best if we sit."

Sitting was the last thing Felipe wanted to do. But the two nearest assassins—he saw at least three more to either side—advanced, blades dripping—maybe poison, maybe blood. Felipe said, quite loudly, "Fine," then retreated into the box.

Onstage, Reina was down to her knees, staring at the blade, tears streaming down her cheeks, all her makeup ruined and running. The audience cheered. They were on their feet, enraptured, enthralled, giving the strongest, longest, most devastating ovation of a lifetime.

Other actors on stage didn't seem to know what to do. The man playing the writer—maybe actually the writer, who could say?—moved between them, sharing words, thrusting pages at them.

Reina let loose with a mighty scream. It was hard to know how she pulled the breath for it. The applause dropped. The writer paused and looked at her. One of the actors ran behind the curtain. Everyone staring at her as she panted and gasped. Looking more beautiful than she'd ever been, Reina—no longer acting—said, "Don't let me die here."

Felipe met Maria's eyes. She was—surprised? concerned? confused? resigned?—she was not moving, not reacting, not doing much of anything except providing an anchor to hold Felipe in place.

But Felipe refused.

He couldn't go back through the hall, but he couldn't stay in the balcony. He shook free of Maria's hands again— she'd taken his without him realizing—and climbed over the balcony's edge. Curtains ran down the wall, from ceiling to floor, thicker stronger curtains than might have been in place when *The Palace* had originally been constructed. He used them like a rock climber, grabbing fistfuls, lowering himself carefully, bracing his feet against the wall behind them.

Halfway down, one of the other spotlights clicked on and found him. It made the descent easier. He dropped the last few feet, landing in the aisle on the side of the theater next to a teenaged usher who stared at him like a puppy. The kid looked strong but dumbstruck, and his eyes were like a deer's as the spotlight lingered.

Felipe grabbed him by the arm. "C'mon." He dragged the usher toward the stage.

From the audience, a scattered clapping followed him, but most were silent as Felipe ran up the steps, usher behind him, and across the stage. He knelt beside Reina. She looked at him. She looked at him with sad, brilliant eyes, the shadows around them sparkling in the spotlight. She clutched his hand. With his other, he held her head steady.

"Get back," the teenaged usher said to someone.

"But I have your lines."

Reina smiled. "I knew it would be you. Of all of them. Who would answer when I called." She said it loud enough for the audience to hear. A moment later, the curtains swung closed, and the audience erupted into applause as Reina kissed Felipe full on the mouth.

Then she got up, yanking two pieces of the prop sword away. She gave Felipe a smile, then squeezed and released his hand. "I really meant it."

"Meant what?" Felipe asked.

"All of it."

And with that, the first act of *The King in Red* concluded.

15.

Felipe was ushered out of the backstage area. Todd, the director, would have started yelling at him, but the playwright—or the actor playing the playwright—tried to pull him aside and pointed at script pages still wet with ink.

"I don't care if you *own* the place," Todd said.

"I do."

"What did I just say?"

And Felipe was thrust, without ceremony, into the public area of the theater, where mingling theatergoers carried wine and champagne and canapes. He went upstairs, to the balconies, and found no assassins. His private balcony was empty; his guest, Maria, had gone. Ignatius's balcony was also empty.

Felipe surveyed the faces below him in the theater, searching for any that were familiar. He felt on the verge of frantic. He had believed Reina was bleeding on the stage. Real blood. Real sword. Real wound. But none of it was, and he didn't understand how. He hadn't slept well, or had slept too well, over the past twenty-something days, and it was catching up with him.

He retreated to his office. It was the calmest, quietest room aboveground, except perhaps Ignatius's private apartment. He leafed quickly through the program, and read some of the quotes. *Blood so real, I thought the King was*

truly dead, said one critic. And under that, in the smallest
typeface: *Too bad about the third act.*

The lights flicked off and on. Felipe gave up on the
program, ventured out among the crowd, and made his way
back to his balcony. There, on a small table beside the two
chairs, was an open bottle of champagne and two glasses.
Maria had just poured them. She smiled. She said, "That was
a very brave thing to do. Almost valiant. I didn't know you
had a role in the play."

"She was dying," Felipe said.

"Is she dead?:

"No. No, not at all, it wasn't real."

"She's quite good, then," Maria said, handing Felipe one
of the glasses. She clinked, and drank, and glared at Felipe
until he took a sip. It tasted extraordinarily sweet. In the
orchestra section, and on the loge, people were returning to
their seats. The lights blinked one last time. From the
orchestra pit, unseen, a single violin took up where the music
had left off at the end of the first act.

"Who is she?" Felipe asked. "Who are *they?*"

Maria shook her head. "You ask the wrong questions."

"How do the halls underground lead to theaters in
Madrid and Sydney and Chicago?"

She shrugged. "The god of mazes and mysteries
designed the underground. You'd have to ask him."

"Will you answer anything?"

"Drink," Maria said, "and let's enjoy the show. I want to
see if the King really dies."

The lights dimmed. The curtains opened. Reina knelt at
center stage. She looked out onto the crowd, up to the loge,
to the balconies on one side then the other. She met Felipe's
eyes. He saw fear. He saw trembling. He saw a performance
well beyond the ability of any of the other players.

Reina announced to the audience, "Kings do not die so
easily. A sword? Ha! A sword coated in poison? Ha! It will

take more than that, more than a mere assassin, to throw off the balance of a king and her kingdom."

The play went on. The playwright interrupted again, surprising an actor during his monologue. "There are greater truths," the man was in the middle of saying. The writer gave him new pages.

"This," he said. "This is what you must say, because we've lost someone."

The actor scanned the page. "This?" he asked. "Instead of that brilliant monologue?"

"You and I, and all the world," and here the playwright indicated the audience, "know those words were written by a baboon."

Halfway through the second act, Maria leaned close and whispered, "This is objectively terrible. I blame the actors."

"I blame the writing."

"At least there's one standout performance."

At that moment, Reina strode back onto the stage in full red regalia. A tremendous, brass-heavy fanfare accompanied her. The actors on stage cheered, the audience cheered, even the teenaged ushers briefly joined in. Felipe, however, held back, and Maria merely squeezed his knee.

"Enemies on all sides of me," the King announced. "My family: vipers. My friends: ogres and witches, every one of them. My subjects—oh, my very kingdom, my life's blood, my reason for breathing—infiltrated by schemers, connivers, liars, madmen, poets, and thieves. You're an abomination. A blight on these, the last days of my dynasty."

"I can help you," a voice said from offstage.

"And who are you?"

A fresh actor walked onto the stage, a man in flowing white with heavy eye shadow and bright red lips. "I am a humble servant, but I know the words."

"The words?"

"Words of deliverance."

"I would give my kingdom for its deliverance."

"Oh, you shall." Then he laughed, and all the lights on the stage went dark except the spotlight on him. He recited words, strange and unnatural syllables, not from any modern language. The words were coated with dust, layers of death and decay, mold and rot and ichor.

The actors, the members of the court and the King herself, poured out from the shadows to grasp the humble servant by his legs and arms, to put arms around his chest and drag him back from the audience. They tried to put hands over his mouth, but he continued to speak.

"Spare us!" Reina, the King, cried out before a terrible crash of cymbals and the thunderous roll of the timpani.

A tinkling came from above the stage—above the audience—from the chandelier, a thousand tiny shards of crystal and filaments of light. It sparkled and sang like bells, and it trembled. The audience gasped as one. Reina cried out, reached out, struggled to free herself from arms that now held her back as well as the servant. With another crash of cymbals, the chandelier shuddered. With another crash of cymbals, the theater lights darkened further, and all that remained was a chandelier glowing like a thousand stars in the night sky.

Then the orchestra crashed into silence. The humble servant reached the end of his litany. The actors trying to restrain him gave up their efforts and slipped soundlessly into the darkness. The curtains behind Felipe parted as a third person stepped like a whisper into the private balcony; Felipe saw the movement in his peripheral vision.

One of the assassins carried a thin blade as long as Felipe's forearm.

The chandelier vibrated and swirled. Smoke drifted around it, reaching in and reaching out, reaching for the balconies and the loge and even the musicians in the orchestra. Lightning flashed within a void opening over the chandelier.

The assassin struck, plunging the knife through the back of the seat, straight into Felipe's heart had he not moved. He spun, but the blade cut him anyway—slashing, rather than burying itself in his heart. Maria receded into the dark. The assassin vanished as quickly. On stage, Reina screamed. It was the only sound in the theater as the vortex widened and tendrils of smoke entangled the audience.

The cut in his side burned and bled. Felipe tumbled over the front of the balcony, crashing through tendrils of ash and smoke, bouncing off an unsuspecting woman in pearls. The thunder that followed came from somewhere other than the timpani, somewhere more distant, somewhere more fragile. It shook *The Palace, The Gris Theater* if you preferred, from its highest towers and spires to its lowest, deepest dungeons.

Reina's scream gave permission to everyone else. A deafening noise rose from the audience, from the walls, from the spinning maelstrom Felipe found himself staring into while on his back.

"It's alright!" the writer called from the stage. "This is in the script!"

Reina knelt at Felipe's side. She leaned low to be heard over the noise. "Can you move?"

"I think so."

She helped him sit up. He could barely keep his eyes off the portal above them. As it hauled in members of the audience, it released winged horsemen and gray dead kings and evil sorcerers from forgotten ages.

"Can you close it?" Reina asked.

"How?"

"It's *your* theater," she told him.

He had no idea how to close the portal. The humble servant laughed from the stage, pieces of the chandelier cracked and broke apart and whirled in the ether, and darkness shot through it like beams of light, devouring whatever it touched.

Reina hooked an arm under Felipe's to help him to his feet. She supported most of his weight. "We have to get out of here."

"The tunnels," Felipe said.

"We'll be safe there?"

"I don't know that," Felipe said, "but we'll be away from here."

To escape the theater, they tumbled inelegantly into the orchestra pit. They descended into the basements, rounding corners and throwing open doors at random, until they burst into a room occupied by hooded figures seated around a great mahogany table.

16.

"Felipe Gris."

She lowered her hood, revealing familiar green eyes and red lips on a desert of a face. "What have you allowed?"

"*Allowed?*"

She slapped him with an iron palm. He felt the red she left on his cheek. Reina cowered behind him, not as though he might protect her—he was physically incapable of protecting anyone—as though she might hide in his shadow. But shadows under the theater worked differently than those under the light of the sun.

"Go back," she told him, "and see to your theater. Prove your worth."

"I don't know how..."

Behind him, Reina whispered, "The third act."

The cultists—the Parliament?—faded into the tunnels, into the darkness and the light, into the dirt of the floor and the cracks of the walls. The ancient woman stared at him through all this, until all of them were gone, until she herself had vanished, though the eyes lingered longest.

Felipe took a breath to gather courage and resolve. He didn't know what he was going to do, what he had to do, what he could possibly accomplish, but he said, "Come on."

"We'll die," Reina said.

"If we must."

"It was just supposed to be a role," Reina said. "My first lead role. My big break. After this, I was supposed to find Broadway."

"Maybe you still will." Already, Felipe headed back, toward the theater and toward the stage, toward Maria and the assassins and the interdimensional eddy that had been brought to life over the thousand crystal lights of the chandelier.

The storm inside the theater howled. The musicians had fled, abandoning instruments and scores. The conductor's baton looked most like a weapon, so Felipe snatched it off the floor before climbing out of the orchestra pit. Reina rose behind him, the two of them like warriors into the tempest. Wind buffeted him. Some of the audience sat rapt in their seats, unable to move, unable to take their eyes off the performance.

On the stage behind Felipe, the playwright said, "And thus begins the third act of *The King in Red,* as the king returns with her chosen hero to face all the demons of Hell!"

Felipe stared into the face of the abyss. Surrounded by the stars and constellations and images from lost mythologies on the ceiling, the abyss stared back with elusive eyes and ragged teeth. He turned to Reina. "Says something regal."

"I'm just an actor."

"You're the King in Red," Felipe told her. "Be the king."

Someone in the audience screamed and ran from his seat. The abyss plucked him out of the aisle with a murky tendril. Lightning flashed. Thunder roared. The curtains tried to tear themselves free of their bindings. The playwright clutched script pages in his hands and ranted about equations and prophecies and sleeping giants.

"I am your King!" Reina yelled up at the maelstrom. It thundered in response, so she raised her voice. "I am your sovereign! Bow before me, your King, your Queen, your Emperor, and your God!"

The maelstrom roared. A tentacle launched from it, a thick sinewy thing of nightmarish ooze. Felipe got in the way, thrusting the baton forth as though it might actually do something. *And it did.* The tentacle receded. The baton tingled in his hands. The King, behind him, continued her soliloquy. "I have ruled this kingdom for all of your life, and I shall rule it until you are nothing but ash and dust!"

"You're adlibbing!" the playwright cried from the stage. The orchestra pit separated them, but he had a gun in his hand now, something heavy and metallic and filled with deadly lead.

Felipe turned the baton on the playwright like a magic wand.

"The King in Red perseveres!" Reina yelled. "And you are nothing but an empty, vacuous, shell of a memory!"

The gun went red with heat and the playwright tossed it aside. The edge of the baton glimmered and winked like magical sequins.

A voice emanated from the abyss above the chandelier. Dark, booming, deep, it scratched the lowest reaches of the souls of all who heard. Members of the audience fainted dead away. Paint throughout the theater curled and dissipated. Blood streamed from Felipe's nose. The voice said, "But mother, we are so very ravenous."

Reina turned away from the abyss, tears streaming down her face, her makeup smeared and frightening, her eyes wide and pale. "Oh, God, it thinks I'm its mother!"

"You are!" the playwright cried, stepping to the very edge

of the orchestra pit. "And for our third act, your children will feed upon the very earth and all its souls."

By instinct alone, Felipe whipped the baton back and threw it, like a knife, at the playwright. It struck the center of his belly and protruded there. Briefly, the playwright looked down at it. Turning his eyes back to Felipe, he grinned — then toppled forward, plunging into the orchestra pit at its greatest height.

"Consume another world!" Reina commanded. "Leave this one forever!"

It used its voice again. It was a choir, a legion, a tenebrous abomination, shattering glass sconces up and down the walls of the theater, shattering all the remaining crystals of the chandelier, shattering bones and eyes and brains and spirits. "As you wish, *mother.*"

The smoke, wind, and tendrils of darkness retreated into the maelstrom, dragging whatever last audience members and actors it could. It reached for Reina even as it receded, but she stepped into Felipe's arms and out of its reach. The pressure in the theater shifted as the tempest closed in on itself, popping ears and the last pieces of glass that had been left untouched.

Reina slumped unconscious in Felipe's arms.

On stage, the remaining actors staggered like broken marionettes. A piece of wood fell from the front of the stage, landing on the timpani, bouncing in a final kind of drumroll that signaled the end of the third act. *The King in Red* concluded. The houselights flickered, but mostly failed to come alive. Applause rippled through the audience. A standing ovation. Felipe carried Reina out of the theater, away from the audience, into his office. He laid her down on the couch, wiped blood from her face — his blood, still dripping from his nose. When he left the room, he locked the door and went straight up to the balconies.

The usher was nowhere to be found.

His own private balcony remained empty.

Down in the orchestra pit, he retrieved the conductor's baton, which lay bloodily on the floor between folding chairs that would have been used by flutists and oboe players. They had been disturbed, but the playwright—or his body—was gone.

17.

As clocks throughout the city struck 3am, Felipe sat in a folding chair onstage. He looked out on the theater, the mess of restored wood and gold leaf and red upholstery. The audience had gone, the survivors somehow believing the whole thing had been some sort of performance—which of course it was, even if it had also been entirely real and unscripted, playwright be damned. One of the stagehands had cleaned the fake blood from the stage. The shredded curtains, the damaged seats, the shattered chandelier hadn't given any of the audience pause.

The cast and crew had laughed and joked with each other, what cast and crew remained, and had cleaned not just the blood but all other remnants of the play. Greg, the contractor, had said there'd be a lot of work to do before the next performance, which was already scheduled for next weekend. When Felipe asked the name of the play, Greg had shrugged and said, "I don't know, some sort of ballet, I think. Ignatius arranged it."

Of course he had.

Musicians had returned to retrieve their instruments. One of them had even rearranged the chairs for the orchestra. The conductor never returned, which was fine by Felipe. He still clutched the baton, and he still saw echoes of the maelstrom that had nearly overwhelmed the theater, the city, the world.

Occasionally, Felipe looked up to the balconies, half

expecting Maria to reappear, sitting in the same seat from which she'd watched *The King in Red*. Or maybe Ignatius would reclaim his balcony and stare down at him disapprovingly. He waited for an army of hooded cultists to emerge from underground to lead him away, perhaps to the Theatre of Dionysus, in Athens, where they could enact the truest and oldest of tragedies.

One of the rear doors of the theater opened. Reina, dwarfed by the doors and the theater itself, a waif of a thing, half the size she'd been on the stage, slipped in. She paused to look around. The curtains on one side of the theater looked as though they'd been shredded. They hung in tatters, reminding Felipe of a long ago theater that presumably no longer existed.

She said, with nothing by way of projection, "I'm sorry." Her words stretched thinly over the space of the theater.

"Watch your step," Felipe said. "There's glass everywhere."

She made her way down the aisle. A few of the seats had been mangled, but most remained intact and only one twisted into the aisle. Slowly and softly, the former King walked. She was barefoot. She'd shed the red cape of her costume. She said, "I don't feel very good."

"Neither do I," Felipe admitted.

She reached the edge of the orchestra pit. It divided them like a chasm. "There was never a third act," she said. "Todd, he insisted there would be, but he was lying. He didn't know. *The King in Red* was a lie. They made it up as they went."

"The story on the program?" Felipe asked.

"They made that up, too."

Felipe looked at Reina. She had shrunk. She had paled. She wasn't lying, not exactly, but she didn't know the truth. The usher had said things, Maria had said things, the play itself had said things, and all of it contradicted the young actor. She was practically a child. She said, "I guess I was right about one thing."

"What's that?"

"I made a real killer king." Whether the tears slipping down her cheek were real or not, Felipe would never know.

"You really did. You're going places."

She shook her head. "I should probably just go back home."

"For what it's worth," Felipe said, "I thought you did a phenomenal job."

She smiled. Half smiled. She said, "I could kiss you for that, I really could, but that would doom us both, don't you think?"

Felipe didn't answer that. He didn't have to.

Reina turned and went back the way she came. She pushed out through the same door and disappeared from the theater. Half a minute later, the sound of the outer door slamming shut behind her echoed through the theater.

Felipe found himself alone. The longer he stared at the ruin of his theater, the less he could focus on what he saw or what he didn't see. He flicked the baton once or twice. Its edge sparkled with energy he didn't understand. He looked up toward his balcony one last time, knowing this was the moment Maria should make her appearance.

She didn't.

Neither did Ignatius.

Felipe retreated backstage, descended to the orchestra pit by the stairs, and walked through the shadows that remained until he left *The Palace* behind. He didn't know how to navigate through the designs of the god of mazes and mysteries. It didn't matter. He knew enough to know, when he opened a particular door—he didn't know which particular door—he would come upon the cult, the Parliament of Ushers, the hooded woman and her compatriots, and even Ignatius.

Maybe he walked for hours. Maybe for days. Eventually, Felipe opened that door, and inside found exactly what he expected: a heavy table around which a dozen hooded men and women gathered. Two hoods were lowered. Ignatius and the old woman. One seat at the table was empty.

"You were invited to request admission," the old woman said, her voice aged since last time and now like sandpaper. "Now we will decide."

There was no discussion. The ushers in attendance crossed their arms over their chests and lowered their heads. Some turned their backs to the table. Some did not. Felipe counted twelve of them, as though that number was somehow significant. The empty space was most significant.

When all the votes were cast, Ignatius and the ancient matriarch both facing the table, six of their brethren faced away.

"One vote remains to be cast," she told him.

"I have questions."

"Questions eventually find answers."

"Ignatius. Where's your daughter? Where's Maria?"

Ignatius gave him a sad smile. "I've seen Maria a hundred times since I was young. But she's a phantasm, Felipe Gris. A flicker. An unrested spirit. She was never my daughter."

"I saw her first at the Pitt. The day I first met you. The day you started watching me."

"You'll probably see her again," Ignatius said. "I never implied our work was without peril."

Felipe nodded. He was ready to cast his vote. He crossed his arms in front of his chest. He lowered his head. He turned his back on the table and waited. Finally, the old woman said, "The invitation, once given, is rescinded. Felipe Gris, you are not one of us."

Felipe inhaled deeply, let it out slowly, and exited the room. He walked the maze. He rose, eventually, and found a relatively flimsy aluminum door. It led to a hall. The hall led to an alley outside a theater. The alley led to 42nd Street and the lights of Times Square, to a wall of posters advertising plays and musicals, one of which featured the face of a woman he had known, once upon a time, as The King in Red.

SECRET HISTORY
PART V

The Final Curtain Call of the Palace Theater

PART I
OVERTURE

1.
Now

An army of creatures dark and foul, their breath rancid and corrosive, their touch acidic, their blood ink dark and staining: they rose from sewers, they rose from tunnels, they rose from shafts of moonlight cutting the night. With deliberation, over the course of hours or even days, the creatures surrounded the theater. Something wolfish. A kind of serpent. Clawed creatures with sharp fangs. Creatures with venom running through their veins. Creatures without veins. Nearly insubstantial. Creatures with the weight of a thousand elephants and creatures with the weight of a thousand butterflies. They perched atop adjacent structures which decayed under their weight. They emerged from the shadows of alleys and arrived on motorbikes and ebon steeds. Smoke drifted from the nostrils of those horses, and the tailpipes, smoke from the very fires of hell. The creatures gathered. The creatures surrounded the theater. They stomped their feet and rattled their swords and reveled like ravers in the dark. But they waited on someone's call.

2.
Then

The Palace Theater had changed ownership frequently during its life. It had hosted plays and operas and musicals and ballets. Rock stars had strutted across that stage, and also four year old ballerinas, actors famous decades past, and angels from faraway lands.

Tonight, the new owner, a young woman of means, whose name might be well known but who wished to remain anonymous, took the most elaborate of the balconies for herself and her guests. In truth, she considered every soul in the theater her guest—all but one. The audience, even those who had paid exorbitantly for the privilege, obviously. The actors, who had been invited to put on this show for her. The crew, the concessions keepers, the tuxedoed women at the box office. Even the ushers. Everyone except Ignatius, who insisted he came with the theater, and oversaw every aspect of renovation. He made her feel she couldn't invite him anywhere.

This was an event that could not be missed. See or be seen. None of that meant anything to the theater's owner and patron, and presumably to her friends. For the audience, though, it was a chance to be close to her—and a small part of her reveled in that. A small part of her grew enormous anytime someone entered the room and cast eyes upon her. She'd been born to play this role, though secretly she might have liked a shot at Juliet, star-crossed though she may be.

The audience included socialites, musicians, actors, famous producers from Hollywood—even a writer, god knew why. Oil money, arms money, drug money, all of it was represented. But also in the audience were people who had strode across those boards before, former caretakers and crewmembers, actors, even patrons, drawn to see this final performance.

It wasn't billed as a final performance. But anyone with a history tied inexorably to the theater knew the truth of it, even if it couldn't be explained.

Reina, an aging actress, who had won awards for Broadway performances but shunned the screen, sat in one of the balconies with her young paramour. She peered across the vast auditorium, at all the seats which looked nothing like they had in the past, at the aisles, the new chandelier. She looked into the patron's balcony, swept her gaze across the dozen or so gathered around her like moths to a flame. No one noticed Reina, whose star had shone and faded many years ago. Her first memorable performance had been here. She had been King.

She saw, in the small balcony reserved for Ignatius and his guests, a man she recognized. He had hardly aged. The years had been kind to her but had ignored him entirely. His hair was longer, his beard was longer, and something unimaginable burned in his eyes. He sat alone, back rigid, perhaps reliving their last night in this theater. She should have stayed with him. All of her life would have been different. She'd never recaptured the thrill of that one night.

He met her eyes. He smiled. It was a gesture of acknowledgement, not of joy. She had been foolish then and remained foolish now. She averted her eyes, looked instead to the orchestra pit, where musicians tuned their instruments and took their seats and looked out on the audience with a kind of wonder reserved for artists. Did she recognize the faces behind the flutes, the oboes, the trumpets?

Momentarily, she'd forgotten she was not alone. Her paramour—she had to work to recall his name—Anthony Something—leaned over, pointed discreetly, and asked, "Is that who I think she is?"

Reina looked but hardly noticed. She nodded curtly. "Probably everyone is who you think they are," she said, "and none of them matter."

Directly ahead of her, under the patron's balcony, Reina noticed the S in the wood. It was hidden, had remained hidden, and had survived the renovations intact. Reina sat on the northern side of the theater facing south. The stage itself was west. She had never found the cardinal labeling the direction of the stage. Had she not been so young, so reckless, so vivid, she might have taken a moment to wonder if it was important.

The lights dimmed and rose to hurry the audience to their seats. The layer of murmuring floating through the theater settled into something lesser, and the orchestra began.

Once upon a time, Reina had floated across that stage. She could almost make out the bloodstains in the wood.

Elsewhere in the audience, in the back of the loge—the cheap seats, if any could be described that way—Nicholas fidgeted. As a stage magician, he had performed here not so very long ago. He had performed here, had shattered a mirror on that stage, had pulled from it one of his own reflections. In his mind, he saw precisely where the mirror had been. He felt the heat of the spotlight. He saw the red eyes of dogs, or doglike things, prowling the shadows; and when the lights dimmed, he saw them again. He tapped a finger against his knee, repeatedly, maybe not even aware of it, until the goddess next to him put a hand over his and whispered, "You'll spoil it for the rest of us."

He said, "I don't know why we're here."

She reached into his jacket pocket, her fingers brushing hotly against his chest, and withdrew the invitation. It was fancy, embossed, addressed to *The Man Without Reflection. Cordially invited*, it said. *A spectacle you will not want to miss.*

"We don't even know who sent the invitations."

Devi smiled as she might for a child. "You know."

The lights dimmed one last time. The pre-show music reached its end. The conductor tapped the top of his music stand with his baton, raised his hand, and with a flourish launched the orchestra into the overture.

Elsewhere in the theater, below the orchestra, below the green rooms and dressing rooms, below the makeup and the props, a robed man held his own invitation. It had been similarly addressed to him, though it had contained only a single ticket. His name was Frederick, though very few people called him anything at all. He had not come alone. He and his companion had not arrived in a car, but had walked through the maze of basements and subbasements, a conduit that might have taken him anywhere in the world. His companion, once his maid, now his student and lover, leaned close and said, "It's begun."

3.
Then

In another theater, under a New York City cathedral where once upon a time, should the stories be believed, a gargoyle had come to life, a band of actors prepared to give a prestige performance to an audience of almost twenty. They were in a secret room accessed from another basement and nestled between the corridors and crypts of St. Lazarus' Cathedral, where even now Father O'Leary was weighed down by religious texts.

The actors wore rags meant to be abstractions of actual costumes, but at least the King's robes were a brilliant cherry red, just as the playwright had imagined a hundred years before.

The young director, Joshua, scowled as he flipped through pages backstage. "I don't understand this," he said to the playwright. "This isn't even your play."

"It's how it was written," the playwright said, "and how it must be performed."

Joshua thrust the pages back. "No."

"You don't get to say no," the playwright told him.

Joshua took a breath. He was a big man, once a wrestler but not professionally, once a weight lifter, once a great many things, and only in his twenties so there was plenty of time to be a great many more things. "I say no."

The playwright, however, refused to take back the pages. "Don't make a mistake."

"Don't make me crack your ribs."

The playwright wasn't really a playwright. He was an actor, barely more than a teenager playing at being an actor. In reality, he was probably destined for a desk somewhere, papers to be pushed and numbers crunched, but he meant to delay that as long as possible. Everyone called him Ethan but no one knew his real name. He had spent a lot of time researching this play. He knew it better than anyone alive — better, anyway, than anyone alive who hadn't been involved with it before. He knew, or at least suspected, *The King in Red* had been put on sometime a few decades ago, and the actress playing the King had walked away. The stories, the legends, the *myths* built up around the play, were just that.

Ethan had taken ownership. The director, Joshua, had merely wandered in like a holy man from some Tibetan mountaintop. Ethan had allowed it only because the role of playwright was most important. He wasn't about to let some two-bit nobody from Brooklyn upset the delicate architectural balance required by the play.

"You know," Ethan said. "At this point, we don't even need you."

Joshua dropped the pages at the floor. They spread out like a deck of cards. He didn't say anything more There was no need. Any words would be pointless. Ethan watched him go, watched and folded his arms over his chest, watched and muttered curses under his breath. As Joshua disappeared in the maze of tunnels that connected the theater to the real world, Ethan said, "I hope you get lost."

4
Then

Joshua got very lost.

The labyrinths under theaters were unique warrens of dressing and storage rooms, armories, apothecaries, and enigmas. He stormed out of the secret theater—the *Secret Theater*, as if that was its name, as if it had a name—furious and relieved and sad. The pages made no sense. The character of the King made no sense. Joshua had never even seen the third act. How was he supposed to direct—how were they supposed to debut the show *tonight*—if the director had never been allowed to see the ending?

Because he had never been the director.

Putting on the play had been a performance.

Joshua didn't like the play, didn't trust the playwright, didn't even know what he'd been doing. Learning something? What, exactly, he didn't know. He followed his fate, the cards, the stars, the voices in his head. He did the things he was supposed to do. On this particular night, he was meant to abandon all his preparations and wander the maze.

The maze led through darkness and shadows. He heard other footsteps, then chanting, then the strings of a dying violin. He saw figures dancing in flickering firelight, but couldn't see the flames. He followed the sound of his own feet on the stone floor until another sound, a click of talon or claw on the stone tiles, made him pause. This wasn't a stray dog he heard, nor even a wolf. He ducked into an alcove. He became one with the shadows. And he watched as something indistinct, amorphous, heavy, and hungry stalked out of the depths.

He didn't see where it came from. He held his breath as it passed, its haunches as tall as him, its four legs the size of men, its tail long and straight and barbed at the end. It was in no hurry, but it moved in the same direction as Joshua, and it licked its jagged teeth, and it growled from somewhere deeper than its throat.

Joshua allowed the thing to disappear into the darkness ahead, then waited another thirty seconds before daring to take another breath. Part wolf, part dragon, part demon — he didn't know what to call the thing.

Regardless of what it was called, it would at least be a better lesson than *The King in Red.*

Joshua, in no hurry, followed the beast.

5.
Then

On stage, in front of nearly twenty people, *The King in Red* was off to a terrible start.

6.
Now

The show progressed. At the interlude, the audience dispersed to the bathrooms and bartenders. Some went outside to smoke, braving the brisk air and chilly winds to feed their addictions or see who there was to see. The patron, the woman who owned the theater, never went outside, though she had the coat for it, and she had the gloves. They were black gloves, brilliant satin, and they covered her arms all the way above her elbows.

If she had gone outside, she would have seen figures in the alleys and in the windows across the street. She might've noticed the moon's shine had yellowed, creating crisp shadows. The audience who saw these things didn't think any more about them. They didn't recognize the threat. They failed to taste the sting of doom on the air.

As the interlude concluded and the audience filed back

to their seats, a few of those seats stayed empty. From her seat in the balcony, the patron noticed this, and she was not pleased.

7
Then

Alyssa strode down the long corridor, her dress flowing about her like a cape, as the orchestra started to play. Whether intentional or not, her pace matched the rhythm. Behind and above the stage, she could stop and peer out through tiny peepholes, from which she could pick out individual members of the audience, in the orchestra, loge, or balconies. She noted one seat in particular remained empty.

When she turned the final corner, she moved like liquid. She rushed like a river changing direction. She reached a door that had remained virtually unchanged in the theater's every incarnation. No matter how much reconstruction occurred, no matter what transformations were undertaken by the very soul of the theater, one constant remained.

She knocked, unconcerned with the sound. It wouldn't carry over the orchestra, wouldn't reach the audience. She knocked three times, bare knuckles on the wood. When no one answered, she knocked again. She listened for any sound from the other side, any indication of life.

Hearing nothing, she tried the door. It was locked. She fished keys out of her little purse. The set was special, but she tried several without success. She frowned, but not bitterly, and she refrained from uttering curses. She didn't fear the sound of knocking, but her voice might carry too far too quickly.

The keys were silver, platinum, steel, and iron, but none worked, and none would work. She had suspected they wouldn't. She reached into the purse and withdrew another, this one obsidian, blacker than night and sharper than steel. It wasn't the original. She'd fashioned this one herself, partly as a test of her skills, partly as a challenge, partly as proof of vitality. It slid through the keyhole and infiltrated the locking mechanisms. She returned all her keys to her purse and stepped back to allow the obsidian to work. Inside, the lock dissolved and disintegrated, piece by piece, until something cracked.

Alyssa pushed the door open and entered Ignatius's apartment.

She had never seen his apartment before. It was sparse, occupied mostly by books but not many. There was a lamp and a chair and a table. She had expected more. Secrets, maybe. Maps. Insignia from the Parliament of Ushers. Something more, something useful, something enlightening.

Alyssa pulled the door shut behind her. It settled into its place, though there was no longer anything to latch with. At the center of the room, she bent to one knee and touched the floor. She felt the vitality of the theater itself, its lifeblood, pulsing through the bones of the architecture. More than merely the music from the orchestra, this was primal and archaic. She registered the pattern, the rhythm, the accents, and took all this into herself.

Once upon a time, she had walked across that stage, though at that time the theater had been rundown, decrepit, shuddering near a last breath. How it managed to persist, even Alyssa wasn't sure. It was a kind of magic like a virus. It infected people. Like the patron, out there now, watching her actors perform for her audience—like all the previous wardens—they were helpless against this type of magic.

It was a kind of magic Alyssa didn't fully comprehend.

She tried to breathe it in. She absorbed it. How else might she understand all the mysteries? The play, downstairs, continued without her, despite her, regardless of her.

By the time Ignatius entered the room, pulling open his

own destroyed door, she could not be surprised. She had felt his every step, his every breath. "What do you think you're doing?"

She didn't remove her hand and didn't turn her head. She released a full breath before saying, "You know me."

"That was a long time past," Ignatius said, stepping closer to intimidate her, "when this theater wore a different face."

"The theater often wears different faces," Alyssa said.

Alyssa's sister, her twin, her reflection from another world, stepped into the room behind Ignatius. The old man was built like a brick wall. He was strong, solid, immoveable, unstoppable, and his blood tied him directly to the Palace Theater in ways no patron ever dared to dream. He loomed large over Alyssa. His shadow engulfed her entirely. Lissa, on the other hand, all chalky flesh and coal-like eyes, altered the balance. She slipped a knife between Ignatius's ribs, quickly and quietly, without a breath of sound. The blade moved as if enchanted. When she removed it, she put it between two other ribs, and punctured internal organs. A third thrust severed his spinal cord. Finally, she reached around and slashed his throat. The spray of blood altered the color of Alyssa's dress.

PART II
CHOIR

1.

When the lights dropped again for the second act, Reina's paramour had not returned. She imagined a number of possibilities, including that he was still outside enjoying a smoke or a drink. Perhaps he had been tempted by a younger woman, someone his age, whose acrobatic abilities might be greater than hers but who lacked other skills.

But she didn't believe any of this. She assumed the

theater had swallowed him.

She sat uncomfortably in her chair as the performers wandered the stage, but she no longer noticed them. They weren't particularly captivating. She looked across the way at the patron, adored by her entourage like a queen, like a goddess, but nothing about the woman seemed right anymore. Reina, once and always the King in Red, took two more slow breaths before leaving her seat.

She disrupted no one.

She had an understanding of the Palace Theater most would not. She'd been born here, in a way. Spilled blood here. Reined as King for the duration of one show. She'd seen the universe split apart. And she knew these corridors, even if they had been made over in someone else's image.

She strode through the halls, back, deeper into the theater, out of the way of the dime store ushers and concessionaires and ticket takers. She circled around the back of the theater. When she couldn't hear the actors, she at least heard the musicians. It seemed so very familiar to her.

She turned a corner, reached another balcony door, and quietly opened it. She slipped inside and took the empty seat next to Felipe Gris, who once upon a time owned and remodeled this theater. That opening performance did not go well.

"You shouldn't have come," he whispered as she sat.

"How could I not?" He smiled. He hardly looked at her. She resented it, and already was beginning to regret coming to him. "Is it happening again?"

He looked down to his lap. In one hand, he held a conductor's baton, not dissimilar to the one being used in the orchestra pit, a weapon and tool she had seen him wield before. "I'm not the same man you knew."

"You are."

"Why are you here?"

Reina shook her head. "Memories are a funny thing,"

she said. "The past calls to us. Draws us in. Like a black hole, you might say."

He smiled again, but this time it seemed sincere. "I know what you mean."

"Why are you here?"

"This place is still in my blood," he said. "I tried to get away from it, tried to exist somewhere else entirely, but always a remnant of the Palace remained with me."

"The *Gris* Theater," Reina told him.

He shook his head. "That was never my intention."

They watched the performance for a little while. Nothing spectacular happened. The music shifted. The faces on stage changed. Reina glanced toward the patron's balcony. The woman seemed oblivious of everything. "Where is your usher?"

Felipe shook his head again. "Ignatius is older than rocks, I think. But this was always his theater more than mine."

"You never answered me. Is this *The King in Red* again?"

A breath, a shake of no, a glance toward the patron—even Felipe Gris sensed something was amiss—before he said, "No. This is different."

2.

Nicholas sat between Devi and an empty seat, where presumably Lissa should have joined them. The goddess remained calm and quiet. It felt like forever since they'd seen each other. He remained uncertain, uncomfortable, unprepared. He smelled ozone in the theater, the buildup of electricity or something like it. Lightning. Fire. Danger. He wasn't sure. He didn't know. He was years past his prime.

Devi glanced at him and smiled. He had underestimated her, back when they'd first met. They'd met on the other side of a mirror; she shouldn't be here at all. Nothing made sense to Nicholas. Nothing ever had. After the magic with the mirror, his mind had cracked. It was hard to keep track of reality.

And he saw no sign of his former assistant.

He leaned close to Devi to whisper. "Something's not right."

"Nothing's ever right," the goddess told him. "The secret is to accept that."

She didn't understand. She was so far above mortal concerns, it frightened him. Once, they'd walked together, and briefly she'd loved him, but her path had always been divine and his had already been shattered. He reached inside his jacket, not for the first time, to touch that invitation. It was a piece of magic, typographical magic, a link between him and the woman who had sent it. His assistant. Lissa.

Nicholas hardly noticed the actors. He had looked at them long enough to confirm none wore Lissa's face — or none were Lissa wearing another's. He scanned the audience, sure his senses were well-refined, extraordinary, better than human. Doglike, even, though the thought made him shiver.

Devi put a hand on his knee. She whispered, "Relax."

"It's easy for you," he said.

"It's *easy*," she said.

It didn't feel easy. His blood pressure was up. The nape of his neck tingled. His fingers itched. His ears burned. He scanned the balconies, as best he could, seeking meaning in the faces, seeking familiarity, seeking reassurance. There was none to be had. Finally, he got up, excusing himself, apologizing to the people around him. Devi followed him to the aisle, to the back, into the richly upholstered hall behind the loge.

"She's here," Nicholas said.

"Of course she's here."

"Where?"

"She'll reintroduce herself to you at a time of her choosing, I'm sure." Devi still spoke at a whisper. She kept cool. Calm. Composed. "But there is something else, isn't there? Something I've been trying to ignore, but I really can't. There's a hint of my brother here."

"Your *brother*?"

She shook her head. "Not him. Not at all. But, there's something in the wood, in the halls. Something in the basements that links...there's a maze, of course, underneath. Connecting the theater with—with other theaters? Of course. That makes sense."

"No," Nicholas said. "It does not."

"My brother, my twin, was the god of mazes and mysteries. He was with me in the White City so very long ago. He *connected* the theaters. I never even knew."

"What does that mean?"

"We're at something of a conduit." Nicholas had never seen Devi's eyes light up as they were now. "We're at a junction point between places, between situations, in a pocket of reality difficult to describe." When Nicholas didn't respond, Devi shook him and said, "Do you know what that means?"

"We can walk to Madrid?"

"I can descend to the underworld," Devi said, pulling Nicholas into a powerful hug. "I can bring Dale back." She grabbed Nicholas by the hand and ran down the stairs, away from their seats, and into the basements of the theater.

3.

The maid, the former maid, now a famulus herself, an acolyte and student, a devotee of the magician called Frederick, once had a name. Chloe. Her mother had given it to her, but she'd lost track of it in the mountains. She thought of it only in times of trouble, when threatened, when the perils she faced were beyond her understanding. Beside her, Frederick, who considered himself the mightiest of all magicians, stood tense and rigid, clutching a paintbrush in one hand, an invitation in the other.

She hadn't been part of that invitation. She was meant to throw the situation off balance. But her skills were minimal; as a student, she worked more in books than craft. She could manage simple illusions, but little else. She had once made a broomstick dance. It had made her laugh, but Frederick was not big on laughter. He wasn't big on much of anything.

Chloe clutched her name, and her illusions, and Frederick's arm. "It's a play?"

"It's not just a play," he told her.

She knew this. She knew, too, who had sent that invitation. She'd recognized the color of the magic invoked. It permeated the lettering, which had all been done by hand—with a fountain pen—as was the other woman's style. *To survival*, she had once toasted, but now she wasn't sure that was possible.

Frederick was so invested in what was happening in the theater, he hardly seemed to notice the labyrinth behind them. They had arrived via those twisted paths, had risked shades and phantasms to get here, rather than reveal that invitation to someone at the box office. So he didn't notice the gathering of darkness, the oppression in the shadows, the temporary life in the faces carved into the apex of stone columns. Eyes blinked redly, then were gone, and it was no mere illusion.

She said, "We should do something to protect ourselves."

He looked down at her. He always looked down. It wasn't just that he was a head taller than everyone else, it was his nature. "You'll learn to protect yourself," he said. Maybe he meant tonight. Against her better judgement, she crowded closer to him. But while his senses were all trained on a stage and auditorium she couldn't see, hers continued to explore their immediate environs.

Shadows had thickened into slavering jaws and rippling flesh. Shapes slithered through the mists of gloomy obscurity dripping from the walls. When the heat of their breath touched her, she let loose a cry and a wave of her hand to create a bloom of carnivorous nightshade. She whirled to face the creature, purple flowers like teeth lashing out ahead of her, but the creature—a lupine thing with glistening teeth and gleaming eyes - reached through the illusion with a single paw.

Chloe fell as Frederick finally turned to see the creature. He lifted his paintbrush defensively, grinned, and said something to the beast even as the nightshade dissipated into dust.

It might be magnificent to see, Frederick battling a creature conjured from ash and umbrage, but Chloe didn't like her own chances. Innumerable shapes moved in the darkness, closing in on the theater and its occupants, the magician and his assistant among them. Chloe scrambled backwards, and when she was able, shot to her feet and ran. She reached the backstage in a heartbeat, ran into one of the actors within the space of a single breath. The man glared at her as she rebounded from him. He said, simply, *"The show,"* then strode out onto the stage.

4.

Frederick faced the creature, the beast, the thing risen from unfathomable depths, and saw immediately it was not alone. The invitation had never been to parley, or to negotiate, or to reminisce about old times—he had never believed any of these—but a trap, and the trap had already sprung.

The creatures, the one before him and its brethren,

uncountable and impossible, crowded the corridors under the theater, under other theaters, perhaps under all theaters. They snarled, showing teeth and fangs and claws and talons, some dripping with gore, others dripping with venom. Eyes of crimson, of putrid yellow, of lustrous onyx.

Frederick did something he almost never did. He backed away. Only one step. He had to be sure. The creatures did not advance. They bided their time. They waited for prey to come to them, to cross the line—the threshold of the theater.

The creatures made a cage of murderous shadow with muscle and sinew and malignant intent.

"So," he said, to the creature but also to the woman who had summoned it, "there is to be no escape."

The creature gave no sign of understanding.

5.

Joshua took refuge within an alcove and watched more creatures in the tunnels. One had turned to look at him, its eyes like yellow fever, but it did not deviate from its resolve. They weren't merely here to feed, but at the bidding of someone, presumably someone powerful.

Joshua liked to think he was powerful. He had more than just a handful of tricks available to him. He conjured a ball of light, a white light, pure like snow, bright like citrus, sharp like diamonds. Holding this before him, he entered the stream of creatures. He walked among them. Some of the creatures growled. Some barely glanced at him. One stretched a claw in his direction. He lashed at it with a tendril of the light. Whether it was the light or not, the creature did not press at him.

He walked beside them, in their direction, until he reached a place where the creatures stopped and drew their line. Here, they said, but no further.

From above, the sounds of an orchestra dripped down to

him, and the feet of actors upon a stage, and the quiet of an expectant audience. The creatures hadn't drawn him here. There was something else. Something greater. The theater above, the Palace Theater—he recognized this immediately—had once upon a time hosted *The King in Red*—and it had ended disastrously.

Behind him, in the theater they jokingly called The Lazarus Theater because of the cathedral above it, that same play threatened to begin again.

He turned. He meant to go back, to stop the play, to kill the playwright, Ethan, before the show had a chance to reach the third act. But the creatures behind him were thick and deep and restless now, and not at all put off by the ball of light which faded in Joshua's hands.

6.

In The Lazarus Theater, *The King in Red* had begun. The playwright, Ethan, substituted pages on stage, interrupting the performers. The lights flickered. The heat had stopped working, so cold leaked in through the stone all around them. There was never supposed to be a theater tucked under this cathedral. It was merely an empty space someone had carved a path into. One by one, the audience gave up and left, until only half a dozen souls remained.

Ethan, the playwright, pressed on. Aaron, the king, refused to waver. They went back and forth on the stage, improvising, which was a talent neither possessed. Someone heckled from the audience, someone hidden in shadows—it was easy to hide in the shadows of a theater consumed by them.

They raced to the end of the first act, and barely paused for an intermission.

PART III
SOLO

1.

Alyssa walked away from the usher's apartment. She had gone through everything and left her poisonous mark upon it all. Every book, every surface, every molecule of air dripped with it. She closed the door and sealed it—not merely locking it—making it so the room could never be accessed again, not by human hands, not anyone living.

She weaved through the theater like an expert, though it had been many years since she worked it. Then, she'd been merely an assistant to a stage magician—which meant, of course, she did all the work and reaped none of the rewards. Now, she controlled the theater in its entirety.

She went first to her seat in the loge. She merely entered the loge and saw that the seats were empty. She smiled. Nicholas and the goddess were off on their own adventure, presumably. But he was only a secondary target.

She paused, then, noticing something she hadn't expected. There were a dozen separate balconies in the theater, some on either side, some larger than others, many of them private boxes owned by wealthy patrons. One, the biggest, was occupied not by a mere patron but the most important of them, the woman in whose hands the theater currently belonged. She had renovated the Palace Theater, had redesigned some of its hallways without ever losing the soul of it. Ignatius, the late Ignatius, had seen to that.

In her balcony, the patron was a magnet of attention and desire. Men swooned at her side, women fawned over her, even the cast adored her. She was a light in the darkness, and Alyssa might require words with her. But in the next balcony, the small one reserved for Ignatius and the other ushers, a balcony often left empty, the two seats were occupied, one by a woman Alyssa had never seen.

In the other, a man—no, not merely a man—The Maestro—looked back at her.

He saw her. He smiled, though it was enigmatic. Did he wink, or was that a trick of the light? Alyssa swallowed involuntarily. She had not anticipated his arrival. She didn't know his connection to the theater, but obviously there had been one.

He looked young, younger than she'd ever seen him. She hadn't been sure he was still alive. Time was a devious beast, especially in a place like this, a palace of wondrous deceit and unfettered passion. Maybe the Maestro who looked back at her now hadn't yet struggled with an unstable portal. Maybe he hadn't yet died.

Alyssa nodded an acknowledgement. That seemed to satisfy him. He turned his attention once again to the stage, though it was of course a mirage. An illusion. The basest, easiest, stupidest form of magic. Alyssa tried to think of a worthy curse for uttering, but language failed her.

She left the loge.

Alyssa descended stairs and took to the arteries of the theater, the hidden veins and lymph nodes, alongside air conditioning ducts and tubes of speaker wire and electrical cords. Below the main auditorium, below the entire audience, there was a pool. It was a long rectangle, not deep, a hundred meters in length but only two in width. It ran below the center aisle of the theater, and at its very center, through the ceiling and floor and into the air, was the newest chandelier to dominate the Palace Theater.

She strode alongside the length of the pool, listening to the fish and koi and other things that swam in its waters. Her crimson dress whirled around her like a cloud, like a cape, like a mist of red death. Ahead, down a set of stairs, she walked among the dark creatures and beasts and animals. She ruffled their fur, stroked their hides, scratched behind their ears. They purred in response, growled and moaned, a symphony that reverberated through the beasts. Below the theater, they were like a sea, thick and undulating.

"One of mine has escaped," she whispered to the spidery beast beside her. "Please find him, and bring him back."

The spider, no bigger than a Volkswagen, with a dozen eyes and a mat of black fur, chittered—that may have just been its legs on the stone floor—and disappeared among the others. It followed a scent as well as any wolf.

Alyssa extended her arms and breathed deeply. Her other guest had not come into the theater until recently. He'd been wise. He was her primary target. She yearned for vengeance upon him most vehemently. She detected his foul stench, now that he'd crossed the threshold. It wrinkled her nose and turned her stomach.

On the stage above, the performers played their parts. The musicians kept the melody. The conductor kept the rhythm. The conductor, no Maestro, was a man named Abraham, and he was about to die.

Here, she was under the orchestra pit. The music resonated through the wood and through the stone. She let it seep into her bones. She reached up, seeing through wood and stone as though they weren't there, and through the flesh. She reached through the bones, under the ribcage, gripping an illusion of the heart of the conductor. It pounded with the music, and it pained her, briefly, to destroy such beauty.

But it had to be done.

She flexed her fingers, squeezing slightly and to the rhythm, matching the music and the heartbeat so no one, not even the Maestro, could notice her machinations. She curled her fingers, her fingernails, and pricked the walls of that muscle. She caught the first drop of blood on her lips, consumed it with a flick of her tongue, and now her lips matched the color of her dress.

2.

Lissa left the Usher's room and strode through the bones of The Palace Theater. She descended, circling around the front of the theater and descending a spiral stair no one had used in an age. It remained hidden, but she'd always known about it. It had existed on her side of the mirror; its existence here had been a certainty.

The stair let her out in a chamber far below the theater. It stretched infinitely in all directions. Thick columns supported the low ceiling. The floors were stone but not well kept, studded with cracks and holes and crevices that maybe descended to realms other than this.

She tore the edge of her dress, unraveling a single white thread. She wrapped it around a stone in the stairway twice, tied it, then wrapped it a third time for the appropriate number. She walked through the vast hall. When she circled a column, which she did more than once, she ducked under the thread which stretched out behind her. It could lead her back to the theater. Just as easily, it could lead someone to her, but she was unconcerned. She strode between the columns seemingly at random but with deliberate purpose. Eventually, she reached the farthest end of the hall and entered a wide-mouthed corridor.

It was stone, as well, but no longer crumbling beneath her feet. She turned here and there, and passed none of the creatures her sister, her twin, had summoned.

Lissa selected certain intersecting hallways. She heard the faint echoes of musical numbers, soliloquys, black and white movies. She caught a hint of the dialogue. *Casablanca*, she decided. One of her favorites.

When she paused to look back, to check on the thread that had once been half her white dress, the straight, taut line gave off a neon glow. The colors shifted. That was okay. That was expected. They were a part of her, and her world had always been a study of black and white but it had always been trimmed in neon. It felt like she was giving up a bit of herself in the process. The dress now was short and getting shorter, the thread traveling farther afield than might seem possible.

Finally, she neared her destination. From above, fumbling voices reached her, and they were enough to make her cringe. She climbed the final set of stairs, stepped into the darkness of The Lazarus Theater, and with a fingernail cut the thread loose from her dress. Once long and flowing, it was now nearly immodest, but with an audience of half a dozen people and a cast of fewer than that, there was no one to care. With her chalky complexion, she melded into the shadows. She tied the final thread to the doorknob, wrapping it thrice, and pulled the door shut.

Behind her, the thread was taut.

She took a seat. There were plenty to choose from. On stage, the King in Red said, "My family: vipers. My friends: ogres and witches, every one of them. My subjects—oh, my very kingdom, my life's blood, my reason for breathing— infiltrated by schemers, connivers, liars, madmen, poets, and thieves. You're an abomination. A blight on these, the last days of my dynasty."

Lissa smiled as someone offstage said, "I can help you." The *King in Red* was proceeding on schedule.

3.

The conductor, running away with the music, convulsed quietly and invisibly, then slumped forward, over his music stand, over all his notes. When his baton and hand both came down, the musicians faltered. On stage, the actors stumbled. The audience gasped—not as one, as they didn't all immediately know what had happened.

The conductor dropped off his dais, blood streaming from his eyes like tears, and expelled his final breath.

PART IIII
RECITATIVE

1.

The Maestro rose quickly from his seat, Reina with him. She seemed stunned but unable to resist. The Maestro leapt over the edge of the balcony. He landed softly on his feet, leaving Reina, the former King in Red, alone in the usher's balcony.

He swept up the side of the theater. Quick as a heartbeat, he was in the orchestra pit, at the side of the fallen conductor. A touch of the man's skin, and he knew the heart had been stopped. He raised his baton, whirled the edge, sought the source of the conductor's ailment. It had been planted in him before today. The ailment had grown thickly and blackly in his chest. It had wrapped around his heart like ivy, and when squeezed...

The Maestro frowned. This wasn't merely murder. It was a trigger.

"Blood magic," he muttered under his breath. Only Reina heard him, and maybe the violinist. The actress had reached the edge of the orchestra pit and leaned over it.

"What do we do?" she asked.

"You're the King in Red," he told her. "Be the king." Even as he said the words, he heard the echo in them. He had said the same thing once before. What more could he do?

Reina stood and turned to face the audience. "I am your King!" she called. "I am your sovereign! Bow before me, your King, your Queen, your Emperor, and your God!"

2.

Alyssa said, "I knew you would come."

Frederick turned to face her, putting the creatures to his back. He obviously liked nothing about the situation. His grip tightened around his wand—his paintbrush. Colors sparked at the edge of each hair of the brush. "My debt to you is paid."

"You *bought* me," Alyssa said, shaking her head, "as a famulus. You owed me more than day old bread and cheap wine."

"I gave you run of the house."

"You set your staff upon me. Your cook. Your butler. Your maid." He winced at the last word. She noted that. He had brought her with him tonight. Fine. She was already in the trap, and she was going nowhere. "You were required to teach."

"You learned."

"Did I?"

"And you tricked me," Frederick said. "Cheated me. You wronged *me*, famulus, not the other way around."

"Do you even know my name?" Alyssa asked.

In response, Frederick hurled a spell at her, a burst of colorful energy from the edge of his brush, with all the grace of a donkey pitching a knuckleball. Alyssa caught it. Barehanded. It hurt. She wouldn't lie about a thing like that. It hurt a lot, burning and scratching and eating into her flesh like acid. She looked at it, considered tossing it back, but instead let it fizzle out in her hand.

"And what of Veronica?" he asked. "She sold you."

"She actually helped me," Alyssa said, "but you're right, she used me. Manipulated me. Might have destroyed me, had I stayed."

"You've obviously learned much since then," Frederick said.

Alyssa stepped closer to him. One step. It was enough to be both promise and threat. "I reserved a seat for you," she said. "In the orchestra section. Front and center. You should have been watching the show."

"It's a magic act," Frederick said. "I've seen it."

"Not this one, you haven't." Alyssa offered her best smile. She saw in his reaction, the brief glimpse of terror, the resignation, and fury, that it had the affect she wanted.

3.

Chloe watched from the side of the stage as the magician—the magic illuminated his veins—examined the conductor. There was nothing to do be done. The man was dead, not merely killed but sacrificed.

She scanned the faces of the audience, none of whom even noticed her. They were rapt by the new show, no longer interested in the actors or the stage. So she returned in the direction from which she'd come. There were two performances tonight.

She stopped short of her goal, though. The creatures remained at the threshold, preventing both escape and rescue. Her mentor stood with his back to those things and faced the greater threat: the famulus who had once lived in their house.

They were arguing. Talking. Fighting. Sometimes, it was hard to know. Chloe lifted her wand. It wasn't much of a wand. She'd carved it from a winter birch outside the house. It had been strong and flexible. She conjured an illusion. A trick of mist and shadow. She rearranged the moisture in the air, and the air itself, to bring form to her vision.

She created a monster.

Its carcass dripped with yellowed venoms. It moved heavily, unevenly, without grace and without support. It made no sound, but the creatures, dark and foul as they were, saw it and reacted. They snarled. They slavered. They rattled their talons and swords against the tiles. Those weapons cracked the floor. Marble dust rose in the air, intermingled with the acrid corrosion of the creatures. They were not illusory.

Chloe's monster lumbered one step forward. It was enough to attract Alyssa's attention. Although illusion-based, the venoms were real, albeit temporary, and permeated the air.

Alyssa came toward her anyway. She grinned like a devil. She raised her wand—a pen with a sharp nib, it dripped magic and ink—and stabbed it toward Chloe.

The pain was immediate and complete. Every muscle, every tissue, every fiber of her being burst into white fire. Time slowed for Chloe, so she could feel the fervor building in every cell, until finally the membrane that kept her whole and kept each cell complete ruptured. She saw it happening, even as her eyes were liquefied. Nothing remained of her but a pile of sludge, and she was aware of it until the very end. With the last of her voice and the last of her breath, she said, "I'd shown you a kindness."

"Only the once," Alyssa said. After that, Chloe and her illusionary monster ceased to exist.

4.

Alyssa whirled on Frederick. "You shouldn't have brought her. You knew my intentions."

"She," Frederick said, "was under my protection." He lashed forward with a stream of terminal colors. Alyssa withstood the assault. It tickled, but there was something else underneath it. It picked up traces of the girl's illusory venoms. The monster had succeeded in agitating her creatures, but the only thing about it that persisted beyond the fracturing of light was that venom, and the very touch of it burned.

Alyssa was infected. So she would not survive this night after all.

INTERLUDE

1.

Nicholas never imagined how deep stairs might go. At first, it was one level, then four, then ten, but it now seemed like they'd been descending for half a lifetime. The carvings in the walls became more ornate as they descended until what had been paintings and engravings became figures reaching out of the stone. At one point, he almost said something about how lifelike they were, but realized they were, in fact, alive, just moving too slowly to see. He touched one to confirm this theory. Though the surface of his body was cold as marble, blood moved underneath the flesh and muscles rippled with life.

They had descended far below the Palace Theater, below the network of corridors that joined all theaters, no matter the size or the show, and into realms of mist and shadow. The stairway opened on one side, revealing a chasm that reached far beyond the limits of torchlight. Nicholas hadn't said anything when the electric lights were replaced by gas, and again didn't comment when those gave way to torches that should not have kept burning. But when the stairs narrowed to force them to walk single file, he asked Devi to wait.

"What is it?" Devi asked. "Oh, I forget, you're merely mortal."

"I'm thirsty," Nicholas said. "And my legs ache. How much further do we have to go?"

"All the way to the bottom," she told him. She tapped the wall beside one of the statues. A stream of water shot out of the marble-like mouth. "It's fresh," she said, "and from neither the rivers Lethe nor Styx, so it is safe."

Nicholas hesitated, but drank from the fountain. It was strangely intimate. He tried not to think too much on it. When he finished, he pulled away and wiped his mouth. The water stopped flowing, and the statue—with one eye—began the slow process of winking.

He nearly fell back. Devi caught him by the arm. "Be smart," she told him. "Nothing is real, and nothing is illusion here."

"Here?" Nicholas asked. "We're already here?"

"We've been here for a week," Devi said.

"It can't have been that long."

Devi smiled. "Time," she said, "does not work the way you think it does. What's about to happen has already happened, and I can do nothing to change that."

"What do you mean?"

"The paths to the underworld have been closing," Devi said. "Every time I return from one with my lover, Dale, at my side, that way is closed to me forever. It was a matter of good fortune, and fate, that you brought me to this theater tonight."

"We're not still in the theater," Nicholas told her.

"We never truly left," she said. "I've been told, a hundred times or more, you cannot drag this soul back from Hell, not again. The lord of mists, my uncle, forbids it. He talks of balance, but he doesn't understand a truth about balance: love is the balancer."

Involuntarily, Nicholas retreated one step up. Something in her words, something in her eyes, revealed a particular truth to him, and he didn't much like it. "Why did you bring me?"

Devi grinned. She still had a hand on his arm, and he could not resist her strength as she pulled him down. "Balance."

2.

Devi dragged Nicholas into the depths of hell, into the lands of mist, over a gorge a mile above a river he could hear but not see, over a wall she should not have been able to scale. He hung, dangling, clutched in her hand like a handkerchief. He considered options, he struggled futilely against her, and he even began to hope the spider would snatch him before she introduced him to the lord of mists.

He didn't know when he'd noticed the spider. It shadowed them, it closed the distance, and it seemed to lock all its eyes on Nicholas.

By the time they stopped descending and the path leveled out, the mists had grown too thick to see the spider, or even to see the walls, if indeed there were walls around them anymore. He almost saw the sky, and certainly saw the moon, full, not bright but strong enough to pierce all those layers of cloud and fog and smoke.

"You know why I'm here," Devi said.

A figure appeared in the mists. Nicholas hadn't seen him. Twice the size of a man, pale like a ghost and as ethereal, he wafted rather than walked as he emerged from nothing. He did not look happy. "And this is your trade?"

"You demand balance," she told him. "I understand it."

"You've never understood."

"Bring him."

"He's in the pits," the lord of mists said. "Held down by a host of the jealous dead."

"Because no one ventures into the depths of hell to revive them?"

"Because they loved you, all of them, in life and in

death," the lord of mists said. "You engender that."

"They call me a goddess of love." Her grip on Nicholas's arm tightened.

"They call you a great many things."

"They demand to be rescued?" Devi asked.

"They demand nothing," the lord of mists said. "They refuse to surrender him, is all."

"I can deal with them."

"And with me?"

Devi smiled. Grinned. Snarled. Growled. It was hard to describe her reaction, because Nicholas was merely mortal. She dragged him forward, through the lord of mist, who dissipated as they passed, to the edge of a pit.

The pit was only deep enough for a grown man to stand just below the lip of it. Inside, a thousand souls crowded around the one Nicholas recognized. Dale. He sat in the center, arms wrapped around his knees, tears dripping from insubstantial eyes. In the pit, every soul was transparent, and every soul was translucent, and every soul was clearly visible. Nicholas saw more layers of detail than his mind could process. A wave of vertigo shuddered through him. Devi squeezed his arm and pulled him to the edge of the pit.

"Give me my lover," Devi said, "and I'll give you this one, still alive, whose flesh I have tasted."

A murmuring arose among the souls.

"Give me my lover," Devi said, "and I shall leave you here, content, un-abused, to enjoy whatever remains to you."

"Nothing," one of the souls said.

"Take me," said another.

"We can serve you."

The dead souls sang when they spoke, their voices like angelic chords, triads echoing over triads, bells and butterflies, harmonious to the point of fever.

Devi's grip on Nicholas tightened. He felt it in the bone of his arm, in his blood, in his very soul. Until he'd faced his own reflection outside the mirror, he had never given much thought to souls, to life after death, to parallel universes and paths untaken. Now, he saw all of it in the silvery blue faces of the dead, the reflective eyes. In all the pit, at the center, where Dale sat and hugged himself and cried, only those tears had any degree of physicality. Almost hesitantly, at barely more than a whisper, he said to Devi, "There's another way."

3.

The lord of mist gathered himself from the mists and rose behind them. "I advise against it."

"You always do," Devi said, then turned her full attention on Nicholas. "Do it." She didn't bother to ask what it was.

"You have to let go," he told her. "I have to go *in*."

"In the pit?" Devi asked.

"I advise against it," the lord of mist said again.

"Give me your blessing, then," Nicholas said, "or a boon, something, so that I might survive."

"You'll have nothing from me," the lord of mists said.

But Devi kissed Nicholas, hard and passionately, furiously, with all the power of a goddess of the second age, such that he still felt her lips and tongue after she released him. He dropped featherlike into the pit, and walked among the souls of the dead. They touched him, all of them touched him, their fingers like icicle needles driving through his skin, but the lingering touch of the goddess sizzled inside him. He barely saw the dead, ignored the abysses of their eyes, and walked straight to the one among them whom he'd known. He knelt beside Dale, put an arm around his shoulder in comfort, and produced a glass vial.

Maybe he hadn't had it on his person, but Nicholas was something of a magician, and his skills were intuitive. When he needed the vial, he had it. He placed it under the dead man's eye and said, "That's it, Dale. Let it all out."

And in that manner, pressed close by a thousand dead souls in a pit deep within the realm of mists, Nicholas collected the physical tears of a dead man. He remained until Devi's fire inside him dwindled, until the last vestiges of warmth faded entirely. Then he stood. He stoppered the vial. He shook it, and said words that sounded like an invocation but basically translated as, "I hope this works." He turned to face the goddess, a thousand miles away at the edge of the pit. He lifted the vial. He said, "I haven't got strength enough to return."

Devi, moon goddess, dust goddess, dragon of the white city, stood smiling at the edge of the pit and said, "You do."

A shaft of moonlight tore through the mists and struck Nicholas. It invigorated his muscles. It revived his blood. It pulsed through the vial of tears, so that they sparkled and glimmered and burned and transformed. He lifted the vial up—it needed more of the moonlight than he did—and held that pose for half an age. Civilizations rose and crumbled to dust during that moment. Great romantic sagas ended with heartbreak and death. Finally, exhausted by the sheer intensity of it all, Nicholas dropped to his knees beside Dale, put an arm around his shoulders again, and said, "Drink."

Dale lifted his head, lifted his mouth, and allowed Nicholas to spill a single drop of the moonlight-infused tears down his throat. Physicality came to him like a mist, until Dale was whole again, himself, and alive. He looked at Nicholas, smiled, and said, "I knew I liked you."

A thousand souls crushed in on them, all clamoring for the vial, reaching, pushing and shoving, swiping and stabbing. In the midst of this, Dale saw Devi and smiled and said, "You, I love." She reached for him, with a moonbeam, lifting him from the center of the pit.

She might have left Nicholas to rot, but the spider, when

it moved, did so swiftly. It scampered on the underside of the moonbeam, leapt into the center of the pit, ignoring the souls and shattering the vial of tears. The spider bit Nicholas on his back, releasing its venoms to paralyze the man, then grabbed him with two legs and leapt again. Returning to the moonbeam on a thread, it scurried into the darkness.

From the edge of the pit, Devi and the lord of mists watched, but did nothing. From the overside of the moonbeam, Dale reached for Nicholas but it was a futile gesture. The spider was quick. The spider eschewed the paths of torches and gas lights and electricity. The spider took to the shadows, to the darkness, to the crevices in the skies over the realms of mists, and carried Nicholas away.

PART V
ACCOMPAGNATO

1.

Music ceased. There was only the sound of a flute being moved through the air—a hollow tuneless note that fluttered into and out of existence—and discordant strings not being struck so much as trembling within their violins and cellos.

Felipe Gris examined the conductor as Reina, the King in Red, commanded her audience. The spotlights followed her because she'd stolen their focus. The singers and players had fled the stage—down into the orchestra, back behind the stage, wherever they were able to run to—and none could have resisted Reina's domination.

She delivered the same lines she'd recited when she'd been decades younger. They revived her, something inside her. She strut across the aisle between the orchestra pit and the first row of the audience, and every eye, even the eyes of the farthest balconies, looked nowhere else.

Except perhaps the patron. She had abandoned her seat

and her entourage. The balcony seemed tremendously lighter without her.

When she was young, a girl, in her first starring role right here at The Gris Theater, or whatever else it was called, Reina had known nothing of life, nothing of love, nothing of the mysteries, nothing of her art. She had been naïve, foolish, frightened, arrogant in the power of her youthful beauty. Now, she was merely confident, skilled, nuanced, and at the height of her power.

Behind her, Felipe gave orders to the musicians. He sent one for an ambulance, one for towels, one for water. But his voice betrayed the truth of it: the conductor was dead.

Reina issued her commands to the audience, and drew their eyes from the spectacle behind her. She worried about the patron. Had the woman escaped? Run away? Was she responsible?

"Another place, another time, worlds were consumed," Reina said to the audience, "and I, the King in Red, reined over them, and I had to protect them."

2.

In the Lazarus Theater, the King in Red, Aaron, told the audience, "I am your King! I am your sovereign! Bow before me, your King, your Monarch, your Emperor, and your God! And from the depths, I call forth my children, wretched and disfigured though they may be, to consume your very souls!"

Five people in the audience gasped in utter contempt. Lissa merely smiled. She glanced toward the ceiling. It supported the weight of an entire cathedral above them, but it served the purpose well. Thick wood beams, bare and old, rippled like the surface of a lake. There were no children left to emerge, merely a void, an abyss, a great expanse of crushing darkness. It widened without a sound. It vibrated like the string of a violin along the length of a pulsating neon thread connecting theater to theater. The portal grew, nearly to the size of the theater ceiling, and still no one noticed the darkness in the shadows.

"The King in Red perseveres!" Aaron yelled. "You shall be but an empty, vacuous, shell of a memory!"

Someone in the audience yawned audibly. It was time to intervene, time to reinforce the language of the play and the spell craft. Lissa rose to her feet, the fabric of her dress electrified around her, and shouted over the actor. "But father, we are so very ravenous!"

With that, the King in Red bowed big, as though he were an icon and the adulation limitless, and swept off the stage. The playwright, Ethan, trembling and eyeing the ceiling, said, "For our third act, the King's children will feed upon the very earth and all its souls."

The audience gave no adulation as the players left the stage and the curtain was jerkily pulled shut. From backstage, the sounds of an argument—between king and playwright—could be heard. A couple, a man and woman, rose to leave, but Lissa barred their exit. She shook her head, let them see the gun in her hands, and said, "There's no magical solution more volatile than gunpowder."

Even as she said it, she felt ice running through her veins—not hers, merely the echo of icy venom in the blood of her sister, her twin, whose world this was. For the pain to reach her, it must be intense at the source. She frowned. She didn't know if either of them could survive without the other.

She used the gun to point at the seats the couple had quit. "Might as well stay through the finale," she said. "But now you've pissed me off, and I can't promise not to shoot you just for the thrill of it."

3.

Joshua stood within the confines of the Palace Theater, beyond the reach of the darkness and the creatures it contained. He listened, not to the sounds of salivating, not to the grinding of teeth through the flesh of someone who had tread too close to the threshold. He listened to the sounds of the orchestra, which were miniscule and defeated, single painful notes that were byproducts of something other than music. He listened to the beating of a heart that had stopped as it struggled to regain its rhythm. The muscle had been suffocated. He listened to the words of the actress, who he recognized as a former King in Red, who therefore should not have been alive, who had instead aged gracefully and even lustrously. He listened to the conflict, one basement above him, a battle between magicians, in which both were already doomed.

He listened, too, to an underlying note, a musical thread existing below and beneath everything, too low for human ears to hear. His ears, all his senses, were more attuned than most. That note, more than any other sound, intrigued him. He tried to isolate it. It defied his understanding. The timing was off. The timing was off, and yet somehow connected to the play—*The King in Red*—not the actress above, whose delivery hid her fear—but to another king elsewhere in the theatrical labyrinths. The Lazarus Theater.

A porcine creature outside the grounds of the Palace Theater swiped at the air between them, snorted and grunted, edged closer. Its tusks dripped with blood, but its eyes said it wanted more. Joshua flicked a piece of light from his diminishing ball at the creature, merely burning it.

The key, of course, was understanding that note, deciphering it, interpreting it, translating it into something he could use, but it might already be too late. Blood had been spilt. Blood magic was strong. He smelled it in the air, a co-mingling of protective blood and venom and sacrifice.

He withdrew a pen and a piece of paper to scribble a quick series of letters. He swirled them around each other until they were illegible, except to certain eyes. He pressed the note shut—it said, *To the Parliament, Blood has spilled in the Palace Theater. Urgent.*

He reached through the air, snatching a sparrow from elsewhere. The poor thing trembled amid the throng of creatures, monsters, and foul beasts that snuffed and shuffled at the threshold of the theater. "I know," Joshua said to the sparrow, attaching the note to its leg, "and I'm sorry, but five hundred souls are counting on you."

The sparrow sighed, in the way sparrows do.

"I'll lend you a flicker," Joshua said. He opened his hand, releasing the sparrow, and flicked his wrist. The creatures responded, rushing, shoving, straining to reach the point where the sparrow appeared to fly, but it was merely an illusion, a reflection of the sparrow beside itself, and it flew instead thirty degrees west of that mark. The darkness still swiped at it, but the sparrow flitted through the foul beasts and stenches and deeper into the tunnels of the labyrinth.

4.

The sparrow flew through the labyrinth with an unerring sense of direction and purpose. Through grasping claws and trunks and tentacles, diving and darting in every direction, the sparrow escaped the reach of the foul creatures though its little lungs were filled with their stench. She wasn't perfect, the sparrow, but she was smart and single-minded and absolutely reliable.

She maneuvered the tunnels, rising through stairways, ignoring doors and favoring cubbyholes that joined adjacent tunnels. The maze, if that's what it was, could never confound the sparrow or its kin.

She reached a chamber where a man sat alone beside a candle reading a book of some sort. The sparrow never understood books. What kind of message could require so much weight in paper, when a few brisk words ought to be enough to alert anyone to danger, inquire about any concern, or issue statements of import.

She fluttered briefly in front of the man before alighting on the table beside him.

"What's this?" the man asked.

The sparrow sang.

The man smiled, though he was not a man accustomed to smiling. It made his face crease in places it shouldn't, but the sparrow didn't mind. She wasn't judgmental. She appreciated the sentiment.

"Well," the man said, releasing the note bound to her leg, "your kind don't usually take to the tunnels, do you?"

She sang again. He didn't pretend to understand her. He read the note. It was short, much shorter than his book, but it pulled down his lips on either side. That seemed more appropriate for his face.

Abruptly, he rose from his chair and sniffed at the air. The sparrow sang again, a warning this time, and the man understood the tone if not the details.

And that, for the sparrow, was enough. She'd done her job. She took flight, exited the man's brooding chamber, and circled underground in search of an exit. But something was wrong, something confounded her, something in the maze had been changed and she couldn't escape the web of that wretched theater.

5.

Olivia Mason, patron, owner, proprietor, whatever title a person might bestow, knew more about her theater than the average patron, owner, or proprietor would. So when the conductor collapsed with a whiff of blood magic, she excused herself from her balcony and immediately sought Ignatius, the usher, the Palace Theater's fist of the Parliament of Ushers. But his room had been sealed, again with blood magic, so deftly she hadn't detected its odor until she was mere steps from the door.

She knocked anyhow. Three times. Loudly. With the butt of her fist rather than her knuckles. She knew she'd get no response, but she felt obligated to give him a chance.

She got what she'd expected: nothing.

Okay. She left his room and descended to the theater floor, through the backstage area so she wouldn't have to cross the entire theater to get to the magician.

Of course she'd known he was a magician. The very fact that Ignatius had allowed him access to his balcony was suggestive. Also, she'd seen him float to the ground. He was a little too old, and physically imperfect, to be ninja, so what else might he be?

When she reached the orchestra, the conductor had already been moved, into and through the pit so as to avoid disturbing the audience. Seventy musicians instead of four hundred guests, that seemed somehow considerate. But they were all her guests, including the conductor—Raymond Broadhurst, who had led orchestras in Richmond, Baltimore, and D.C., who had recorded a remarkable selection of orchestral maneuvers, who had lent his baton to the efforts of a half dozen animation studios. He had been murdered, violently and maliciously. She wanted to know why.

She passed within inches of the actress, Reina, who had

come for personal reasons; and despite her elegant dress and jewels and tailored coiffure, Olivia hopped into the orchestra pit and found the magician.

"Tell me."

"He's dead," the magician said. "His murderer is on the premises."

"Can you locate him before he leaves?"

"I'm afraid," the magician said, "no one will be leaving."

Olivia Mason looked at him, considered him, and examining him in the space of a breath. She didn't consider his words a threat, so she said, "I know you, don't I?"

"You're Ms. Mason."

"And you're Mr. Gris."

He smiled, nodded, and said, "They call me Maestro."

"Then you can lead the orchestra," she told him, despite that half the players had abandoned the pit and disappeared into the underbelly of the theater.

"Reina has control up there," the Maestro said. "That will have to be sufficient. No, our theater is under siege." She didn't insist it was *her* theater; that wasn't how ownership worked. She wasted no time with arguing semantics, disbelieving her senses, or any other such foolishness.

"What do you need me to do?"

But the Maestro gave her one slow shake of the head. "I'm afraid whatever's been done cannot be undone."

Olivia nodded once. "What can we do, then?"

The Maestro closed his eyes a moment, assessing the situation, weighing the options, deciding how best to answer her. Finally, he said, "I count four hundred ninety two souls within the Palace Theater. Fewer than there should be, and there will be fewer still before the night is done. A spell has been cast."

"What kind of spell?"

"Transportational."

"You make it sound like the theater has been converted into some sort of railway."

The Maestro said, "Nothing quite so comfortable."

6.

Unable to move, barely able to breathe, Nicholas couldn't even close his eyes. He had a spider arm's view of his entire journey. It seemed to last forever, but he soon realized he hadn't been gone from the theater very long. The noise and vibrations of the theater grew more apparent as they rose through darkness.

The return from the realms of mists was primarily in darkness. The shapes he saw, the shadowy forms which maybe didn't exist, imprinted onto his memory. He would carry those for the rest of his life, however short it may be. The smells turned his stomach. At one point, the spider put him down to spar with another creature. All Nicholas saw of it were yellow eyes and gleaming teeth, and the occasional spark of their natural—unnatural—weapons clashing.

When the spider retrieved Nicholas, its legs had been spattered with black ichor, presumably blood.

He'd been coiled within the spider's webs, so if control of his muscles ever returned, he would still be unable to move.

The darkness of the depths gave way to the firelight of tunnels. They scurried past a group of actors smoking and drinking and gambling. Nicholas attempted to call out for help, but could only manage an unintelligible groan. They passed an adventurer with a long thin sword in one hand and a torch in the other. They came perilously close to a priest examining a neon thread. But no one and nothing saw Nicholas curled in the arms of that massive spider. No one heard them, and no one felt the disturbance of air.

When they reached the rearguard of the army crowded around the theater, all those beasts dark and foul as the spider, they scrambled across the roof. Nicholas felt the blood rush to his head. His face flushed with heat. His eyes burned, and finally he was able to shut them.

It wasn't much, but it was movement.

Eyes closed, pain thrumming through his veins, the sounds of monsters all about him, Nicholas concentrated heat—what he felt, what he could conjure, what he could draw from his own flesh—into his palms. Heat, light, energy of any sort, into a point no bigger than a black hole, an inverted singularity restrained within his hands.

Finally, the spider reached the line beyond which the creatures wouldn't pass, the edge of the theater. From here, upside down, Nicholas saw his former assistant, Lissa, in a brilliant red dress made of blood and sweat as well as fabric, facing a man he'd never before seen, a magician, a hermit, a wizened young man who had abused his own body and intellect. Nicholas saw it in the way he moved, as though every muscle revolted with searing pain.

Nicholas couldn't imagine what it would be like to live like that.

He also saw the remnants of a woman, a girl, a former maid. The ghost of her persisted over a puddle of variegated sludge. She was surprised, shocked, hardly aware she was dead. The liquid bits of her physical remnants maintained their shape only by inertia. The image of her persisted only because Lissa held the pieces in place.

"She," the magician said, "was under my protection." He lashed forward with a stream of terminal colors. Alyssa withstood the assault. An array of colors swirled around her, agitated by the attack. It was black like obsidian death, jagged and sharp, broken into its component colors.

"I," Lissa said, "do wish you'd have taken your seat. I wanted you to witness the show, the extravaganza, to its conclusion." She raised a fist. With it, a chunk of earth burst from the floor, swallowing the magician, and continued rising through the ceiling into the theater above.

The last vestiges of the girl's image fell apart and drifted away. Lissa, his assistant, whose reflection had been with him on the other side of the mirror, turned her full attention to him and the spider.

"Very good," she said, stepping toward the arachnid and stroking its head. "Daughter of Arachne, I thank you."

The spider made a noise not dissimilar to a purr.

"Nicholas," Lissa said. "Stage magician extraordinaire."

He grinned. He felt like he grinned. He didn't know what else to do, but he felt the urge to defy her.

"You didn't think I'd forget you, did you?" she asked. She touched his cheek. There was warmth in her touch, and a bizarre, supernatural heat. Her body fought infection. During the brief touch, Nicholas didn't even have to think about it; he drew some of that heat from her. Not the poison in her veins, the venom that was already eating her up from the inside. He didn't want that, didn't need it, didn't think she deserved to be released from it.

"I've thought about you a lot," she told him.

He managed to work his mouth. The words came out slurred. "I loved you."

"Ha!" It was dismissive and angry and unbelieving all at the same time. "You loved the skimpy costumes you made me wear. You loved the look of me, and how I made *you* look. Your audience, such that it was—it was me they loved, Nicholas, not you."

It required a lot of effort to speak through the paralysis. Nicholas didn't try to respond.

"Then you dragged me into your delusions," Lissa said, "and I knew they were more real than you imagined. I took what I could from you, dear Nicholas, but you really had nothing to give me. Your magic, your fumbling attempts at magic, were never anything but infantile. I studied, Nicholas. I studied and I learned, and I withstood greater indignities than you."

Nicholas gulped a lungful of air. It was the first full breath since the spider's bite.

"I didn't want you here for vengeance," Lissa told him, leaning close. "It's true, you believed you loved me, and I didn't *want* to hurt you. But you're tied to this theater inexorably, Nicholas, and I needed three forms of blood to complete the casting."

"What casting?"

She smiled. "I'm sorry you won't see it." She withdrew a blade from somewhere in her blood-soaked dress. Smiled at him with blood-soaked lips. He saw it all now. Even her eyes were blood-soaked. All other color was gone from her. "It will be spectacular. I don't know that anyone's ever tried a magic on this scale. I'm going to send this theater, and my only surviving tormenter, into a pocket universe outside reality."

The blade was obsidian, black as a coal-smeared soul, gleaming like a mirror. Nicholas knew something of mirrors. He had experience. He had terrible, inescapable experience with mirrors. He saw his own eyes reflected in the blade. He wanted to do something, anything else; there was nothing left but to release the conflagration he'd gathered in his palm.

Lissa drew the blade across his throat, spilling his blood, already cooled—and maybe it would be enough to complete whatever spell she'd conjured—as he released the explosion.

PART VI
ENSEMBLE

1.

The explosion shook the Palace Theater. It was felt in the very deepest chambers, in the dressing rooms, in the lobby. On the rooftop, an unkindness of ravens, birds reputed to shuttle the souls of the dead into the realm of mists, scattered at the disturbance.

But in the basement, where Nicholas's blood had been spilt, where the spider had taken him, where Alyssa completed the necessary work, the explosion rent the flesh of shapeless beasts, incinerated monsters with the intensity of its light, and splintered the bones of the structure.

Architecture relied upon particular points of pressure, just as magic often did. The central column, the single column upon which the weight of the theater rested, cracked. Dust fell away in the wake of the concussive burst of flame. If the fire caught anywhere, it was not in these stones. But pieces crumbled. Fell. Shattered.

The entire theater groaned. Little cracks formed in places where nothing should be cracked. Bigger cracks spread like fragmented lightning in the walls and floors and ceilings.

The explosion had thrown Alyssa off her feet. If she hadn't already had defenses up, it might have left nothing of her. But the spell was complete, the third taste of blood given—always the numbers, three being ever so important—so even if she died now the spell would run its course.

She realized her fingernails were now the color of Nicholas's blood.

She allowed herself a quick grin. It was supposed to be a smile, but she'd never been particularly skilled with those. In his final moments, Nicholas had managed to impress her. She felt a tinge of sorrow, that he'd had to die.

None of her pets in this section of the subbasement had survived the blast. Instead, striding through the dust and smoke and ash, there was a man Alyssa had not expected to see again. He was nearly a twin to the usher she'd sacrificed, with strong hands and darkly tanned flesh, despite that he subsisted in this underground labyrinth. Getting to her feet, wiping dust from her dress, she said, "Algernon."

He nodded in acknowledgement. "I had not expected to see you here again."

"You hadn't expected us to survive."

"No matter. Here you are, and I see what you've done."

"What have I done?"

He nodded toward the shattered column, which continued to break apart and crumble. "You've destroyed the theater foundations."

"That was not my intention."

"I've seen your silk," the usher said. "And I smell the blood of my brother on you. I know your intentions, Alyssa, and they were never good."

"What do you know or care of *good?*"

He shrugged. "I care about the soundness of the theaters under our charge."

"*Our?*"

Algernon shook his head. "Don't play dumb, Alyssa. It doesn't suit you. Now, will you help me save this building and its soul, or will you leave me to do it on my own?"

"If I don't?"

"You die, no matter the circumstances," Algernon said. "The venom in visible in your veins."

She looked down at her hands, her arms, and saw the yellowed outlines under her skin. Seeing it allowed the burn to break through.

"Focus on me, Alyssa," Algernon said. "Or did you intend to slaughter over five hundred fellow human beings tonight?"

"Collateral damage."

Algernon shook his head. "Your concept of balance is flawed."

Above them, the theater creaked as its stones shifted.

"The theater is already doomed," Alyssa told him. "I'm moving it, all of it, every stone and every chasm. Every breath of air, every piece of wood, every insect and every person. That weight, physical and biological, is necessary."

"*Balance*," Algernon said. "You cannot move a pile of rubble and dust."

2.

Someone plucked a note from the neon thread.

Lissa heard it over the action of the third act, but there was nothing she could do. If she left the Lazarus Theater, she risked breaking the thread and severing the anchor.

She stayed on her feet. She kept the gun pointed in the general direction of the audience and the cast. But she no longer saw them. She listened, instead, to the priest, a priest of St. Lazarus' Cathedral, examining the thread that connected it to the Palace Theater.

On stage, the King, Aaron, faltered in his lines. Lissa snapped her attention, and the gun, back on him.

"It's alright," the playwright, Ethan, said. "It's in the script."

The King said, "Do I die in your damned script?"

"Everybody dies," Lissa said from the audience. "But not today. Finish the play."

The King swallowed his will, his pride, his fear, whatever was necessary, and recited the next line from his script page with volume but without authority. "I am your King, and I require..." He faltered, looked at that playwright. "I require what, exactly?"

"You *require*," the playwright said. "What more do you

need?"

"I require."

"Again," Lissa said.

The King turned to her, and gave the strongest performance of his life. "I *require.*"

The priest, from somewhere within the labyrinth, pulled another discordant note from the thread. It startled Lissa. She pulled the trigger. The bullet ripped through the King's chest, tearing his heart and lung, ricocheting off the back of one of his ribs to do even more damage inside. She saw its path, saw the surprise on his face. One of the women in the audience screamed. It didn't matter who. All that mattered was she matched the note made by the priest. Lissa felt the reverberation through every fiber of her dress, a combination of indescribable pleasure and unbearable pain.

Someone in the theater audience moved. She turned the gun. Her expression said everything she needed to say. On stage, the playwright said, "And thus, the blood of the King runs red." He dropped the last page of the script. It fluttered. Drifted. Dissolved. In the darkness above them, in the gaping abyss that had formed, a flurry of lightning exploded. One arc—only one was needed—escaped, burning through the Lazarus Theater. It struck the playwright, so that both the actors were dead upon the stage. It jumped from one audience member to another, scorching their faces, burning their lips and hair, melting their eyes, and charring their flesh. The bolt struck the gun in Lissa's hands. She dropped it, snatched her hand to her chest. The bolt escaped the Lazarus Theater through the door, through the neon thread, racing at the speed of light to the Palace Theater on the other end of that thread.

3.

A chunk of rock and dirt and metal thrust through the floor of the stage. Until then, Reina had the audience captivated. At the top of the upthrust fist of earth, in a cage haphazardly formed of the same materials, a magician, bloody and torn, had been trapped. He stared at the audience, appearing insensible, and screamed in pain. Some of the teeth of that cage had impaled his flesh, piercing one leg, his abdomen and shoulder, and both arms. In one hand, he clung to what appeared to be a paintbrush.

Olivia Mason, current owner and proprietor of the Palace Theater, stared with her mouth agape. The Maestro snapped his fingers at her to regain her attention. "The only thing we can do," he told her, "is change the velocity."

"Can we get everybody out if we slow it down enough?"

The Maestro shook his head. "We can't slow it down. But if we disrupt the speed of transition, and the direction, we can at least alter the destination."

"What's the destination now?"

"Oblivion."

"That," Olivia Mason said, "does not sound promising."

"Do what you can to help Reina. Keep the audience calm. We need them calm."

"Why's that?"

"Panic is a distraction we haven't time for."

But it was too late. Panic had erupted in the midst of the audience when the earth erupted through the stage and the theater shook with all the power of a Pacific volcano. The Maestro turned away from Olivia, from the entrapped magician, from the musicians still scattered about him. He reached through the air, through a portal of his own — dangerous, as just such a portal was growing to envelop them now — but he needed something from his stores. He couldn't reach his own house, distant as it was, so he sought an abandoned mine in Ethiopia, the first to come to mind, and withdrew a sliver of obsidian glass.

He squeezed it in his palm, cutting his hand and drawing blood, and had to hope that amalgamation of ingredients would be sufficient. The abyss was already about them.

4.

Olivia Mason rose from the orchestra pit. The spotlights had been abandoned, left pointed randomly at the stage. With a glance at the actress, Reina, a former King in Red, Olivia stepped into one of those spotlights.

She took control.

This was her theater. These were her guests. They were loud, raucous, fearful, but she would not abandon them. She raised her hands. She glanced backward into the orchestra pit. One of the remaining musicians nodded and, in an instant, was striking thunder on the timpani.

Not all at once, the audience quieted.

"Guests!" Olivia called. "Friends! Look at me!"

Some did. Some ran, stumbling, struggling with their seats.

"Listen to your Kings!" Reina commanded.

Olivia glanced back at the musician again. The timpani proved insufficient. The musician, realizing this, went for the gong. The note rung out through the theater, reaching the farthest depths, the deepest alcoves, the darkest corners. The chandelier quivered under the sound—or for other reasons Olivia wasn't prepared to acknowledge.

"Breathe!" Olivia yelled. "Breathe, and drink your wine!" She turned to Reina. "Do they have wine?" She continued. "I have news, and it is not the best of news. The theater is surrounded. If you try to leave, you will find nightmares made flesh."

"How is that supposed to calm anyone?" Reina asked, not for the audience to hear.

But they didn't need the audience *calm*; they needed to be still, instead, and if fear prevented their flight, Olivia would use it. "We've already lost a dozen or more of us," she told the audience. "I can't abide that. I won't. I refuse."

The audience, for the most part, seemed to listen, though some of the balconies had emptied and screams echoed from the lobby.

"There's nothing we can't overcome," Olivia told them. "But we can't run until the nightmare is ended." She glanced at Felipe Gris, magician, down in the orchestra pit. She didn't know what he was doing, but he was doing something. "We are in good hands," she announced. "Protected."

On stage, the magician in the cage mewled piteously as the theater began to tremble.

5.

The Parliament of Ushers, a certain number of them, arrived at the site of the Palace Theater to find a crater. The monsters were gone, the theater was gone, all its occupants were gone.

They found the thread. It had been scorched, shredded, torn, left to waft through the tunnels in lost and lonely strings as though cut by a wild, dervish-like Atropos.

They found a sparrow, lost in the tunnels, who had escaped the gravitational force that had swallowed the theater. She was thankful to find the sky again, even if the air wasn't fresh.

They traced the thread back to the Lazarus Theater, where the smell of copper mixed with ozone. But this theater, too, was gone, and all that remained was a hole, and a priest,

Father O'Leary, hands burnt and eyes smoldering, who insisted someone had stolen his church and he would not rest until he'd found it again.

6.

At the central foundation of the Palace Theater, Algnernon, of the Parliament of Ushers, reassembled pieces of the column. Alyssa stood at the center of it, supporting the whole of the theater on her shoulders, preventing the inevitable collapse long enough for Algernon to do the work.

She suspected he worked more slowly than he might. He would refer to it as methodical.

He applied a kind of magic Alyssa had never seen. She studied it. Questioned him. "Is that a kind of mortar?"

"It's like that, yes."

"Does it draw from the earth?"

"And also fire. And also water. It's quite potent."

"Could you use that magic to mend flesh, as well?"

"Do I strike you as a healer of flesh?"

"What's the purpose of this Parliament, anyway?"

"Question the gods," Algernon told her. "When you reach the realm of mists."

The effort drained Alyssa's strength. She was already drained. The venom burned her veins and organs. The pain doubled every few minutes. She forced it back with every ounce of numbing magic she could muster, but she had never studied mending and repairing.

By the time she faltered and finally dropped to her knees, Algernon had finished. He tilted his head as he looked at her, examining her like a mysterious curiosity you might find in a museum with a placard reading *unknown origin, unknown purpose*. He said, "I have a question of my own."

Alyssa slumped to the tile floor. The dust of the column bit angrily into her flesh. "You want to know why."

"I don't care about why," Algernon said. "I want to know where."

"Where?"

"Where have you taken us?"

"A realm of oblivion," Alyssa said.

Algernon nodded. "So the theater will disintegrate. But the air will escape first, and everyone dies."

"Everyone dies," Alyssa told him. "Inevitability."

"And what of your menagerie?"

Alyssa shook her head. "They guarded the perimeter, and should have been left behind to do as they would."

"They were not left behind," Algernon told her. "You'd made them a part of the theater in its final minutes. They were dragged into this darkness with us."

"Then they should feel at home."

"They will feed."

"Let them," Alyssa said. "Frederick will get a chance to see it all. The lengths I went to on his account."

The winds of oblivion made their way into the Palace Theater. Algernon knelt at Alyssa's side and said, "You've left me in a quandary."

"How's that?"

"I must protect the people inside the theater," he said, "as well as the beasts. That's the quandary. But you—I don't believe I'm obligated to protect you any longer."

She smiled. Grimaced. Something. "I can't be protected. The bitch's venom is strong."

"Thank you for that," Algernon said, rising and walking away. "I shall feel no guilt when your body fails you."

PART VII
ARIA

1.

The Maestro used the obsidian to carve into the floor of the orchestra pit. It was stone, and not easy to cut, but the Maestro was not an easy man to deny. He bloodied his hand as he worked, forming geometric shapes in the tile, blowing dust away, well aware of his audience.

The theater's audience listened to Olivia and Reina, in front of the orchestra pit, though a great many probably stared in horror at the ensorcelled and entrapped self-proclaimed magician. The Maestro recognized what linked them—not what, but who—Alyssa, his former famulus, whose heartbeat faltered in the bowels of the theater.

He heard other sounds, too. Talons and claws and feet on stone and tile as a dark army of unspeakable foulness cautiously explored the edges of the theater. They were inside, because the outside had become a realm of Oblivion, an infinite expanse of nothingness. Footsteps, too, of someone walking through the tunnels, someone who belonged here as much as any other man. As much as Ignatius, but the Maestro did not recognize the rhythm of his tread or his heartbeat.

And someone else—and something else, too. He looked up. "Reina!" he called.

She came to the edge of the orchestra pit.

"Look outside. Use a window, not a door. Tell me what's out there." He paused. "Look in all directions, until there's something to see—because we're not alone in this void."

2.

In the void between theater and cathedral, Joshua clung to the remnants of a neon thread and dragged his body across the aching, penetrating vacuum. There was nothing to breathe, and no hope of reaching the cathedral before consciousness left him.

At the edge of the theater, amid the charred remains of beasts already deceased, a man—no, an usher—grabbed hold of the neon thread, Joshua's lifeline, and added his strength to the effort.

Approaching the threshold, Joshua inhaled half a lungful. It was all he could get. Once across, he let go of the thread and gasped. The air was weak, thinning, tinted with odors best not examined, but full of oxygen.

"Our problems," the usher said, looking out at the cathedral, "have multiplied."

Joshua, careful not to swallow too much air, closed his eyes to limit stimuli and calm himself and said, "This is Oblivion. Look, the edges are already starting to dissolve."

"The edges of you, as well."

Joshua looked down at himself. All color had been drained from his clothes. His fingernails were red with blood, and more wetly stained the cheeks under his eyes. He touched the thread, looked back into the nothing, and said, "The Lazarus Theater. And St. Lazarus' Cathedral. That was some powerful craftsmanship."

"The thread's been cut," the usher said. "If we are to save these structures and the souls within them, they must be reconnected."

"How do we do that?"

The usher held up the end of the neon thread. Color bled out of it. "In the exact same way." They looked, the two of them, through the expanse of the void and the immeasurable distance between two places that should not be there.

3.

Lissa sat at the edge of the Lazarus Theater. Already, the air thinned, and the extremities of the structure dissolved into the Oblivion around them.

This wasn't supposed to happen.

The Lazarus was meant to be an anchor. Through that thread, they were supposed to swing the Palace Theater, and only the Palace Theater, into Oblivion. Something had gone wrong. She knew the magic required extraordinary balance and delicacy. Her sister had gotten it wrong.

She looked through the void at the side of the Palace Theater, from its highest towers and spires and antenna down to its deepest basements and subbasements and hidden rooms. There was more weight to it than Lissa had realized. Though some of the walls had been retained, she saw through the darkness to her sister, sprawled across the floor of a lower level of the theater—not the lowest, not by far. Alyssa was dying, but Lissa felt nothing about it.

Physically, they were linked, but apparently not so greatly that either required the other for life. Lissa wouldn't have to die with her sister.

She saw other people, strangers mostly, and ghosts gone mad. She saw the dusky indistinct pack of wolves and snakes and demons they had invoked to guard the perimeters. Some drifted into the void, but a great many ventured into the theater. Nothing prevented it any longer.

Lissa was alone.

There might be someone in the cathedral, but she had no direct access to it without risking the corrosive void. It would be a short eternity. She watched the last wisps of the thread, made from her dress, drifting and disintegrating.

She felt the intensity of the magic being conjured inside the Palace Theater and rose to her feet. Someone intended to fling the theater back into its own reality. But surely, someone with that kind of knowledge and skill would realize it was impossible. And nothing would happen at all without the thread linking the two anchor points.

"Have you had your revenge, sister?" she asked. She didn't imagine her voice reached far through the void. Still, Alyssa lifted her head to look in her direction, and maybe the other woman smiled—Alyssa and everyone here would claim Lissa was the reflection, but she knew better—maybe she smiled, and maybe she grimaced, but maybe she just pushed out her last breath.

Alyssa slumped to the floor.

Leaving Lissa alone to listen to almost five hundred frantic hearts pumping in the Palace Theater. Every upstroke and downstroke of each of those hearts weighed on Lissa. She fell back into her seat, unable to withstand it. A single tear rolled free of her eyes. She wiped it away. The drop was neon orange and already fading. She stared at it a moment, then flicked it into the abyss. It floated away, continuing unhindered in that single direction, though the line through Oblivion was neither straight nor certain. Eventually, the nothingness eroded the tear. Lissa felt it as strongly, or as weakly, as she had felt Alyssa struggling to purge herself of the venom.

The void wouldn't instantly destroy her. That gave Lissa confidence, and also a deep, soulful dread and despair. She wasn't ready to die.

She got to her feet again. She tore the end of a thread of her dress, wrapped it three times around one of the lights just offstage, and with a running start, leapt into the void.

She rocketed across the darkness, trailing a neon thread. The path between theaters was more direct now, and would not require all the fabric of her dress. It unraveled behind her much more rapidly than when she had walked.

The line between theaters was not straight. The darkness ate at her, cracking her fingernails, singeing her eyelashes, needling her skin, tearing her hair. She tried to swim, to redirect herself toward the Palace Theater, and for a brief moment it seemed to be working.

But the chasm between the two theaters was great, and her senses unreliable. Something inside her ruptured, an artery in her brain perhaps. The pain was subtle, by comparison. She closed her eyes, unable to draw a last breath. Maybe death wouldn't be such a bad thing.

4.

Joshua and Algernon stared at the woman streaking through the emptiness. A thread linked her to the Lazarus Theater and St. Lazarus' Cathedral.

"She means to connect the theaters," Algernon said.

Joshua shook his head. "Her trajectory is wrong."

"Even in Oblivion," Algernon said, "straight paths are crooked."

"She's not going to make it."

It was true. She would pass far to the west of the theater. She had been maneuvering with intention a moment ago, but they could clearly see she'd lost consciousness if not life itself. The thread of her dress continued to lengthen behind her.

Algernon looked back at Alyssa, who had ceased to breathe. If it was possible to say, he smiled. He tore at her dress, wrapped a fistful of thread around him, and said, "I'll get her."

"You can't."

"*You* can't," Algernon said. "I'll have more time than you." He dove into the thick noir, pulling the blood-soaked thread from Alyssa's dress behind him.

Joshua knelt at the edge of darkness and understood. The two women, sisters or twins or something indescribable—reflections?—had crafted this transportation, so there were advantages to harnessing their energies, however weak and spent, to do whatever was next.

And what was next? Saving the Palace Theater? Saving the cathedral? Saving the almost five hundred people inside?

5.

From his prison, pierced in a dozen places by dirt, metal, rock, and stone, bleeding and losing more than blood, Frederick saw something more clearly than he'd ever seen. The games of his life were coming to an end. His mother, Veronica, had died naturally—had she died naturally, or had Alyssa rejoiced in the shadows as his mother's life escaped her?—and he would die most unnaturally, here in the midst of this void, this cavity outside of reality. He would die with an audience, though Alyssa had intended him to witness all the deaths that made up that audience. Even now, even here, dark and foul creatures, amalgamations of lupine and serpentine and arachnidan and bovine and ursine and avian, distortions of nature, abominations, some of them armed with swords, others with claws, pincers, talons, and teeth, reached the doors to the theater. They emerged from the shadows behind the balconies, through the doors at the back of the theater, from behind the stage and from the orchestra pit. They came through emergency exits and they came through walls, a hundred or a thousand of them, an uncountable number, nothing less than a legion.

There was a reason he'd never liked that self-proclaimed famulus.

He called every color to him—every ounce of red that was visible, every shade of blue, the verdant and the creamy—from the walls, from the chandelier, from the clothes of the audience, from their eyes. One or two or ten fell to those obscenities. That couldn't be prevented. But with a great gasp, his final breath, he released all the colors as a sunburst.

A sunburst in the darkness of Oblivion.

It rained over the audience like mist. It pelted the creatures like an avalanche. It penetrated the walls and floors and ceilings. It covered the entirety of the theater, every backstage room, every frontstage area, and ripped the foul creatures apart at their most basic levels. Few of the beasts would survive. He would not.

6.

The Maestro, bathed in light, had done all he could do. The Palace Theater remained in Oblivion, and there it would remain forever. Something was missing, something from the original spell, an anchor point by which they had been shifted out of reality.

Reina, from somewhere above, called out, "There's a cathedral!"

He couldn't see her, but heard her voice over all the other sounds. "Where?"

"Far," she said.

"How far?" the Maestro asked. "How can we bridge that distance?"

"There's a woman," Reina said, "a woman in white, shooting through the void."

"From the cathedral?"

"She's connected."

"Connected, how?"

"A neon thread."

The Maestro stood suddenly, violently, explosively. "Will she reach us?"

"No," Reina said, "but there's someone else."

"Who?"

She didn't respond immediately, then said, "He caught her!"

7.

The collision of bodies within the void was far from a catch. It shattered Lissa's senses. Briefly she was aware outside of herself again, and thus could grasp at the body of the man even as dust fell from her fingers.

Algernon grabbed her with the strength he had left. The void of Oblivion was a horrible, corrosive place, and he had nearly lost himself. He clutched the woman, and in the midst of nothingness they twirled like dancers. It was the only way to join the two threads. She might have smiled then. He might have, too, had there been time.

8.

The collision, the union of threads, the linking of theaters gave the Maestro the final push he needed. He caught onto the last of the momentum of the swing from reality and pushed the Palace Theater and its anchor one frame further afield. They crashed into a city and became part of the city—a city of darkness but not the unrelenting emptiness of Oblivion.

The Palace Theater settled in Midnight, the City of Night, tucked between two mountains in such a way, the sun never shone there. The effort had been costly. The Maestro collapsed, his baton splintered, his hands scarred, and he didn't want to see his face.

Olivia Mason, in the spotlight, collapsed of exhaustion. Many in the audience fainted. On stage, nothing remained of the magician in his cage but shredded flesh, dripping blood, and stray flecks of insubstantial light.

Belowground, beside the body of a dead magician's assistant, Joshua dusted himself off. He picked up the thread which connected to Alyssa's body but had been torn at the very threshold of the theater. Tunnels continued into the city from here, into this dark, unimaginable city teeming with life.

With a sigh, he entered the city's underground. He ascended somewhere distant from the theater but not far from the cathedral. He could follow the ghost of the thread, even though they were no longer physically connected. He found no trace of Algernon or Alyssa's reflection; maybe they had died in the void; maybe they had been flung further afield, maybe they were just lost within the catacombs of Midnight.

He entered St. Lazarus' Cathedral, surprised to find it had suffered so little damage. No one lived inside.

The walk had given Joshua mysteries to solve, specifically questions of time, which apparently did not work the way he had thought.

PART VIII
UNDERTURE

1.

The Maestro woke in a comfortable bed in an apartment somewhere in the Palace Theater. He recognized it immediately and easily. He'd been ill, but the fever had finally broken. He sat up. On the other side of the room, in a chair reading a book of magic, sat Olivia Mason, the current patron and proprietor of the Palace Theater. She looked up from the book and smiled.

"How long was I out?"

"That's difficult to answer."

"Try, please," the Maestro said.

"You brought us out of Oblivion," Olivia told him. "No one believes it was solely your efforts, but what you did was essential. Without you, we would all have died a slow death."

"We all will die a slow death," the Maestro said. "That's the nature of life."

"Don't get into semantics. I've something difficult to tell you."

"How difficult can it be?"

"We can't go home, none of us."

The Maestro shook his head. "Unfortunately, that's not a surprise."

"It's not just a matter of place."

"I'm not a child," the Maestro told her. "Speak plainly."

She nodded. She smiled again and put down her book. "I'll get us both some whiskey."

"It's time, isn't it?" the Maestro asked. "We were flung into the future?"

"Not the future." She poured two glasses and brought one to the Maestro's bedside. He had never noticed how gray her eyes were. "The year is 1902."

2.

Someone knocked on the big doors of St. Lazarus' Cathedral. Joshua made his way there, though they weren't locked. Outside, a group, a congregation of sorts, had gathered around the doors.

"Is this cathedral a gift from God?" one of them asked.

Joshua considered the question. But since he wasn't sure how to answer it, he didn't.

"Are you the priest?"

Joshua shook his head. That, he knew how to answer. "I'm just a wanderer."

3.

In the cavity that had been the Palace Theater, an ancient woman in a hooded robe presided over a funeral. Her face was wrinkled, leathery, dry and cracked. Her red lips and green eyes shone. The theater was acknowledged, its long history and untellable future—there were books that provided hints and suggestions and even legends—as well as the ushers who had died defending it. Ignatius. Algernon. Others without names had been inducted posthumously into their ranks. They acknowledged the past proprietors, all of them, a long line of men and women who had done much to maintain the bones and soul of the theater. They specifically named Olivia Mason. Like a captain, she had disappeared with her ship.

Elsewhere, a priest, Father O'Leary, who had seen miracles in New York and now beyond, followed paths, underground and over, untraversable to most, in search of his stolen cathedral. He would find it, in the unlikeliest of places, with a history almost a hundred years old, and would take residence there once again.

4.

In the realm of mists, Nicholas's soul was plucked from obscurity and delivered from the depths of death. The lord of mists frowned. He said to his niece, "You cannot make a habit of simply retrieving anyone you want."

"Of course not." Devi smiled as she said it and stroked Nicholas's cheek. "But I owed this mortal man a favor, and you, above all others, know the perils of ignoring the demands of balance."

Dale said, "It's good to see you again, Nicholas. It's been far too long."

"How long?" Nicholas asked.

Dale shook his head. "You'll learn to stop asking questions like that."

Nicholas walked with Dale and the goddess out of the realms of mist.

FINI

ACKNOWLEDGEMENTS

Enormous thanks to Mary Lescher. I started this project in Virginia, and like so many projects before this, you were there at the start. I miss you.

I wrote parts of this in Virginia, Florida, and Spain, unique environments which helped develop this project.

Thanks to everyone who helped and supported me during the process. My influences, my teachers, my friends, my lovers, and my bitter enemies all contributed to make me who I've become: the person able to tell this story.

I will forget people if I list them all by name. My support system for this book included Brent, Brian, Mary, Mike, Mikey, Coop, Gina, everyone in Madrid and at SPA Studios, a few people in Virginia and Florida.

Extraordinary thanks to Morgan, who keeps my best and worst secrets.

As always, special thanks to Sabine and the Rose Fairy.

ABOUT THE AUTHOR

John Urbancik wrote the first draft of *The Secret History of the Palace Theater* in pieces between 2017 and 2019. They were volatile years in his life, in which he moved between two states and another country (Spain) and lost his partner of over 20 years (Mary Lescher) to cancer.

His first novel, *Sins of Blood and Stone*, came out in 2002. Numerous other novels, novellas, short stories, and poetry collections have followed.

He hosted the *InkStains* podcast for almost two years. That led to his first nonfiction book, *InkStained*.

Born on a small island in the northeast United States called Manhattan, he has lived in Australia, Spain, and a number of states. He suffers from an insatiable wanderlust. Currently, he resides in an undisclosed location along the Susquehanna River.

www.DarkFluidity.com

ALSO BY JOHN URBANCIK

COLLECTIONS
Shadows, Legends & Secrets
Sound and Vision
Tales of the Fantastic and the Phantasmagoric
The Museum of Curiosities

POETRY
John the Revelator
Odyssey
Annabel Lee, in Shadow

NOVELLAS
A Game of Colors
The Rise and Fall of Babylon (with Brian Keene)
Wings of the Butterfly
House of Shadow and Ash
Necropolis
Quicksilver
Beneath Midnight
Zombies vs. Aliens vs. Robots vs. Cowboys vs.
Ninja vs. Investment Bankers vs. Green Berets
Colette and the Tiger
Madmen, Poets & Thieves
Clockwork Ravens
The Night Carnival
La Casa del Diablo

ALSO BY JOHN URBANCIK

NOVELS
Sins of Blood and Stone
Breath of the Moon
Once Upon a Time in Midnight
Stale Reality
The Corpse and the Girl from Miami
DarkWalker 1: Hunting Grounds
DarkWalker 2: Inferno
DarkWalker 3: The Deep City
DarkWalker 4: Armageddon
DarkWalker 5: Ghost Stories
DarkWalker 6: Other Realms
Choose Your Doom

NONFICTION
InkStained: On Creativity, Writing, and Art

INKSTAINS
Multiple volumes

NEXT BY JOHN URBANCIK

JOHN URBANCIK

CLOCKWORK
RAVENS

www.ingramcontent.com/pod-product-compliance
Lightning Source LLC
Chambersburg PA
CBHW072120250626
47159CB00007B/2514